W9-BXY-722

THIS BOOK WILL NOT SAVE YOUR LIFE

Michelle Berry

Enfield & Wizenty
(an imprint of Great Plains Publications)
345-955 Portage Avenue
Winnipeg, MB
R3G 0P9
www.greatplains.mb.ca

Great Plains Publications gratefully acknowledges the financial support provided for its publishing program by the Government of Canada through the Book Publishing Industry Development Program (BPIDP); the Canada Council for the Arts; the Province of Manitoba through the Book Publishing Tax Credit and the Book Publisher Marketing Assistance Program; and the Manitoba Arts Council.

Design & Typography by Relish Design Studio Ltd.
Printed in Canada by Friesens
Author photo by Sarah Thomson

FIRST EDITION

Library and Archives Canada Cataloguing in Publication

Berry, Michelle, 1968-
This book will not save your life / Michelle Berry.

ISBN 978-1-926531-04-5

I. Title.

PS8553.E7723T55 2010 C813'.54 C2010-903229-2

ENVIRONMENTAL BENEFITS STATEMENT

Great Plains Publications saved the following resources by printing the pages of this book on chlorine free paper made with 100% post-consumer waste.

TREES	WATER	SOLID WASTE	GREENHOUSE GASES
10	4,431	269	920
FULLY GROWN	GALLONS	POUNDS	POUNDS

Calculations based on research by Environmental Defense and the Paper Task Force. Manufactured at Friesens Corporation

*This book is for my brilliant daughters, Abby and Zoe,
and for my agent, Hilary McMahon, who never gives up.*

ALSO BY MICHELLE BERRY:

Short fiction:

How To Get There From Here

Margaret Lives in the Basement

I Still Don't Even Know You

Novels:

What We All Want

Blur

Blind Crescent

Contents

A Letter to the Reader of This New Edition

Dear Reader,

Any way I look at it, it is hard to know where to begin.

My life—anyone's life—is harder to explain than you think. There are so many complications. Life isn't straight or even curvy. It's more like one of those roads in the cartoons. The kind the Roadrunner picks up and shakes in the desert to out-fox Wile E. Coyote, a looping and rolling, shaking and twisting road. Was the Roadrunner magic? All those black holes he painted on the roads that Wile E. fell into. Can you out-fox a coyote?

Magic. Cursed magic. White rabbits and magic wands. Abracadabra and presto. Thimbles and coins and matchsticks and long sleeves and fake boxes and stooges and deception.

When it's finally time to explain my life, it feels as if there is something stuck at the base of my scalp, something pressing into my brain—and it's not the rock-hard pillow the paramedics here in the ambulance have put under my head, but some kind of little lever that, when pushed, turns off all the stuff I'm meant to think about, all I want to say. I'm a blank slate. *Tabula rasa*, as my grade seven teacher used to shout. I feel wiped clean. There is nothing inside of me anymore. No past, no present, no future. Nothing but me, Sylvia Swamp, travelling with three strapping paramedics in the back of an ambulance down the highway.

When I tell one of the paramedics I feel empty of thought, he tells me that this feeling might have something to do with my condition. The Pulmonary Embolism. Capital P, capital E. But what does he know?

I suspect he's thinking it has everything to do with my size. He doesn't say this, but I can tell by the way he's looking at me, like he's trying to digest a particularly gassy meal. Like he can't decide whether to blame me or feel sorry for me. Seems to me everyone believes that the size of a person, her weight on a scale, explains everything about her. Her social status, her mental health, her upbringing, her inability to say no. When an object has weight it means it's impressive and large-scale and a thing we should all pay attention to. A weighty issue. Or a weighty book. But when a person has weight it means the opposite. It means greed and guilt and fear. It sometimes means you're hiding something. It means something we should ignore, look away from, feel disgusted by. Judge.

My sister Sadie had no patience for any talk about my size. I'm not sure my size had anything to do with all that happened. Maybe in the long run it did, but I'm not positive. But it certainly controlled my life.

I'm looking at the ceiling of the ambulance when the paramedic puts his head down close to mine and says, "How ya doing?" He has godawful garlic breath. But I can smell mint too and I'm touched. He's made an effort. For me. I pretend he did it only for me, brushed his teeth after lunch because he knew we'd be together in close quarters. Lately my sense of smell has been weak, I don't know why, and so even this horrible garlic and mint combination, instead of making me feel nauseous, actually makes me feel good. I can suddenly smell something again. Maybe the shaking of the ambulance has opened up my nose. Everything in here is shaking. The ambulance. The three men. The platform I'm lying on, my pillow. Me. Bumpy spring road, rough ride. Potholes from the harsh Ontario winter. I'm wiggling.

"I'm OK," I say. "How are you doing?"

It pays to be polite to the people who take care of you.

I suppose Sadie would like it here, in this ambulance. She would certainly like the look of these men. It took five firemen to lift me onto the moving platform at the hospital, five gorgeous men grunting and heaving, one man shouting, "On the count of three," like he was hoisting a piano (I guess he was). And now it takes three paramedics to drive me down the highway. All these men are simply glorious. Two muscular paramedics are in the front of the ambulance, chewing gum and laughing at something. One poor guy with garlic breath is stuck back here with me. He's smiling nicely. All of these men are strong and lean and muscly and tall and their skin glows with good health. They are handsome and their handsomeness makes me blush, it makes me feel alive. I've seen men like this on TV, but not often in real life. It occurs to me that firemen and paramedics are nothing like police, who always seem kind of dumpy and out of breath. Stressed, over-anxious, dough-nut-eating police. I know it's a stereotype, but the ones I know are like this. And I do know a few police.

With that thought—police—the little lever holding in my thoughts dislodges slightly, lets some of my past in. A policeman. That policeman. I can see him clearly, strangely, standing in our apartment years ago, searching for escape from the crazy lady, my mother, who was screaming and throwing things at him, telling him he was lying. And then he was back again, a few months later, smelling like smoke. And then again, full of condolences. Was it the same policeman? Could that be possible? Surely Toronto has more than one? Or maybe the Swamp family just had one policeman assigned to us permanently. One nervous, chubby policeman assigned to give us bad news.

After all, we were a handful.

Maybe if I just relax a bit, don't push too hard with my memories, I'll be able to begin. My mother always said, "Begin at the beginning, Sylvia," when I came running home from school anxious to tell her about my day. Because I always jumped straight to the punch line (oh my God, to think suddenly of jumping and running, what it felt like. I used to run. I used to jump. But now I have become the punch line of a fat woman joke—Sadie's favourite: "There are two fat women in a bar, having a drink. One says to the other, 'Your round.' The other replies, 'So are you!'").

Where is the beginning? How far back is the beginning? Adam and Eve or cavemen or dinosaurs? Black holes and space? Or God, if that's what you believe in. Me, I'm not sure yet. I always figured that I would decide about Him when I got older. And now I am only twenty-eight and I'm balancing pretty close to God or to the end, to a nothingness or a somethingness, and I'm still not sure what the answer is.

The beginning is my grandparents. Or my mother and father. The beginning is my mother's obsession with Dr. Spock's book, *Dr. Spock's Baby and Child Care*. The book that defined who we were and what we did. The beginning is also Marvellous Marvin, the magician.

I can barely breathe. I have pains in my chest. At the hospital, the anticoagulant medication didn't work. The doctors told me that my fat, my size, is responsible. Of course it is. I'm fat, not stupid. I could have told them that. Fat is always responsible, responsible for more than half of North America's problems I developed a deep vein thrombosis in my leg from being stationary for so long. DVT, they call it, because everything is an acronym, even a clot. The clot became dislodged and travelled through my veins and "embolized to a pulmonary artery." Or to my lungs. I don't know. These doctors, they talk so fast. Most of it cannot be understood. I remember the word *embolize* because it sounds hot and red, an ember from a fire, and it brought me back in time to that painful moment. I have shortness of breath all the time and rapid breathing and chest pain. Lately I've been coughing up blood. The doctors say a chest x-ray and CT scan are necessary. And, since I don't fit into any of the machines in the hospital, I'm being driven to the closest large-animal veterinary hospital to climb into their CT scan like a sick elephant. Is there a waiting room at the veterinary hospital? Me and several horses, a cow or two, waiting our turns.

The heaviest man in the world weighs 1,244 pounds.

My clot dislodged. Moved along. It's good to know that while I've been bedridden something inside of me has been travelling. Even if it is just a clot, my body is on the move.

After the veterinary hospital, then what? What happens next? I'm not sure. The doctors have told me they won't staple my stomach until I lose half my weight, which is really impossible. Even if the fattest man in the world is losing weight for his wedding, I can't. I've tried so many times. Besides, I'm not getting married, so I don't have that motivation. When I asked what might happen in the future if I just do nothing, if I just carry on the way I am, a doctor, rushing through on his rounds, said, "sudden death." I think he meant that kindly. A not-so-subtle warning to fix things quickly, to make peace with the past. And so, you see, it now seems important for me to remember and for me to start at the right place. It is necessary for me to face my life. To understand why I did the things I did. To figure out the beginning so I can understand the end. I really need to forgive myself.

I wonder often what will happen to this thing surrounding me, this bulk, this hugeness of skin and blubber. What is done with the body of a morbidly obese woman when she dies? What can someone do with that? Two burial plots? A specially-made casket? Or is it possible to cremate me? Is there an oven big enough? Think of the cost. My urn could take up an entire living room.

"You're crying," my smelly paramedic says. "And humming. Are you having trouble breathing, Ms Swamp?" He leans over me and wipes at my eyes with a Kleenex. I'm both crying and laughing—I always hum—imagining my urn and all those ashes. Funeral guys, dusted with soot, shovelling my ashes into a wheelbarrow, wiping the sweat from their brows like miners. My paramedic threatens me with an oxygen mask. Dangles it in front of my face and then straps it around my head. There is nothing I can do. "Don't you worry, Ms Swamp, we'll be there soon and then you'll be all fixed up."

All fixed up. How is that possible?

He is the only one who will talk to me. The others look away quickly.

Their eyes say Freak, Monster.

Here it is. The truth:

I am a woman who is so large she doesn't fit in a human CT machine. Last weight estimated: 700 pounds. Remember, the fattest man is almost twice as fat as me. I'm a woman who needs to be rolled onto an ambulance by five firemen and a moving platform and then transported to a veterinary hospital. I'm a woman who needs a horse CT machine, a cow, hippo, elephant-sized one. Do elephants get CT scans? I imagine they would. If they were sick and Ringling Brothers were in town.

Why don't they just shoot me? Put me out of my misery. I'm not a race horse or a circus animal. I have no worth.

Without even trying to know me, people always decide they already do.

All fixed up. I wonder what that would entail. Messiness, probably. A lot of hard work. A lot of heavy lifting and thinking and doing.

OK, so the one paramedic is driving, he has to look away. I'll give him that. The other one is up front and it may be hard for him to turn his neck. Maybe the humiliation is all in my mind? My mother used to say that all the time: "Sylvia, people are not paying any attention to you. Stop worrying. It's as if you don't exist."

The thing is ... what it comes down to if I'm honest with myself ... this really doesn't bother me all that much. I expect it. Being invisible. Being fat. Truth be told, what would bother me is if the paramedics were all suddenly very nice to me. If they looked me straight in the eyes. People have been avoiding looking at me for so long that becoming visible again would be painful. The one nice, garlic-mint paramedic, my paramedic, is enough of a big issue. A weighty one, to be precise.

This is why the beginning must be perfect. Because I'm about to start the whole mess up again. That's the thing about memories. You can't just think them, you have to relive them. Carefully. One thing leads to another, like one cookie leads to the whole box, or any other food or non-food related metaphor. I do compare everything to food but when you live in this body, what else can you do? I haven't many other interests. There really is nothing wonderful a cream doughnut can't compare to. A bright summer day is like the butter cream filling spreading over your tongue.

See. Taste it.

"Fatty fatty, two by four..."

When I wasn't invisible, I practically glowed.

The paramedic stops wiping my eyes, lowers the oxygen mask, and sits back down. I can't see him from here, I can't lift my head, but I can hear him adjusting himself, getting comfortable. The ambulance lurches through traffic, rain pelts down outside. The windshield wipers have a sticky squeak to them—weeeeeaaak, weeeeaack—rhythmical.

Judging?

"Swamp Monster," my nickname in school. One of many nicknames.

I can tap my finger slightly even though the straps are holding my arms down so I won't roll off the platform. I follow the sound of the wipers for a while and I listen for the three lovely men to breathe, for them to clear their throats and begin talking. We have a long way to go yet and I hope they talk to each other. Traffic is thick. It is early spring and the air is full of the stench of left-over winter.

I'm not all sadness and gloom. I'm not all about food or death, although food does play a major part. And so does death. My life is also about magic (or magicians, precisely), which can be exciting or extremely boring depending upon who you are and what you believe, and my life is about fires and arson and attempted murder. And family too. In fact, some of my life is quite upbeat. Life is like that, isn't it? When you think you shouldn't laugh it's funny, and when you are laughing it's often not so funny. For example, I'm so fat and Sadie is so skinny, well, that's funny when you put us together in a room. If she turns sideways she disappears. And if I turn sideways I squish her flat like a pancake.

I think that's called black humour. Perhaps because it makes you feel uncomfortable, dark. But black is a lovely shade. Slimming.

My life is also about love. Because I'm best at that. I can love better than anyone. Honestly. You wouldn't know that if you just saw the surface of me, but if you took the time to look down inside this skin, behind this mass, you'd see it. True, unending, pulsing, beating, red love. Holy love. For my sister, for my father, for my grandparents, and even for my mother. I can love them until it hurts. I can love them until they feel the love covering them, smothering them. My love is reflected in my size. I've blown up into a blimp full of love.

I guess the best way is to start with the actual beginning. The beginning of me, Sylvia Swamp. Start with my mother and my father, Ruth Mileford and Benjamin Swamp.

And then, of course, with Sadie, but that may actually be the end of this story instead of the beginning. I'm not quite sure.

I'm not a mind-reader. I'm not able to see what is not in front of me. And so I'm leaving a bit of this up to my imagination because, as my grade one teacher once told me, I have a wild one. "Always making things up, Sylvia Swamp. Always telling half-truths and lies." I can create things that seem right, that fit into the story the way I'm going to present it and, well, you'll just have to take my word for it. What else can you do? If I feel my father felt a certain way or that my mother noticed a twitch in her side every time she took a breath or read a book, well then you will just have to trust me.

"Stop lying," Sadie would say. "Get the facts right." But it isn't lying to me. It is creating, exaggerating, making everything bigger and more interesting than real life.

If things had been different in my life, I think I could have been a writer.

This is my memory. This is my voice. My lovely, deep, gluttonous voice. My hum. What I want to remember is important to me. So listen up. For now, this is me. This is my perspective.

This is a large chunk of me to keep. There is so much I need to make peace with. My life was full of everyone else. I did what I thought was the best for us. For our family. This is our story, the Swamp story, and it is enough to fill a library. Our story is the icing on millions of cherry cakes—the kind Mother used to make for Marvellous Marvin's birthdays before everything changed. The Swamp story will begin like a light bulb flashing on in a pitch-black room. It will begin like the spark of a lightning bug in a jar, or like fire climbing the curtains and ripping through an apartment. Heat and light and action. Our story will begin just like this.

Or this.

With much love,
Sylvia Swamp

•••

IF RUTH COULD look back on her life and apologize for all she did, she wouldn't. There is nothing she regrets. Really. Sure she feels sorry for Mr. Swamp and Sylvia. Sure she isn't too pleased with Sadie these days, but there is nothing she really feels guilty about. Ruth hears other mothers talking about guilt as if it were something you naturally attained when you gave birth. Push the baby out, feel guilty. But Ruth feels nothing of the sort. She never has. It's not her fault the way things turn out.

"If you think you're so powerful as to change the way of the world, or to change how people view themselves," Ruth says to anyone who will listen, "then you're really quite proud of yourself, aren't you?"

Mr. Swamp and Ruth sit across from each other in the diner. Mr. Swamp is eating a bagel smothered in cream cheese. He uses his fork to spread it. Ruth sips her coffee and stares meaningfully out the window.

"There they are," Ruth hisses.

Mr. Swamp looks. A spot of cream cheese on his chin, his fork held above the bagel.

"Where?"

"How can you miss them? How can you miss Sylvia?" Ruth points out the window at their daughters, Sylvia and Sadie, as they walk towards school. Sylvia's gait is rolling, she swings her arms to move her bulk forward. Sadie is looking down at her feet, her long blonde hair moving like a waterfall down her back. They carry their backpacks over their shoulders. Sylvia's pack looks absurdly small balanced on her immense back, like a child's toy. Sadie's pack gets lost in her hair.

"How—"

"Ruth, don't start," Mr. Swamp says.

"Start what?"

"You know." Mr. Swamp continues to eat. The girls pass by across the street and disappear around a corner. Even though their parents have breakfast in the diner every morning the girls do not acknowledge them. Both girls look steadily away from the diner's front window. A wind whips up and a stray bag follows them along the sidewalk.

"But they are just so different."

"They are sisters, Ruth, they aren't supposed to be identical. Every morning," Mr. Swamp says. He sighs.

"Coffee?" The waitress bends over them and refills their mugs. Ruth picks at her manicured nails.

"I really have to get these done today before the show."

"What time do you have to be there?"

"I have to be on stage at three o'clock. A bus load of seniors from New York."

Mr. Swamp raises his eyebrows. "To see Marvin? Why do they come all that way just to see Marvin?"

"Marvellous Marvin," Ruth says. "And me."

"Huh." Mr. Swamp stands, his bagel finished. "I'll see you tomorrow then."

"I'll be home after midnight."

"I'll be asleep."

Mr. Swamp stares at his wife. Ruth looks again at her nails. And then she looks out the window towards where her daughters disappeared.

She feels suddenly as if she's going to be sick. She feels melancholy, like an actress in an old movie, or like a character in an old book. Old. She feels old. Who knew that aging was so horrible?

"Don't you feel so old?" she whispers.

"What?"

"Well, I won't wake you up then. When I come home."

Mr. Swamp opens his mouth to say something but changes his mind. He leaves the table and pays the bill at the cash register. Ruth doesn't look at him again. She continues to stare out the window into the wind, into the image in her mind of her receding daughters—one fat, one thin—leaving her, moving forward, moving off into the world.

Without her.

Everyone is always moving forward without her.

But at two o'clock she's with Marvellous Marvin and he is spinning her around in his dressing room, marvelling at her lovely sequined body, her long legs, her high, full breasts, and Ruth is feeling like a million bucks.

"Wonderful," Marvin says. "Simply wonderful."

A new body suit, a new costume for the show. Picked out deferentially by Marvellous Marvin. "I went to the seamstress on Gerrard," he says. "She knows exactly what I like."

Gold sequins atop black. Low neck, lower back, high cuts up the legs, fishnet stockings.

"I really don't feel my age," Ruth says, "when I'm around you."

"Now let's see how easily that comes off."

At the end, after it all plays out, Ruth is alone. She is in the hospital. Sylvia drove her powered wheelchair out the door to get dinner in the cafeteria. Sadie is back at the condominium alone, most likely dusting. Ruth watches the nurses walk back and forth past her room as they move around doing their business. Everyone is busy. Ruth thinks that she was always busy in her life. But, even so, no matter how much she took on, she never felt busy enough. Ruth knows that life is good when it's busy, that when you are lying on a hospital bed about to die you wish you were busy again so that you wouldn't have to think. Thinking is not good. It's never best to think too much.

"You OK, honey?" A nurse pops her head in the door.

Ruth is making sobbing noises, trying hard to stifle them, but they are coming up and out just the same. Keening moans. Sad sounds.

But she nods to the nurse. What else can she do? She is not OK. She is not hunky-dory, she is not even just fine. She's dying. Cancer. After all she's done in her life, after all that has happened, this feels oddly anticlimactic.

One minute Ruth is there, all alone. The next minute she is gone.

•••

DEAR READER,

School sucks. It always does. Everything sucks. I'm in history class and we're learning about friggin' wars and all I can think about is magic. Out on the school grounds I can see the phys ed class, the grade fives, doing all their stuff for track and field. There's my sister. Look at her. Or don't look at her. Everyone is laughing, pointing, staring. She's wearing my father's shirt and some boxer shorts and her breasts are sagging and bouncing and her stomach is jiggling. Breasts? More like fat.

Marvellous Marvin touched me the other day. He was backstage, alone. I was waiting for my mother. He ran his hand over my head, down through my hair, along my back. I got tingly all over, as if he was performing magic, as if he were putting a spell on me. Abracadabra.

There she goes, trying to run the track. Oh shit, look at her. But don't look at her. She's twenty feet behind everyone, her face is beet red and she's dripping sweat. I can see the glow from here.

"Sadie Swamp, please pay attention to the board," Mr. Reebird coughs out from the front of the class. "We're discussing civil war not watching the track stars."

Right when he says this everyone looks out the window, everyone looks at my sister as she collapses on the track, out of breath, as every kid out there laughs and the phys ed teacher comes running down the field to make sure she is all right.

Marvellous Marvin touched me. He looked right in my eyes. No one ever looks right in my eyes.

Except Sylvia. She's always staring at me. Through me.
I raise my hand. Mr. Reebird coughs again.
"I have to go to the washroom."
"Hurry back," he says. "You don't want to miss too much."
But I disappear out the front of the school. Into the sunset (although it's only just before noon). Out into the wild streets of Toronto. Who knows what will become of me? Who knows what I'm capable of? Who cares about civil wars or track and field runners or fat sisters?
Magic. It's all about the magic. My mother knows this. And now I do too.
Black magic. Card tricks and rabbits, top hats and paper magic. Silks and threads and ropes. Disappearing boxes. Optical illusions. Mental magic. Stooges.
"A stooge," Marvin says, "is your assistant. He is someone you can trust to keep the secret."
"I'll be your stooge," my mother says.
"I'll be your stooge," Sylvia shouts because she is young and stupid.
"I'll be your stooge," I say, and I mean it.
"You can all be my stooges," Marvellous Marvin says. "Even you, Mr. Swamp."
Daddy turns away. He's definitely not Marvellous Marvin's stooge.
But we are.
Especially me. I can keep his secrets.

xoxo,
Sadie Swamp

•••

It seems to him, lately, that he's always crying. It's as if his eyes leak, as if there is a faulty tap somewhere, a drip, drip, drip. He needs to tighten it somehow. Tighten himself. Buck up. Stand straight.
Benjamin Swamp doesn't know what has happened to him. He used to be so happy, so larger-than-life, so full of himself. How can two daughters and an unhappy wife change all that?

When he was a boy he was in the school plays. He was always one of the main characters or the narrator or the master of ceremonies. He sang in the choir. He worked on the school yearbook and wanted to be a journalist.

Now he's an overworked accountant with leaking eyes, a heavy heart and a wife who is perpetually angry at him.

And his daughters. Three and one, both completely lovely and adorable, but both hellishly loud and demanding. Sadie always hollering for something—milk or cookies or up, up, up. "Now," she shouts. "Up now."

Sylvia is always crying. Ruth ignores her. Sadie hits her, knocks her over when she tries to stand. Says, "Go away. Go back to where you came from." Benjamin comes in from work, wipes his eyes, and tries to get everyone to calm down. He props Sylvia up. Puts pillows behind her.

"I won't have this," Ruth shouts. "This is not what I want."

Benjamin isn't sure what she means. She doesn't want her children? She doesn't want him? Sure, Ruth has always been loud and difficult, but now she's something out of a bad black-and-white movie. Her mouth wide and painted red. Her eyes lined in black and open wide or shut into slits to glare at him. Her hair stiff and dangerous above.

"Up, up, up," Sadie shouts. Pushes Sylvia over again and again. "Up, up, up, Daddy."

Sobbing Sylvia. Stick a bottle in her mouth. Give her a cookie. That'll soothe her.

Benjamin cries on his way to work. He cries on his way home. Not loud, open crying, but soft inside crying. No one would know he's crying if it weren't for his eyes being wet, but inside he's howling in pain. He disappears into himself, each day a little farther down. There is nothing he can do about all of this. He isn't Dr. Spock, he's just Benjamin Swamp. He isn't Marvellous Marvin either. This makes him cry even more.

Benjamin Swamp has lost his life to a one-year-old girl, a three-year-old girl, a book of pediatric advice, and a magician. When all he ever wanted in the world was for everyone to be happy.

Trust yourself, Mr. Swamp recites. *You know more than you think you do.*

At the end of it all, though, Mr. Swamp trusts himself completely. Who else is there to trust? In the end, when things settle down, when life becomes an achingly slow but satisfactory routine, when he spends his evenings settled in to watch TV with Sylvia and Ruth and Sadie, Mr. Swamp knows that the only person in the world he should trust is himself. And that suits him just fine.

Part One
Sylvia

Trust Yourself. You Know More Than You Think You Do.

The Parent's Part

"Parents are human. They have needs."—Dr. Benjamin Spock

RUTH MILEFORD, MY MOTHER, married my father, Benjamin Swamp, in February at a small United Church in Toronto, Ontario. I assume they married out of a profound love for each other. Isn't that why people marry? For companionship, too, and because they respected each other, perhaps. But in my lifetime I rarely saw this between them. I saw mostly indifference. Sometimes spite. Occasionally little kindnesses, white flags raised. But more than all that, I saw each of them blame the other for what became of their lives. My father more subtly than my mother.

Fifteen steps away from the church was the diner they would eventually eat breakfast in, off and on, for the next twenty-odd years. Fifteen steps was all they wanted to take to get to their wedding reception in the minus thirty degree wind chill, the snow whirling around their heads. One hundred and thirty steps away, give or a take a few depending on the length of a person's gait, is the apartment they rented, and eventually bought and paid off—"the condominium," Ruth said, even before they owned it, "not apartment." They decorated the place with overstuffed chairs, a large Christmas ornament collection, Daddy's TV and TV *Guide*s and Ruth's Avon products. At the reception in the diner there was coffee and cake. There were people I never knew, my mother and father's friends. By the time I was born the guests had long gone and it was only my parents and grandparents. My mother sometimes found people—Mrs. Randall from across the hall, Mrs. Duffy from the diner—but more often she lost people—she told Mrs. Randall that her son was retarded, she borrowed, broke, and never replaced Mrs. Duffy's crystal wine decanter. "Pettiness," Ruth would say, slamming the door. "People are petty." My father supposedly played cards at the Rotary Club on Tuesdays for the first year of his marriage, but Ruth soon put a stop to that.

I can't imagine my father playing cards and laughing or smoking a cigar, drink in hand. Surrounded by other men. I can't imagine him having fun. No matter how much love I sent my father's way, he was never fully happy. Only my mother could make him smile and she rarely did that.

But on that day, their wedding day, they were happy, they were in love and they were young and hopeful. This is how I think of it anyway. A white dress, a charcoal grey suit, flowers, coffee, cake. Benjamin Swamp insisted on being called Mr. Swamp by his new wife, Ruth (even in bed, she told Sadie later, even when they were in the throes of love-making), even after the children were born and they stopped making love. He jokingly said he would be Mr. Swamp to her, in the diner just after their marriage, a small crowd of their friends gathered around the buffet and the coffee urn. He held up his mug. "I will be Mr. Swamp to your Mrs. Swamp." He laughed ferociously (back when he did laugh, it was always ferocious and loud, "A bark," said Ruth), but Ruth didn't think it was at all amusing.

Sometimes I think that this was the beginning of the end. The whole Mr. Swamp/Mrs. Swamp thing. With the world on the cusp of feminism, my father made a joke that changed the way my mother saw marriage, the way she saw her life. I'm sure my father meant it as a joke, but the joke backfired and everyone took him seriously. Everyone always took him seriously. Ruth listened carefully to her swaggering, happy, caffeine-high husband, and decided right there that she'd had it. Before it even began.

At the time Ruth smiled nicely; it was, after all, her wedding day and she was willing to give a little, but from that moment on she decided not to be Mrs. Swamp. She didn't like his last name anyway (she told Sadie that once, but she never told me; she rarely told me anything important and a lot of what I've pieced together has come from what Sadie said. And, even though Sadie says I lie when I actually just exaggerate to make a story more interesting, Sadie actually really lies often. My information is not always reliable) and so Ruth stayed with plain old Ruth. My father called her Ruthless when he was in a particularly jolly mood (which was rare), or when he had a drink (courage) in his hand. He supposedly used to pinch her rear end and shout, "Ruthless Ruth Swamp," into our over-crowded apartment. Imagine this? I can't. This was all before they had children. This was all in the first year of marriage.

Swamp names either took on an importance in this family or were given because they were important. My name, Sylvia, for example, has more meaning than a person would think. I think my name is an omen, a curse, a foreshadowing of my life. I am named after Sylvia Plath, Ruth's favourite author, who died years before I was born. Sylvia Plath was Ruth's favourite because of the way she killed herself, not because of what she wrote. Plath placed bread and milk on the table, sealed the kitchen with wet towels and blankets so the gas wouldn't harm her sleeping children, and stuck her head deep in the oven. This appealed to Ruth's romantic side. ("She does have a split personality," my father said to me. "Your mother is always half this and half that.") This appealed to her sense of foreboding, her sense of the martyrdom of women, mothers especially. "What we won't do for love," Ruth was fond of shouting. Ruth loved the idea of women who saved their children from doom and disaster, even though I'm sure she never would have done the same herself. I'm pretty sure she wouldn't even have thought of her sleeping children and she most certainly wouldn't have left us any breakfast—I can't remember a day in my life when breakfast was ready and waiting for me, when I didn't have to pour out my own cereal, or make my own toast or eat the pizza from the night before. If Ruth were Sylvia Plath, the gas would have seeped through the apartment and we'd all have been better off.

Ruth never read anything of Sylvia Plath's. Not the poetry. Not the novel. When I was twelve I went through a Plath stage (don't all girls?) and I was reading *The Bell Jar*. Ruth picked it up off the coffee table and held it quizzically before her. She squinted at it. She said, "Would that, perhaps, be a jar one puts bell peppers in? Is this book about cooking? Why are you always thinking of food, Sylvia?"

Names: my father was always Mr. Swamp to Ruth, Daddy or Dad or Father (if we were angry at him, which wasn't often) to me and

Sadie. My mother was always Ruth. We thought of her as Ruth, but we called her Mother or Mom or sometimes, rarely, and only when we wanted something (food, or, in Sadie's case, money), she was Mommy. When Sadie was a teenager she called our mother Fuckhead and Dimwit and other angry names I would rather not remember. Sadie also sometimes called her nothing. Sadie sometimes refused to acknowledge her. And Sadie called our father Shadow Man. But never to his face.

Sadie is Sadie because it was the name of our father's childhood companion, a small golden dog who followed him everywhere, a golden dog who rode in the front seat of his car when he was young and full of hope, when he was not married and unhappy. The dog's head would loll out the window, tongue flapping. He was a dog who charmed the pants off our father. A dog who represented all he wanted in life: simplicity and ease and devotion. His first love, he said to us, fondly, and Ruth sighed and said, "Your father always had a thing for blondes."

Sadie's name is a foreshadowing of her life too. It's not hard to imagine Sadie now with her head out a car window on a warm spring day, sniffing the breeze, her long blonde hair flapping about her like golden puppy ears.

But back to my parents' marriage, which began as uneventfully as most marriages begin.

Benjamin and Ruth both worked in offices downtown. My father (accountant) made twice as much money as my mother (secretary) even though his job required half the skill and much less responsibility, but that was fine with him and he often said so. You see, in the beginning of that first year Ruth let my father think he was the boss, the man in the family. She let him think highly of himself and of his maleness. She used a bicycle pump to fill him up as far as he could go (ironed his shirts, darned his socks, fed him well) and then stuck a pin in and popped him.

Ruth worked in a law firm. In a secretarial pool. There was no swimming involved. She also sold Avon on the side to the other secretaries. She began collecting Christmas decorations at church and yard sales and she fixed them up and re-sold them. "They add a little sparkle to our lives," she said. Even with all of this she worked the hardest at getting pregnant. "It's all I've ever wanted," she told anyone who would listen (the harried lawyers at the firm, the women swimming in the pool, her mother, the waitresses in the diner). Her marriage, she liked to tell the secretaries, was a perfect excuse to have babies. "Don't get me wrong," Ruth said. "I do love Mr. Swamp, but it's the babies, the millions of babies I'm going to have, that will make me adore him." Sure, women got to vote. They got to work. They wore pants. But wasn't having babies what women were for? Ruth thought so. Making babies, having babies, raising babies. Simple rules: love, marriage, that old, squeaky-wheeled baby carriage. Even kids in the schoolyard knew this. You didn't have to be an accountant to figure it out.

It wasn't about Mr. Swamp then? It wasn't about true love and devotion? It was about procreation. Simple. Or was it?

Even though they weren't close, my mother had tea with her mother once a week. That's the kind of thing you did when you were first married. You had tea with the mother that always drove you crazy, you humoured your husband to make him feel big and strong and virile. My grandmother told Ruth to wait at least a year before getting pregnant. "That's how it's done," she said. "Marriage. Set up house. Baby. That's how I did it and I did it right."

Grandma Mileford bustled about her cluttered kitchen, her large hips sashayed around the small space, knocked into things—magazines on the table, a dish teetered on the edge of the counter. Ruth held her hands out in front of her and looked at her manicure.

There was a time she would have listened to her mother. There was a time the quiet, heavy woman sweating before her would have made her weak and nervous. But Ruth had married. Things had changed.

(Grandma Mileford once showed me the nail in the kitchen wall where she had hung the strap. "She called it Gerty," my mother said shrilly. "Can you imagine naming a strap?")

"Honestly, why should I wait a year?" Ruth said.

Grandma Mileford rolled her eyes. "Besides, you're too skinny," she whispered. "Unhealthy."

My mother shouted. My grandmother whispered. It was impossible to imagine one strapping the other. It was hard enough to believe that one came out of the other. But that's the problem with being a child, isn't it? Try imagining your parents as kids. It doesn't always work. It's virtually impossible.

Ruth laughed. "If I want a baby now, I'll have a baby now. There is nothing you can do about it."

"Ruthie, you need time to get used to being married before you have babies. Love each other, make some money, a nest egg." Her voice sounded like ruffling in the grass, skittering of mice feet, hushes.

"I'm getting pregnant."

Ruth stomped in her high heels out of her mother's house (I can see it now. Even when I was young she would stomp out of her mother's house. She would never leave quietly and politely), but not before she patted her silenced, grey father on his head as he sat at the kitchen table working a crossword puzzle and grinding his teeth.

Spite: three months into the marriage Ruth was pregnant with Sadie. "I told you so," she shouted.

"Pish," Grandma Mileford said. "You'll screw up. You don't know half what to do."

Until Sadie came along, my mother always got what she was after. There was something about her eyes, the way she tilted her head at you, the volume of her voice, there was nothing you could do to resist. Ruth was beautiful and vicious. She was sexy when she wanted to be. She was cold and determined. Ruth was ruthless, competitive, demanding and spoiled rotten. If she wanted a baby, dammit, that's just what she would get.

I've met a few people in my life who are like that. People either love them or hate them or both.

It's easier than you think to hate someone you love.

Believe me, I know. I push the love out of me. It grows stronger by the minute. It seeps from my pores.

"You stink, you fat pig."

"Stink, pink."

The kids at school tried to push me down, step on me.

"She can't get up."

They hated me. But I loved. I still was able to love.

•••

"At best, there's lots of hard work and deprivation—this is our visible immortality."

RUTH FARED WELL during her pregnancy with Sadie. I was, supposedly, quite a difficult, awful baby. I kicked, for one. A lot. And I had the hiccups for an entire week. Ruth said her body jerked continuously, that she never slept well when she was pregnant with me. She had indigestion, heart burn, acid reflux and gas (hey, that's everything I have right now). Her breasts ached and throbbed, her nipples were so sensitive she couldn't wear a bra. The doctors stitched her up after I came out and the stitches got infected and leaked pus and smelled like blue cheese. I heard no end of complaints.

But Sadie was a dream baby. A little bundle of pink joy wrapped safe in the cocoon that was Ruth's womb.

Ruth neglected to mention the depression. She never said she was sad when she was pregnant with Sadie and forever sad after she gave birth. She never told anyone about the thoughts of suicide, the thoughts of the damage she wanted to do to herself, to Sadie. She didn't know why. It just washed over her most days, this sadness. It just made the days grey and gloomy and listless. It turned Ruth from a flame, a spark, into someone angry and tearful, someone who sometimes couldn't make a decision. Pregnant, swollen, she stood listless before Sadie's new crib or the stroller, not comprehending anything about a baby. Nothing made sense. And she turned into someone for whom nothing mattered one day and the next every little thing bothered her. Some days were good. Others were horrible. Ruth told us, when we were older, that these feelings were why she didn't have any more babies, but Sadie reminded her then that I came along three years later.

"She was a mistake," Ruth said, looking away.

Before Sadie arrived, Daddy, feeling his wife's sadness and anxiety, came home from work one day with two baby outfits to cheer her up: a blue sailor suit and a pink, frilly, lacy one.

Ruth, who quit her day job as soon as she was visibly pregnant (even the Avon people told her to take time off—a visibly pregnant sales rep wearing makeup was never in their books), had been bored and angry for weeks, crying and complaining, sometimes tossing things. But when she saw the outfits, she kissed her husband on the cheek and spent half an hour hanging them on the wall in the living room with push pins. "I'll take down the one we use," she said. "In the meantime they will remind me of what I've got in here." She patted her belly.

Those small outfits stayed on the wall for the rest of the pregnancy. And then for two years. And then for twenty-odd years. Ruth considered them art after a certain point. Sadie never wore the pink one, or the blue one, and neither did I.

They are still hanging there. I'm not quite sure what they represent anymore, other than the obvious: Ruth had hopes and these hopes were dashed.

"Those are the last nice things Mr. Swamp ever did for me."

The last thing he did, really, before she put him down constantly, argued with him, disrespected him, ignored him, and he faded into the man we knew and loved. Those outfits represented the end of a wife who cooked and cleaned and took care of him. Those were loaded baby outfits.

Marriage ain't all it's cracked up to be.

Mind you, neither of them worked at it, and, from what I've seen on TV from my constant position in bed over the last many years, you have to work hard at a marriage for it to succeed. The world is a complicated place. There are a lot of temptations, a lot of choices, and everyone is too darn busy. No time for sex. No time for love. There is selfishness and greed lurking behind every building. There is dissatisfaction and self-absorption. No one ever really means it anymore when they say "How are you doing?" No one listens for, or wants to know, the answer.

Except for my lovely, smelly paramedic. He seems genuinely interested. He's asked me three times now. I can't complain, really.

When you see that the world has gone to hell and no one has time for love, when you see corruption and filth everywhere, maybe you can understand my life.

•••

The Mother's Part

"So enjoy your imaginary baby and don't feel guilty if another kind arrives."

PREGNANT, RUTH IMAGINED Sadie as a warm lump of skin floating within her, swimming like a feathered amoeba. Like sea monkeys or lava lamps. She imagined Sadie's fingers and toes as stumps of pink cold wax, her nose a silver button, her eyes two pieces of black licorice. She imagined life would be perfect once this baby arrived, that she wouldn't be angry anymore, that Mr. Swamp would, miraculously, be different, that the baby would make all her pre-conceived notions happen. Somehow Mr. Swamp would stand up and look tall and strong and beautiful, somehow he would be a man of mystery. They would drink champagne and travel and have dinner parties. Ruth wondered if she had settled. Had she settled? Her mother always thought so. But Ruth wondered: what was it about him that she once loved? She wanted to remember things about him I could never know—how he made love to her, how he held her, what he whispered in her ear. Ruth thought that once her amoeba baby arrived, fully formed and lovely, everything would change.

One of the other things that I've learned from TV is that you can't sit back and expect things to change, you have to make them change. You. No one else can do it. And also—you can't change anyone. Ever. No matter what you do or how much you try. Part of me thinks that if only Ruth had watched more TV her life would have been different.

While my mother was suffering from depression and worry, while she was sad and fuming, my father was adding up the bills that were slowly coming in and he was sighing and scratching his head so that most of his hair fell out. Only thirty-one and our Daddy was old. Ruth either made people old or she made them young and immature. No one who met Ruth ever felt just the right age around her. My father spent his days before Sadie was born becoming a caricature of a nervous father. He began to wear cardigans with patches on the elbows, and brown pants with the fly open by accident, as if he was too tired and beaten down to zipper up. You can chart the change in the family photographs. From business suits to crumpled clothing, he slumped about in loafers that were two sizes too big and he always smelled like mothballs. The virile

Mr. Swamp of his wedding day, loud and confident, quickly turned into the over-worked, grumpy accountant Mr. Swamp, meek and grey. In time, his name fit him fine. In time, there was nothing anyone would consider strange about my mother calling my father Mr. Swamp.

Throughout her pregnancy Ruth wore high heels, Avon red lipstick, Avon black eyeliner and Avon false eyelashes. Ruth went to a hairdresser to get her hair set several times a week—a permanent once in a while, depending upon how she felt. A dye job. Sometimes she looked like Marilyn Monroe, sometimes Jackie Kennedy, other times she looked like Ruth Swamp. There were small bags under her eyes that she covered with foundation. She wore bright colours, blues, lilacs and pinks, to offset the grey of her husband. She went to the dentist when she was five months pregnant and had him bleach her teeth so bright it hurt your eyes when she smiled. Ruth drank white wine from thin crystal goblets (red wine stained her new teeth) and took to calling her ever-dwindling posse of friends Dahling, and Sugar Plum. She was unhappy but determined. Spoiled herself (Sadie says food is spoiled, not people. I, for one, have never left food long enough for it to spoil. But that is beside the point).

According to Ruth, nothing made Mr. Swamp wonderful. Nothing made Ruth's world liveable.

Ruth's hormones and outlook kept shifting.

"What is happening to me?" she cried.

Thinking of all of this is a bit like pulling teeth. There is no give. Only straight tension. I've pulled out a loose tooth before, Sadie's, yanked it hard, put all my weight behind it, and so I know what I'm talking about.

This is not coming out as easy as I thought it would. The lever in my head clicks and shifts with every jangling kilometre we drive in the ambulance, but still there are gaps and blanks and huge teary wet spots to overcome. There is a smell to all of this. Of urgency. Thick and acrid, like smoke.

My mother was depressed. My sister was nearing birth, her grand entrance. Mr. Swamp gave up. There was no point in trying, he thought.

And then came The Book. *Dr. Spock's Baby and Child Care*, by Benjamin Spock, M.D.

Almost at the end of her pregnancy with Sadie, Ruth came upon this book one day in a second-hand bookstore. She was out shopping for bananas, craving them. She was crying slightly, angry at herself for being fat and then more angry at her tears for running her mascara. But she saw The Book on a shelf and she thought Help, and grabbed it, managing to knock several other books to the floor at the same time.

And along came a man. Not just any man. A man with bright neon lights shining over him, flashing arrows pointing. This man helped her pick up the tipped-over books. Ruth held her large, Sadie-full belly, the man laughed. Ruth wiped tears and mascara streaks. She smiled. He smiled back.

Sometimes people mention that one small thing that can change your life—opening your car door on a bicyclist, letting go of your child's hand in a crowded mall, closing the door on your lover's face—that one small thing that can make all the difference. Well, this neon, arrow-flashing man was Ruth's one small thing.

This man was Marvellous Marvin, the magician.

Life is mostly about guilt and regret. I regret a lot of things: world wars, the Holocaust, starving children, child abuse, fast food binges, but mostly I regret this bookstore moment. Sadie thought it was a fairy tale. The Marvellous Magician meets the sad, beautiful princess. Happily ever after?

When she was young, Sadie asked Ruth to tell us about the bookstore meeting over and over again. Sure, I got caught up in the story like any eight-year-old would, but all I could think about was what might have happened if Ruth had not met Marvellous Marvin. All I could think about was the alternate ending, about how she might have raised us if she hadn't obsessed over Dr. Spock's book and looked deep into the eyes of the magician. Is it possible our lives could have been worse?

"How you doing?"

My paramedic.

The others up front are looking at me.

"I'm fine, thanks." My body jiggles as we hit a bump. It's raining harder. We are slowing down in traffic. I sigh. The paramedic sighs too and lets off a sad whiff of garlic, a bit of onion. He stifles a burp and looks away. I distinctly smell Greek salad.

In the bookstore Ruth thanked the magician, her eyes shone, her cheeks pinked, and she quickly bought Dr. Benjamin Spock's book and left the store. She felt something. A twinge in her belly—Sadie?—a pain in her heart?—a blush of love?

Love: I'm in the schoolyard and I'm kissing Matthew Finkler and all I can think about is Sadie. My love, my true love. Sadie. My big sister. Protector. Oh, her hair shines in the light. Golden. Her eyes are sharp blue and when she looks at me, her little sister, my world spins in upon itself and collapses.

"Fatso," Matthew says. He has been dared to kiss me. He spits.

But when Sadie walks me home she walks ten steps ahead, always too fast for me to catch up, always too fast for me to breathe.

Ruth knew it was love. Even though she left the bookstore rather rapidly, our mother told us she couldn't stop thinking about the mysterious man who picked up the books. "He was wearing a top hat, would you believe it? And tails. Tails in a book store."

"He put a spell on her," Sadie whispered. "With his magic wand."

Ruth bought this second-hand copy of Dr. Spock's book. It was a third edition, published in 1957. I don't know why the Book Barn was selling this book that day—found in the basement of the store? But after Ruth read it she claimed it had called to her on the shelf. She took off the black and pink dust jacket and found the hardcover was a salmon pink colour. This meant that Ruth would have a girl. She was so sure The Book talked to her, jumped off the shelf to tell her that there was a baby girl inside of her, to have her meet Marvellous Marvin, that if you reasoned with her she became hysterical. "Wipe your tears away," The Book shouted. "Cheer up. I'll help you through it all." The Book actually glowed in the store. I don't know if it was the fluorescent lights or what. The Book's dust jacket was set afire.

When Sadie was small she spent days trying to copy that shine, holding The Book up to all the lights in our apartment whenever she was allowed to touch it. The Book never glowed for Sadie, in fact it didn't even shine at all. The dust jacket was finger-printed and dirty. Sadie wondered if The Book was magic. She thought The Book only glowed for those who believed in it. Years later, when she began to change, or when I realized that she wasn't my Sadie anymore, she said she thought our mother was "a fucking idiot."

We usually weren't allowed to touch The Book. But Sadie would sometimes put on her woolly blue mittens and ask Ruth if she could please touch The Book. Eyelashes fluttered. "I'll be so careful. Just once. Just kindly and softly, please, and I won't ever damage any of the pages." Blink blink, those lashes like butterfly wings. "Oh, please." Even Ruth, who was an expert at this kind of manipulation, wasn't immune to it.

Armed with her book, Ruth felt sure of herself suddenly. The advice it gave. The comfort. Having a baby would be a piece of cake. Ruth read The Book over and over—only a little time left until the baby arrived—Ruth studied it, began to believe in it like she believed in herself. Grandma Mileford was no help, and even if she was, Ruth would never have asked her for it. But The Book certainly was.

"My God," she told Mr. Swamp, "This is like an instruction booklet. Everything you need to know is in here. If you just follow this advice everything will work out fine."

My father shrugged. "Don't you know this stuff already?"

As if women were born knowing this stuff, as if it is just part of our anatomy—vagina, breasts and the ability to give birth and raise perfect children. Simple. Ruth swatted him hard and told him that children are more complicated than he could even imagine, that he'd better be ready to help out, he'd better be ready to read The Book.

"Children should be seen but not heard,"said Grandma Mileford. "Don't you know anything?"

"What's that?" Grandpa Mileford at the kitchen table, sleeves rolled up. "Did you say something?"

There was Ruth and there was The Book. And there was nothing else. Through his writing, Dr. Spock spoke to Ruth. You know how there are Scientology believers today, all the movie stars, and you know how they believe that aliens will come down and save the world? Well, Dr. Spock was Ruth's alien. He was her religion. Maybe because she was depressed, maybe because she was always a little crazy (Grandma Mileford said Ruth was crazy as a kid too: "fat, thin, fat, thin, starving herself, talking to herself, always wanting things, stupid girl"), maybe because she was lacking something in her life, maybe because she was lonely. But it was not just baby advice she needed. Dr. Spock educated her on how to run her own life too. He told her how to be a strong, independent woman, how to be a good mother, how to draw strength from her weakness and take her anger and turn it into kindness. He taught her how to change diapers and express milk and train her children to be good, to be little human beings with ethics and morals and skills. "*Children like to be kept good,*" she read. "*Parents should expect something from their children,*" and "*Needless self-sacrifice sours everybody.*" My whole life she quoted him, not even realizing she was doing it. "*Parents do the best they know how,*" she said to me much later when we were in the hospital with Sadie, "*with the kind of child they receive.*"

This was a case of words speaking louder than actions.

By the time Baby Sadie was pushing to be born Ruth had read *Dr. Spock's Baby and Child Care* four times. Front to back. She took notes in the margins in case she lost her mind during labour and needed to refresh herself quickly. She underlined and highlighted and folded down the pages. She wrote out things that appealed to her and plastered them all over the burnt orange refrigerator in the apartment. "*Love for the baby comes gradually,*" it said next to the grocery list: milk, cheese, eggs, butter. "*Parents are just as human as their children.*" Ruth was prepared. And The Book became so fragile that the pages sometimes wafted out and floated to the floor.

Blame The Book? Blame Ruth?

I guess I could always blame Grandma Mileford. She was pretty ineffective and unhelpful, as mothers go. Whispering. Giving old-fashioned advice. Never listening—probably because her daughter was so damn loud it hurt to listen—everything with Grandma Mileford was always black or white. Only two ways. There was nothing in between, and there was never any forgiveness. If you did something wrong, just once, you were never forgiven. Perhaps Ruth had no one else to turn to for help.

By the time Ruth picked up Dr. Spock's book, by the time she bent her knees and tried to reach far down to the side of her large belly, Ruth was good and ready for it. Grandma Mileford didn't need any books when she had Ruth—after all, she raised her two sisters almost by herself—but our mother needed it. Ruth felt that Dr. Spock gave women permission to think for themselves. He gave them the option to trust themselves and not listen to all the wrong advice. This, Ruth thought, was monumental.

We hit another bump in the ambulance and my head shifts on the hard pillow. "Hold on," says the paramedic. A white flash, some pain, and then—

When Ruth was pregnant and reading The Book, she didn't yet know the consequence of having a baby, of having a Sadie. A Sadie is what she became. One of a Kind. Hard to look up in a Book. Our Sadie, we called her.

At first Ruth merely used The Book to help her figure out breastfeeding and toilet training, but soon she was using The Book to help her interpret her daughters. The Book was a Magic Eight Ball. It was a Crystal Ball.

But I'm jumping ahead.

First there was the pregnancy. And Daddy's hair loss. And then The Book. Then there was Marvellous Marvin and his Magic Show. Marvellous Marvin, the man who bent to pick up the shower of books from the floor of the Book Barn on Yonge Street. Marvellous Marvin in his top hat and tails. On his way to work. On his way to woo the blue-haired audience at his show. The white rabbit under his hat.

Then there was me. All of me and all of my love. Sylvia Swamp.

•••

"The maidenly figure goes gradually into eclipse, and with it goes sprightly grace... No more hopping into the car on the spur of the moment, going anywhere the heart desires and coming home at any old hour."

ONE WEEK TO go before Sadie's birth and Ruth was in the doctor's office waiting after having blood taken, after peeing into a cup. She was reading the paper when she saw him again. Marvellous Marvin. There on page three of the Entertainment Section of the *Toronto Daily Star*. He was performing at a local hotel on Thursday nights. Limited Run, it said (although he performed in that same modest hotel, the one with the musty conference room, green carpet, a sticky bar, and an uneven stage, the entire time I knew him. It always said Limited Run in the paper. Limited in talent, sure. Limited magic, perhaps. Just plain limited).

"He's a sleight of hand genius," the advertisement barked. "Come see the amazing close-up tricks and spell-binding optical illusions. Using everyday objects like cards, matches, silk, rope, thimbles and money, Marvellous Marvin will astound."

Ruth was ordered to sit in the waiting room for ten minutes to make sure she wasn't going to faint—she had once already, low blood pressure—before she could get up and waddle out. She had been thinking of this mysterious man ever since the day in the bookstore. She would read The Book and superimpose Marvellous Marvin's face onto Dr. Spock's—his advice, Marvin's features. She was sure this book-picker-upper looked at her a certain way that day, she was sure there was something sparking between them, a gleam in his eyes. The more she read The Book, the more she thought Fate, Destiny. When she left the waiting room she headed straight for the hotel. Her round belly, close to term, led the way. In this way my sister was present the first time Ruth and Marvin connected. Peeking out of Ruth's belly button? She was there both first times, I guess. In the bookstore and again at the hotel.

It all began with Sadie then. Did it? It's hard to know.

The ambulance clatters along. Swishing windshield wipers. A bumpy road. I do what I always do: I imagine myself 600 pounds lighter. I imagine a body strong and long and lean, a body angular with bones protruding. A flat stomach. Small, perky breasts. Legs that go on and on, miles of legs. If I squeeze my eyes tight closed I can see me.

If I open my eyes I see him. Marvellous Marvin. I need to stretch and mould him, like clay, to get him right. First impressions are important. It is critical that I remember him as he really was, before all that eventually happened. Only, like the Sylvia-Body of my dreams, I never really knew him. Did any of us really know him?

"A slap-dash magician with brown eyes and only a little charisma," is what my grandmother called him. "The only thing he has in his pants is a small rabbit."

(I imagined it, white, curled up there, keeping warm, nibbling.)

"You're jealous," Ruth shouted at her mother.

"Wouldn't the rabbit bite?" I asked. "Wouldn't that hurt?"

Ruth shouted "You're jealous" all the time. At least ten times a day. Everyone, everybody, everything was always jealous of Mrs. Ruth Mileford Swamp. But Ruth didn't let it bother her. "It doesn't bother me that you're jealous," she said. "Not at all."

Can you see why Ruth had no friends?

"I don't need friends. They are always jealous of me."

I didn't need friends either. My Sylvia-Dream Body didn't need friends.

Cloakroom, grade six. Pushing and shoving.

"Get your hat, Sylvia. It's cold." The teacher is lovely, fresh and young, full of energy.

I place my hat on my head. A toque. It rips. Has my head grown? A hole in the seam. My brain is bigger, I think. I'm almost pleased with this thought. I've learned so much today that my head grew.

"Fat Head," Tommy shouts. Pushes me. "Fat Head."

My legs are huge. My girl-breasts sag. My arms shake. My stomach wiggles. The only thing I think is fine is my brainy head.

Tommy throws the toque on the floor and steps on it. I walk home. Cold. Sadie walks me home. Ten steps ahead. Says, "If you'd just stick up for yourself, Sylvia. Jesus." She doesn't look back at the school or at me. She always looks forward.

Ruth left the doctor's office, belly out front, and went straight to Marvellous Marvin's dressing room. She followed the ad in the paper. The hotel staff was familiar with sending women up to Marvin's suite on the fourth floor of the hotel, although they'd never sent hugely pregnant women, or even young women before. Usually blue-haired women wearing lots of jewellery. Ruth banged on his door, breathless though she took the elevator. The band-aid from the blood test fell off the minute she knocked on his door. "Fate." (All my life Ruth had the tendency to interpret everything thrown at her as signs and she interpreted these signs any way she wanted to. Sadie called it Selective Interpretation or SI for short. When Sadie was still being nice to me and Ruth was being Ruth, she would look secretly at me, raise her eyebrows, and say, "SI.")

But is Fate something you control? Do we make our own Fate? Was it my Fate to be fat or did I make myself fat because of Fate? Chicken or egg.

All Ruth knew about Marvellous Marvin was that he was capable of bending over quickly ("So athletic, his knees don't even crack") and picking up the books for her at The Book Barn. He touched the actual Book she bought, the one that saved her life, made her strong, energized her, when he said goodbye to her. Put his hand on it, like he was blessing it. And then a bouquet of plastic flowers magically appeared from his hands. And a quarter from her ear. She remembered this on the way to his hotel room and blushed. He must have been feeling something too, she reasoned ("Pregnancy hormones?" jaded, teenage Sadie asked. "He was feeling your damn pregnancy hormones?").

Ruth finds out later that, when bending to pick up The Book for her, Marvellous Marvin stole her watch and picked the pocket of the sales clerk standing close by. But by the time she discovered this, she couldn't stop thinking about the magician and so she made the whole thing one big joke. She forgave him with a laugh. "He gave me back the watch," Ruth said to Mr. Swamp when he found out. "Right away."

"He was just fooling around, Mr. Swamp. Honestly. You're so stuck up. You have absolutely no sense of humour. You sit there on the couch and watch TV. What do you know about magic?"

It was always complicated. Ruth wanted to love herself, she wanted to love her baby, she maybe even wanted to love Mr. Swamp. And she really wanted to love Marvin and so she did. The watch he returned to her after she discovered it was missing was not hers, but she was too proud to say anything about it. Mr. Swamp noticed though. "It says, My Beloved Rose on it," he said. "What does that mean?"

Ruth loved Marvin because of Daddy's Loss of Hair and his Accountant Job and his Inability to Be Romantic. She loved him because, like me, she needed to love something fully, wholeheartedly. She needed to love herself and she loved what she became when she was with him. She fell in love with what Marvellous Marvin represented: Magic. And one crummy stolen watch, one small mistake, was never going to change that.

Ruth was knocking on Marvellous Marvin's hotel room door. Sealing her Fate. He answered wearing a black tuxedo. He had plastic flowers up the sleeves. He was getting ready for a late afternoon show. "Yes?" he said, "Can I help you?" He smelled like cologne, like spice and cigarette smoke and whisky. He sent shivers up her bent-back spine. How could she resist?

What I think is this: I think he must have been worried that she was there for her watch. Imagine him, can't you, panicky brown eyes scouting the exits, how do I escape? Perhaps he'd already sold it, perhaps he'd given it to a lover, perhaps he'd lost it—just one of the many items Marvellous Marvin acquired over the years. Women and objects. But then women are objects, aren't they? I just happen to be a rather large one.

Sadie always said that it was the blood test that did it, that made them come together. "She was just dizzy," Sadie said. "Blood loss." Although the first thing Ruth did when Marvin answered the door was to fall into his arms in a swoon, I'm not sure if I believe that it was just blood loss. To me, Marvellous Marvin and Mother were always meant to be together. It wasn't Fate, it was just a matter of timing and energy and the *Toronto Daily Star* and need. It was just a matter of Mother's desire, her selfishness. Underneath these layers of flab, I'm sort of a romantic. It's the Plath in me, I guess. There was a spark of electricity in the air whenever Marvellous Marvin and Ruth were together, and it wasn't just because of the thick, plush, green carpets or the dry heat in the hotel.

"Sylvia," Sadie said once. "Don't be stupid. He just wanted to fuck a pregnant lady. All guys do. Just to see what it's like."

Hum, hum, I hummed. Block the words.

"Oh my," Ruth said as she fell into Marvin's suite.

As we got older the story kept changing, depending on Ruth's mood. Ruth said that Dr. Spock wrote about *"blue feelings"* and wrote that *"you just weep easily." "Go to a movie,"* he suggested, *"or to the beauty parlor, or get yourself a new hat or dress."*

"Mother," Sadie said. "He didn't say to get a boyfriend. He said to get a new hat."

"Perhaps a hat is a metaphor for something else? Perhaps that was not exactly what he was suggesting? Did you ever think of that, Sadie? Dr. Spock is a genius. Sometimes he doesn't say exactly what he means. And Marvellous Marvin is not my boyfriend. He is just a good friend." Ruth slammed the bedroom door in our faces. "You'll never understand." Sadie rolled her eyes.

If a hat is a metaphor for having an affair then I don't know anything. Nowhere in The Book does it say to fall in love with a man who is not your husband. Believe me, I have looked.

Ruth always slammed the bedroom door in our faces. Once she slammed it on Sadie's fingers. "I'm wasting a perfectly nice Sunday afternoon in this hospital," she said later. "A finger cast for my clumsy, snooping daughter." Ruth talked in a megaphone voice and slammed doors. Sadie howled and I hummed.

On the other hand, Grandma Mileford only whispered. Daddy said that the loud gene skipped a generation. I'm not loud. Sadie isn't. Although maybe my loudness comes out in my size. "Here I am," my body shouts, "listen to me." Sadie is so slim she slides into nothingness. Her voice, no matter how hard she tried to make it loud, was always tiny. It chimed like bells. She may say loud things, but she can't be loud.

This is what life was like. The Swamp sisters, large and small. Mother and Daddy and Marvellous Marvin. There is more. Levers shift. Memories collide.

"Sylvia, Sylvia, Sylvia Swamp,
All we hear is chomp, chomp, chomp."

Skip rope songs. Chants. Sadie walked me home. Ten feet ahead. She always walked me home even if she hated it. My Sadie.

Two days after Ruth met Marvellous Marvin in his hotel suite she asked him home for dinner. When my father came home from work to a singing, pregnant, cooking woman, he smiled as he stood at the door to the apartment. He thought, ah, she's not angry right now. Ruth was in the kitchen, apron tied around her huge waist. Ruth sang. Something upbeat and cheery. My father stepped into the kitchen and saw his wife so happy, lipstick on, high heels, perfume scenting the air, cooking up a storm, and he said, "What's going on?" with a smile. Things were going to change, he thought, things were going to get better.

That was when the doorbell rang. Initially Daddy thought that Marvellous Marvin was selling something. A white rabbit? We don't need one, thanks. A bouquet of plastic flowers? Nope. Cologne? Perhaps.

But how did you get in the apartment building? No, Marvin was there to have dinner. And Ruth was bustling around, her face flushed. She didn't look pregnant suddenly. Suddenly my father noticed that she could still sashay those hips when she wanted (Some of the Mileford women are famous for their sashaying hips). Her legs were long and lean and shapely. Her breasts were swollen, large, popping out of her blouse.

"What's going on?" he asked again, this time with different inflection.

Marvin entered and Ruth kissed him on both cheeks (Ruth liked to pretend she was in Paris). Marvin shook hands with my father, put the white rabbit down on the coffee table where it remained completely still for the whole evening ("Oh, isn't he adorable?" Ruth said. "I think he's a she," said Marvellous Marvin, winking at Ruth), and raised a toast to Dr. Benjamin Spock's book. "Without which," he said, "I wouldn't be here with lovely Ruth Mileford—"

"Swamp," my father said.

("This is why I think the rabbit is fake," Sadie said when we were told this story by Ruth. "He doesn't move throughout the whole dinner. That's not possible. Rabbits move. All the time. Their noses twitch.")

"And her wonderful, bea-utific baby body—"

"My baby too," my father said. "My body—"

("He's a she rabbit, Sadie. You heard Marvellous Marvin.")

"Quiet, Mr. Swamp," said Ruth. She flashed her eyes. She giggled towards Marvellous Marvin.

"That's all I wanted to say," Marvin said. He patted—yes patted, (Daddy told us this another time when he had too much to drink, when he was lounging in front of the TV with his top pant button undone and his depleted hair sticking up as much as it could, his grey sweater worn at the elbows)—patted Ruth's bottom as she sailed back into the kitchen to bring out the first course.

"No, he didn't," Ruth said. "He never patted my ass."

("How dare he?" Sadie said, and giggled.)

The rabbit, the one Sadie thought must be stuffed, chewed on my father's stamp books and pooped on the coffee table ("I told you it wasn't fake," Sadie said.)

My father, greyer suddenly, sadder, whispered, "What's going on?"

What is going on?

Recently I saw a TV show about people who are narcissistic, who have NPD—Narcissistic Personality Disorder. These are people who need to be constantly admired, who need to feel they are grander than anyone else, and who lack empathy. Lots of movie stars and rock stars have it. Especially the new reality TV ones. "Look at me!" they shout.

Empathy: the ability to understand someone else's emotions or state of mind.

Ruth's stories were always bigger than real life, everything that happened to her—whether it was taking the bus, or in a line-up at the grocery store—was more impressive, exciting and interesting than could be possible. The things she said, the things she did, the way she treated others... it was always someone else's fault. Never her own. People existed in order to take care of Ruth's needs, she wasn't put on earth to take care of anyone. Even her strict mother had to drop everything when Ruth called. She had to fly to the rescue, or sit quietly and hear the wild story. And Ruth's children? We were never allowed to be better than her—not prettier, smarter or more sophisticated. Our stories must be pale in comparison.

The TV show mentioned that people with this disorder lose lovers, friends, spouses, that it affects their jobs—they are always getting fired for being too self-involved and never thinking they are wrong or at fault. The funny thing is, the show encouraged people to see a doctor if they think they have NPD. This made me laugh. How is that possible? Why would anyone who thinks they are perfect suddenly see that they aren't?

Supposedly the spaghetti was overcooked and mushy, the sauce had too much garlic in it and made Ruth burp, the rabbit pooped a lot, and Marvellous Marvin talked about himself all night.

My father scratched his head and more of his hair fell out. Ruth stormed around the kitchen, her head full of magic and tricks.

"I have a plan for my life, Mr. Swamp, and you have to fit into it. You have to stop slinking around all sad and boring."

"I don't know what you want," Mr. Swamp said. "I don't know what I'm supposed to be or who I'm supposed to be."

"Anyone other than who you are."

•••

The Father's Part

"He can sit in the waiting room with some old magazines and worry about how the labour is going, or he can go to his unbelievably lonely home... It's no wonder that a man may take this occasion to drink in company at a bar."

I'M JUMPING AROUND. I know. That's ironic, isn't it? I can jump around with language, with story, with memory, with life, but, sadly, tragically, drastically, I can't do it with my legs. I'd probably break them or crash through the floor. I don't know, I've never tried. I stopped jumping when I was young. I never skipped rope. I never made it around the track or leaped the hurdles or bounced on the trampolines. I waddled around the gym, the field, smiling widely.

Things aren't coming to me in any sort of order. Memory is like that—a mash of images and thoughts, one thing layered next to the other, one thing setting off the other. There's no sense to anything. Why is it that when you are stationary, when you are lying completely still, your mind still races wildly along? Thinking takes my breath away. It exhausts me to try and keep up.

Marvin watches, watched, is watching. Daddy, oh Daddy. He merely sits, sat, was sitting. I wonder if I could sum up all our lives like that. Just one word in three tenses. What would be my word? Sylvia ate, eats, has eaten. Ruth shouts, shouted, was shouting. Sadie changes, is changing, changed.

Imagine what my father went through:

Before Sadie was born, every day, when he came home from work, another thing was added to the apartment. "Dr. Spock says we need," Ruth said. And then she would list everything. All laid out on the living room floor. Ready to go. Ready for Sadie.

"Aren't you going to breastfeed?" my father asked. "I think my mother breast-fed. I'm not sure. I wish I could ask her."

"I don't know yet," Ruth said. "I'm just getting ready for all possibilities. Unplanned eventualities. Perhaps the baby won't want a breast. Perhaps the baby will want a bottle instead. Who knows? Stop talking about your dead mother. What do I care what she did or didn't do?"

"Ah," said my father, in his usual way, as he settled in front of the TV with his newspaper and his grey cardigan sweater and grey hair. He probably thought that she was just hopped up on hormones. He probably thought things would get better. He probably worried about the money spent. For now, he watched TV and ate the meal Ruth had prepared and went to bed and got up the next day and worked and then did the whole thing over again. Maybe he went to the bar down the street for a beer once in a while? Maybe he had some friends, someone he talked to? His family, his mother and father, were gone, both dead in a car accident when he was newly in Toronto. Ruth had never even met them. My father didn't have a brother or a sister. And his dog, Sadie, was long gone.

When Our Sadie was born, Ruth screamed bloody murder in the hospital. (The nurses finally sedated her because they couldn't take the noise. "That's the one with the mouth on her," one nurse said, as Ruth was being wheeled out of the delivery room when it was over, a beatific smile on her face, a babe wrapped in a pink bundle in her arms, her face flushed. "Look at her now. You should have heard what came out of that hole in her face when she was pushing.") My father said he could hear her from the waiting room. He said all the men in the waiting room turned their pale faces to the floor. One man started pacing.

"What did you do, Daddy?" Sadie asked.

"Oh, I don't know. I read a magazine I suppose. I drank my coffee. I looked out the window and thought a bit."

Sadie looked disappointed at this response. "But what did you do?"

"What do you mean?"

Sadie took to the breast right away, to Ruth's horror.

"What will I do with all those bottles?" she cried. "What will I do with all the advice? How will I follow it? I can't skip the whole section on bottlefeeding."

"There's always weaning," Grandma Mileford said. "I never breastfed you. It just wasn't done in my day. It's primitive, if you ask me."

"I'm pretty sure my mother breast-fed," Daddy said. "I'm almost certain, but I don't remember, of course." He laughed nervously.

"Lucky you," shouted Ruth, Sadie stuck to her tit like a kitten, sucking wildly. "This is beyond me. I feel like a cow."

"Everything is beyond you, Ruth," Grandma Mileford said with a sigh. "You were always sensitive. That's why I'm here. Grandma Mileford is here, Sadie love. When your mother messes up, I'll be here."

"Having a baby," Ruth said, "is easier than taking care of one."

"Don't I know it. Wait 'til she grows up and turns into a shrew."

"A shrew?"

Grandpa Mileford was in the corner of the room, doing a crossword puzzle and occasionally staring out the hospital window at a rain-soaked street.

"Dr. Spock does say breastfeeding is natural," Ruth said. And sighed.

My father remained still. Perhaps shell-shocked. Or perhaps because he saw Sadie, so perfect, nestled there next to her mother. It was enough to scare anyone. A baby. Anyone would sit up and take notice of his life, anyone would think beyond the here and now, wonder what had passed and what was to come. He sat so still in the other corner that everyone forgot he was there. He balanced his one ankle on his other knee and jiggled his foot mercilessly. He cleared his throat. Ahem. Ahem.

"Stop that."

In pictures we have of Sadie she was perfectly formed. Her head so round and sweet and downy. Her eyes bright and intelligent. Her lashes long and thick. Nails tapered. Silky small paws. Sadie was the cat's meow Ruth said, ruthlessly, to anyone who would listen.

Occasionally our father picked Sadie up and coddled her and giggled and cooed and gaahed. As fathers will do. But most of the time he worked downtown in his drab office, in his drab clothing, with his drab hair and grey face. Looking at my father was like looking at a white wall for a long time. You faded into it and saw behind it to the things in your imagination. Daddy, when I looked at him, became the circus, or a white polar bear, or Mrs. Leard, my grade three teacher. He became a mouse in a glass jar, a peanut on the floor. He was so quiet that "You can hear a pin drop when that man is around!" Mother shouted, and we all jumped.

Mr. Swamp married Ruth because of her wildness, I guess. He married her because she was colourful. She balanced his greyness, took it up a notch. But, somewhere along the line, my father realized that his grey was cancelled out by her colour. Ruth overwhelmed him.

This is not to say that my father didn't have a life outside of us. I'm sure he did. I'm sure (I hope) he had a quiet secretary at work, someone as muted as he was, and I hope they kissed softly behind closed doors. I'm sure (I hope) his mind was full of his own memories and of things he wanted to do, things he wished he'd become, happy thoughts, stories he told himself of what he was capable of doing. My father came home every day from work because he had two children, because he had a wife. There were reasons for his faithfulness that I think I can understand. He was a man of that generation. He was not selfish. My father was a kind, full-hearted person. He had morals and responsibilities.

He took care of us without asking for anything back.

I remember Daddy laughing at the TV. Mouth open, head back. I remember him holding my hand to cross the street. Or forcing me to walk the stairs. He had a powerful scent, muskiness and soap, gin, a smell that made me think of warmth and comfort. Once in a while he read to us. Once in a while he took us out for dinner or to the park or for a walk in the snow.

Ruth said Daddy was fresh and bright-faced at the wedding. She said there was something about him that attracted her. "For God's sake, I married him, didn't I? There must have been something." But by the time I thought to ask him what made him so shadowy, he was long gone. He had disappeared into the chair in front of the TV. With hardly a sound.

Sometimes, when Ruth stormed past us as we watched TV, I would see Daddy reach out with his eyes and caress her body. I would see his eyes linger on her breasts or her legs. And she knew it. Whenever my mother (or Sadie, as she got older) wanted anything, she would use her body to get it. Move a little more suggestively, sway her hips, unbutton that top button on her blouse, shorten her skirt, soften her powerful voice.

Sadie said they only made love twice. "Me, you," she pointed us out. "Duh." But I like to think my father became someone else behind their closed bedroom door. I like to think he threw off his cloak of greyness and underneath he was a rainbow of colours and lights and strength. Underneath he glowed.

"God, you're stupid," Sadie said. "Do you honestly think that?"

I knew my father as TV companion and potato chip lover. I knew him as the only man (the only person, actually) who ever looked right at me and didn't see through me. He was my Daddy. I loved him, adored him, but, just as easily, I forgot he was there. It was so hard to focus on bland.

It was so hard to see him when everyone else was so blindingly visible.

•••

Relations with Grandparents

"The parents must have confidence that the children will be cared for according to their beliefs in important matters (that, for instance, they won't be compelled to eat food they don't like, be shamed for bowel accidents, or be frightened about policemen)."

For a while, when Ruth was pregnant with Sadie, Dr. Spock's book told her to *"lift herself by her bootstraps."* And so Ruth did. She bought new boots at Canadian Tire, the mountain-hiking kind. There is one picture of her in them and it still makes me smile. It's as if she was a different person wearing them. As if she was real, not an act. She threw out all the high heels she had accumulated over the years. These boots were lined with sheep skin and were waterproof and good for minus forty. Good for hiking to the top of Mount Everest. Ruth knew they were boots you would wear exploring the Arctic, but she didn't care because Dr. Spock insisted that she lift herself up. Feel good about herself. Be comfortable. No one ever insisted she do this before. These were solid boots, boots meant to conquer the world. And Ruth's mood, her feelings about herself had been plummeting since the moment she became pregnant. The way Ruth took herself, and the world around her, much too literally, was one of the things both my father and Marvellous Marvin loved about her.

It was one of the things that infuriated her mother, my Grandma Mileford. One of the many things in their tortured relationship.

Dr. Spock wrote about a woman patient who said of her children, "*This one always rubs me the wrong way.*"

Grandma Mileford and Ruth never saw eye to eye. Ruth told us that Grandma Mileford was a horrible mother, that she was demanding and bossy and never let Ruth do what she wanted. When I saw Grandma Mileford there, so silent and meek, Grandpa Mileford in front of his crossword, forehead creased in concentration, I could never imagine this. Neither could Sadie.

"Mother's problem," Sadie said, "was that Grandma Mileford never let her do everything she wanted to do. And Grandpa Mileford never got involved. So now that she has her own kids and a husband she can do whatever she wants."

"Even if it's bad?" I said.

"Especially if it's bad."

There were stories of Ruth's childhood. A lonely one, she moaned. A violent one. Ruth said the godawful quiet demanded in her house was oppressive. She said she had to tiptoe through the house, avoid all squeaking floorboards, never have friends over. Grandma said, "Hogwash. You didn't have any friends. Besides, you were loud enough on your own for a hundred kids."

"What's a four letter word for creation?" Grandpa said, fiddling with his crossword.

Grandma Mileford told me that Ruth was born bitter. She said that my mother felt the whole world was out to get her and that everything she did was perfect and that people just didn't understand that. "Your mother thought no one ever appreciated her the way she thought she deserved. She was demanding and controlling. It was always about her," Grandma said, "never about anyone else."

"Sounds about right," Sadie said.

Ruth was fat. That's where I get it, I guess. Grandma Mileford used to take me on trips through her photo album (she had one album—Ruth from birth to age fifteen. "What happened to her after fifteen, Grandma?" I'd ask and Grandma wouldn't answer, she would roll her eyes and sigh, as if the oppressiveness of a teenager still weighed her down). We would start with a pudgy baby, swaddled, pink bonnet. Then a toddler—legs with so many creases, so many layers, they looked like elephant legs. Fat arms. "Look at Ruth's wrists," Grandma would laugh. "We'd have to separate that fold in order to clean in there ... if we didn't, oh my, the smell ... do you remember the smell, Grandpa? Like old cheese." Then there was sour-faced Ruth (I can see her slowly becoming the woman I know, the beautiful woman), sitting on the porch steps, her hands on what would be her hips if there wasn't so much blubber. "She's about twelve here," Grandma says. "Hard to believe that in the three short years after this picture she lost all that weight."

"How? HOW?" I needed to know.

Grandma Mileford served me Kentucky Fried Chicken in front of the TV—her soaps. She patted my greasy paw. She mopped the drool off my chin. "You'll grow out of it," she said. "Don't you worry."

But I didn't. And Ruth worried.

"I starved myself, Sylvia," Ruth shouted. "How the hell else do you think I did it? I wouldn't settle for looking that way. That's why you and I are different. I have willpower."

Even though she wasn't happy with her parents, Ruth still visited Grandma Mileford once a week. Ruth always, without fail, patted her father on the head while he did his crossword puzzles at the kitchen table. Her hand hovered over his bald spot as if considering bashing it in.

"Life, Grandpa," I told him. "A four letter word for creation is life."

"Smart girl," Grandpa whispered.

If they were given a chance to speak now, if they were still alive, what would Grandpa and Grandma Mileford have to say about all of this?

Grandpa Mileford was a lot like my father. I can't remember him that clearly. I can only remember a figure crouched over a wooden table, pencil at the ready, worrying an eraser. His short laugh and quiet smile. I remember a bald head, stiffening for the pat. I remember a grey cardigan with holes in the elbows. But sometimes I think I'm confusing my father with Grandpa. It was easy to do.

The women in my life have generally been loud and bright. And the men have been grey. Dr. Spock would have had a field day with the men in my life. No wonder you are so fat, he might have said. Why would you ever want to attract anyone when all the men you've known (two really, if you think about it. Well, three, if you consider Marvellous Marvin as someone I knew—and I don't really consider him this way because, really, I never knew him) are so unbelievably boring? That's what he might have said to me.

"Never," Ruth said, "put words in Dr. Spock's mouth."

Sometimes I think this is all a dream. Me in the ambulance. The paramedics, the firemen (now, *they* are colourful and lovely and strong and definitely not boring). My huge unwieldiness. How could I have become this large? This sick? Rolls upon rolls upon rolls of me. I'm not just a fat woman, I'm a caricature of a fat woman.

We are still a long way from the veterinary hospital. My paramedic is nodding off. His head lolls on his shoulders, his arms are crossed in front of his chest, his legs are stretched long across the floor almost touching my thighs as they rock back and forth with the motion from the ambulance. The two up front are chatting amicably, laughing about something or other—not me, I'm sure of it. One says, "Fourteen laps, can you believe?" "Circuit?" the other asks. "No, just constant. Nothing new. One minute each set."

Nothing new.

I fart. The (wonderful, bright, beautiful, strong, garlicky, Greek salad) paramedic wakes and looks at me. I shrug. So sorry. My body gets away from me. I have no control. The smell is overpowering. A window is cranked at the front of the ambulance and I can feel the breeze rush over my hot red face.

Grandma Mileford knew about Marvellous Marvin and her daughter and she hated it. She hated that Ruth met him when she was still pregnant. This disgusted her—a visibly pregnant woman conducting an affair. The fact that Ruth was also married was merely an afterthought because Grandma Mileford wasn't particularly impressed with my father.

"The whole thing," she said, mildly, "just plain stinks."

"No, it doesn't."

"What about your husband?"

"What about him?"

"We paid for the wedding."

"It's always all about you," Ruth shouted. Slammed the door.

Every Thursday, six weeks after Sadie was born, Ruth dropped Sadie off with her mother. She would pat her father on the head, and head off to perform magic in bed with Marvellous Marvin.

At least, when we were older, that's what we assumed she was doing. That's what Sadie said must have happened.

"Play with Sadie, Mother," Ruth said. "Bond with her. She is your only grandchild." Ruth took off. Her black bra strap showed. Her lipstick was deep red, her nails freshly lacquered. Those old Canadian Tire boots were now in the garbage and her high heel sandals click-clacked down the front walk.

Grandparents: "*They want to hold him, joggle him, tickle him, jounce him, waggle their heads at him, and keep up a blue streak of baby talk.*"

But Grandma Mileford did nothing of the kind. After all, she never read Dr. Spock. She didn't joggle or tickle or jounce. She would place Sadie on the floor and return to watching her afternoon TV shows, the soaps, and picking at her teeth with her pointy silver nail scissors. Occasionally she would get up to stretch or blow her nose. Sometimes she cried or laughed quietly. Depending on who was shot or killed or divorced or missing. Then she would sit down again and adjust her butt on the squeaky vinyl chair. Sadie and I both remember the squeaking sounds. And the TV. Other than that, the silence.

Grandma Mileford's kitchen always smelled like baking even though she never baked. She merely heated up take-out food in the oven. Sadie liked the quiet the most about the Mileford house. Every little noise startled Grandma. A car door slammed outside, a dog barked, the mail came whooshing through the slot in the front hallway door, a doorbell chimed on TV. Sadie Baby lay on the floor staring up at our grandmother and watched her tense and fidget and jump at every small sound. She was a one-woman show. A class act. She was Sadie's first performance art. Bang. Jump. Settle in. Bang.

What did Ruth do with Marvellous Marvin? Even though I've spent almost half of my life in a bed, I haven't ever really been there. With a man that is. The closest I've come to snuggling is in the last several years when Sadie would snuggle next to me to stay warm. If she did that today

I know I wouldn't be able to feel her there. My skin seems to have lost its sensitivity and all I can feel these days are my aching bones, my rolls of flesh. The insides of me, deep down there, under it all, my insides are always pained.

Ruth on top of Marvellous Marvin? Or on top of Daddy? Or underneath or behind or standing up or in a shower stall or on the kitchen table or on the floor? I can't remember what my private parts look like so it's impossible to summon anyone else's up in graphic positions. Breasts. Thighs. Legs. Groin. Pubic hair. All I know of breasts and thighs is chicken. From what I've seen on TV, I could look all of this up on the Internet. That's what they say the Internet is for. But I don't have a computer.

Do you suppose I might go home? Do you suppose I might ever be the kind of person to get a computer and attach it to this Internet thing?

Can you see me moving my sausage fingers together on a keyboard? fadsjkl; jkl;asdfa

Sometimes I think I know so much, when really I know so little.

My body gets away from me. It farts again. In his half-sleep my paramedic puts his hand up to his nose.

Grandpa Mileford often farted. Perhaps this is hereditary?

Grandma Mileford was always feeding me. I guess I can blame her for who I am and what I've become. If it wasn't for all her store-bought cookies and her trips to Kentucky Fried Chicken and McDonald's, then maybe I'd be a normal weight. Maybe?

But Sadie ate just as much as I did back then at Grandma Mileford's, filling the silence with food, and she still managed to be rice-paper thin and beautiful.

I've spent my whole life trying to rationalize my weight, trying to understand it. Sadie, at the end, became my enabler when I finally couldn't move to feed myself, and I was the body that enabled. I chose to eat. She chose to feed me. Suicide or murder?

And did she really choose anything?

Fat people are jolly. Anyone can find comedy in the morbidly obese, right? Like a bowl full of Jello. Santa Claus. Dom DeLuise. John Candy. Show me an unhappy fat thing. Fat things are funny.

•••

He had white rabbits in cages. Sixteen or twenty of them. They all looked the same and, before Reggie came along to take care of them, his hotel room always smelled like sawdust and cedar chips and shit and urine and rotting vegetables. He had many hundreds of plastic flowers in all colours of the rainbow. Like an old lady's living room. "Even indigo," Sadie said. Before Mother and Sadie worked for him, Marvellous Marvin employed stooges that he sent into the audience to read minds and pick pockets during his act. He cut a small boy from the audience in half with a chainsaw and then put him back together just as cleanly and nicely as you please. No blood involved. He waved his magic wand, plastic, white-tipped, in the air and presto all of his hundreds of colourful handkerchiefs were tied together. Card tricks galore. Double lift and turn over, snap change, the Braue reversal, the glide, square and glimpse. Cards moved rapidly through his hands. He performed magic with matchsticks and silk scarves, spoons and ropes to tie complicated knots that fell away under a spell. ("What has the potential to tangle, will always tangle," Marvin said.)

Rubber bands and vanishing acts. A disappearing woman—sometimes she was our mother, sometimes someone lucky from out there, beyond the spotlight, or sometimes the daughter of the manager of the hotel. Never me because I was too big to fit in the box. ("If we put Sylvia in," Ruth said, "we'll never get her out.") It was funny that I could not be made to disappear even though I spent my whole life invisible. Irony, I guess. Or sad. Sometimes the volunteer who disappeared didn't come back (drinking at the bar?) and Marvellous Marvin, wiping his brow, got a little angry. "Where are you?" he sang. "Come back, my darling." Once Sadie vanished and didn't come back for an hour. We could feel the anticipation, the nervousness in the crowd. "I was going to the bathroom," she said, sheepishly. One time Marvellous Marvin changed a rabbit into a grey dove but the dove got free and flew up to the ceiling and perched dangerously near the whirring ceiling fan. The dove shit on anyone below. The crowd gasped and cringed, waiting for the blades to strike, the blood to splatter. Would the dove stay alive if the fan made its mark? Like a chicken with its head cut off? Or would it fall to the ground, fall on us below? I was in the audience that day and I couldn't help but clap with delight and anticipation. It took a large ladder, four men and three pellet guns to clear everything up. The bird didn't get hit by the fan, but he did die of shock, of stage-fright. In my opinion, this was one of Marvin's most successful shows.

He was a B Magician. Screwed up as much as he performed flawlessly. We were as astonished when a trick worked as when it didn't. Marvellous Marvin wore a black toupée that stayed on so tight it didn't move when he was making love. Or so they said.

"Do you think he uses super-glue?" I asked Sadie.

Sadie shrugged.

His eyes were a shocking brown, like chocolate milk sprinkled with gold, and his teeth were slightly uneven and gummy. More yellow than white. He tended towards chubbiness, but sometimes he was lean. Sometimes Marvellous Marvin was actually fat.

Like me, but not like me.

He ended each show the same way. With fire, a poof of smoke, and ta-da, he was gone. Ruth stood on stage, as spell-bound as the audience. She bowed to thunderous applause and exited stage left.

What my mother (and Sadie) saw in him I will never know. It's incomprehensible.

"What you see in a dish of butter pecan ripple ice cream, I'll never know," Sadie countered.

My thoughts always return to Marvellous Marvin and the magical effect he had on our lives. The disaster he created and played through until the end. The fear he instilled. In me, in particular. There was a draw to Marvellous Marvin. A pull. Like the magnets he used in his show, he sucked you into his vortex. Spun you. Spat you out.

I made Mother and Sadie take me to several other magicians' shows over the years. They were all much better than Marvellous Marvin. No one caught fire, no rabbits died, they were all more astounding and colourful, more professional and smooth. But there was something about Marvin I could never put my finger on. He was like velcro. Once he stuck, you had to use force to rip him off.

When I was thirteen I was convinced that Marvellous Marvin was truly magic and had put a spell on my family. Now I know that he was merely momentarily charismatic, he was a reality TV star, we were insecure and looking for something and he used us to fill his ego. I know now that magic is fickle, magic is absurd. Every trick in the book can be explained and rationalized. We were his stooges. We kept his secrets.

Ruth said that a person has lost their innocence once they stop believing in magic. Ruth said they might as well be dead and buried when they stop feeling awe and surprise.

•••

Callers and Visitors

"Limit the visitors at first." "They have just gone through the equivalent of an operation..." "The doctor says I can see only one visitor a day for fifteen minutes, beginning tomorrow."

THE UP-FRONT PARAMEDICS are joshing each other, laughing and slapping their knees. Something is really funny. The smell in the ambulance has aired out, the windows are back up.

I never had a friend. I thought Sadie was. But she wasn't.

Out in the playground at school there are children gathered around me, circling me, chanting, throwing things. I look down and see a rock, a stick, someone's half-eaten apple in the dirt by my feet. A teacher is running over.

"You should all be ashamed of yourselves."

My lips are bleeding.

"She is eating her lips," a boy shouts. "She's so hungry she eats herself."

"Quiet." The teacher is horrified with me for biting my lips until they bleed.

"Come with me, young man." The teacher has the boy by his wrist, as if all of this is his fault and not mine.

"Why can't you just die?" Sadie asks afterwards, walking home.

I love her with all my heart. Even though she doesn't love me. Why doesn't she love me? My love envelopes her, I can see it slide like liquid in the ten-foot gulf between us. My sister. Shoulders slumped up ahead of me. Angry at me. Angry at the world.

There was a period of time when Ruth had what she called friends. They appeared when she first heard about Sadie and Marvellous Marvin in the baseball dugout in the rain. When she heard about it, but didn't believe it, from the police officer who brought Sadie home. It was as if Ruth had somehow conjured up a coven of witches, other women who were lurking in the woodwork, waiting for Ruth to need them to listen to her. They were there, suddenly, in our kitchen, having coffee, drinking wine, doing their nails or doing each others' nails. Ruth leaned on the counter, her wet-polished fingers held high. She led the discussion. She paused and looked at me when I came in to get another cookie, or a cream soda from the fridge. Jello was always tilting on angles in wine glasses on the second shelf in those days. Solidifying in shifting layers. The talking continued only when I left the room, the door swinging shut behind me. Glimpses of Ruth through the in-and-out of the door. Each slice of her more animated then before. Flashy.

I grew wider and wider with each year. But just because I kept quiet it didn't mean that I kept everything inside. Grade five, 180 pounds. Grade six, 220 pounds. Onward, upward.

The women hung out in the kitchen.

"Where," Sadie asked when she came home from school one day, "did she find so many friends all of a sudden?"

"Get out of that fridge, Sylvia," Ruth yelled.

"Always with your head in the refrigerator."

"Sylvia, if you are not careful you will be as big as a whale."

Beluga? Killer?

But I wanted to hear what they were saying about my sister. About my sister and Marvellous Marvin. And the only way to eavesdrop was to tiptoe to the food, take it out, eat it silently. My world had previously been so small (that's funny), so quiet (that's funny too). Now, suddenly there were women in the apartment. Friends. Imagine that.

Ruth was the ring-leader, bright and vivacious. But, at the end of each day, when the women trailed out—exuding cigarette smoke and perfume smells—Ruth crashed at the kitchen table, her fresh fingernails ripping through her hair.

"Jesus, I'm beat," she said to Mr. Swamp, to anyone who would listen. "Those women wear me out. All they do is complain. I want to shout: do something about your problems. Don't just complain about them."

Often, in the elevator, one of the kitchen-neighbour-women, if I wasn't invisible that day, would pat my head and say something soothing like, "Poor dear," or "How you holding up?"

Soon the women left. Ruth treated people nicely up to a point and then was disdainful. Everything is wrong with everyone. That was her opinion. The human race was going to pot. No one was good enough for Ruth Swamp. Ruth wanted to be alone and, in the long run, she was. Besides, one of the women had suggested that, perhaps, Marvellous Marvin was sleeping with Sadie, perhaps this really was what was happening, and this sent Ruth into a horrific rage. "Get out. Get out of my condominium."

Maybe if we all had friends?

Sadie didn't have any friends either. Did Daddy? Maybe at work?

I have a friend now. I smile at my paramedic. He smiles back. "Getting there," he says.

"It's better not to have friends," Mother told me and Sadie. She was dusting a styrofoam ball with glitter, creating a sparkling snowman. "You can't trust anyone these days. Remember what happened last week? On the news? That girl was killed by a schoolmate."

"It was her uncle, Mom," Sadie said.

"Still. He was a friend. After all, Dr. Spock says, *'It's frightening to most children to waken and find a stranger.'*"

"*For* most children. Not *to* most children," I said. I hummed.

"But he was her uncle," Sadie said.

"Uncle, stranger. Friend. It doesn't matter how he says it. And Sylvia, stop sniffing the glue."

Sweet smell of glue. I grinned, hummed. Mother sighed.

•••

Help for the Mother

"This is a good time to simplify housework by putting unnecessary furniture and furnishings in a store room for a couple of months or a couple of years."

I HELPED IN the kitchen. I did the dishes (and surreptitiously ate whatever was left on the plates). I vacuumed, but eventually got too big to lug the vacuum far. I did everything I could to make things better. After the incident in the baseball dugout, the did-she-or-didn't-she-Marvellous-Marvin-incident, Sadie and Mother were always at each other's throats. Bickering. Nothing was good enough for either one of them.

"Take off that blouse, Sadie, it's see-through."

"It is not. You bought it for me."

"To wear with an undershirt."

"I'm fourteen. I don't wear undershirts."

"What is going on here?" Daddy said.

"She's half-naked."

"I am not."

No one ever noticed that I was home from school. I was huge but I was as see-through as Sadie's blouse. People walked through me. If I closed my eyes I could feel them push through my skin and come out the other side.

Ruth was busy. She took Dr. Spock seriously and shoved the furniture in our apartment up against the walls. Crowded into square rooms Dusty. Her Christmas ornaments were scattered on all surfaces—glitter and glue and shiny pieces—but the last time we had a Christmas tree I was seven and Sadie was ten. Ruth decided then that we were definitely too old to celebrate.

My father said, "What's going on here? I mean, with the furniture."

And Ruth shoved Dr. Spock's book in his face. "Seriously, Mr. Swamp, don't you ever read anything? Don't you ever think? I'm simplifying my life."

Daddy looked around for his sofa, too far from the TV. He had come home to Mother and Sadie screaming at each other in the kitchen. Running his fingers through his thinning hair he raised his voice to a shout. For the first time ever.

"What the hell is going on around here, Ruth?"

We all stood still. And then Ruth came around.

"What do you care where the furniture is?"

She was shocked. He, Mr. Swamp, had raised his voice. I left and cowered in my bedroom, my head under the pillow. Sadie took off down the hall and changed her blouse. She threw the see-through one in the trash.

All night we heard Ruth grunting as she moved the furniture back. She swore at him. At herself, at the "fucking state of this condominium and my life," but then, in the morning, the living room was back in place and Ruth was settled on the sofa, waiting. For what I didn't know.

If Daddy had that effect on Ruth when he yelled then why didn't he yell more often? Why didn't he yell all the time? Why didn't he put Ruth and Sadie in their places when they fought? Someone needed to.

I went to school. But sometimes I spent the days looking for Sadie on the streets of Toronto. She was sixteen and she was fighting with our mother and she spent the nights out a lot. I didn't know where at the time. I was losing Sadie, my sister. When I went to school there was no one I knew across the playground, no one to walk me home. I was in a constant state of fear, of shock. Sadie had her part-time job with Marvellous Marvin. I searched the hydro poles for posters of his Magic Act. He was always at the same hotel but his posters were constantly new and exciting. He was still a Limited Run. I occasionally spent my allowance watching other magic shows if they were in town. Good ones. Nothing like Marvin's shoddy performances. I wanted to believe again and I almost did. Sometimes. Almost. I went to movies and ate popcorn and drank extra large Pepsi-Colas and Root Beers. I ate Snickers and Mars Bars and huge packs of red-cherry Twizzlers.

The apartment was often empty when I got home.

"What is a teenager?" I asked my father one night.

"Sadie," he said. "Sadie's a teenager."

"Yes, I know that. But what is a teenager?"

"Shhh, honey, I'm watching this show."

Teenagers. Sadie came and went for a while. She took her full Self with her. And her hair dryer and make up. Teenagers. She took everything she was—the clothes, the records, the curling iron. She never left a note. Even when she was around she was gone. Doors slammed shut. Music on too loud to talk. She was missing-in-action.

And my heart ached for her.

When we were little, one and four, Sadie and I had spent countless hours in front of our father's old tropical fish aquarium. We sat in the living room on the big loveseat. Me with my bottle, Sadie with her juice in a sippy cup. We snuggled there, the two of us, and watched the fish swim round and round the Christmas ornaments that Ruth put under water (glitter floated to the surface). It was like watching TV. Squished up warm and full with someone you love. A tropical, sparkling, beautiful, colourful show. It was a world that was generally clean and orderly, contained and lovely. The fish looked content. Around in circles they swam. Most of all, it was spellbindingly quiet and the heat from our bodies mingled and passed between us.

We did this up until I was almost three and Sadie was almost six. We did it everyday, watched those fish, until one day Sadie told me to feed the fish a whole can of their food to see what would happen. Sadie held me up so I could reach the top of the aquarium, so I could lift the lid (she has always been my enabler). And then we curled up together on that loveseat, hands clasped, and we watched them eat and eat and eat. They never stopped eating.

Sadie laughed. "Pigs," she said. Gleeful laughter. "They are piggy pigs. Like you, Sylvia."

One at a time, they bloated, floated to the top, and died. Amidst all the glitter.

(I still think it had more to do with the glitter from the Christmas ornaments than the food, but everyone always blamed me.)

"I knew that would happen," Sadie said triumphantly. "Sylvia killed the fish."

Equipment and Clothing

Getting Things Ahead of Time

"Then a little job like buying half a dozen nipples looms as a real ordeal."

IN THE AMBULANCE, I lie here. Dr. Spock, a mantra, a prayer: *"Don't use soft pillows for a mattress. There's a slight risk of the baby's smothering in one...."* I think about the bathtub and how it should be *"high enough so that you don't break your back bathing the baby."* Other equipment you'll need: *safety pins, rectal thermometer, absorbent cotton, vitamin drops, soap, diaper pail. Sweaters and sacks, diapers, shirts, nightgowns, waterproof sheeting.* I say these things to myself over and over now. I say these things to myself when I am sad, or hungry, or upset. I repeat a million times, lists. Always Dr. Spock. Am I becoming my mother?

Or am I missing my mother?

Ruth said he was a genius. The history books say he started something—a new way of raising a baby. Dr. Spock wrote that it was just plain common sense. Something a lot of people don't have.

Ruth's obsession with The Book was intense and complete. Nothing was left out. She loved the cover, the spine, the pages. She loved the table of contents and the blank pages at the back. There was nothing he wrote that she didn't eventually do in one way or another. Nothing she didn't buy.

From the day she was born, Sadie was the lunar eclipse over Ruth's moon. She was the shadow cast on the mirror. As Sadie grew more beautiful and stronger, Ruth shrunk and collapsed in upon herself. She fought it for years: Oil of Olay, pedicures, manicures, facials, hair appointments, diets—Scarsdale and grapefruit—new shoes and hats, coats and pants, skirts and blouses. But she couldn't keep up. Who could? Youth always wins. And there was nothing Dr. Spock could do to help her.

I was thirteen years old when Sadie began to hang out with Marvellous Marvin, but it seemed as if my whole life through I could see this happening. I had just been waiting for it. The tilt of Sadie's head towards Marvin on stage, the way she pressed her hands across her sweater to get the wrinkles out before she moved upstage and disappeared into his magical box. "Pick me, pick me," she called out from the audience, even when she was very young. Eyes shone. The pitch in her voice was high and lilting. He began using her in his act more and more. Less Ruth. More Sadie. And there was Ruth, sitting in the audience as the stooge, or behind the stage curtains. Scowler extraordinaire. Ferocious. "If looks could kill," Grandma Mileford would have said, if she had been there.

Grandma Mileford: "I'm not so sure about that girl," she confessed to me one afternoon in front of the soaps. "I think she may be trouble. Like her mother."

The ambulance brakes and swerves in the rain. The paramedics up front are quiet. I'm so sleepy. I feel disoriented, confused. Black spots dance in my vision.

Ruth wanted Sadie—remember how she said she wanted hundreds of babies? But when she finally had her, Sadie was more than she bargained for. Even though I hated Sadie at times, even though she was always mean to me, I think she was worth more than a hundred babies. But Ruth couldn't be Ruth with a baby. The biggest part of being a mother is giving up who you are, being selfless, and there was no way Ruth could be anything less than 100% Narcissistic Ruth. After all, her life, our life, was all about her, wasn't it?

"You're talking to yourself, Ms Swamp. Do you need more oxygen?"

I nod. The mask is placed on my mouth.

Ruth was depressed when she was pregnant and she stayed depressed after Sadie was born for a good long time and there was nothing a new purse or a drive in the country or a magician for a lover could do to prevent the sadness. It crept in and took over and often showed itself in the form of anger, rage, sullenness, hatred for our father, and eventually for Sadie, and disdain for me.

Don't get me wrong, it wasn't all Ruth's fault. We all played a part. Didn't we? We all contributed to what became of our family, the mistakes we made.

And I was the biggest mistake of all.

"Breathe, Ms Swamp. It won't help if you are crying."

"Everything OK back there, Mike?"

"Yeah. She's moving in and out of consciousness but I've put her back on oxygen."

"You need help?"

I hear movement, I feel warmth. Two paramedics now, on either side of me, squished into our little travelling box heading down the highway.

Medical and Nursing Care

"Your child's health is more important than the doctor's feelings or your own feelings."

MARVELLOUS MARVIN SAID, "Sadie, honey, come work for me. Your mother is run-down and tired."

"I am not tired. Nor am I run-down."

"Ruth, let the girl talk."

Sadie sat by the open window of our apartment, looking out. She was bare-legged, tanned, her hair sunny-blonde. "Yeah." Gum chewing. "Yeah, I could use a job."

"Sadie. Your school work."

"What's going on here," Daddy said.

"Sadie is getting a job." I was standing in the kitchen, watching.

"A job?"

"Mr. Swamp. Don't you think Sadie is too young to work?"

"Doing what?" I said.

Daddy looked at Marvellous Marvin. He looked at his wife. His two daughters. He shrugged. "I'm not sure I understand. What's going on?"

Sadie grinned.

•••

Frankness Works Best

"The mother will have five or ten questions that she wants to ask, with her first baby, anyway."

RUTH WAS TOO open with us, her daughters. She told us too much. Things a mother shouldn't tell her daughter. I didn't realize it at the time. I thought it was normal for a mother to talk about sex and her lover to her four-year-old. And bodies. Too many bodies. Too much about female parts—blood and mucus and stench. I had no way of knowing what was right and what was wrong. I had no friends. No way to compare. No one to ask. I wanted to ask Sadie but she didn't talk to me very much. Sadie's breasts happened—just happened, one day she didn't have them, the next day she needed a bra—she got hips and the hormones coursed through her body and Ruth kept talking and talking and Sadie went wacko. That's what Ruth said, at least, "Sadie, you're wacko. You're hopped up on hormones."

Marvellous Marvin was always in the background, looking, admiring.

"Mother," Sadie whined—she rolled her mascara-thick, eye-lined, heavy-lidded eyes. Sexy eyes. I always loved that, Sadie's eye rolling. She had this way of starting her eyes at the floor and then moving them slowly up, both eyes following the same direction, until we could only see the whites. Right around. A big, funny circle. It always made me laugh. Remembering it makes me laugh right now, in the ambulance. The mask is tight. The garlic-paramedic and his friend think I'm choking. More oxygen. Concerned expressions. I would wave my arms, stop, if I weren't tied down.

"We're almost there," my paramedic says. I settle down. Breathe. In, out, in, out.

"Shut up, fatty," Ruth said to me when I laughed at Sadie's eye rolling. I was moving up to 200 pounds then. Which, come to think of it, actually seems thin now.

"Oh, God, I'm sorry, Sylvia. I didn't mean to call you fat. I'm sorry."

Ruth meant well. She just couldn't help herself.

"Do I yell at her for being fat?" I heard her say to Daddy one day. "Or do I just ignore it and hope she gets better? What do I do? Tell me."

"She's not sick, she's just a little overweight."

"Dr. Spock says that kids get chunky when they are going through puberty. He says not to worry about it."

"You could talk to a real doctor."

"Mr. Swamp. That's enough. Dr. Spock is a real doctor."

"Well then," Daddy sighed. "How can anything I say compete with that? You've got your answer."

Sadie's sweaters got tighter and tighter. Her lips went from chapped and bitten to coated blood red. Our mother tried to get her to tone it down. She said things like, "You'll never be taken seriously," but Sadie had a hard time not laughing. In fact, she did start to laugh. Loudly. Ruth was wearing bright red lipstick. Tight sweaters. High heel shoes. They were mirror images of each other. Sadie was just a bit blonder. Ruth was just a bit hippier. A bit breastier. Ruth had a bit more perfume on and her mascara often globbed in the corners of her eyes.

Really, they both scared me.

I can see now what Marvellous Marvin saw. When Sadie was sixteen the magician offered her a job and got two for the price of one. It was just like magic. An optical illusion, identical twins. Sort of.

Can you see me? Can I see me? My body is not really Sylvia Swamp. It's not who I am. My body is not a body anymore. I don't think it ever was. It's a mountain. It's a brick wall. It's a wicked, sad house for my soul, my thoughts. My body isn't flesh and blood and bones. It is something to scale, to climb over, not through.

No one could ever love me. And no one did.

Oh sure, I feel sorry for myself. But I can't blame the world for my fatness. Can I?

I am now Morbidly Obese. My body is the petri dish, the bell jar, the container for a pulmonary embolism. My body is a shit-factory. My body leaks and jiggles and shakes and drips. My body smells and puses with rotting bed sores. My body makes people stare. My body scares people. And, frankly, it scares me. Jiggling and rolling, how did I get so big? How did it happen?

I cannot see my feet. I cannot see my knees or my belly button. But at one point I could see all of that and more. Because I always saw more when I looked in the mirror. Even when I was OK, even when I was just chubby. I would look in the mirror in the bathroom and see this.

THIS. All of it. I knew the future. I could see it. At one point I was a girl watching her mother and her sister and trying hard to understand. My role models were unreachable, untouchable, unmentionable. *"The mother at least knows that she is the centre of attention."*

"You're just like your father," Ruth said to me. "He's big-boned."

Daddy was anything but big-boned. Daddy was skinny. Even Ruth could take her fingers and weave them around his wrists, his bony ankles. He was tall, sure, but he was a beanpole.

I did figuratively shrink. I was invisible under Ruth's gaze. Sadie couldn't see me anymore. She didn't protect me. She didn't love me. No matter how big I got, I was always small and insignificant around my family. I always disappeared.

If I didn't understand Sadie or Ruth's behaviour, my father was twice as confused.

•••

"The poor father is a complete outsider. If he wants to see his baby, he has to stand outside a nursery window and look beseechingly at the nurse."

"THEY FIGHT ALL the time," Daddy said to me in front of the TV where the two of us spent most evenings together. We were hiding from the wild women. We had come together in a quiet way, a safe way. We shared potato chips. Me with a Cola or a Tab and my father stirring his gin and tonic or a vodka and soda with his finger tip. Short sentences occasionally. Never anything too serious or complicated or emotional. We watched reruns together—*Hogan's Heroes, Laverne and Shirley, Happy Days*. All the girls at my school were in love with the Fonz, but I knew I would marry Scott Baio one day. I had a poster of him under my bed. Chachi and Sylvia. I would be stick-thin like Joanie. I would perm my hair and wear tight jeans and drink chocolate milkshakes without any worry about gaining weight.

"Teenagers," I said. Because that was what I heard the teachers say about the kids they caught kissing at the side of the school. "Their hormones are crazy. What can you do?"

Daddy raised his eyebrows at me. "Crazy hormones, eh?"

"Yep." I rolled my eyes.

He nodded and smiled slyly. "You're kind of funny," he said. "I guess I sometimes forget that."

•••

When To Call The Doctor

If your baby "looks different, acts differently, fever, colds, coughs, earaches, etc."

RUTH CREPT OUT most afternoons to be with Marvellous Marvin in his hotel room/dressing room. His Limited Run was a steady gig there. He impressed the blue-haired women who accompanied their husbands to conventions, he kept them occupied with his treachery and fakery and white rabbits. This, in turn, impressed the hotel owner and Marvellous Marvin became a fixture.

Marvellous Marvin, at the height of popularity. Why? Who knows. This was when he made enough money to live on from his performances (and not just from stealing watches and wallets from the audience). Ruth, Marvin assumed, was good luck. People lined up to drink at the tables and to watch Marvellous Marvin and his sexy assistants. He had a way about him—a banter that was charismatic and appealing. Marvellous Marvin knew how to make the women come back to see him over and over. A quick smile here, a nod to the ladies. He touched their shoulders as he passed their tables. And the women's husbands were there to see the assistants in their body suits covered in sparkles, to see their breasts push out of the cone cups they were squished into. Sparkly Playboy Bunnies. They were there to see his original girls, and then they eventually came to the show to see Ruth. Many years later it was Sadie who attracted the crowds.

Think: swimsuit covered in sequins and sparkles and beads and feathers, high cut at the hip, blues and greens, golds and reds and silvers.

Think: plunging, lightly freckled cleavage, fishnet stockings, high-heeled shoes. Think: ruby red lips, black eyeliner, Marilyn Monroe hair. A spritz of perfume. Las Vegas, baby. Call girl. Escort. Prostitute.

Ruth came out draped in a black velvet cape tied at the neck with a satin ribbon.

She flung off the cape. Stood in the lights sparkling, proudly beautiful. She took your breath away.

I think Marvellous Marvin held onto Ruth because of this success, because the moment she arrived in his life, even before she worked for him, his Limited Run turned into a Permanent Run, because he was given a hotel room to dress and live in, and he suddenly commanded a lot of attention. Women began thrusting themselves on him at the bar. "Are you a magician?" Without even knowing him anyone could see that he attributed this to Ruth, to having her around him, to bedding her. His confidence sky-rocketed. I was sure of it then and now. He called her, "My good luck charm, my rabbit's foot, my four-leaf clover." Marvin was not one for words. "I'm more instinctual," he would say. "I'm more feely and touchy. Aren't I, Ruth?"

Daddy groaned. "Why is he here for dinner again?"

"Silly man," Ruth said. "You're very smart. He's smart, isn't he, Mr. Swamp?"

But why else would Marvellous Marvin want Ruth Swamp? A pregnant, married woman. She had a husband and eventually two children. Not too much money. Enough to get by. What was possibly attractive about that? Her body, I guess. She was extremely pretty. And when she was in a good mood she could light up a room.

How do you explain attraction anyway? The fattest man in the world, after all, is getting married.

When the magician gave Ruth a job, put her in a skimpy outfit so that others could see what he saw, suddenly things got even better. He fired his regular girls, who were getting tubby and looked like the strippers they were anyway, and he focused all his energy on training Ruth. Soon she could astound the audience as much as Marvin could, soon she could move her arm gracefully and reveal the disappearing box, the top hat, a bunny, wave them out of thin air. Her loud voice called out, "The Magnificent Magician, Marvellous Marvin," over the crowded, noisy bar. My mother looked like a dream on stage. She looked like a movie star, an apparition.

Ruth thought of Marvin as her Fate, Marvin thought of Ruth as his Luck.

"You have a job?" Daddy said to Ruth as we sat in front of the fish tank together drinking our drinks. He was astounded.

"It's a money-making thing, Mr. Swamp," Ruth said. "Don't you want money? Besides, haven't you ever heard of women's liberation?"

"But you have to wear that? That thing? That's not liberating, is it?"

Ruth stamped her foot.

"What do you want from me? Do you want me to be barefoot and pregnant in the kitchen all my life? Is that what you want?"

"I just want you to be happy, Ruth," Daddy said. "That's all. Just be happy."

Sadie and I looked down at our mother's high-heeled shoes.

Ruth stood in the living room, having just thrown off her trench coat. She stood there, half naked in front of her husband, her chubby baby daughter, her just-beginning-to-be-beautiful older daughter, the still-alive fish, our sippy cups. I remember Sadie laughed delightedly and left my side to stand up and touch the sparkles, to run her hand down our mother's long legs. "That's a beautiful bathing suit. When I grow up I want one just like it."

Ruth left the house at 1:30 most afternoons. She worked until 11:30 every night except Sundays. Daddy said that he missed her, he needed her to make the dinner, to take care of the kids, but she just laughed.

"I never made this kind of money selling Avon," she said.

"What money? I don't see any money," Daddy said.

We never saw much money, nothing really improved.

"I have to buy pantyhose every day. I have to have my hair done. My nails," Ruth shrieked. Our TV was always the same one, the hole in the living room couch never got fixed.

Ruth turned on the crock pot in the mornings. She sometimes dumped us at Grandma Mileford's house in the afternoon and headed off to the magic shows. Or sometimes Daddy picked us up after school and shepherded us into the apartment. He scooped out macaroni and cheese, chili, sloppy joes, or sometimes made toast with ketchup on it, grilled cheese, peanut butter and jelly sandwiches. He sighed a lot but rolled up his sleeves and took care of us.

"The extra little bit of money will help," he said. "In the long run. When she brings it home."

It was not as if I could wear Sadie's hand-me-down clothes. Even my feet were two sizes bigger than hers were at my age. We needed that money. But Ruth must have spent it on herself.

Did Ruth and the magician have sex every day? I couldn't imagine it. Sadie said she didn't think that every day was possible. "Every day?" But that was before she herself spent time with Marvellous Marvin. Before the magician's dressing room couch was so comfy and before she was caught in the baseball park on the bench in the dugout. The bench that was so hard and demanding on that particular rainy night.

"He is Marvellous," Sadie said, dreamily.

Maybe not marvellous to everyone, but he was sort of tall. He was hefty. His nose was crooked. His toupée was windswept. Black. Yes, even though he wore a toupée—thinning on top—women still seemed attracted. He walked with one hand in his pants pocket at all times, sometimes fiddling with change (our money?), or spare keys. His fingers were thick and buffed and he had manicured nails. After all, Marvellous Marvin did work with his hands, they had to be perfect. His eyes were brown. The brownest brown arresting eyes. I gave him one point for his eyes. Sadie said they reminded her of this border collie we used to see on the way to school. Quick and watchful. An almost black brown that turned to chocolate-gold in the sun. Clear though, not milky. Wild animal eyes, feral. Even though his toupée was jet black, Ruth said he was blonde everywhere else (a perfect example of the kinds of things she should never have told us). The hair colour made the eyes more bizarre. He had a gummy smile that somehow attracted people. He put his whole self into this smile and, although I knew he was always hiding things, it seemed when he smiled that he was open and transparent. After Ruth hooked him, his teeth were polished and bleached like hers. Some crooked, some blindingly straight, but all white. He lost a lot of weight. Then gained it back. He had a baking smell, doughy and cinnamon-like. Often he smelled of Old Spice or strong colognes. Ruth said nutmeg, Sadie said allspice, I said gross. Sadie said, "Grow up, Sylvia." He reeked.

A corner is turned, a deep slanting turn, we are off the highway.

"Almost there. I know I said that before, but this time I mean it." The paramedic laughs.

"And then we have to go back," I say. He looks shocked, as if he had forgotten that we had to return to the hospital, as if he assumed they would leave me at the veterinary hospital and head back to their homes. "You are taking me back, right? I'm not being put to sleep?" I laugh through the oxygen mask. "Like an old dog."

"Ha ha," he says, nervously. He pats my hand.

"Did you tell them at the hospital that you found a better home for me in the country? Like they tell the kids whose pets have died? You know, 'Spot has gone to live in the country, Joey.'" I giggle.

"You're funny. That must mean you are feeling better."

Another deep turn, the ambulance tilts slightly, I watch my body slide one way and then the other. We slow down. Turn signals click. Turn right.

I try so hard to remember what Daddy looked like. Beautiful in his own way, but too skinny and stooped. He was a delicate man. All bones and angles. At the end, when he rose from his chair in the living room it took him ten minutes to stand straight from the osteoarthritis in his spine. He would groan and his back would crack. His cardigans were always holey and covered in little fuzzes—I would pick them off sometimes, as we sat side by side in front of the TV, I would make a pile on my lap. Daddy was a sad man, and thinking of him as sad makes me sad. I wish now that he had had someone else to love, that he had noticed what was happening with Marvellous Marvin (did he? How could he not?) and had divorced Ruth. Wouldn't we all have been better off? Me and Daddy, Sadie and Ruth. We'd have split in two sets, we'd have divided like amoeba.

Sadie suddenly came home wearing one of those body suits and Ruth stood frozen in the kitchen, her hand raised, about to chop a carrot (or a finger) on the cutting board. Grandma Mileford was with us, having tea.

"What in the hell are you wearing, Sadie? Is that my suit?"

"I've taken the job Marvin offered. He bought me this. Your suits are too big."

It was red and silky. The sparkly bits outlined the legs, the breasts, the arms. Spaghetti straps. There was a black belt cinched tight around her waist. She was wearing Ruth's shoes, her highest, her click-clackedy-est. Nude stockings. A seam down the back of her mile-high legs.

"You are naked, dear," Grandma said.

"I told you. There is no way you are working for him. This is simply ridiculous." Ruth threw her arms in the air.

Sadie looked beautiful. Better then Ruth. Mirror mirror on the wall.

Grandma Mileford and I, we were in the kitchen too, but no one had noticed me. I sat at the table snitching cookies off Grandma's plate.

"Honey," Grandma Mileford said to Sadie. "I hate to say it, but you look like a whore. In my day, girls dressed like that were going nowhere in life."

"But Mother wears this to work." Sadie smiled slyly.

"That's different," she said. "Sort of."

"Ha," Sadie laughed. "Are you saying you've already given up on her? That I have some potential still?" Sadie paused. She looked closely at Ruth. "Perhaps Grandma has seen a whore before?"

My face heated up fast. I hummed, turned pink. I ate and considered this.

"You know what she's doing with him, right?" Sadie turned to Grandma. I shrank farther into my chair, farther towards the few remaining cookies. I watched Sadie's suit sparkle as it caught the kitchen fluorescents.

"I work for him. I have a job. I'm a liberated woman." Ruth stomped her small feet. She dropped her carrot.

"You call it work? Work? Do you? That's really interesting." Sadie took one of my cookies and nibbled. One bite. Then nothing else. How did she do that, my sister? How did she take only one bite of a cookie and then put it down?

"Take that off right now, Sadie. Honestly, I don't know what's gotten into you. I told you before, you are not going to work for that man. You are in school. You are ... What are you doing? Sadie?"

And my sister, my Sadie—my God—she peeled the outfit off right there in the kitchen. In front of me, Grandma and Ruth. I remember this so clearly. The spark in the air, the feeling that time had stopped, as if the oxygen in the room had been sucked out. I hadn't seen Sadie without clothes in so long—since we were little and I would perch on the closed toilet lid and read her books while she was in the bath. Years ago. Now I watched her lovely body appear, her flat stomach and long, lean, muscular legs and jutting hips. Breasts. Nipples dark. They were erect from the chill in the air. Sadie's long blonde hair hung over her shoulders. Grandma Mileford couldn't stop looking either but she managed to say, "Oh my," over and over. Ruth stared at her daughter. The pretty one, the thin one. Our Sadie. And she exploded.

"PUT YOUR CLOTHES BACK ON!"

"Make up your mind," Sadie said, but she was frightened, I could tell. "Clothes on. Clothes off. Which is it, Mother?"

Sadie scooped up her outfit. Hands shaking. As she bent we all saw it, the hickey on the small of her back. Suck marks. Marvellous Marvin's lips leered at us. Ruth turned suddenly towards me. As if it was all my fault. She could see me now, I was there in the kitchen, witness to her decay. My lovely Sadie, so pretty, and Ruth so angry. Ruth raised her hand high, knife still in it. (Was she going to stab me? Did she want to stab me?) Put her hand down again. Cried.

"Stop eating, Sylvia. Stop, stop, stop eating."

Marvellous Marvin stole my mother.

Marvellous Marvin stole my sister.

Marvellous Marvin made playing cards shuffle rapidly, spread like a fan and back again. He made money appear behind our ears and he tied knots in silk scarves that came undone with one, two, three quick tugs. He balanced water glasses on eggs and he shattered our hearts and read our minds and confessed to nothing. Marvellous Marvin was brilliant at some things. Especially stealing: money, watches, wallets, love, lives.

There were many days when I would come home from school to find Ruth hunched over at the kitchen table reading *Dr. Spock's Baby and Child Care*. Oftentimes she was taking notes and drinking white wine.

Other times she was folding down the pages. Ruth read with a stretched smile on her face. Her holy bible. Sometimes there was a candle burning beside her. An apron over her tight dress. Her hair was done up on her head like Audrey Hepburn in *Breakfast at Tiffany's*. Her nails were long and sharp. She said to me, "Get yourself a snack, honey," and never noticed that Sadie wasn't with me, that Sadie hadn't walked me home in a while. Sadie was supposed to walk me home, she was supposed to protect me from the world, but she didn't and then I pretended that it didn't matter anymore.

When Ruth was reading The Book, it absorbed her. You could do anything, you could eat anything, you could play your music loud and dance around naked, and Ruth wouldn't notice. Sadie told me that Marvellous Marvin had a copy of The Book in his hotel room too, but it wasn't until about a year later that I remembered that comment and wondered what Sadie was doing in Marvellous Marvin's hotel room. (Although, really, by that time I didn't have to wonder. I knew. It was just that the synapses were firing into place then.)

Ruth found her religion in Dr. Spock. "It's pure rubbish," Grandma Mileford said when Ruth dropped me off to stay with her some weekends. "In our day we toilet trained kids in a matter of months. Now he wants you to wait years. And then just ask them. 'Do you want to shit now or would you rather wait 'til you are ready?' How ridiculous is that."

"I don't need to be toilet trained," I said. "I'm thirteen years old."

"Still."

"Mother don't say shit in front of Sylvia. She's still young and innocent."

"I'm old enough."

"She hears that kind of word every day on the playground, Ruth."

"Mother. And besides, in your day you were animals. Sheer animals. Dr. Spock has taught us to respect our children."

"Poop then. Do you want to poop in the pot? Is that what you are supposed to ask?" Grandma Mileford cackled.

"Poop," Grandpa Mileford echoed from the living room, his crossword puzzle at the ready. The sound startled Grandma Mileford who clutched at her heart and sat smack down on the vinyl kitchen chair. It squeaked. "Oh my," she said, "I always forget he is here."

•••

"Both parents, I know, can get the wrong idea from the masks that are worn in many maternity hospitals."

"WHO ARE YOU?" I heard Ruth saying to Sadie one night. "It's like I don't even know you anymore."

"Sadie Swamp, duh," Sadie said.

"You've changed. You know he doesn't love you. He loves me." This last bit was a whisper. Ruth's first. She was as surprised by it as we were. Wide eyes. Startled. For some reason, though, we heard the whisper louder than her normal voice.

My father looked up from the television. Then he looked back at the television. His face flushed. I ate my chips and drank my Tab and turned up the volume. He didn't say anything to me, but I knew he heard it.

"All right, since you asked. I'm sweet," Sadie said. "That's who I am. Sweet and young. Young, Mother. Not like you."

"Sweet is not a who, it's a what. You don't know anything. And you'll be old one day, mark my words."

The door to the apartment slammed and Sadie was gone. Ruth was crying. Big, loud, all-capitalized SOBS.

"More chips?" Daddy said to me and I nodded but he didn't move. He handed me the bowl. "You'll get them then. All right? I'm a little afraid." He tried to smile. Ah, the effort it took. His face cracked. He cranked his head towards the kitchen and the bellowing sounds.

I was afraid too. This happened all the time now. Loud noises, shouts, doors slamming. I was as jittery as Grandma Mileford on a bad day. Ruth was leaning up against the fridge, that look in her eyes. She was hot angry. Crying and angry all at the same time.

"More chips?" I mumbled. I held out the bowl. Ruth was filling the crock pot for the next day. Carrots and mushrooms and white wine and onions and chicken and rosemary. The aroma was lovely.

"Get out. Get out. Get out." Joan Crawford with the coat hangers. I cringed and ducked and scurried out, past my father, past the TV.

I took the elevator down to the lobby and out onto the street. Daddy wouldn't mind that I was going out for a while. Mother told me to leave. So I left. There was Sweet Sadie up ahead of me in her tight leather pants and a jean jacket, moving through the small crowds of shoppers and teenagers and drug dealers on the street in the pre-dark. She was smoking and walking slowly, her head down, storm clouds coming out of her lips, her nose. I half expected lightning. I always did with Ruth and now I was expecting sparks with Sadie. She was headed up the street away from Ruth and towards the hotel. Long hair flapping around her head. Suddenly this guy who worked for Marvin, Reggie Reynolds, was there, following her, talking to her. She blew him off, smoke everywhere, her arms flapping and she moved fast forward. Towards Marvellous Marvin. Under her jean jacket, under those tight leather pants, was her costume. A scheduled show tonight to accommodate a group of insurance men from Quebec and their wives who had spent the day visiting Niagara Falls. She was wearing the yellow suit with the sequined purple breast plate and I followed closely behind because I wanted to see her, I wanted to spend time with her, I wanted to see the show.

"So tell me," my paramedic says. "How did this happen?"

"Huh? What?"

"This. You." He waves his strong arms around my bulk.

"How did I get so big?"

He grimaces. "Yeah, I guess. I mean, why?"

"Why or how? Those are two completely different questions."

There is silence from the two men up front. The windshield wipers squeak. I wonder if they dared him to ask me. My paramedic clears his garlic-and-mint-scented throat. "Are they?"

"Are they what?"

"Are they really two completely different questions?"

How?

Why?

I'm not sure.

During that period Marvellous Marvin had been imitating Houdini. Or trying to. He had locked himself up in all kinds of contraptions and had tried to get out of them on the stage. Turned himself into a bit of a comedy show. Tricks of the trade: vaseline and K-Y Jelly and butter helped him slide from the handcuffs. Ruth always turned pink when she saw the jars and tubes of lubricants on his dressing room table. She tried to block them from our view. When I picked up the K-Y Jelly and studied it, having no idea what it was, she would say, "Here's some money, Sylvia. Get yourself something to eat."

And now Sadie had burst out of our apartment onto the street, had pushed Reggie Reynolds away, and, with me following, she was in Marvin's hotel room. She was helping him liquid up his wrists. She had thrown her jean jacket on the floor and had stepped out of her leather pants. She rubbed lubricant in, all the while looking him straight in his brown eyes. Marvellous Marvin was watching her, his eyes wide open, smiling at Sadie.

I remember this Sadie. This girl who could look a man straight in his brownest eyes without flinching. I remember a strong, proud, haughty Sadie. So many years later now, and I can still see her taking off her jacket and pants and stepping out into the lights wearing so little. Her legs so long. Sadie's legs "go all the way to China," said Marvellous Marvin. He would clap her on the ass. She would sashay out onto the stage just like our Mother. Cherry lip gloss smacking. Scrumptious Sadie.

Believe it or not I was under a food trolley outside Marvin's open hotel room door, watching Sadie holding Marvin's wrists. I don't know how I had squeezed in, but I was pretty certain I couldn't get out. Suddenly I could hear a herd of rumbling rhinos. Coming down the hall straight at me. One hippo really, her heels thumping, her angry snorts. It was Ruth, all crazed and wild, her hair falling out of her clips, her lipstick skewed purposefully— drawing outside the lines helped to heighten the anger. It exaggerated the whole effect. I was certainly scared. Sadie looked shocked, with her hands on Marvin's wrists and Ruth bounding towards them slapping Sadie's hands away. I was invisible in the hallway, hiding outside of the open hotel room door—sandwiches half eaten, a bottle of beer—I reached up to grab something to eat below. A chewed-on pizza crust, a tater tot. It was, for a bit, almost like being at the movies. In the action scene.

"Damn you, Marvin. She's just a child. Leave her alone."

"What are you talking about, Mother?" Sadie said. "I'm just getting Marvin ready for the show."

Sadie's beautiful face was pink and warm. It suddenly occurred to me: Sadie was in love with Marvellous Marvin.

Marvin smiled slyly, his eyes flashed. He took Sadie's hands off his and pretended he hadn't heard Ruth. "I've got vaseline on my wrists. Do me up, won't you, honey?" Marvin looked down at his pants and his zipper was undone. "I'm all sticky."

We all stopped breathing. The Swamp ladies. He was challenging our mother. Sadie's eyes widened. And then they narrowed slyly.

"Do *yourself* up," Ruth hollered. She made a grab for Sadie's wrist but Sadie slipped out—the vaseline worked. She escaped like Houdini. One quick zip and Marvin's face flushed and Sadie swung her sexy hips out of the dressing room.

"Oh my God," Ruth cried.

"Yes," Marvin said, dreamily, shaking his head. "Oh yes."

"She's just a child," Ruth said. "Leave her alone, Marvin. I'm warning you. She's only sixteen years old."

Marvin wiped off his wrists and took Ruth by the hand. "I don't know what you are talking about," he said. And then he reached up behind her ear, pushed her hair aside and whispered, "Voila." Fingers stretched out. On his palm was a quarter.

"Wow," said Ruth. "Really? A quarter? Do you think that impresses me?"

"Darling," Marvin whispered. "If I had more money...." The hand went back up her neck, massaging, touching, a warm hand on her naked skin.

Ruth was like liquid. Like jelly. All I could think of there, under the trolley, was the oozing of jelly when you bite into a doughnut. That thick jelly oozing out the hole in the centre, dripping slowly out. Like a bullet hole leaking blood. Powdered sugar coating.

And then there was my mother, Ruth Mileford Swamp, on the couch. I looked away and then I looked back. Marvellous Marvin was over her. I looked away. I looked back. Her legs circled behind his back. I was thirteen. I felt horribly sick. And then there was Sadie behind my trolley. She was standing behind the trolley and I was underneath it. My mouth stuffed with pizza crust. Stale. Hard. Dry. I was going to choke on it. I couldn't swallow. The door to the hotel room was open for all to see. In the heat of the moment I guess they forgot to close it. Ruth was making these sounds. Marvellous Marvin was quick. Less then Marvellous? Perhaps. Half-digested tater tots came up my throat. I swallowed them back down with the dry crust. All I wanted to do was run, but I was stuck there, and besides I couldn't run.

Mother? There is a book called *Are You My Mother?* Remember it? The little bird hopping from place to place, from animal to animal, asking, "Are you my mother?" He was so hopeful, so determined. All he wanted was to find his mother. I can't remember what happened at the end, did he find his mother? He must have or the book wouldn't have been so popular. I can only picture his tiny body, the little cartoony bird looking lost and miserable.

It wasn't Ruth in Marvin's mind, it was Sadie—eyes closed, he was concentrating. I could see this. Under the trolley, thirteen years old and I knew what was going on in Marvin's mind. It was the beginning of something big for all of us, for Sadie and Ruth and for their relationship. Because Ruth sensed it too. And Sadie knew it. There was something in the tilt of Ruth's head, the way her eyes were squinched closed tight, that suggested she knew that Marvellous Marvin was not fully with her. He was really, truly with Ruth's long-legged, powdered-sugar-sweet, young daughter. The one who was watching from the hallway, eyes flashing to match the sequins on her body suit.

Sadie reached down, under the trolley, and pulled me up. "Come on, let's go. What the hell were you doing there, Sylvia? You are such a freak." We disappeared down the hall together. We rushed home, Sadie ahead of me, as fast as my fat legs would move.

Ruth didn't come home until late that night. She filled in for Sadie at the show and, although I was sure she was beginning to understand that she was losing the fight, there was nothing in her mask-like demeanour to suggest it.

Your Baby

Enjoy Him—Don't be Afraid of Him

"Your baby is born to be a reasonable, friendly human being."

THERE WERE THE times Sadie and Ruth got along quite well. They baked and cooked together and I ate whatever they made because they were always on some diet or another. They liked to watch old movies together and cry. They shopped together and shared lipstick and got their hair done at the same place. Ruth loved to buy Sadie clothes—mini-skirts, platform shoes, jean jackets—but Sadie didn't always wear the clothes in the way Ruth intended them to be worn.

"Do up that top button," Ruth shouted upon seeing Sadie with her shirt unbuttoned almost to her navel. Her Farrah Fawcett hair poofed. Blue, thick, raccoon-like eyeliner.

My father came and went. Mysteriously. He paid for the food on our table. He put money in the jar on the hall table for odds and ends, snacks and treats. He bought us an answering machine when they became popular and he splurged on a VCR. He watched a lot of television with me.

Ruth and Sadie made an agreement. For a few months they decided to try to politely share the job on Marvellous Marvin's show. Sadie would work weekends to give Ruth a break. Ruth would work during the week when Sadie was in school. The tension was palpable in the apartment when Ruth caved in. Did she just give up? What could she really do to keep Sadie home and away from Marvin? Lock her up? Maybe she thought that the only way she could hold Marvin to her was if she let him have something that he wanted. I didn't know (men). I wasn't sure about anything.

I turn towards my paramedic. I look him in the eye.

"You ask why? Because I was spoiled with an embarrassment of food."

The paramedic nods.

"You ask how? Because I just couldn't stop eating."

Grandma Mileford suddenly shrunk without dieting. She got sick. She stopped being able to eat and Sadie and Ruth and Daddy and I, we watched her slowly disappear. Like her voice, her whole body got smaller. Ruth was beside herself and let us know that—"I'm beside myself," she moaned. She slammed her bedroom door. She wallowed in self pity which, Sadie said, was a good look for her (and I agreed). Black clothes. Sallow expression, cheeks sunken and lipstick blood red. A middle-aged Goth. Marvellous Marvin fell out of the picture for a while (a month?) while Grandma Mileford succumbed to cancer. Even though Grandma was dying, I loved this time in our lives. Sadie and Ruth had something else to focus on and they focused on it together. There was no fighting, there was no Marvellous Marvin.

There was no baseball dugout yet. Not at that point.

But when it happened their shirts were still on, their pants were off. He sat there on the bench, she crouched over him. I watched from behind a tree in the park. ("What's a dugout?" Ruth asked the police officer who brought Sadie home. "Is the ground actually dug out?") I couldn't tell if there were tears in my eyes or if it was just rain. I knew this was the beginning of something tragic and all I could think about was food. Chocolate sundaes, corn meal biscuits, potato chips.

For someone who has never ever had sex herself, I've certainly seen a lot of it in my short lifetime.

I tried to pretend I was a detective, creeping around, spying on everyone—but Nancy Drew never caught couples having sex, did she? I guess if she did it wasn't in the books I was reading.

When Grandma Mileford finally died, Grandpa Mileford came over to tell us. I think this was the first time I saw him away from the kitchen table. We all attended her funeral and Ruth cried loudly into a hanky supplied by Marvellous Marvin who was there, of course, to support the family. And then it was over. With nothing left to focus on, no more dying relative, Sadie and Ruth began again their old game of "who gets the magician," and eventually we were back into the full swing of things (and the park and the police officer). Both of them going out to "work." Daddy and I sitting in front of the TV, eating. We rented a lot of movies now that we had a VCR.

I remember Grandma Mileford well. I remember those quiet and exciting times in front of her television set when Sadie and I were little, lying on the floor in the muted silence, waiting for a noise, any noise, that would make her jump. The anticipation was thick in the air. For such a quiet woman, she was generally pretty exciting to be with.

I wonder what my father was thinking when Marvellous Marvin came to Grandma's funeral? I wonder how he felt deep inside. Surely he must have been holding his broken heart together with paper clips? Surely he must have been dying all the time? Collapsing like a balloon with a slow leak?

When Grandma Mileford was alive she took me aside often and told me that I was special. She told me that Sadie was a problem child but that I was good. She told me I was nothing like Ruth. Or my father even. That I was an individual. She told me to take care of my family. "Any way you can, sweetie. You just take care of them. They need you."

So I did that. I took care of all of them in the only way I knew how. And myself. I also took care of myself. I put on my armor. And I survived.

Until now.

•••

"The child who is appreciated for what he is, even if he is homely, or clumsy, or slow, will grow up with confidence in himself, happy."

RUTH WAS BEGINNING to notice my size. She was beginning to (finally) worry. I was moving slower and most of my clothes didn't fit. Bathing was becoming an ordeal. My balance was off and I slipped getting in and then getting out of the tub. I fell often. I cried often. So I stopped bathing and then I stunk. It was all too humiliating. I was watching my body become some alien thing. I didn't know how to control it. Two hundred and forty pounds. The Incredible Blob.

My grade seven classroom was on the top floor of our school. I panted and wheezed when I got there. And then the bell would ring for lunch and I would have to go back down the stairs. Our cafeteria served chocolate pudding and French fries and coke. There were candy and chip machines in the halls. I sat alone, my tray loaded. I spent my days thinking of Sadie, of how I wished she were still in my school, how I wished she were still there to walk me home. Occasionally someone noticed me and threw something at me. The names they called me were uninspired and I soon stopped listening.

When I made it home after school, Sadie was often out. "Working." She came home when she needed a change of clothes or a good hot shower. I noticed that she had begun to pat our father on the head when she passed by him. Ruth rarely went to see Grandpa Mileford after Grandma died. I heard from my father (late at night, one too many gin and tonics, he was in a talkative mood) that Grandpa Mileford wasn't doing well. He was going to be put in a home. One of "those homes," Sadie whispered. Everything about Sadie was in quotation marks those days. She wore her "uniform" to "work." She "fell asleep" on Marvin's couch after a show and didn't make it home. "Sorry." She went to "school." She ate "lunch" already.

Ruth worried about Grandpa Mileford, but only to a point. She worried about how his old age would affect her. It was always all about who would eventually take care of Ruth, who would cater to her every whim, who would listen to her stories, her tall tales. Most of all, who would react to them. Grandpa Mileford merely scratched out the answers for his crossword puzzles with a stubby pencil and nodded once in awhile. He was not the audience Ruth needed anymore. Ruth's mother was dead and her father was a useless old man. Ruth had better things to do than visit him.

I went over sometimes to see him. With my father. We would sit at the kitchen table and throw out words for him to put in his crossword puzzle. He would pat my hand and say things like, "Such a nice girl you are. Nothing like your mother."

"That man needs someone to feed him," Ruth said. "And it sure as hell won't be me. You three are hard enough to take care of."

Did she ever take care of us? Our father dished out the crockpot stews after work, he washed up after our meals, he helped me in and out of the bath, averting his eyes. He bought me the clothes I needed. He bought me dresses that looked like tents, and stockings for huge women and, best of all, he didn't say anything about it. Just put the bags of clothes on my bed and left the room. One size higher every time. "I thought you'd look lovely in yellow," he said. He bought me my wonderful running shoes that were for wide feet and so comfortable and he let me wear them unlaced. Three hundred pounds. I could finally sneak. I had sneakers now.

My stomach was huge. I couldn't see past my waist unless I bent forward and when I bent forward I lost my balance. I had a short stature, which didn't help. Big bones. My back ached and my hips and legs gave out on me every so often. When I looked in the mirror I saw my eyes becoming thin slits peering out from my oversized cheeks. Like a squirrel with nuts in its mouth. I saw rolls under my chin. I was nothing like my svelte sister. Nothing like my toned mother. Nothing like skin'n'bones Daddy. I was not my Grandma Mileford or Grandpa. Who was I?

Who am I?

"The rain is stopping," my paramedic says. "Just in time."

"In time for what?"

"I don't know," he says. "In time to get you out of this ambulance? We wouldn't want you to get wet."

I smile. "You're very nice," I say. "Not many people are nice to me."

"Hey," he says. He is blushing. "You're nice too. I'm just sorry you're sick."

"*Strictness or Permissiveness?*" Ruth read in Dr. Spock one of those many times she decided to stop ignoring me and do something about my weight. "*This kind of severity produces children who are either meek or colourless or mean to others.*"

"What does he mean?" Ruth railed. "Should I be strict or should I be permissive?"

Daddy left the kitchen. He was always competing against the men in Ruth's life. Dr. Spock. Marvellous Marvin. Why didn't he just walk out and never come back?

I voted for Permissive. I'd rather be mean to others. I was already meek and colourless.

Sadie shouted from her bedroom, "Strict. Diets only work when you are strict. I should know."

"*Stick to your convictions,*" Ruth quoted. "I've got to be strong, Sylvia. No matter how hard it is. This is for your own good."

This became a pattern. First Ruth couldn't see me. My own mother passed me in the hall without even nodding. Then she would get all energetic and decide to "Do Something" about my weight.

"We must do something about this," she shouted at my father, at me, at Sadie. "Everyone must help." Ruth took things away from me. Deprived me. She took away my potato chips, my pop, my Slurpee allowance (but my father, after scotch on the rocks in front of the TV, still pushed money into my hot, wet palm and whispered, "On the way home from school tomorrow, get yourself something. A small treat. You deserve it"), and frozen pizzas. She took away my Easy Bake Oven. (Those late-at-night small cakes lit up with a lightbulb in the dark of my room. Gone.) And for some reason she took away my stuffed turtle beanbag chair. I was never sure why.

"Face it, Sylvia," said Sadie, as we watched the beanbag chair head out the door. "You can't get out of it anyway."

She was right.

And worst of all, Marvellous Marvin was called in to try hypnosis on me. After all, he was marvellous, surely he could fix anything. Even me.

"Look me in the eyes, Syl," he said. I could smell his stale breath, so close to my nose.

"Don't call me Syl."

"Mellow out, Sylvia," Sadie said. "Be nice." She giggled.

"Sorry. How about Ms Plath?" Marvellous Marvin laughed. Sadie and Ruth smiled. They were standing behind him, pushing to see who could get closer to the brilliant man. "How's that?"

"Not funny." Although I kind of liked this. I had been reading Sylvia Plath and thought she was a genius. In fact, the only stupid thing she ever did was to kill herself because of tainted love, because of a man. Why she didn't just kill him was beyond my comprehension.

"You are getting sleepy," Marvellous Marvin said. I watched him as he tried to get a steady rhythm with his watch on a fake gold chain (stolen?). His hand was jerky. Old age? Onset of Parkinson's (I was hoping)? I was not hypnotized but I decided to play along until he made me cluck like a chicken or roll on the floor like a fool, in which case I would let them know that his magic didn't work. It wasn't magic, anyway, it was all tricks. It was all lies. It was sleight of hand. Not genius. I was old enough to know that there was no such thing as magic. My innocence was gone.

There was a time when I believed. I remember clearly the thrill of the rabbit coming out of Marvin's hat—how did it get there?—I remember my mother being cut in half. I cried copiously. She was put back together. Thankfully. My mind whipped around, my head ached from thinking. How did he do it? Scarves, beautiful silk scarves, so many of them coming out of his sleeve. Endless scarves. Millions of rainbows.

I was young then. And stupid.

"Stop eating," Marvellous Marvin droned, his voice soft and low. Tempting, but not quite.

"No, don't stop," Ruth said. I jumped she was so loud. "Just eat healthier stuff. Dr. Spock says..." I faded out. Ruth was stuck that day on the sections about *Infant Feeding*. (Remember: I was thirteen years old.) Behind Marvin I saw Sadie open the top button on her shirt. Wet her lips with her pink tongue. I sighed. She had learned everything from our mother.

Ruth saw it too. She slapped Sadie's hand. Stood up straighter. Put her hands on her hips.

Of course Marvellous Marvin's hypnotism didn't work. He didn't even try to make me cluck like a chicken. He didn't make me stop eating. He was impotent (it figured). His magic was a sham (lies, all lies). I was beginning, at this point, to hate him with an unparalleled passion. The more I hated him, the more I ate. He consumed me. And I consumed.

"That's not nice," Sadie said later, when I confessed that I didn't think Marvin was magic. She was standing in front of her full length mirror trying on clothes. In one tight pair of jeans and out of one tight pair of jeans. She was painting them on. Stretching herself into them. Sucking in her breath. Admiring her butt, her thighs, her stomach. "You just aren't willing to believe, Sylvia, and so you didn't fall under his spell. It's not because you hate him."

Was that it? I hadn't fallen under the spell Marvellous Marvin had cast on the rest of my family?After that hypnotism crap, I decided to start following him. To see what he got up to when we weren't around. I'd do my Nancy Drew. I'd do my Charlie's Angels. I'd sneak and skulk and spy. This was how I caught my sister having sex with him in the ball park. I decided that even though I was large I could slip easily in and out of things. And because I decided this, it happened. I sucked in my stomach and disappeared. No one seemed to notice me. Ever. I could watch and follow, I could sleuth. I was good. The pair of Nike running shoes my father bought me, size ten, sneaked. I wore a lot of black (which was beneficially slimming) and grey. I faded into the Toronto scene.

In school I spent my time thinking about how to slide into shadows and duck behind buildings and trees. I would eat at my desk and imagine sneaking around. It was a drug, like Cool Whip. Sometimes I would take my lunch money and buy Cool Whip in a can and spray it into my mouth until my mouth filled up so tight that I could hardly breathe. I'd do that with the entire can, over and over until it was empty, and still I didn't feel full.

Wouldn't that be a lovely way to die? Suffocating on Cool Whip.

Marvin saw me sneaking only once. He was walking onto the stage during one of his daytime performances and he looked back at the black curtain behind him and he saw me peering out. I was in the wings, offstage. I should have been at school and he knew that. I was large and obvious. My sneakers glowed white. He smiled, though, and waved. I waved back. What else could I do?

I had been so invisible for so long that his wave felt like I'd been shot. He had noticed me. He had waved. He had smiled a smile that looked so familiar and almost comforting. I stumbled offstage.

What Feeding Means to the Baby

The Important Sucking Instinct

"Spoiling comes on gradually when a mother is too afraid to use her common sense or when she really wants to be a slave and encourages her baby to become a slave driver."

WHAT I FOUND out about Marvellous Marvin was complicated. Facts were illusive. No matter how much I followed him, I couldn't seem to understand him. He was on all the time—the showman. Every move he made was controlled. There was no down time. I mostly found out about his daily activities. But what was he really like? I didn't ever know. The only real magic Marvellous Marvin ever succeeded at was concealment. Who was he? Where did he come from? Where was he going?

Years later, I still have no idea.

"Look," I say to my paramedic. "I can do a magic trick if you release my hands."

"I don't know." He shrugs and runs his hands through his hair. "It's dangerous. You might roll off the bed."

"Is that what you call this thing? A bed."

"Yeah, well..." He has taken off my oxygen mask but I'm starting to breathe heavily again and so he holds it above my face. "Do you want this?"

Do I want to breathe easily? I ignore the question. I'm sucking thick air.

"I can do card tricks. And a few other things. You don't have three cups and a ball around here, do you?" I laugh again. I suck in my breath. Let it out. Suck it in.

"Only our coffee cups," he says.

He laughs. The two up front look back, surprised that we are enjoying ourselves.

"What are you?" he says. " A magician?"

"Yeah," I say. "A really big one. The biggest damn magician you've ever seen."

Marvin was a cheat. He was a fake. There was no magic in the man. Not even an ounce. Not even imaginary fake romantic magic. Nothing he did could astound anyone. Rabbits always died on him. That was why he had so many. That was why Reggie Reynolds was so important. Reggie would substitute rabbits in the middle of a performance and no one would know the difference. The rabbits suffocated under Marvin's top hat, biting his head and his plastic hair, scratching at his scalp as they struggled to breathe.

Marvellous Marvin failed out of school. He told us this when everyone was worried that Sadie was skipping school. He never graduated from high school. "And look where I am now," he said. I, personally, wouldn't have been surprised to find out he didn't know how to read. I always felt as if he was more than just a joke, more than just dumb, I felt as if he was missing something crucial. And it was not just empathy (for my father, for our family) or common sense. It was that little connected wire that makes someone human. That little spark of awareness.

The same sort of thing that was missing in my mother.

Narcissistic Personality Disorder.

Here I was in the audience: a matinee show. I was watching Marvellous Marvin for about the millionth time. His show never changed. A few card tricks. A woman cut in half. A boy who disappeared in a box. Sparkly costumes. Top hats. Rabbits and scarves and multi-coloured plastic flowers. The audience hooted and hollered, oohed and ahhed. Even though it was early in the afternoon, most of them had been drinking. Heavily. Marvellous Marvin bowed low, his toupée crept forward. He stiffened up. Looked older suddenly. Looked straight at me. Grinned or grimaced, I was not sure what. Disappeared in a puff of smoke. His assistant exited stage left.

As usual, I followed. That day I lucked out. That day I hung around by the back door of the hotel until he had had his shower. Then I followed him towards Yonge Street. Sadie must have been in school. Ruth must have been resting at home or working on her ornaments or worrying about herself or exercising or phone-selling Avon. It was her day off, there was another assistant on stage, a woman who substituted sometimes when she wasn't tending bar. I followed Marvin and wondered about Ruth—what did she do all day when she wasn't working? My father was most likely sitting at his accountant desk in his accountant cubby, working on his accountant work, perhaps trying not to make an impact on anything. Trying not to leave behind a fingerprint. A smudge.

We trudged down the street. Me behind Marvin. Marvin walked quickly.

That fine day Marvellous Marvin, the Deceptive Magician, ducked into a door adjacent to a shoe store on Parliament Street. I was far behind and panting from the exertion. He climbed stairs (I assumed), as I saw a light go on in the front window of the second floor. An apartment? He had used his own key. Pulled from the hip pocket of his dress pants. He had put it in the lock naturally, like he belonged there. I stood outside, watching, looking up. I crossed the street for a better look and because my head hurt from stretching. I saw Marvin near the front window. He took off his coat and placed it down across the top of an old-fashioned, high-backed chair. And then, like magic, just what I wished for, I saw a woman (a woman other than Ruth or Sadie or the bar-lady assistant or the hotel maids or, or...) come towards him from the back of the apartment and they stood together in front of the window and looked out. They were laughing. The woman threw back her head, her mouth wide. I ducked back into the shadows but looked once, twice. No, it was not Ruth, it was not Sadie. I made sure of it. The woman moved to stand behind Marvin, her arms wrapped around his chest, her chin rested on his shoulder. Comfortable love pose. I slid into an alley and looked out from behind a dumpster. Their movements were what fascinated me, so I couldn't tell you then what the woman looked like. Just the way her hand was on his chest, the way she pulled into him, the way he wrapped around her. And then Marvellous Marvin manoeuvred the woman around in front of him and kissed her tightly, almost sucked her into him.

They were kissing. It was a true love kiss, a romantic kiss, the kind of kiss you see in the movies. Full body kiss, every part of each of them was reacting to the other.

I was hot. Out of breath. I was scared. I was confused.

Wait until Sadie and Ruth hear about this, I thought.

I was happy.

Life in our family would get better from here on in. I was positively sure of it.

I used the spare change in the bottom of my coat pocket and bought a banana popsicle on the way home. Why not celebrate?

I walked as quickly as I could, all the way home. I had big, exciting news to tell and so I felt lighter, my body reacted to the news. Everything would be good now. Marvin would be out of our life. Wouldn't he? Wasn't that what this meant? A true-love kiss. How could Ruth take him back after this? How would Sadie react? Would she be nice to me again?

What you don't realize, when you are thirteen years old, fat, unloved and ignored, is that things don't wrap up cleanly like in the movies. Life is more complicated than that. Things can change on a dime, things can twist and turn and shoot out at you in all kinds of unforeseen directions. Like trying to bathe an angry cat or put an octopus to bed. There is no happily ever after.

•••

Breastfeeding

"...is natural. On general principle, it's safer to do things the natural way unless you are absolutely sure you have a better way."

I CAME HOME with the wonderful news of the woman and Marvin but the tension in our apartment was as thick as smoke. Ruth was not talking to Sadie. Sadie was locked in her room, music loud. My father sat by the TV trying to watch his favourite shows, trying to shut out the noise of anger, a seething, quiet noise. Oppressive. It was sometimes hard to breathe.

For some reason, on this spectacular, good-news day, when I walked into the kitchen, Ruth looked straight at me. She stared at me, the banana popsicle still hanging out of my yellow mouth, and she said, "Where have you been?"

She had rarely taken notice of me lately. I caught my reflection in the hall mirror. Mouth open. Yellow stain on my lips. Jaundiced.

The fiddler, the fusser, the sleeper, and the waker was written on the blackboard in the kitchen. And, *"Special Problems of Breastfeeding."*

Ruth caught me looking at this and read aloud to me. She said, *"Most Babies Love Orange Juice And Digest It Easily. Some Young Babies Always Vomit It."* She held up The Book. Tapped it with her nails. "Where have you been? Eating again? It's early in the afternoon."

I pointed at the chalk board. "We aren't babies anymore, Mom. We're teenagers."

"What does that have to do with good advice?"

I shrug.

When Sadie first got her period, I remember Ruth said, *"It is common for undigested vegetable to appear in the bowel movements when a baby is first taking it."*

"What are you talking about? A period is not undigested vegetable." Sadie was angry and frustrated and embarrassed.

"Spinach causes chapping of the lips and around the anus in some babies."

"Christ, you're sick, Mother. Dad, make her stop."

Part of me, now, sees that Ruth's quoting of Dr. Spock was the beginning of what was to come. As her desperation to make sense of child-rearing got worse, or as we got worse no matter what she applied to our lives, she sunk deeper into her depression. Dr. Spock's words were rapidly becoming better than anything she could think up herself. His words replaced hers. And then, years later, when she became so sick she couldn't think straight, his words took over and became hers. But when I was thirteen years old I thought nothing. Back then I thought it was normal to swallow a book like *Dr. Spock's Baby and Child Care* whole. I grew up with it and I didn't know any differently.

"Have you ever said anything you regret?" I ask my paramedic.

"Sure, yeah, of course. You?" He sits back, leans his strong frame on the jolting ambulance wall.

"Never."

"Never? That's not possible. Everyone says things they regret."

"Not me." I look up at the ceiling. "I've done a lot of things I've regretted, but I've never wanted to take back anything that I've said."

"Huh. That's weird."

"If you can't say exactly what you mean," I say, "then you shouldn't say anything at all." I think that's from *Alice in Wonderland*, but I'm not sure and my paramedic doesn't look interested anyway. We roll on in silence.

From her bedroom, Sadie's music blossomed and wailed, shook the walls. I had news to tell. Big news.

Ruth was still on me about orange juice and babies and digestion. I was throwing out my popsicle stick. I opened the cupboard door under the sink. Then I turned, slowly, cleared my throat grandly, waited for Ruth to stop talking, and made my joyous announcement.

"I've been following Marvellous Marvin," I said, very quietly, but somehow everyone in the apartment heard me and suddenly there was silence all around. I paused. But then I let it out, "and I've found out that he is… get ready for this… married." Ta-da. I wanted to open my arms and sing.

It's not over, I wanted to shout, until the fat lady sings.

But Sadie tore out of her room. Music off. Ruth stood up and the kitchen chair fell backward onto the floor. Daddy turned off the TV and spilled his bowl of Fritos from his lap.

I couldn't help it, the reactions were better than I had imagined, and so, just to push in the knife a little farther, to twist it, just because I had never had this kind of power, this attention before, I added, "And she's very, very skinny."

I didn't regret it at the time. There is no use regretting it now. It seemed, back then, such a perfect thing to say.

•••

"A big factor in giving solids earlier has been the eagerness of mothers who don't want their baby to be one day later than the baby up the street. They put strong pressure on doctors."

NEVER BEFORE HAVE I made such an impact on so many people.

I have since. When I was rolled into the hospital with five firemen surrounding me I caused quite a stir. When it took five of them to lift me onto a bariatric mattress, I shook up some lives. And then, today, when the same five men put me back in the ambulance and waved me on my way to the veterinary hospital, when the three paramedics settled in beside my bulk, I could see people whispering, eyes bulging. Freak show at the circus. Animal at the zoo. Can you imagine what they will tell their families when they go home for dinner? Can you imagine the image I have created? Will I be good dinner time conversation or will the thought of me turn stomachs? Good weight-loss trick: imagine the fat lady in the hospital.

But nothing like what happened that day. Nothing like Sadie and Ruth and even my father, all gathered around me and my burgeoning bulk in the olive green, orange and brown kitchen.

"You're kidding," Ruth said. "Married?"

"That's not possible," Sadie said. "We'd know."

"We would, wouldn't we? We would have known," said Daddy. "Surely we would have known, Sylvia?"

Did I really see her? The Mrs. Marvellous Marvin. For a moment I doubted it. Did I? Or did I imagine it because I needed to change the way we were headed? I needed to take our family and shift it a little. Focus us on something else.

I had been following him for weeks in my sneak, sneak, sneakers. I wanted to bring something back to Sadie and Mother and Daddy. I wanted us to start all over again, have a new life, without the Magician. And what better way to do it? If he was married then we were free of him. Free of his tricks. Sadie and Ruth could come together like mother and daughter again. They could stop fighting. My father could get off the couch and turn off the TV, maybe even begin wearing bolder colours—yellows and oranges. Even Grandma Mileford might magically rise in her coffin, dig herself out of the ground, and come home all dirty and hungry. A Mummy. After all, someone needed to look after Grandpa Mileford. And me? I might suddenly become thin. Don't you think? Couldn't it happen this way? If only Marvellous Marvin was otherwise occupied. If his spell was broken.

Who was to blame? Me for my vision (which was prophetic in the long run, wasn't it)? Sadie, for her fierce hatred of our mother? Ruth for her spiteful anger and self-centeredness? Or my father for his quietness?

Personally, I always thought Reggie Reynolds was to blame. And, luckily, the police and justice system sided with me.

They were gone. Sadie, Mother and Daddy. They left. I stood there, in the empty world. Sound and thought seemed to echo around me. The TV was off. So was Sadie's music. It was quiet and sad. I was lonely. I thought that something was supposed to change, something was supposed to be different after I told them the news about Marvellous Marvin. Our family was supposed to be a family, a REAL family, for the first time. Together. Marvellous Marvin was not free or single anymore, not for either one of them. So where did they all go? What happened?

Why was it that no matter what happened, no one ever worried about me? Why did no one ever think, "I wonder how Sylvia feels about all this?" "I wonder if Sylvia is hungry for dinner?" "I wonder if Sylvia would like to come with me to wherever the hell it is that I am going?"

It seemed to me that no matter what happened, nothing changed. I ate to get noticed—I disappeared. I gave Reggie the bra—he blew his nose on it. I spied on the magician and found out he had someone else—and everyone left without so much as a nod in my direction.

What more could I do?

"I am only thirteen years old," I said to the empty apartment.

•••

The Reluctant Weaner

"Think how you'd feel if a big bossy giant who had you in his power and who didn't understand your language kept trying to take your coffee away and make you drink warm water out of a pitcher."

THE BRA.

For a few months before I saw the mystery woman in the window, Reggie Reynolds was hanging around Sadie. Occasionally he walked her back home from wherever she was to the apartment. I saw them outside the window. I saw him sometimes in the lobby saying goodbye to her. She was not interested in Reggie ("He smells like rabbits," she said, "like cedar chips and shit"), but she liked the attention. Besides, Ruth, ever since the police officer brought Sadie home in the rain, had been monopolizing Marvellous Marvin. Reggie was a way for Sadie to see Marvin. He was the excuse she needed to duck out of the apartment and disappear into the night.

"He's more your age," Ruth said. "Twenty-five is closer to sixteen."

"Closer than what?" Sadie said.

"You know what," Ruth shouted. "Just shut up."

Reggie was awkward and ugly. He hadn't grown into his nose, which was huge and bulbous and scattered with pimples. He owned a pet store and he walked with a limp from the time he fell off the stage after passing Marvellous Marvin a new rabbit. He was always trying to stay out of the spotlights. Reggie had a creepiness to him that bordered on psychotic. I would see him staring, always staring, at Sadie. I would see him slinking up behind her. She never knew when he was there. I would see him scratching at his groin and moaning like a dog. He reminded me of the snakes he sold in his store. Narrow eyes, tongue flicking in and out.

Sadie said he was harmless. She said he knew she didn't like him "in that way." But it looked to me as if Reggie would do anything to get her to like him in any particular way.

One day Reggie stopped me on the way home from school. He was wearing a fringed suede jacket which rustled when he turned. "Hey, fatty," he hissed. "Do me a favour."

"I'm not fat," I said. It was all right if my mother called me fat, or my sister, but when someone out of the blue, someone I had no respect for, reminded me of my weight, it infuriated me. I had been in plenty of scraps at school (all of which I won just by sitting on my opponent). I knew how to defend myself.

"What are you then? Skinny?" Reggie laughed hard. "That's hard to believe."

If that was a way to get a thirteen-year-old girl to do you a favour then I wasn't sure I knew anything.

"What are you then?" I countered. "A zit-faced idiot?"

Reggie's eyes shot darts. "Get me something of your sister's," he said. "Like clothes. Or underwear. Or her toothbrush. I'll give you some money."

Reggie was the name of the cute guy in Archie Comics. The dark-haired one. The rich one. It was hard to put this Reggie together with that one.

"What are you going to do with it?" I challenged.

"Voodoo," Reggie said. And then he laughed. "I'm going to sniff it, fatty. I'm going to sleep with it and rub it on me. What do you think I'm going to do with it?"

He was so disgusting that for one of the first and last times in my life that I remembered, I lost my appetite. I threw down the cookie I had been chewing on. A pigeon clucked over and took it from the street. I thought of getting Reggie something good: if he was going to rub it all over him I should give him some of that itching powder you see advertised on the back of comics and tell him it's Sadie's bath powder, or get him one of her new safety razors for her legs, or get him her deodorant and fill it with mouse poison or termite killer or lice treatment.

But instead, for some reason I didn't even know (the money? To buy food? To see what would happen?), I did get him something. It wasn't as if I was planning anything that far in advance, it wasn't as if I knew what was coming, but it turned out later to be a useful object. I got him something that I thought wouldn't hurt anyone, but in the long run hurt him.

Sadie was arguing with Ruth one night about whose turn it was to wear which sparkle costume. Ruth was shouting, "You are not working for him anymore," and Sadie was saying, "You can't stop me," and I was just so sick of the loud screaming, the shouting, the mean words, that I snuck into Sadie's room and took one of her bras out of the drawer. She wouldn't notice, I was sure of it. I stuffed it under my shirt. In my room, I examined it. I was touched at how delicate and simple it was. It was pale pink, almost white, and there were small hearts embroidered into the seams. A lacy part in the front made me think of all those doilies around Grandma Mileford's old house. There were sweat stains on the sides and it smelled like my sister and something else. Old Spice?

The next day I gave it to Reggie, who just happened to be hanging out in front of my school. The kids were calling me names, walking with their hands out wide, doing rolling walks, pretending to be fat. I tucked the bra into my sleeve and the clasp stuck on my sweater and pulled the wool apart. Reggie didn't care. He was delighted. He told the kids to fuck off. He said "Boo!" and they scattered. He untangled the bra for me and then chucked me under my chin and said, "I won't call you Fatty no more. Besides, you get enough of that." He handed me five dollars (was that worth it?) and sauntered off down the street, Sadie's bra shoved into his pocket.

Did he feel sorry for me? Was Reggie protecting me?

I smelled rabbit. Distinctly. A wood-chip, cedar smell. A piss smell. It followed him.

I went right to the Grocery Mart and stocked up on as much as I could get for five dollars.

I didn't know what I had done then. I was just hungry for something to happen to someone. I was mad because when Ruth and Sadie were around the apartment back then everything was always loud and angry. I was upset because Sadie made our mother mad. And then Ruth would turn on me, try to fix me. I was all alone, adrift. I didn't know what Reggie would do. I didn't know that Sadie's delicate bra would be used as evidence. How could I have predicted that?

Circumcision

"Maybe he's masturbating because there is discomfort from a little infection." "The trouble is that this theory often puts the cart before the horse."

After I gave Reggie the bra, he would not leave Sadie alone. He was worse than usual. He hung out behind the stage at Marvellous Marvin's show and fondled the bra. He rubbed it between his skinny fingers like he was wiping the dirt off of them with it. The germs and grime. Wiping the sweat away. The bra began to look disgusting. Dirty and ripped. I swear I saw him wipe his nose with it. Sniffed. Like he was sniffing glue. A look of pure addictive determination in his eyes.

It was easy to see why he was charged with the crime. Reggie played the part of a criminal perfectly. He never tried to look normal. And, even if he tried, I'm sure he couldn't convince anyone he was innocent. He was too strange.

At the time I thought that, by my giving him the bra, Reggie would make everything better. I thought he would take Sadie away from Marvin and let Mother have the magician. But instead Reggie ended up making everything worse.

It was really my fault. Perhaps no one would have been hurt if I hadn't given him that bra. Perhaps. It's hard to know. Reggie was on a path of destruction from the moment he met my sister. It's hard to know if I did anything to speed it up—or if it would just come charging, that destruction, as fast as possible no matter who got involved. Like a train right at Sadie. Right at us.

•••

How Do You Unspoil?

"Make out a schedule for yourself, on paper if necessary, that requires you to be busy with housework or anything else for most of the time the baby is awake. Go at it with great bustle—to impress the baby and to impress yourself. When he frets and raises his arms, explain to him in a friendly but very firm tone that this job and that job MUST *get done this afternoon."*

THE FIRE BURNED through the apartment building. It sucked up oxygen and created a mask of black smoke throughout Parliament Street. It was spring, late afternoon, and people came out of stores to watch. They carried coffees outside and stood there and admired the blaze. The fire truck swerved and two people were knocked down and under. An ambulance screamed and people shouted. A fire hydrant burst. Water was everywhere but on the fire.

I was thirteen years old. Sadie was sixteen.

No one saw my father, Ruth or Sadie anywhere near the scene. Or me, for that matter.

Later, a lot of people thought they saw Reggie but that might have been only because I said he was there.

The fire took a few hours and then was rubble and smoke and ash.

When the fire was out, everyone stood in the living room breathing heavily. We didn't look at each other. There was too much to digest. The police officer rapped on the door. He didn't notice the smell in the air, the singed smell of our clothes emanating throughout the apartment. He didn't notice our wet shoes or the ash on my parents' hands, or the crazed look in my sister's eyes. He didn't notice me, over two hundred and fifty pounds of me, blocking the sun.

"Marvellous Marvin," he told my sister, looking straight at her, "has been burnt up in a fire. A tragic accident. We thought we should tell you because you worked with him. There was no one else to notify."

"I worked with him too."

Sadie wailed. Like those women you see in Arab countries. Head back, tongue out, wailing.

"Was he alone?" Ruth asked when she could be heard again. Her mouth was a picture of horror. The Scream with lipstick. Eyes wide and vacant.

"Yes. Luckily. I'm awfully sorry for your loss."

"Luckily," Ruth echoed. She turned towards me. She turned on me. The police officer left and I wanted to follow him.

I said, "Wasn't that the same policeman who was here the night Sadie ... in the dugout..."

"Hush," Ruth screamed. "Your fault. He was alone. You made it up."

Daddy settled into his chair in front of the TV. He put his head in his hands. His shoulders were shaking—was he laughing? Crying? Sadie blew her nose and slunk to her room, the mournful sound of her music soon moved over us.

"You," Ruth said. "You." And she pointed at me. As if I was the one to drop Dr. Benjamin Spock's book in the Book Barn sixteen years ago. As if I was the one who met Marvellous Marvin. As if I was the one to push Sadie out the door and into Marvellous Marvin's bed. As if I was the one who went over to the apartment and lit a match and started the fire.

"Me?" But my voice was weak and drawn. I knew I was to blame. If I hadn't said anything, if I had just sucked on my popsicle and kept it all inside.

Sadie signalled me from down the hall. Ruth was beginning to bubble over. She was on the war path. Pacing up and down, hands shaking. She was pale and twitching. Marvellous Marvin was dead.

"Come," Sadie said. Her eyes were swollen. I think she was in shock. She seemed ethereal at the time, as if she was floating. Her eyes were so large, and she was rarely blinking, only staring. The wailing had stopped.

I was nervous, but when was I not nervous in this apartment? I grabbed a bag of chips, a leftover sandwich from the fridge, a Tab, and headed around my mother and towards Sadie.

"Oh, just walk away from it," she shouted. "You're just like your sister. Only larger." And then Ruth sobbed. Big animal-sounding sobs. And my father got up from his position in front of the TV and attempted to comfort her. He patted her on the top of her head. He tried to hug her. She swatted his hand away.

"Don't worry," he said, clearing his throat. "It's a shame, I know. But you'll get another job soon."

"We're almost there," my paramedic says. "I know I keep saying that, but this time it's true."

"I'm still here," I say. "I haven't gone anywhere." I laugh. He laughs. We're having fun back here. My back aches with each bump in the ambulance. The rain has stopped but the wind has picked up and I can hear it whizzing around the ambulance. I can feel it pick the ambulance up occasionally, little tugs. Come with me, the wind says. Fly away.

In her room Sadie lay on the bed on her back and stared up at the ceiling. There were posters of unicorns and fairies on the walls, leftover from a more innocent (magical) time, pictures of teenage rock stars, men cut from GQ magazine, a few pictures of old friends. On my walls there was nothing. Just pink paint. The occasional greasy fingerprint. I never found anything worth hanging. I disliked clutter. But in Sadie's bright, cheery room, I lowered my bulk to the floor and began to eat. The music was loud. Heads together, we whispered over it.

"I can't believe he's dead."

"I know," I said. "Dead."

"Burned up. For real. In tiny ashy pieces right now. No more magic. No more Old Spice. No more rabbits." Sadie rolled over on her stomach. "Oh my God, what do you think happened to his rabbits?"

"I'm sure they are OK," I said. I was eating quickly, pushing down the bile that was creeping up into my mouth. The imaginary smell of singed rabbits seemed to be everywhere. "I'm sure he doesn't keep them in his apartment. Don't you think?" I had heard rabbit tastes like chicken.

"They are usually in cages in his dressing room," Sadie sobbed. "Or at Reggie's store."

Reggie, I thought, with his damp and sticky bra, with his erection, with his nicotine-stained fingers and his limp and pimples and greasy hair. Reggie.

"Do we have to tell Reggie?" Sadie said. She had written the word Foxy on the headboard of her bed and I stared at it for a while.

"I'm sure he knows already. The TV news crew was there."

"Someone should tell him anyway, I guess," Sadie said. "He should know he is out of a job. He should know what happened to any rabbits that were with Marvin. Can you tell him? I don't want to see him." Sadie shivered. "I hate him."

We heard Ruth crying in the kitchen. Banging pots and pans around. Bowls. I hoped she was making dinner. Or dessert. Or something. I was starving. Hopefully Dr. Spock had reminded her enough that her family comes first, that she had to take care of us. Seriously, his book said that everywhere. When would she notice?

This was the last time we were together. Sadie. Me. Hanging out in her bedroom. See. I knew that after Marvin was gone we'd be a family again. I was right. We were quiet and sad and lonely together. The two of us. I was on her floor, digging through her thick carpet to catch the crumbs that were falling. Sadie was on her stomach on the bed, or her back. Flopping back and forth. Staring up at the ceiling and then down at me. She was sad and wet-eyed. I wanted to say, Marvellous Marvin was only your first love. I wanted to say, you'll have many, many more. You're Foxy. You're beautiful. You're Sadie.

I didn't know then that this was one of the last times Sadie would be the way she was. Fresh and vital. Alive. Crazy alive. Full of over-charged hormones and teenage despair. A small pimple on her nose. White surrounded by inflamed red. The smell of watermelon lip gloss lingering in the room. Her hair was soft and long and flipped back like Farrah Fawcett's.

"Did you love him?" I whispered.

"He's dead, Sylvia. Oh God, he's dead. It's not true, is it?" Sadie rolled off the bed and slid towards me and gathered all of my bulk into her thin arms and hugged me hard. She cried then. And I cried too. I was being touched again, by my sister.

Ruth was sobbing in the kitchen. Sadie was sobbing in her bedroom. My father probably wiped away a tear or two. Happiness? He was, after all, rid of his enemy.

"I'm starting to think he wasn't married," I said to Sadie. "I think I made a mistake." And she pushed me so hard away and smacked me so seriously across my fat face.

"What? What?"

My cheek stung like a million bee stings. "I just mean, maybe I didn't see it right."

I can feel it still. Her slap.

"There was a woman," Sadie hissed. "You said there was."

"Was there?" I backed away from her.

"In the window. You said she was sucking on his face."

"I'm not sure anymore. Could I have seen them up there like that? Maybe it was a trick of light, of shadow."

"You said she was skinny."

"I don't know. Was she? I don't know what skinny is anymore. Maybe...."

"Don't ever say that again." Sadie stood. She put her hands on her hips.

"I'm so hungry," I moaned. "I feel faint. I don't know what I'm saying."

"There had to be a woman. He had to have been with someone. That's the only way this all makes sense. That's the only way, Sylvia, that I can live with it."

Did she start the fire? I was confused. Impossible.

She didn't know what she was saying.

I was exhausted and starving. I could eat a horse, a bear, a cow, a buzzard. A barbequed chicken-rabbit. I started humming.

Sadie stormed out of her room and down the hall towards the bathroom. Ruth had stopped crying in the kitchen by this point. I heard nothing but the TV. And then running water. Sadie was in the shower. I don't know why I did it, but I flushed the second toilet. Just because I could. Just because nothing had changed, after all my hard work. My hopes were dashed. Sadie screamed and shouted and danced around in the burning spray.

That night I found myself outside of Reggie's pet store. Staring inside, nose pressed against the window. Greasy fingers. Greasy nose. I didn't know how I got there. One minute I was eating ice cream in the kitchen, listening to everyone crying in every room, the next I was here, staring in. It was late. Dark. Cold. I could see my breath. My legs ached. I was starving. Reggie was there, lit up behind the counter. He was reading something. He was settled in, like he'd been there awhile. Sitting on a stool, his fingers picking at the pimples on his face. He was absorbed in a magazine. It had never occurred to me that Reggie Reynolds could read. A *Playboy*. He held it up in front of his face and I saw the cover. Thin woman, legs spread.

Snakes in glass cages. Rabbits hopping around their wire enclosures. It seemed strange to me to keep the prey so close to the hunter. But then I guess lots of people live on farms with the chickens and cows they eat. The tension felt liquid. Even outside of the store. I could see the bunnies' noses quivering, the tightness of their haunches, their desire to hop quickly away. The snakes curled lazily under the heat lamps.

There was nothing in the world that would make me step inside that shop. It was a horror movie for a thirteen-year-old. How did I get there? And why was I here? One minute there was ice cream in my mouth and the tub was on the counter (I don't think I remembered to put it back in the freezer), the next minute I was there.

Reggie looked up suddenly. And saw me.

Aha, I wanted to shout. I knew it. I was not invisible.

Back in the apartment the ice cream I had left on the kitchen counter melted and spoiled.

"There is such good in Sadie," I say.

"Pardon me?" My paramedic bends down and sticks his ear near my mouth. I'm tempted to bite it. Large, hairy, oyster-shaped ear.

"My sister. Sadie."

"Yeah, um, sure." My paramedic moves away from me and up towards the guys at the front. He whispers something and they both look back at me. I smile and nod.

"How you doing?" I shout.

My first real friends, if you think about it.

Reggie stopped reading his magazine and looked at me. Then he put his magazine down on the counter and looked around him, behind him, at the cages of snakes and rabbits and mice—I saw the mice now. Small and impish and curled in balls of fur, shaking their wood chips with fear. He signalled, come in. I shook my head.

"Come in," he mouthed.

"No."

Reggie shrugged and stood, stretched. Came outside, stood in the darkness on his store doorstep and looked down at me. Hands in his pockets.

"What do you want?"

"Nothing."

"Then what are you doing here?"

"Nothing."

"Fuck," Reggie said. "You're so stupid."

I nodded because, at the time, I believed him. I looked down at my hands, which had black ash on them. I sniffed them. I looked up at Reggie.

"Are you here because of your sister? What did she tell you?" Reggie swallowed. "I told her I was sorry. I didn't mean to hurt her."

I leaned against the store window and looked out into the empty street. I could hear sirens in the distance, some other fire. I wondered if Marvin was happier dead than alive. I wondered if he was doing cheap tricks in heaven. Or hell?

"I didn't do it," Reggie said. "She's lying." Reggie's hands were in his pockets now, touching that dirty bra. His left hand was bandaged. And suddenly I understood what he was talking about. The night that Ruth let him in the apartment. Sadie's broken tooth. There was more, wasn't there?

Sadie's silence.

"Did you?"

"Did I what?"

"Ah," I said knowingly. Like a detective. Like my hero, Nancy Drew. I started to walk away.

"Did I what?" Reggie shouted.

He deserved, I thought, whatever he got.

And he was about to get it.

Common Nervous Symptoms

"One father solved his baby's head-banging by sawing the headboard out of the crib and tacking a piece of canvas in its place."

THE POLICEMAN CAME back a few times.

"Where was Reggie Reynolds during the fire?" I asked. No one heard me, of course, but much later we found out my words must have registered. Snake man? Bunny Boy? Where was he?

Marvellous Marvin was officially declared dead. The newspapers cried out, bells tolled, flags at half-mast (no, not really, no one cared about some crappy magician except Sadie and Ruth). Burned up in the fire. Nothing left.

Under my bed were pizza boxes, milkshake cups, potato chip bags, boxes of empty food items. Crinkled paper, soiled napkins, pop cans.

There was a funeral, of course. There always is. People can't just die. Everyone has to stand around in the rain and cry and remember and eventually carry on. Ruth's head wouldn't stay on straight. It kept falling forward on her neck. It was too heavy. Too full of prescription medication.

"She's such a head-banger, ha ha," Sadie said.

I hummed a lot that day. Hummed into myself. Shut myself up with my own buzzing.

A hum drowns out the world, makes you focus only on what's inside. I learned that when I was little and to this day I hum when I need to get away.

At the funeral there was a crowd of women over the age of sixty-five. A Marvellous Marvin Fan Club. All teary. Sniffling and blowing noses.

Coughing into embroidered hankies. Sadie sat next to Reggie. Or, actually, Reggie sat next to Sadie and Sadie moved over to the tip of her chair and almost fell off. She hated him, that much was obvious. When I saw her cower beside him I felt better about dropping his name in connection with the fire. Reggie smelled and so I sat as far away as possible.

There was no "other woman" at the funeral. There was no one but us, the Swamp family, Reggie, and a few old biddies. He didn't have much, did he? But then who would I have at my funeral?

I was feeling awful, of course. Thirteen years old and I felt like it was all my fault. I was eating, but I don't need to mention that.

I was eating because I was hungry. Just basic hunger. A stretched stomach. The bigger I got the more I disappeared. The bigger I got the less people saw me. They turned their heads and looked away.

I realize now how funny that sounds. Get big in order to disappear. Most people spend their lives trying to shrink down into nothing in order to be seen. I have spent years getting bigger. Trying to take up the space that everyone else left behind. Skinny, loud Ruth. My poor Daddy. Wild Sadie. Reggie in jail (he's still shouting to be heard, but no one is listening). I wanted to get so big that I exploded. Like that Monty Python sketch that Sadie and I recently watched on late night TV, both of us curled up in my bed. "Bring me a bucket," the fat man shouts. And then he explodes. Guts and food and internal organs everywhere. Sadie bust up laughing.

"It's funny, so funny," I said.

"Funny," she howled. "So so so funny."

"Just a wafer-thin mint, sir," I imitated. We laughed. We always laughed. "Just a wafer-thin mint." My belly rolled when I laughed which made Sadie crack up even more.

Now, on my platform in the back of the ambulance I want to take it all back. I'm scared now. I'm terrified. I'm heading down the highway towards the veterinary hospital, all the hundreds and hundreds of pounds of me jiggling and jostling and twitching and jumping over the bumps in the road, the paramedics all around, and I'm really really worried. Too big, my brain finally says. It's too late. "Just a wafer-thin mint" and I will explode.

There was a reason those kids tortured me in school. They were little early-warning signs. Like on the Weather Channel when the little flashing box at the bottom of the screen comes up to tell you a tornado is on its way. Those kids in my school moved around me like wind funnels, they harassed me like lightning, they picked on me like wind. I guess they tried to make me realize that what I was doing—eating to explode—was not the way to win in this world. Kids are cruel, but sometimes what they are saying is nothing but the truth. Sadie protected me from those kids for a while, but then she stepped back. She finally saw what I should have seen, the warning flash, the "typhoon coming" sign, the rolling black waters boiling and bubbling. And now it's too late. I am drowning in my own body fat.

"Look what you've done now," Ruth would say if she were still around.

Look what I've done now.

The lights go out sometimes in my head. My breath hurts as it comes out of me. The sores on my body leak fluids. I can't wash or go to the bathroom on my own. I smell horrible no matter who bathes me or how often. I certainly have made an impact, an impression. On someone. On something.

On a CT scan made for a horse. On five lovely firemen and three paramedics. On a handful of nurses and some very fine doctors.

On Sadie. Poor Sadie.

On myself. I've certainly made an impact on myself.

When all I really wanted was to disappear. Like magic. Marvellous Marvin sliding his hand over the marbles. One, two, three, they are gone.

"You always do everything opposite," I can hear Ruth saying. "If you wanted to die, it would have been easier and faster to just gas yourself."

Absolutely nothing changed after Marvin was gone. I need to reinforce that. I need to justify it.

The sequined body suits still hung in the closets. Twinkling.

The Book was abandoned for a while on the hall table. But not for long.

Sadie still stormed out of the apartment. Screaming, fighting, crying, laughing. No one even knew why.

And Ruth? She talked even louder than before.

Let them grieve, I thought. Give it time. Soon we'd be a family. Something was bound to change eventually.

But then my mother turned to me again. From The Invisible Fat Girl to Centre Stage. Ruth had no more work to do for Marvin and so began again to consider me her job. She weighed me. She pleaded with me. She yelled at me. She starved me. She fed me. She pulled at my hair, my arms, she poked my stomach. And I had enough.

"What happened to you? It's like I turned my back for only one minute and you ballooned."

Sadie came home. And watched. She snickered and smiled and acted like my mother.

And then that horrible day happened.

Sadie was sitting at the kitchen table eating French fries from McDonald's. I was drooling. I was trying not to leap out of my chair and lunge at her, trying so hard to sit on my hands. I hadn't eaten since the night before. Ruth had denied me breakfast.

"Look at her," Ruth hollered.

Sadie shrugged.

Help me, I signalled to Sadie but she turned away.

"I've decided to make it my mission in life to cure her," Ruth said.

"She's not sick," Sadie said. I smiled. "She's just stupid." My smile fell.

"Obesity is a disease."

Sadie? Help me, Sadie?

"If you would just help out," Ruth said. "Be a good sister to her." Yes, I thought. I agree. Ruth placed a plate of carrot sticks and celery in front of me. I gagged.

And then I dove for the fries. I finally had enough. Of Sadie. Of Ruth. Something inside of me burst. I upset the kitchen table.

"You stole my fucking fries," Sadie shouted. "You pig."

I grabbed the fries from off the floor and I stuffed and swallowed them as quickly as I could. They were hot and salty and burned my lips. I pushed them down. Sadie and Ruth were hollering at each other and at me. So loud I couldn't even enjoy my food. So loud that the neighbours pounded on the walls.

And that was when it happened. That was when I finally figured out that our life had nothing really to do with Marvellous Marvin. It had nothing to do with Reggie Reynolds. Our life was about Ruth and Sadie. They were both so loud that I suddenly hated them. I had spent my whole life loving them and just like that I hated them. I stopped chewing and looked up at them and the fries started to churn and boil in my stomach, they moved up my gullet, they came into my mouth (all squishy, salty, biley, greasy) and they shot out between my lips to the floor, to the walls, to the kitchen chairs. I turned and vomited.

Ruth and Sadie stood still. Quietly, they looked at me. Everything was so loopy I wanted to laugh. I stopped vomiting. I had thrown up my love for them right there in the kitchen.

That's how I figure it started. If I need to explain myself. Here in the ambulance, I figure that I threw up everything that day. I mean everything. My soul, my heart, my love, my guilt, my grief, my childhood. A light bulb went off in my head. Lightning. I threw up Sylvia Swamp and I opened my new eyes. I was born again. And things were definitely going to change.

Sadie turned on me and shouted, "You are a cow, Sylvia. C-O-W. Cow. Why can't you be normal like the rest of us? I've always been embarrassed to be seen with you. You're disgusting. You're huge. You make me so ashamed. Sick. You make me sick. I hate you, Sylvia Swamp. I hate you."

School children always danced around me in the gymnasium. Taunted me. Hurled insults at me. Stabbed me with their words. Not a single person out there wanted to be my friend.

But I always thought that deep down inside Sadie loved me. After all, she had to. She was my sister.

"You are NOT my sister," Sadie said. "You have never been my sister and you will never be my sister. From now on don't even talk to me. Don't even look at me. I. Hate. You."

Inoculations

"Any vaccine has to be made from the germs of the disease."

THE WIND RIPPED through the streets that day. I could hear it from where I stood in the kitchen staring out towards the living room, towards the windows that looked out on the city. Sadie had stormed out after I vomited. And Ruth was putting on her coat, her outside shoes, and heading out for a walk. I watched her walk down the hall towards the door and she looked so much like Sadie. Or Sadie looked so much like her. They had the same walk, the same hip-swaying movement. Their lean legs were longer than their torsos. Their waists were tiny. Hair that was styled and luxurious. They could have been twins. Sisters.

Marvellous Marvin was dead and buried.

I did the dishes. I cleaned the vomit off the floor. I cleaned the walls. I swallowed the greasy bile that was still moving up my throat. French fry taste. My own poison.

"I hate you," she had said.

"You are NOT my sister."

I didn't intend to do anything. Honestly. I was just walking in the wind.

It's hard to believe a morbidly obese woman, isn't it? There's something about the eyes, the shifting, beady eyes, sunken in the head. The lids so swollen. There's something about the fat around the jowls, like it's covering up the truth.

"She's talking to herself," my paramedic says.

"Sorry," I say, and he startles. "I was just thinking aloud."

"You OK?"

"Right as rain."

"Hmmm," he says. "I've always wondered what that means. Must be left over from early farming days."

It wasn't my fault when one month ago Sadie up and left me in the apartment to fend for myself. It wasn't my fault that no one took care of me. I lay in bed and I waited and I waited. I called out. I tried to reach the phone but it was too far away. I couldn't move my bulk even that little bit to the dresser in the corner where the phone sits. I couldn't steady my breathing. For all that I did for my sister, she eventually left me in the lurch. To stew in my filth. To starve. To stop breathing. She deserted me—like Ruth, like Daddy, like Grandma and Grandpa Mileford, like Reggie Reynolds and Marvellous Marvin.

They were all gone and I was invisible again.

Twenty-eight years old. Over 700 pounds.

But I am invincible too.

Still, now, as I ride on my back in the ambulance to the veterinary hospital, Sadie is probably out there somewhere, dancing to the music in her mind. With no thought to me and my future. No concept of how the neighbour below eventually heard my bellowing (he said, "bellowing," as if I am an elephant) and called the police. No thought as to the front door of our apartment and how the firemen and police had to sledge-hammer it in (who will fix it? Has it been fixed already? Is the air from the hallway creeping into our apartment?), how they found me there and how the smell of me, the sight of me lying in my filth, made them gag. They turned from me and gagged. I had no way of relieving myself. What did they expect? Sadie gave no thought to how many men it took to get me out of the apartment and into the hospital. How many lives were affected. Not only the police and firemen, but their families waiting for them to come home from work. And Ruth called me selfish?

Sisters.

Mothers.

If there is one thing I have learned in my short, distressed life, it is that sisters and mothers don't amount to a hill of beans. They aren't worth anything. You see sisters walking down the street together—same hair, same body build, one slightly taller than the other—and you think that they must have so much in common, that they must love each other deeply. They must share so much memory and history. After all, they are attached by heart and hip and blood. You'd think that, wouldn't you? You might also think that pigs fly?

And mothers? Mothers and daughters together, holding hands, arm in arm, shopping bags over shoulders. Sharing a laugh. A smile. A look of love. Isn't that the way you see it on TV, in the movies? The way you read about it in books? There is supposed to be a willing-to-throw-yourself-in-front-of-a-train kind of bond.

But, no. I guess there are times when that is fiction and this is reality. My life vs. TV life. My life vs. Other people's lives. Dr. Spock told Ruth to love her children unconditionally.

Why was this the one thing he wrote that she didn't pay attention to?

Sometimes I think that if I could just understand my mother's relationship to Dr. Spock's book, I could understand everything else. Four times I've read *Dr. Spock's Baby and Child Care*. The last time was a month ago, in bed, before Sadie left me and I ended up in the hospital. I read and ate and read and ate. Filled up my soul and my stomach. I didn't think to bring The Book with me when the firemen broke down my door. I should have asked one of them to grab it from the bedside table, but it was chaotic and everyone was talking at once and I was profoundly embarrassed at the state of the apartment, the dirt, the filth I was lying in, the horrible smell of my own excrement.

What I gathered from Dr. Spock as I read (and his first line is exactly this) is that mothers and fathers have to trust their instincts: *"Trust yourself. You know more than you think you do."* He was saying, You, Parent, you who have given birth to this flailing, screaming baby, you know inside, innately, what to do. If you just stop and think about it. Trust Yourself.

If you need help, sure, turn to The Book and look it up—allergies, inoculations, breastfeeding, everything—but most of the time go with what you feel is right. Your gut. Your first impression is probably the correct one. We are all creatures of habit, we are people who rely heavily on the learned past. Inside each of us we know what our mother's mother's mother did. So we can do it ourselves.

Ruth stuck to The Book like glue.

Sadie threw The Book at Ruth and my mother screamed like she had been stabbed.

I stole a look at The Book one day, thinking everyone was out, and Ruth found me and exploded like a volcano. She refused to feed me dinner. She banned me from the kitchen.

"Why?" I asked her. "What's so important about a book?"

"It's a way of life," Ruth railed. "It's how we all know what to do."

"What do we know, though?" I asked. "I really want to know."

"We know what we need to know."

What did I learn from this? What did Sadie learn from this? I became huge and Sadie became thinner than a mint wafer. We were left alone at the end, in our family apartment, trying to take care of each other. We learned nothing from our mother.

What if you can't trust yourself?

Does that stop the process? If we can't even trust ourselves, if we can't use what we have learned from our mother, then who can we trust? How can we trust?

Ruth's instincts weren't trustworthy.

The Book is still there. It is still our Book. It still makes perfect, common sense. The Book is not wrong. It's the way Ruth read it, it's the way Ruth interpreted it, the way she paid attention to every action, every moment, when she maybe should have just acted naturally. Instinctively. The Book is just advice. Couldn't Ruth see that?

I act by instinct. I always have. I act with my gut.

Where are you, Sadie?

And my stomach growls loudly. The ambulance is slowing down, turning corners. We've reached where we are going. The paramedics are all suddenly very lively—they've accomplished what they have set out to accomplish. They've got the fat woman where she was supposed to go. And the rest is now very exciting. A veterinary hospital. Who knows what they might see. This isn't an average day in anyone's life. More to talk about at dinner.

I'm starving. I'm dying. I'm starving to death.

"Just in time for lunch," my garlic-paramedic says. His stomach growls too. "I'm hungry."

It is raining again. Right as rain.

In my head I see them.

There they are. The sisters. I see them crossing the street in front of the ambulance. We are stopped on a country road just outside of town. We are almost at the veterinary hospital. The paramedics will take me for my test on the huge horse machine and then cart me back to Toronto. They will prop me back up in my airless, white room with the bariatric mattress made especially for fat people. Hook me up to IVs and oxygen. Say, "Goodbye, we've spent such quality time together." And the sisters cross, arm in arm, laughing, before the bright ambulance. Under one umbrella. They both turn and look at the ambulance. I'm sure of it. They must be there, those two sisters. One whose hair is like yellow silk, the other who is shorter, squatter, darker, a little heavy. Perhaps because she is younger and hasn't stretched yet, hasn't fully grown. Perhaps because she still has her baby fat. It doesn't matter how different they look. They are sisters and we all know this. They are coming home from school for lunch. Taking care of each other. Laughing together. Heading towards home. A mother waits for them there. Looking out the window into the rain, wondering if she should come out to meet them with another umbrella. Keep them dry and safe and warm.

It was so windy that day. I stopped only feet from her but she stood there, in my way, and stared at me like she didn't even know me. I was the gruesome monster in a scary movie. She was disgusted. I was a drop of acid on her skin. I was burning pain. I was NOT her sister.

"Ms Swamp? Sylvia Swamp? Can you breathe? Can you hear me?"

I was hoping to be gone before Sadie. It's amazing how long it takes to eat yourself to death. You would think it would be easy. Heart condition, diabetes, high cholesterol and now that clot and a pulmonary embolism. Not to mention obstructive sleep apnea, cardiovascular disease, osteoarthritis, fatty liver disease, menstrual disorders and urinary incontinence. I've refused bariatric surgery and have even thrown out my anti-depressants. There are not enough of them to kill me and I reason that if I'm unhappy maybe I'll commit suicide and save Sadie the trouble.

"I think she's unconscious."

"You are NOT my sister, you are not MY sister. YOU are not my sister," Sadie said that day.

Now Sadie is gone. She left the apartment and I am here in this ambulance. We had some good years at the end, after it all, me and Sadie. We did. Even if she spent those last fifteen years playing nurse-maid to a hippopotamus.

"I did love you, Sylvia," Ruth said to me. "But you were such a disappointment."

"I didn't follow the script, did I?"

"What script?"

"The Book."

"Ah," Ruth said. "Neither of you did. Sadie didn't either. Such a disappointment. But I did love you both."

Sadie was with me when we buried Ruth beside our father. Somewhere in the same graveyard Marvellous Marvin's urn and ashes lay. Sadie kicked around the dirt for awhile on our mother's grave and then pushed me in my wheelchair back to the waiting taxi. It was only us then. Me and Sadie. The funeral director. No one else. All was quiet for once. Ruth wasn't there screaming. Daddy's headstone was growing mould.

All I know is that after years and years of hurting, of being hurt, of aching with anger and sadness and betrayal, I thought it would all be over when my mother died. Instead, it was as if her death tore another hole in the universe.

Why haven't you visited me in the hospital? Has something tragic happened to you? I've reported you missing but no one seems to want to look for you. Everyone just shrugs and walks away, avoids eye contact.

My sister is missing and no one will do anything to help me.

I heard my nickname the other day. They call me "The Mountain." I am a mountain, a force to be reckoned with. How is it that the doctors and nurses can see that but Sadie and Mother never did?

We all told each other that Reggie must have set Marvellous Marvin's apartment on fire. We all told each other that Reggie was to blame for Sadie. The law thought Reggie was to blame too and locked him away. For years and years. Last I heard he's still in there, in jail, crying out for justice.

My father was not impressed with Marvellous Marvin, even when the magician was dead. He told me once, when he had too much to drink, when we were watching TV, that the reason his life hadn't turned out the way he thought it would was because of the sneaky magician, because of the magic spell he cast on Ruth and Sadie. Daddy and I were two peas in a pod. I wanted to tell him that I thought the exact same thing but I was afraid to say it aloud because then it would certainly be true. The spell would be real. I just nodded sagely and we went back to watching TV.

But I don't know now. Who is to blame? Sometimes, late at night, when I can't breathe and my dinner is roiling in my stomach, when I can't sleep, in those pre-dawn hours before someone comes in to help me, that's when I know with all my heart that I am to blame. All of me.

I loved how, after everything that happened, Sadie took up my habit and hummed to herself when she cleaned the apartment, and I loved how she smiled when she brought me my food. She always smiled when she fed or bathed me. She never frowned. It was almost as if her lips didn't know how to frown anymore. I loved how level-headed she was. Never happy, never sad. Just Sadie. Just my sister. My friend. I loved how she occasionally did a magic trick instinctively. She would take a pack of cards and shuffle it so quickly that my head would spin. And then she would ask me to choose one. She would put it back in the deck, reshuffle and find my card. She always found my card.

I love Sadie Swamp.

This is the end, Sadie Swamp. You are missing. I am hospitalized. Soon it will be all over. This test at the veterinary hospital is ridiculous, just added humiliation for me before I die (well-deserved punishment, I guess). Soon it will all be over and you can go back to the apartment and, maybe, hopefully, get on with your life—whatever that may entail. You can make a mean grilled cheese sandwich, you know how to tip the pizza delivery boy, you know how to count out money. You'll be fine, Sadie Swamp. Wherever you are. Just fine.

"Your eyes are open. Did you fall asleep?" my paramedic asks. "You worried us there for a minute."

And so we are back to the beginning. The ending is uncertain again.

One day Sadie was watching a movie on TV with me. What we were watching? I can't remember. The next hour she was gone. I was suddenly all alone. I suffered. I lay in my filth like a pig in the mud.

"We're here. The long ride is over. Ms Swamp, can you hear me?"

Now I am in the ambulance and we have stopped outside the veterinary hospital. The paramedics open the door to the back and begin to discuss how they will roll me out, lever me down, roll me in. They debate the pros and cons. They decide who might be the strongest, who might need more help on his side. A white-coated doctor (Vet? Or do I recognize her from the hospital in Toronto?) is there and she is signalling the direction we should go. She is talking with her hands. I watch her hands flash in front of her face. Her thin, lovely hands. My breathing is scattered, rough. My heart speeds up. I hear birds. It has become a nice day, the rain has stopped and the spring leaves, freed from the snow by the rain, are blowing circles around everyone. My little crowd. I want to laugh with Sadie and say, "Look at all the attention I'm getting." I'm on stage now, under the spotlight of the sun, and here is my audience.

The lesson today, I think, is maybe how to die gracefully. Sadie has been released into the world, but she will only truly be free when I am gone. Trust yourself, Sadie. And I need to trust myself. We both know more than we think.

Life is ultimately one big magic trick, but, like the memory tricks Sadie and Marvin used to do, life only works if you have someone planted in the audience to help you. I had you, Sadie. And Mother. And Daddy. The Swamps. We were, after all, each other's stooges.

Part Two
Ruth

Your Baby's Development

Watching Him Grow

"He's repeating the whole history of the human race."

"DON'T YOU THINK Sylvia did it?" she asks Mr. Swamp at the diner the morning after the fire. Ruth hasn't slept all night. The police came in just after they all crept home covered in soot. It could have been anyone, Ruth thinks. Any one of them could have started the fire. Sadie. Mr. Swamp. Sylvia and her bulk. She was moving around the condominium like a whale last night, the orange juice warming on the counter (doesn't she know it goes bad if you don't put it in the fridge?), a puddle of ice cream on the floor in the morning. "How the hell did we have such a huge child?"

"We didn't have a huge child, Ruth, she wasn't born big."

"Are you implying that it's my fault?" Over and over she tells them all to put the food back in the fridge after they take it out, she tells them all to clean up their rooms or, in Mr. Swamp's case to keep his TV area clean, to shut their curtains before they change, to help out in the kitchen. Over and over and over. Ruth feels as if she's a stuck record. A nag. She's become her mother. No one wants to be a nag. But these children, these girls of hers. This husband.

Ruth was fat as a child, but she conquered it. She starved herself. And she hasn't been fat since. So it's not her fault that Sylvia is grotesque.

Mr. Swamp moves his newspaper closer to his face like he's trying to pretend he can't see or hear Ruth. He peers closely at the stock listings. This husband of Ruth's. She's here with him and Marvin is dead. Ruth is still not sure if this is true. How can he be dead? The police said he was, but Ruth doesn't quite believe anything the police say. They did, after all, make up things about Sadie.

"Jesus. If anyone is to blame, it's you. You and your potato chips and pop in front of the TV. You are immobile. You are stuck, Mr. Swamp. She's copying you." Ruth dramatically thrusts out her section of the newspaper, snaps it, her shiny red nails flash. I'm sharp, she thinks. I'm mean. He better listen. Ruth's hands are shaking. It started last night and she hasn't been able to make them stop.

"I'm not fat," Mr. Swamp says. "Your sugar is low. Look at your hands."

"You're getting a tummy."

"Maybe your mother," Mr. Swamp says. He swallows. "It could be her fault."

"Yes. That's it. Mother." Of course, Ruth thinks. She was fat and it was all her mother's fault. When Ruth stopped listening to her mother, when she stopped respecting her, that's when Ruth finally lost weight. Of course she's the reason. "All those fast-food places she used to buy from when they were little."

"She did babysit a lot."

"What are you saying? I was working."

Mr. Swamp looks at Ruth curiously. He nods. It's easy to blame things on the dead, Ruth thinks. Soon we'll all be blaming things on Marvin. Ruth just knows it. Her magician. Her poor love.

Did he get what he deserved?

"You really should eat some of your food. Your hands."

Ruth forgets for a moment that she is attempting to blame Sylvia for the fire. Mr. Swamp does that to her. He side-tracks Ruth. That's what their marriage was all about in the first place. Ruth was on a straight road and then she got side-tracked.

Ruth snaps her paper again and sees an article about the fire. Mr. Swamp is still focused on the stocks. Shaking his paper around because it won't stand straight.

Dead. He's dead. It won't sink in, not really, until the funeral. Ruth is sure of it. Once she sees the urn, the photos, the flowers, the crying fans in black. Oh there will be fans. Definitely. Maybe that woman that Ruth saw—Marvin's lie. One of many.

"Sylvia thinks Sadie did it," Mr. Swamp says. He's reading Ruth's mind again. She thinks he often does. Says something just when Ruth is thinking it. Ruth studies him. There is nothing there—just Mr. Swamp. Same husband. No spark. "You think Sylvia did it," he says, nervously. "I wonder who Sadie thinks did it? You?" He tries to laugh, but coughs a little instead.

"There is no way Sadie would set fire to an apartment. That's not her style." Sadie is the only one in Ruth's family who has some potential. Although she's been side-tracked lately too, hasn't she?

"Who would?" Mr. Swamp says. "What style?"

"I don't know." Ruth stares. Mr. Swamp has missed a spot shaving. Right there. On his chin. "And maybe, if you think about it, Sylvia is too lazy. Don't you think? Can you imagine her climbing stairs?"

"What stairs?"

Ruth thinks sometimes that talking to Mr. Swamp is equivalent to talking to a brick wall. There is nothing there. He's a dolt.

Coffee is served. Maeve, the waitress, gets their breakfasts without even asking what they want. She knows because they come here so often. Sometimes this bothers Ruth—are they so predictable? Sometimes she finds it reassuring and comforting. Today she doesn't really care. Marvin is dead. Ruth sniffs.

The Swamps' newspapers rustle. Ruth composes herself. She wipes a tear from her eye.

Out the window, Sylvia waddles past. She looks in at her parents. Ruth pretends she doesn't see her. She holds up her paper. But then Ruth must wave because Mr. Swamp waves. Ruth registers her daughter's largeness moving on. Did anyone see her wave? No one is paying any attention. People dig into their breakfasts, sip their coffees.

Ruth is well aware that she shouldn't be ashamed of her child. She is, after all, an expert on child rearing. She's practically memorized Dr. Spock's book. It's just that Sylvia is so out of control. She's become so pudgy and large and roly-poly. It is as if one day Ruth wasn't paying attention and the next day she was huge. Ruth doesn't remember her looking like this a week ago. If the child doesn't take care of herself now, she'll never be able to stop herself. Ruth feels as if she's failed, even though she knows it's not her fault. It is Sylvia's fault (and perhaps Mr. Swamp's?). The child has no self-control. She has no desire to be thin and beautiful. She's just like Mr. Swamp, which is odd—slow and boring and a dolt.

Ruth remembers that when they were little Sadie and Sylvia used to think that was a curious word. "Adult?" Sylvia would say. And Sadie would say, "No, a dumb person. A dolt."

"Adult?" Sylvia would say again.

This could go on for hours.

Ruth thinks of them then. Her two lovely children. Such potential. Sure Sylvia was slightly chubby then, but not like this. Look at both of them now. Ruth wants to put her head in her hands and rip out her hair, but that would be uncivilized. She is in a public place. Chin up, Ruth. Be strong.

"How do you think she got so big? Really. Be serious."

Mr. Swamp says it's fear. He says that Sylvia is afraid of the world. That's all it is. She might as well make something big around her, he says, to keep her protected. A shell. Is that right? Isn't that what he always says, Ruth thinks. He rubs at the elbows of his grey sweater. He pets his thinning hair. Ruth notices strands of grey hair falling out onto his paper. He sighs. He's been using this shell excuse for far too many years. Like everything associated with Mr. Swamp, it is redundant.

Ruth can't help herself. She begins to cry. "Oh my God." She's been crying so much since last night. She places her newspaper down on her coffee cup. The ever-vigilant Mr. Swamp moves it quickly before something spills. "Marvin is dead. He's dead, Mr. Swamp." Ruth just now realized it. Really realized it. What is wrong with her, she thinks? She used to have such will power. Although Dr. Spock would caution her about holding in her problems, Ruth used to be able to hide her emotions.

"Yes. He is, Ruth. I'm so sorry."

"What am I going to do?"

Mr. Swamp sighs. "You'll find another job. Sadie will find another job. Maybe you could get a job in my office? You used to type fast. Remember? Can you still type fast?"

Mr. Swamp looks so hopeful. As if they will really both head off to the office together, maybe have lunch outside on nice summer days, chat at the water cooler.

"I don't need a job." Customers in the diner stop eating and look up. Ruth tries to whisper. "I need Marvin."

This is the closest Ruth has ever come to stating the obvious and she watches Mr. Swamp swallow hard. Come on, surely you know, she thinks. Ruth looks at him quizzically. Don't you? He looks confused. Stunned.

"I mean," Ruth backpedals (what else is there to do when he looks so sad?). "He was a good friend, you know that. He wasn't just my boss." She touches Mr. Swamp's sweater. "You liked him too, right? Didn't you like him? And what a tragic way to die. A fire. Oh my. I didn't think he would die." She cries again. Sniffles.

Across the street Ruth sees her fat daughter moving her body forward down the sidewalk. Sylvia sort of rolls when she walks, her arms swing merrily by her side. Her nose is in the air. What is she looking at, Ruth wonders? Her chest is stuck out far, like a pregnant woman. Her back is bowed. It pains Ruth, physically hurts her, to look at Sylvia. How could Ruth Mileford have let this happen to someone who is related to her? When she had these two children they were going to be perfect, brilliant, beautiful. They were going to be everything Ruth is and more. Ruth was sure, if she just followed The Book. Ruth throws her hands up in the air. She points.

"Look at her, Mr. Swamp. Just look at her. She can't be my child."

Mr. Swamp turns to where Ruth is pointing and looks at Sylvia. Ruth knows what he's thinking. He's thinking, The Quiet One. He's thinking, a glandular problem? Hereditary? He sees her stick her chin in the air, as high as it will go and Ruth is sure he thinks she is just pretending not to notice those people who tease her. She will walk high, walk proud. Or maybe he's thinking that she's walking that way because of all the weight around her middle. It may be a balance thing. Mr. Swamp, Ruth is sure of it, doesn't know. He doesn't know anything. He adores his daughter, doesn't he? Even if she's a walking disaster. A huge joke.

What ever happened to them? To Ruth and Mr. Swamp. Their children were going to be perfect but so was their marriage. Ruth was going to have everything her parents didn't have. She was going to show them that they shouldn't have raised her as an afterthought, she was going to show them that she was better than they were. Ruth was sure she was better than them.

Ruth thinks she should have married Marvin. If only she'd met him a year earlier.

"Benjamin Swamp is lovely," Ruth's mother said. "He's a catch."

Why did Ruth listen to her?

"What will become of her?" Mr. Swamp asks. He asks out loud but Ruth knows he isn't looking for an answer. He never is. Mr. Swamp often says things that don't require any comment from anyone else. Things such as "What's going on?" and "Has anyone seen my *TV Guide*?" and "Soup for dinner again?" In fact, if you don't answer Mr. Swamp, Ruth thinks, it doesn't matter at all. He just goes about his business. Finds his *TV Guide*, settles in and watches TV. Eats his soup for dinner. That's the difference—one of many—between Mr. Swamp and Marvin. Marvin is (was?) always thinking about Ruth, thinking about what Ruth was thinking about, saying things like, "What are you thinking about?" "How are you feeling?" and "Can I get you anything?"

"I'll put her on a diet," Ruth says. She has composed herself. Fresh again. Dry-eyed. "Another one. There's a new grapefruit diet that looks marvellous. Sadie and I were thinking of starting it. Back when she was still talking to me." She tears up again. "Oh, everything is just a big mess. And it can't be my fault, Mr. Swamp. I do everything I am supposed to do. I work hard at it." (Doesn't she? Doesn't she follow Dr. Spock to the letter? What more can one woman do?) "Do you think, now that he's gone, Sadie will talk to me again?"

"Now, now." Mr. Swamp smoothes Ruth's hand with his fingers and almost spills her coffee in the process. Ruth pulls away and uses his napkin to blow her nose. When he touches Ruth sometimes there is a small feeling, a little bit of warmth, a memory of something she doesn't want to be reminded of. "She'll be just fine, Sylvia will. She's a strong girl. It's just a stage she's going through. She'll get taller and then thin out eventually." He takes his hand away, places it back on his newspaper. He doesn't answer Ruth's question about Sadie. Mr. Swamp rarely talks about Sadie. He rarely talks to Sadie either. They both avoid each other. Sadie and her skinny jeans and eyeliner. Sadie and her bleach-blonde, waist-length, feathered hair.

The last night Ruth had with Marvin before Sylvia said he was married to that woman pops into Ruth's mind. He was kissing her under her breasts. He would lift one and then the other (which, if Ruth thinks about it now, was sort of humiliating. She isn't saying they aren't firm, it's just that she was lying down) and he sucked and kissed underneath them. Not the nipple, but the underside, the side Ruth imagines would taste salty, of sweat, if you were a sweaty person. Ruth is definitely not a sweaty person and so hers probably tasted just fine. Later she took her finger and ran it under and licked it and her skin tasted like cold cream. And now he's dead. Burned. No more kissing, sucking. And it's all Sylvia's fault for making everyone so angry. And Sadie's fault for lying to Ruth, for trying to take Marvin away from her. And Mr. Swamp's fault for being Mr. Swamp. If Ruth hadn't felt beholden to these three, so responsible for them all, well, you never know what would have happened. She is pretty damn sure she wouldn't be here right now. There is nothing in Dr. Spock's book that could have prepared Ruth for this turn of events.

Ruth sips her coffee. She's pleased that lately Sadie has been seen with that young rabbit man, Reggie, and she knows she can thank herself for that. It seems that Sadie has finally given up her child-like infatuation with Marvin. If it wasn't for Ruth's match-making, Sadie would be suffering so much more now. Who can blame her for her feelings for Marvin? Really, Ruth thinks. She wants to be just like her mother (they both do, Ruth is sure of it). And Marvin, he is (was) Marvellous. A suave magician—oh God, he's dead—with his tuxedos and top hats and flowers and handkerchiefs. Any young girl would turn her head to watch him walk down the street. Wouldn't they? He was certainly special. A womanizer, perhaps, but special. With Sadie it was an obsession, a silly girlish fantasy. Nothing more. It wasn't true love like it was with Ruth. The police officer who came to the condominium that rainy night saying that Sadie was having sex with Marvin knew nothing. He was just making things up, looking to get Sadie in trouble. Ridiculous. Sadie wouldn't have had sex with Marvin. He was as old as her father, older than her father. And Marvin liked comfort, a bed, a sofa, not a baseball dugout (whatever that is) in the rain. Besides, he loved Ruth.

Only me, Ruth thinks, until Sylvia came home with a yellow popsicle in her mouth.

Now this boy, Reggie, he's like bees on pollen with Sadie. He can't leave her alone. A little obsessive, perhaps?

Ruth studies her nails, looks out the window, and then gladly gives Maeve her plate of half-eaten scrambled eggs and dry toast. Ruth's nails aren't as shiny as they should be. She thinks that they will have to be re-polished, re-filed. The fire really did damage to them. All sooty and chipped. Ruth's nails, Sylvia, Sadie, Marvin, that mystery woman. Ruth has so many things to worry about. If Sylvia insists on eating, well, Ruth will let her eat. She will let her eat until she realizes how disgusting she is. Surely someday soon she'll wake up and see herself in the mirror, a huge teenager, and she'll say, "I need to get my life in order." No one wants to look like that. Ruth is sure of it.

If she's truly Ruth's daughter, she'll wake up one day and figure that out.

If she's Ruth's daughter. Or Mr. Swamp's? Or Marvellous Marvin's? There is always that, Ruth thinks. Thirteen years ago in Marvin's bed, the mattress lumpy, Marvin's feet cold.

Maybe it's Marvin's fault she's fat. After all, he tended towards being thick, chubby, out of shape.

Marvin's cold, cold feet.

Mr. Swamp clears his throat again. He startles Ruth out of her thoughts. Always clearing his throat, blowing his nose, swallowing. There is something constantly stuck in his passages. Another reason Marvellous Marvin was so wonderful. He had very little phlegm. He made very little noise—except during sex. Ruth dabs at her swollen eyes. What a mess. She sniffs like a lady. She orders a refill of coffee. What would Dr. Spock do now?

"I can't believe he's dead."

"Yes," Mr. Swamp says, sounding sort of satisfied. "It's hard to believe."

•••

Care Of The Teeth

"There is no proof that the green film that forms on some children's teeth is harmful."

It happens like this:

Sylvia crashes into the condominium just when Ruth is making up a jug of orange juice. Breathing noisily, sucking noises. It is near dinner time but, typically, Sylvia has a popsicle stick in her hand. Her mouth, her teeth, lips, tongue are stained yellow. Ruth has been transcribing

Dr. Spock sayings all afternoon, thinking to herself that she must put Sylvia on another diet, thinking that she can't give up on her now, the girl needs her mother. Funny that she is thinking this at the particular moment that Sylvia comes in with a popsicle dangling out of her mouth. Ruth does love them, her children, she does all she can. She has pasted the sayings up around the kitchen, taped them to the fridge. No one seems to read them but Ruth. In her bedroom, Sadie's music is playing loud, drowning out Mr. Swamp's TV. Ruth says to herself, I am a good mother. Certainly. Even if they don't listen to her. Even if Sadie won't speak to her. She's just a teenager. Fickle. Hormonal. Angry about Marvin and how Ruth has convinced him not to let Sadie work so much. Some day Sadie will thank Ruth. They will be adults together. They will shop for clothes when Sylvia loses her weight and Ruth will help both of her children raise their own children. She will give them each their own copies of Dr. Spock. Maybe they will take a vacation together—Mexico, the Caribbean. Although Sylvia would have to lose a lot of weight before getting into a bathing suit.

"Where have you been?" Ruth says, not because she particularly wants to know, but because that's what mothers are supposed to ask their children when they come home. If a mother pretends to be interested then maybe she will be interested. Ruth's mother was never interested. She didn't even pretend. "You should be seen but not heard," she would say. Always watching her soaps and telling Ruth to be quiet. Her relationship with her mother—no trips, no shopping sprees. Nothing.

Maybe if Ruth's mother had listened to her. Just once paid attention to what Ruth was saying.

Since Ruth's mother died, she has been comparing the way she was raised to how she is raising her own children. Ruth has made sure to break any similarities, any connections, to rip them apart. She knows that she turned out so well only because of the work she put into herself, not because of anything her mother did. Ruth's children, however, will turn out well because of Ruth, because of Dr. Spock. Ruth is sure of it. It's impossible to do worse than Ruth's mother.

The whole time Ruth has been thinking about this, Sylvia is chatting. Ruth is not really listening, but then, suddenly, Sylvia blurts something out about Marvellous Marvin having a wife, kissing a woman in an apartment over a shoe store on Parliament Street, and the condominium becomes deathly quiet. The TV is silent. And Sadie is suddenly there, standing in the kitchen as if by magic. The music has stopped in her bedroom. The world begins moving in slow motion. Every movement is like running through water. Is anyone talking? Ruth can't hear them. Marvin, Ruth's Marvin? Married? Nonsense.

But part of Ruth has been waiting for this. Hasn't she? Hasn't she always wondered and suspected? When he slips out after a show, claiming he needs time by himself, that he's too tired that night. When he leaves for the weekend, telling Ruth that he is going to Ottawa to perform a private show for an office function, or when he doesn't show up for days and then takes Ruth into his bed and wants only to sleep. Ruth's Marvin has someone else? Ruth knew it. Who is she?

Mr. Swamp leaves the condo. The door slams. And then next, Sadie. And then Ruth knows what to do. She needs to pick herself up (and the kitchen chair which has fallen on the floor) and she needs to get out, to walk out the door. She needs to put an end to this, once and for all. The Swamp family all leave the bearer of bad news alone with her yellow mouth, her popsicle stick, her protruding belly, and the orange juice on the counter.

Ruth needs to speak to him. She needs to ask him if this is true.

So many nights he winks at women in the audience, so many times he smells like cheap perfume and cigarettes. Sadie with her hand on his zipper, his wrists covered in lubricant. How many years of her life has she given to him?

A wife?

An apartment?

"Where did you say the apartment was?" Ruth asks Sylvia before she leaves, and Syvlia tells her mother again, points her chubby arm towards the window.

Ruth doesn't know what to do for awhile. She wanders the streets. She enters some stores. She imagines Marvin on stage, his lovely smile, his twinkly eyes. She stops walking and think of his hands on her body, his lips kissing hers. Neither of them have ever said they love each other but Ruth knows this to be the case. How could it not be? They have been together for sixteen years, since the first day he pulled her, pregnant, into his hotel room. No matter how he flirts, Ruth knows Marvin like she knows herself. He embodies magic. He is brave and strong and mystical. She has seen him happy and sad and quiet and angry. He has thrown vases at her and once he slapped Ruth. He has covered her with flower petals and poured champagne on her stomach. Everyone loves him—Sadie, for one—possibly even Sylvia? Mr. Swamp likes him? Surely? Everyone wants a piece of him.

It's not his fault he has other women.

Married?

Sylvia misunderstood. Ruth is sure of this. It can't be. A woman kissing him? It could have been his mother. He does have a mother, doesn't he?

It then occurs to Ruth that she actually doesn't know that much about him. She doesn't know anything about his mother. Her relationship with him is mostly about sex and magic. It's mostly about Marvin undressing Ruth.

Ruth has a husband. Perhaps it is only fair that Marvin has a wife. Ruth thinks, I just need to speak to him. I need to see him.

Ruth moves through the streets in her own thick fog. She left the condominium without her sunglasses or jacket. She is wearing her indoor heels and she wants to cry but crying will ruin her makeup and she doesn't want to look a mess when she sees him. If she sees him. Maybe Sylvia didn't see him. Maybe she got confused and it was someone else. Someone else wearing tails and a top hat in the middle of the day.

How could he do this to Ruth? After all she has done for him.

Marvin lives at the hotel. He lives in the room that Ruth visits. Doesn't he? Sometimes rabbits are there. A huge bed, stained from their lovemaking. He knows all the maids' names. His toiletries are in the bathroom and rumpled, smelly towels are on the floor. Sylvia is wrong, wrong, wrong.

Where did Mr. Swamp go? Ruth thinks he said something about toothbrushes, about needing to buy them. Then he rushed out of the condominium as if it was his lover who had betrayed him, as if Marvin's unfaithfulness meant something to him. What is all of this to Mr. Swamp? He hasn't loved Ruth in years.

It suddenly occurs to Ruth, out of the blue, that Mr. Swamp's first name is Benjamin. Just like Dr. Spock. Is that possible? Perhaps she isn't thinking straight. After all, Marvellous Marvin is married. Her mind is understandably muddled.

The concert in the park. Violins playing. Ruth is with her mother and father (doing his perpetual crossword) and her mother is spreading a blanket out on the grass, arguing with Ruth about it, "Keep it clean, Ruth, for God's sake." For some reason Ruth went to the park with them that day. She can't remember why. It's not as if she ever did much with them, but it was sunny and lovely and the thought of a concert in the park was intriguing. Cellos. Oboes. A slight summer breeze. Ruth had a new dress to wear. She remembers it was powder blue. Ruth and her mother were on a rare truce. Promising to be polite. And then, out of nowhere, a handsome man walked past, smiled, and bent to help her mother with the picnic blanket, making sure it was spread as wide as it could go for the three of them, making sure there was no dirt on it—and then there were the four of them because he accepted the offer to sit down and eat. A handsome man? Was he all that handsome? Mr. Swamp? He must have been, Ruth thinks, or she wouldn't have married him.

Ruth wanted babies. That's why she married him. She wanted hundreds of children to fill up her life.

Two months later they were married and Ruth took to calling him Mr. Swamp (as per his request). She wanted out of her parents' house. She wanted to get married. She wanted those babies. Mr. Swamp was the way to get what she wanted. Ruth forgot his first name so quickly and then he became greyish and she couldn't remember anything she loved about him. How is this possible?

Ruth thinks: I did love him once.

Or cared about him, loved him like a brother, a family member.

If Ruth had waited one more year she would have been a sparkling, wild Magician's Assistant, perhaps traveling the world with Marvin and his show—their show. Maybe they would have had hundreds of well-adjusted children, children who would also be magicians and shock and surprise audiences everywhere.

Does Marvellous Marvin have a last name? Ruth stops on the street and wonders. Marvin __? Honestly. No last name. How could she not know this? There seems as if there is so much Ruth doesn't know about him. She walks faster, towards Parliament Street. Marvin __? How can this be? Sixteen years with the man, surely Ruth should know his last name.

What happened to her marriage? Was it having babies, like Mr. Swamp says? Post-partum depression? Was it just Ruth? Was it Marvellous Marvin, or did everything fall apart before he came into Ruth's life? Was it Dr. Spock? Mr. Swamp says Ruth uses his advice too often, he says Ruth doesn't think for herself. She does think for herself but she has also prided herself on doing everything suggested in The Book. She follows almost every rule in The Book, although Sadie says they aren't rules, they are just suggestions. Philosophies. But Ruth still thinks about them, and interprets Dr. Spock's writing in her own way. It's not all about being a sheep, a follower. She puts herself into it. And still her life turned out crummy. Her kids are a mess, one is fat and one has her hormones out of control. Her husband is horribly boring and does nothing to inspire her. Just clears his throat constantly. And she is so unhappy. Ruth never feels fulfilled or at peace with herself. She is often sad. And angry.

Mostly angry.

Unless she's with Marvin. Then she is magical.

And here he is with another woman.

There must be more to life. There must be.

Ruth finds herself on Parliament Street. She sees the shoe store. She sees the apartment above. And there he is, in the front window looking out. Ruth makes her arm shoot up and she begins to wave—look at me, Marvin, look at me. But there, behind him, a woman with dark hair appears. She is laughing. She takes his hand in hers and he spins her slightly. They move away from the window and back into the apartment but not before he looks down on the street and straight into Ruth's eyes. Marvin's eyes light up, they widen, his eyebrows peak, and then he is gone. He does not acknowledge her.

Ruth couldn't see her clearly. She couldn't make out the other woman's face.

But there is something in the way they touched, the way their hands clasped, that works on Ruth, that takes her heart and smashes it against her ribcage. She begins to think about Sadie. And baseball dugouts. She begins to wonder about her naïveté, about all she thought was a lie. Is it possible? Ruth doesn't know where she is. She remembers going into a store and buying something but it's not until later that she knows what happened, what she did.

Time moves forward again and Ruth is standing there, her legs aching. There is Mr. Swamp ahead of her. Then Sadie comes. They have all come together to see Marvin for themselves. To see the mysterious woman. They have converged on the scene, but it isn't a scene yet. Not yet. The sun is so bright Ruth finds it hard to focus. There is the shoe store. There, above, is the apartment, the chair that Sylvia mentioned in the front window, Marvin's black coat draped over the back of it. Windows open slightly, a breeze, curtains billow.

Marvin is gone. The woman is gone. Sadie disappears—goes to get gum, she says. Mr. Swamp heads around the block looking for her. Ruth blanks out again for a minute (is she on a fire escape?) and then suddenly she is out front again, looking up, and she sees smoke, a fire breaks out over the shoe store—in the apartment over the shoe store—flames begin to leap from the windows. The chair in the window is engulfed in smoke. Ruth can't see Marvin's black coat anymore. It happens so quickly it is startling. At first she thinks that it is just the sunlight reflecting from a window and then the window explodes and shatters, and the flames leap. Glass is everywhere. Trucks are coming, whizzing down the street, lights flashing, sirens howling. Ruth stands still and watches as a fire truck skids in water from the hydrant, which has burst. Two spectators are hit. An older woman, a young man, do they disappear under the wheels of the truck? Does Ruth really see this? Someone screams. How can this be happening? People move quickly around Ruth at times, like fast-forwarding a video, and then at other times like slow-motion replay. And all she can do is stand there. This is Marvin's apartment. She understands what is happening but she feels nothing. Not yet.

Ruth looks up at the apartment above the shoe store. The curtains are ablaze. That chair in the window comes in and out of focus. The coat that was draped on the back of it is gone. And there is no married Marvin or his fictional wife peering out, shouting, help me help me save me. No one. This is Marvin's apartment. That is his wife, or lover. Ruth knows. Ruth knows that he never loved her. She knows now that he slept with her daughter. She knows. Like that.

Mr. Swamp re-appears beside Ruth. And then Sadie, and she's chewing gum. Together they stand, side by side, and they quietly watch the scene.

"Surely he doesn't live there," Sadie says, finally. "He lives in the hotel. We would know, Mother. Wouldn't we?"

Ruth nods. Yes, she thinks, I would know. Although … she saw him, didn't she? And what is his last name? Marvellous Marvellous Marvellous Marvellous … Ruth saw him there. Ruth saw him. And her. What a cliché, Ruth thinks.

Mr. Swamp says nothing. Just holds onto his elbows, hugging himself. Nodding. Clearing his throat. Creating phlegm as usual.

"Would you please shut up?" Ruth can't stop herself. The noise of the fire, the trucks, the people screaming, ambulances, sirens screeching, burning curtains, wind and smoke, and Ruth can only hear the um um of his throat clearing.

"Fuck," Sadie says. "You two. Get a grip."

"What did you say?"

"Nothing," Sadie grumbles. "It's just that you are always nit-picking him."

"Me? It's not my fault that he can't clear his throat quietly."

"I can," Mr. Swamp says. "I can clear it quietly."

"Then why?"

"Ahem." Softly, he looks bewildered. "See."

Sadie bends down and is looking under the wheels of the fire truck as the paramedics pull out the two people. She is standing ankle-deep in the water from the burst hydrant, the water that should be on the apartment fire. She's too skinny. Too drawn. A skeleton covered with skin. Ruth can count the ribs on her back. Her hair is shiny and thick. Is she anorexic? A middle-aged Italian man is standing next to his shoe store shouting, "My business, my business," and later Sadie tells Ruth that she is sure he shouted, "Mama Mia."

"Not possible," Ruth says. "That's a stereotype."

"I swear I heard him. He was waving his arms and shouting."

Time passes and when they are clearing out the apartment the firemen bring out his props—pieces of a disappearing cabinet, a flexible saw, a rabbit cage, a burned top hat. Ruth's hands are raw and dirty. She feels as if she is burned. She faints. Suddenly Sadie's feet are pushing at Ruth to revive her, as Sadie drips smoky water into her face. Ruth scratches at the pavement with her fingernails and clutches the top hat that she somehow took from the fireman. Mr. Swamp looks forlorn.

"Marvellous, marvellous Marvin," Ruth cries. Her makeup runs in rivulets down her cheeks but she doesn't care. She isn't on stage anymore. She feels she has no one to impress.

Sadie is shaking. She is wet and cold and looks terrified.

Mr. Swamp takes control. He takes his daughter, his wife home. Leads them like lost puppies. Two women, one on each arm. On the way, he ducks into a store and buys them three green popsicles and they suck on them to get the fire taste out of their mouths, to soothe their burned throats. When they arrive back at the condominium it is dark. Sylvia is standing there in the blackness. It is as if she hasn't moved.

But she knows about the fire.

Ruth startles herself in the bathroom mirror—green lips, green teeth, green tongue, mascara streaks down her cheeks, swollen eyes. A look of horror on her face. Who is this woman? What has she done?

And then a policeman arrives to talk to the Swamps and, for some reason, they all work together to pretend that they didn't know what had happened. For some reason, without deciding together, they are all complicit in their lies.

"Marvellous Marvin," the policeman says, "is dead." He has come here because Sadie and Ruth work for the magician. He has come because of Sadie's supposed tryst in the baseball park. He has come, he says, because there is no one else. Do the Swamps know anyone else?

Doesn't he notice the smell of smoke, the ash on their clothes?

"Marvellous Marvin was burned beyond recognition," he apologizes. Head down. He's holding his hat. Ruth sobs. "We found hardly anything. It's as if he never existed. He's gone."

"Like magic," Sylvia says, quietly. "Poof."

•••

Bowel Training

"If his mother becomes more insistent, it increases his conviction that he must hold onto his possession more obstinately. If she becomes cross and tries to get his movement out with an enema or a suppository or if he is worried by seeing it flushed away in the toilet, he may hold back anxiously the next time, as if he were trying to save a part of his body."

BEFORE THE FIRE there is Reggie Reynolds.

Ruth can't understand why Sadie treats Reggie the way she does. He skulks around the condominium building waiting for her to get home from school and, instead of liking his faithfulness or being taken in by his concern or impressed that he owns a store—he's an entrepreneur—Ruth's spoiled daughter moves around him like he's old gum on the sidewalk. He's even taken to bothering Sylvia just to get more time with Sadie. Ruth saw him the other day, talking to Sylvia. She was looking out the condo window at the street below and Sylvia waddled up to the front doors and Reggie was there and he put out his hand to stop her, to talk to her. They exchanged information. Ruth assumed he was trying to find out more about Sadie, because, after all, what could he want with Sylvia?

Marvin hired Reggie to take care of the rabbits after two truly awkward animal events—one was the dove that flew up into the ceiling, narrowly missing a ceiling fan. The other was when Marvin's rabbits began to have diarrhea. Marvin had no idea what was causing this. He was plain tired of taking off his hat only to be covered in wet poop. He stopped the dove part of the show and searched through the Yellow Pages for someone who could tell him something about his rabbits.

"All over the cage? Wet stuff. Aren't they supposed to shit pellets," he says to Ruth as they lie in bed one evening after a particularly lousy performance—both the magic show and the sex. Ruth has PMS (an awful amount of cramping, bloating, overall unhappiness and queasiness) and she has spent the evening stomping around the stage in her too-tight costume. She wanted to kill someone. Marvin, perhaps. After the show, to make matters worse, a young woman in the audience tracked Marvin down and ordered him a drink. He flirted. He always does. Ruth waited in the hotel room, naked, feeling her swollen breasts and watery bloated stomach and thinking, feeling the depression and anger creeping in, feeling it move up her spine and into her mouth. A bitterness. "I could kill him." And when he climbed in beside Ruth, when they made love, he came too quickly—"It's to be expected," he said soothingly, "that young girl had me all worked up." He laughed. Was Ruth supposed to agree? Was Ruth supposed to think this was funny? And then Marvin rolled over on his side and began to talk about rabbit crap.

The rabbits are in the hotel room with them, around the corners of the room in wire cages. Ruth can smell them. Wet rabbit shit. It takes her ten minutes to get used to the smell. She gags when she first comes in. As Marvin talks about shit, Ruth sighs. She wants to go home now, put a hot water bottle on her back, but she knows that if she leaves before he falls asleep he'll be angry at her and he'll ignore her for a couple of days. Flirt with others, have more drinks with fans. So Ruth cuddles him into her and says, "Why don't you just buy a new rabbit for every show? That way you won't have to take care of them all the time."

Marvin ignores Ruth. Rolls over. Thinks aloud that it must be his toupées. The rabbits are eating his toupées under his top hat and it's giving them diarrhea, he reasons. It's certainly doing nothing for his toupées, all chewed up. He constantly has to replace them.

The next day, after a few calls, Reggie Reynolds comes in just as Marvin and Ruth are setting up the stage. Marvin has actually listened to Ruth. He found Reggie's name in the Yellow Pages after a guy at the front desk who owns snakes told him where to look. Reggie is carrying a cage full of rabbits. All white.

"I'll take them," Marvin shouts out. "All of them." He laughs his stage laugh. Big and friendly. Reggie is immediately charmed. Aren't they all?

Reggie picks nervously at the pimples on his face and makes a quick deal. He takes the sick, diarrheic rabbits away and never tells Marvin what he does with them, although he does discount the price of the first set of bunnies for the second. Ruth assumes he feeds them to his snakes. Imagine what Sylvia would say if she knew this, Ruth thinks. Imagine what she would do. She is so overly sensitive.

At every performance there is a rabbit in Marvellous Marvin's hat. Ruth is never sure if they are different rabbits each night or only every couple of months. She doesn't really care. Rabbits aren't anything to her. Just props. She has enough to deal with. She must get her hair done, her nails done. She tones her legs by jogging on the spot for 40 minutes a day. It isn't easy looking as good as Ruth does. Sadie doesn't know how easy she has it. When you are young everything just falls into place, Ruth thinks, everything stays firm and lovely. Your skin is soft and kind.

As long as the hotel room smells less cedar-chippy and rabbit-shitty (although there are often a few still there, in case Reggie doesn't show up for a performance), then Ruth is happy. And so Reggie Reynolds is there to stay. Their rabbit wrangler and whisperer. He's just off-stage, laughing at everything Marvin says. Blushing when Ruth speaks to him. She thinks: he needs a girlfriend.

It takes him about two months to latch onto Sadie. In fact, Ruth is the one who suggests to Reggie that he hang out with her, that he watch out for Sadie like a big brother. Oh, Ruth's no fool, she sees the tent in his pants and she knows there is no big brother stuff going on in his mind. But Ruth feels it would be good to have someone watch (out for) Sadie. Ruth flashes her lovely chest in front of him when she's in her green, blue and yellow sequined costume and she purrs (because she is good at purring and because he practically turns purple when she does this. It makes her feel young again), "Oh, Reggie, I think Sadie likes you. She couldn't stop talking about you last night."

But Sadie is ridiculous. Typical. Bitchy. Like she is to everyone. Reggie is not good enough for her, she says. He is a bug under her shoes. He is spring-time melting dog shit. Sadie's nose is so high in the air. Honestly, Ruth doesn't know where she gets it from. Ruth does have her opinions, sure, she has her pride, but really. Sadie is quite a snob.

"For God's sake, it wouldn't kill you to go out with him," Ruth said to her once. "Would it?"

The One-Year-Old

What Makes Him Tick

"The psychologists call it 'negativism'; mothers call it 'that terrible NO stage.' But stop and think what would happen to him if he never felt like saying No. He'd become a robot, a mechanical man ... He'd never be good for anything."

REGGIE TELLS RUTH that his father left him the pet store when he was eighteen years old. Supposedly, Mr. Reynolds climbed on a stool in the attic of the rooming house they lived in, tied a rope first around the rafter and then around his neck, drank a bottle of whiskey to dull the ache, and kicked the stool out quickly. The bottle crashed. The rope was tight. He did this with no thought for anyone but himself. Reggie tells Ruth this when they are both backstage holding rabbits, juggling them, deciding which one will be less skittish. Reggie says that he always wanted the pet store anyway and that his father was running it into the ground before he killed himself. "So it all, in the long run," he says, "turned out for the best." Reggie turned the store around. Cleaned out the cages, resuscitated the dying animals (or gave most of them away), and now mostly deals in snakes.

"Lots of men like snakes. And a few strippers," he tells Ruth (she is horrified: I am old enough to be his mother, she thinks.) "Besides, simplifying things is the best. The more animals you have, the more they die and get sick."

Ruth pulls on the front of her outfit, which, lately, has been feeling snug. Has Ruth gained weight? Ever since Sadie started working with Marvellous Marvin Ruth feels fat and uncomfortable. Sadie parades around, all lean and young and Ruth's body feels wrong.

"But I had to get the rabbits and the mice. To feed the snakes. It's all a natural progression," he says.

"So the rabbits are food?" Ruth looks at the one in her hand. Its little nose is twitching. A shiver runs up her spine.

"Yeah, I guess. Marvin's the only one who buys them for anything else."

Ruth tells herself, I don't care, "as long as you don't bring any snakes in here," she says. "I may wear this outfit but I'm certainly no stripper." Ha ha ha. She laughs with her mouth open. Red lips flash.

Reggie laughs and shows his crooked teeth. His breath reeks. Ruth has to stand back a bit. He needs work. Ruth squints her eyes—if she does this will he look a little better? Hmmm. He looks a bit like a cartoon caricature of himself, like the politicians in the newspaper, with big noses and chins exaggerated. It's hard for Ruth to imagine Sadie falling in love with this, but what does she know? Ruth, after all, married Mr. Swamp. Mind you, he is certainly handsome compared to Reggie. And Marvin isn't particularly the cat's meow, with all the weight he has gained lately. It's Marvin's inner soul, Ruth thinks, his romantic side, his magical qualities—charisma, Ruth is sure it's called. His eyes are lovely too.

In the audience that day Ruth notices a busload of high school kids from outside Toronto. All boys. A private school—the boys are wearing suits and ties. They look lovely, Ruth thinks, but they are ill-behaved. They are squirming and noisy, hooting and hollering. When she walks onto the stage, she wishes she were wearing something less revealing. The way those boys look at her body, as if they could eat it. Some of them look at her as if she is revolting. An old woman. Their mother. Dressed like that? Ruth is ashamed and aware of her performance and she accidentally drops a pack of cards. Marvin scowls. Three scowls from Marvin and he won't talk to her for a week, he'll hire Sadie to work instead.

Ruth can't concentrate. Perhaps, she wonders, this is what Sylvia must feel like everyday. It startles her slightly. The feeling that you are naked and revealed, as if your body will be injured by these boys, their eyes. It's a hurt that goes deep inside Ruth. She resolves to help Sylvia even more than she already does. Even though she's tried everything.

Look. There, beyond the curtains (Ruth peeks out during intermission), in the audience, is Sylvia. Her daughter. She has skipped school—

again—and is there watching. Surrounded by gangs of teenage boys in suits. A large swath of open seats around her. Boys laughing. Pointing. Why is she here? Does Sylvia have a crush on Marvellous Marvin too? Will both of Ruth's daughters drive her crazy (or to the grave)? Sylvia acts as if her mother can't see her, as if she's invisible (as if that will ever happen, Ruth thinks, she balloons over two seats, plus she is the only female in the whooping, screaming audience). Ruth decides to signal to her so that Sylvia knows she has been caught.

Marvin comes out to see the rabbits. He touches Ruth's shoulder in that possessive way he has and then he puts his full hand on her bottom and squeezes hard. Ruth can't help but jump. Blushes. She'll bruise there, she is sure. He's always pinching and slapping.

"Are we ready?" he says. Second scowl. "Second act."

Reggie's pimples glow white from his embarrassed face. He saw the squeeze, Ruth assumes.

"This little one is good and quiet," Reggie says, handing Marvin a rabbit. "Although I think this might be her last show. She's sick."

"As long as she doesn't shit on my head," Marvin says.

Can you feed the sick rabbits to the snakes or will that make the snakes sick? Ruth wonders.

Reggie laughs long and hard. Ha ha. Two boys sharing a stupid joke.

Ruth sighs. She holds in her stomach. She takes a deep breath. Sylvia's out there. She is watching Ruth. Sadie is at home, at school, somewhere. Ruth doesn't know where her daughter goes. Sometimes Sadie takes off for days. Her teachers have stopped calling. They've given up.

Has Ruth given up?

Ruth turns to Reggie. "Honey, why don't you come over to the condo after the show and see Sadie?"

Reggie touches his pocket where a dirty piece of white cloth is poking out. He blushes harder, almost a purplish red, and says, "Yes, ma'am," and nods his head a disagreeable amount. Marvellous Marvin and Ruth walk out on stage, the audience applauding, and Marvin whispers, "I thought you were staying for a little bit after. I have wine in my dressing room."

It's the wine that is making her fat, she's sure of it, but she says, "Oh, I'll take him back to the condo and then I'll come see you." She smiles. "You don't worry about that."

On stage Ruth points at Sylvia in the audience, flashes her eyes, and that huge girl tries to shrink down into her seat as if she can disappear. But how could anyone not see her?

That night the condo is dark except for the blue glow of the TV. Marvin is waiting for Ruth back in his hotel room. Sadie is in her room, Sylvia is in the living room watching her shows alone. Mr. Swamp isn't home—where is Mr. Swamp?

"It's tax time," Sylvia says, as if that means anything. She looks curiously at Reggie. "What's he doing here?"

"Visiting Sadie. They have lots to talk about," Ruth says.

Sylvia nods and continues with her TV show.

Ruth leaves Reggie in the condo ("Go find Sadie. She must be in her room. It's down the hall") and then scurries out the door, waving. "I won't be late. I just have to run a few errands."

When she comes home after midnight the apartment is darker still. The TV is quiet and black. Sadie's bedroom door is shut tight. But under her door Ruth can see a line of light and so she opens the door slightly, carefully, quietly. Just to talk with her daughter, even if she won't talk to Ruth. But Reggie is still here.

What is going on?

Much later Ruth wonders if it is her fault. Is it all her fault? Ruth told him to visit Sadie. She thinks, sometimes you make innocent decisions that can lead to horrible consequences.

•••

Elements in the Diet—Water and Roughage

"If your baby is sensitive about new people, new places, in the middle of his first year, I'd protect him from too much fright by making strangers keep a little distance until he gets used to them, especially in new places. He'll remember his father in a while."

MARVELLOUS MARVIN'S FUNERAL.

Ruth buys her girls each a hat for the funeral. And one for herself. Ruth's hat is emerald green, Sadie's is beautiful royal blue and Sylvia's is black mourning.

"We have to put on a good show," Ruth says. "The other women there will be looking to us for how to conduct themselves."

"Christ," Sadie growls. "You know I hate hats. They ruin my hair." She has flipped back hair that takes ages to curl. Feathered, Ruth thinks it's called, although it looks nothing like a bird. Ruth keeps telling her she would look so much nicer with a straight bob, or her hair in a twist, but Sadie doesn't listen to her mother. No one every really listens to Ruth. She talks and talks and everyone just does their own thing.

Sylvia seems to like her hat, although from Ruth's perspective Sylvia's head is huge and the hat merely rests on the top of it, like a plate or like a book a model might balance to improve her posture. Embarrassing. But Sylvia looks taller in the hat, Ruth thinks, and that is good.

Mr. Swamp wears all black. Even his shirt is black. He is a priest without the collar. Ruth can't help but stare at him, her mouth open, and then, of course, she starts to cry. Ruth has been crying so much lately. It seems to her that everything she does has horrible consequences. A little jealousy and she destroys everyone she loves. Ruth thinks she never used to get jealous. She never had reason to: she was the most beautiful girl, she got everything she wanted. Even though her mother used to say, "Ruth, you can't be serious? You think you're beautiful?" Ruth did think that. She honestly did. And she was right. She was beautiful. No matter how many times her mother told her she wasn't. Ruth looks back at pictures now and she was sheer perfection. How was it possible to be jealous of anyone if Ruth looked like that? How was it possible that Marvin had someone else? How is it possible that he is dead?

"I can't believe I'm left with him," Ruth mumbles to Sadie and nods towards her husband.

Sylvia munches on a handful of celery. It is all Ruth will let her eat these days.

It has been a week since Marvellous Marvin burned up in the fire and the Swamp family have not been talking to each other. Only short, sweet sentences. Punctuated by sobs or cries of distress. Sadie and Ruth haven't been talking for quite awhile but now no one else in the family really knows what to say either. Ruth certainly doesn't. There isn't anything to say. Sylvia munches on her crisp celery like a rabbit and the sound seems to follow Ruth everywhere. It is driving her mad.

At the funeral Reggie stands close and protective beside Sadie who pulls away from him. Ruth hasn't seen Reggie since the night she left him at home with Sadie. She thinks that after what she saw Sadie should be all snuggled close to him. But her daughter's body tilts away from his until she is almost standing on an angle. Like a stop sign blown sideways in the wind. Ruth watches the two of them closely. Reggie's left hand is bandaged. Sadie is pale and angry. She is wearing makeup that makes her look like she's bruised. A new trend?

The morning after Reggie was there Sadie was upset. But Ruth thought she was merely angry with her. Why would Sadie have let him do what he did to her if she didn't like him? They must have had a spat. A lover's quarrel, Ruth reasons.

How innocent that seems now. Small fights, heated words with the one you love.

Water pours from the sky. Sylvia eats celery. Umbrellas go up.

"Why does it always rain at funerals?"

That night when Ruth opened the door to Sadie's room, she saw something she would very much like to forget. After all, Sadie is her daughter.

Ruth knows she encouraged them to get together. She brought Reggie home to see Sadie. At night. And, yes, she left the condominium. Mr. Swamp was not at home. It was Ruth's fault. But this wasn't what she had intended. Sadie is only sixteen years old and Ruth isn't even sure if she is on birth control. And no matter what that police officer said he saw in the park, Ruth knew that Sadie and Marvin couldn't have, wouldn't have. The officer was mistaken. There are times Ruth forgets Sadie's age and she does wonder. Marvin flirts. He always has. But he is like a father to her. Sadie, especially when she is on stage or when she is yelling at her mother or when she storms out of the condo for days on end, sometimes seems so much older. When her teachers call and say she hasn't been in school for a month and when Ruth finds cigarettes in her purse and once she did find condoms (but Sadie said they belonged to a friend), times like this Ruth forgets Sadie is sixteen. Only sixteen. It's difficult to put all of that together with the idea that this girl has only been in the world for sixteen short years. That's small. That's no time at all. That's impossible. But isn't Sadie sensible? No matter how much of an angry teen she is. She is much like Ruth. Ruth figures a lot of it is all smoke and mirrors. She's trying to hurt her mother by faking things. Marvin laughs when Ruth confronts him about her. He denies Sadie's taunting words. Sadie smiles at Ruth, slyly.

But that night with Reggie, when Ruth is all ready to barge in and pull the boy off her teenage, delusionary Sadie, she can't help but remember Sadie with her hands covered in K-Y Jelly sliding those handcuffs off Houdini-Marvin and she can't help but think that maybe this is good for Sadie. Maybe it'll teach Sadie a lesson about love and appropriate age-conquests and what-not. Maybe Sadie needs this. Maybe Sadie will fall in love with Reggie and leave Ruth and Marvin alone. Ruth is sure, to be honest, that Marvin is bothered by her advances. After all, he is a mature older man. It must be embarrassing for him, Ruth thinks.

Reggie and Sadie are under the covers. Ruth can't see much. He is on top of her. They could both be dressed for all Ruth sees. He does have a shirt on. A little harmless rubbing? She is a teenager. Teenagers do this all the time, Ruth rationalizes. It's only a game with his hand on her mouth. Really, the girls are always saying Ruth is too uptight and that she should leave them alone. Dr. Spock says to give your teenager her space.

So Ruth does.

So Ruth closes the door and tiptoes down the hall to her bedroom, to Mr. Swamp who is lying in bed on his back staring at the ceiling.

"There's a boy in the apartment," he says, as if Ruth knows nothing. "In Sadie's room. She wouldn't let me in when I knocked. She wouldn't talk to me."

"Yes, yes, I know. It's only Reggie. It's late. Don't let the girls wake me in the morning."

"I'm not sure...."

"And it's a condominium, not an apartment."

Mr. Swamp turns towards the wall, his back to Ruth. "In my day," he starts to say but then shuts up. He swallows. He clears his throat. "Ruth," he says. "Remember when we used to be happy together?"

"Did we? Happy? When?" Ruth yawns. Marvin has scratched her with his unshaved face, the skin on her chest, between her legs, burns.

"I remember when we found out you were pregnant with Sadie. Do you remember that?"

"Goodnight," Ruth says. Forcefully.

"I remember when we met." He rolls towards Ruth again, eyes shining.

"Oh, for God's sake, Mr. Swamp. I'm tired."

"I couldn't get enough of you. It hurt when you weren't around me."

"Go to sleep."

Ruth can smell Marvin's Old Spice on her body. She can smell cedar chips and cigarettes. She smells like wine. Mr. Swamp smells like taxes. Ink and bile and stomach gas. Indigestion. Early death. That's what he smells like.

"I would never leave you, Ruth."

"Of course you wouldn't." Ruth pats his head. He's not usually this vocal. And Ruth is tired.

"I have honour and pride you know."

"Like a Frenchman," Ruth mumbles.

"What?"

"Never mind. Why you are talking so much? I need to sleep. Busy day tomorrow."

"I want you to remember me, Ruth. Think of me sometimes. How I used to be. How I used to make you feel."

"You're right here, Mr. Swamp. I don't need to remember you."

"But think of who we were."

"Go to bed." Ruth is not sure what he means.

Ruth lies in bed and thinks about Marvellous Marvin and why she loves him. At times she can't figure it out. He is rough and uncouth. He is loud and demanding. He isn't aging well—distressed small farts, body odour that is rank and putrid after a show, his breath smells.

"I still feel that way," Mr. Swamp says. "It's an ache. Like I don't want to lose you. I can't lose you. I don't know why, though."

"I'm just exciting." Ruth laughs.

"Yes."

It's the magic. A man who can pull flowers so smoothly out of his sleeve, a man who can make fire come out of his fingers, a man who can put a person in a box and wave a wand and, presto, they disappear, that's the kind of man for Ruth. She knows how he does each of his tricks but still he impresses her each and every time. She has ignored his less-than-great qualities for a good long time. She has chosen to be blind to his finances (he's always borrowing money from Ruth—in fact, she tends to pay him more than he pays her), blind to his toilet habits (he stinks up the bathroom several times a day, sometimes leaving Ruth a present in the toilet, and he spits toothpaste in the sink and doesn't wash it down), blind to his sexual nature (always wanting it, but never enjoying it quite enough. Flirting with everyone no matter how old or young). As long as he is still magic, Ruth's magician, she is fine. And, even though she knows his tricks (after all, Ruth has to help with the tricks in one way or another), they are still magical to her. They are still illusions. Marvin is dextrous and quick. He is smooth and suave. He is a powerfully good actor.

Mr. Swamp is snoring suddenly. Heavy breathing. Loud honks. Ruth smells gin. He's been drinking again. That explains all the talking, she thinks.

Ruth used to feel bad about her love for Marvin. At the beginning she did. She used to fret and worry that she would be discovered. She would shower three times a day. She would hide her tracks. She would overcompensate. Now, however, so many years have passed that it seems perfectly natural. What is wrong, really, in the huge scheme of things, with having two men in your life? Ruth thinks. Who is she hurting really?

With Reggie in there on top of Sadie, she is no competition anymore. She is down the hall with her new love. Doing whatever it is kids these days do. Ruth rolls over and stretches. Her mothering self thinks, "go put a stop to this," but her good sense tells her to let it happen, let Sadie find someone her own age. Leave Ruth's magician alone. What's wrong with that?

Sylvia is in bed, no doubt dreaming about food. Ruth is lying beside Mr. Swamp in their marriage bed. He says he still loves her. What more could anyone want? Somehow, Ruth thinks, she has managed to have a normal life and a lover. She has balanced both perfectly. Like the completion of a fine meal, Ruth has managed to have her appetizer, her main course and her dessert. In fact, she's full.

Ruth wishes her mother were alive so she could say *I told you so*. She always said Ruth would never amount to anything, but look at her now.

Ruth sleeps well.

It isn't until later, after Marvin is dead, that Ruth regrets not doing anything about Reggie and Sadie. It isn't until much later that Ruth regrets not really paying attention to Mr. Swamp, not listening to all those things he said.

•••

"Go slow and play safe with the child who has bowel upsets easily."

WHISPER.

In the night Ruth hears some loud noises coming out of Sadie's room. Muffled bumps and thuds. Did someone fall out of bed? And then Ruth hears Sylvia tiptoe (like an elephant tiptoes, loud and thumping) down the hall towards the kitchen. Ruth sighs. Sylvia sighs. Mr. Swamp sighs in his sleep. The fridge door opens, closes. Opens again. Closes. The tiptoe-thump carries on, pauses outside Sadie's room and then back to Sylvia's room, carrying food (most likely).

It is quiet then.

Ruth slowly falls asleep.

Later, the front door of the condo opens and then closes. Reggie has left, Ruth assumes. Drowsily. She wonders vaguely, what kind of a mother has she become? What would Dr. Spock think about all of this? And then she sleeps.

In the morning the world seems brighter, clearer, more hopeful. But Ruth enters the kitchen and Sadie is still sullen, ornery, disturbed. Her face is covered by her wet hair, she's making a mess on the kitchen floor, snapping at her mother. And Sylvia is still watching TV. And eating. No matter what Ruth does, nothing changes.

Does it?

•••

Less Valuable and Undesirable Foods

"They are sometimes called 'deprived' foods. They cheat a child by making him feel well fed when he is being partly starved, and by spoiling his appetite for better foods." "I'd say jokingly that the only safe way to bribe a child about food is to say, 'You can't have your spinach until you've eaten your ice cream.' Seriously, though, never hold back on one food until another is eaten."

THE DAY SYLVIA comes home with a banana popsicle in her mouth and says that Marvellous Marvin is married, Ruth's entire reason for being, her whole world, collapses.

Ruth wants to kill someone. She wants to destroy what she loves.

And then later, when Marvellous Marvin is burned up in his unknown-to-all-of-the-Swamps-apartment on Parliament Street, Ruth's world falls apart even more. She feels as if someone has taken a hammer to glass. Ground it into fine dust. It is as if Ruth has swallowed this dust, as if she is choking on powdered glass.

All she can think is: What have I ever done to deserve this? Am I being punished for letting Reggie and Sadie sleep together?

After the funeral Ruth is stunned and annoyed. Bitter. She lashes out at everyone. She cries constantly. She spends days in bed. And she wonders loudly when she is going to die. There is something about losing someone close to her that makes her question her time left, that makes Ruth realize suddenly that she too will die, and especially how easy it is to instantly burn up in a fire. Ruth's usual motto is to live life to the fullest, not to look too far ahead or behind. But now that Marvin is gone her foot feels one step closer to the grave.

Sylvia begins to eat again—cancelling out all the celery she has consumed recently with ice cream and cakes and doughnuts and pies. ("What a waste," Ruth shouts at her. "What a goddamn waste. Dr. Spock says that ice cream is a deprived food, Sylvia. That means it has no nutrients. Stop eating it.")

Sadie is like a hungry and tortured cat hunting a mouse—she lies low, creeps around with claws extended, lashing out at everyone. Hisses. Her behaviour is often worse than Ruth's. Because Reggie hasn't been around Ruth assumes they broke up.

Mr. Swamp is Mr. Swamp. Maybe a little more quiet. Ruth thinks that's to be expected. After all, whenever he says anything, poor man, they all shout and scream. Sometimes Ruth feels sorry for him, but most of the time his ineffectiveness, his inaction, makes her furious. If he would just stand up for himself. Just once. What does he think he's doing, being so agreeable? How can a poor, sad, wailing group of women depend on a man if he isn't acting like a man?

Ruth finds herself visiting her mother's grave and screeching like a banshee, crying and pounding her fists into the uneven soil. Letting it all out—the anger, the loss, the betrayal, the guilt. When she was alive they had nothing in common. Ruth's mother was always judging her and telling her that she was doing everything wrong. But now that she is gone Ruth finds she actually misses the woman, she feels as if she's missing a limb. Ruth now wishes her mother were there to comfort her, to hold her. Not that she ever held Ruth in her life. A tiny, angry, quiet woman. Nervous.

It doesn't occur to Ruth to visit her father in the rest home, it doesn't occur to her that if she wanted to she could easily go and see him, wipe his drool, pat his head, bring him a crossword puzzle—something he would certainly puzzle over now—and talk. Ruth's father was her mother's slave. He did her bidding and didn't make decisions on his own. "Look at her," Ruth's mother would say. "Your daughter is a slut." And Ruth remembers her father would nod willingly. Now that she is gone Ruth shares nothing with the man, they have nothing in common.

Her parents both grew into old, ineffectual people—people she thinks she could have destroyed if she had wanted to. They loved her children like they never loved her. Sadie and Sylvia knew two people who were not Ruth's parents. These grandparents were nothing like the "back straight, Ruth," "elbows off the table," "don't talk to us until we talk to you," parents Ruth knew.

"Times are different," Ruth's mother said before she died. "Back then we didn't buddy up with our kids like you do now. We treated kids like what they were—children."

"But I just wanted you to love me."

"Oh, Ruthie," she said. "You loved yourself enough for everyone."

Perhaps, Ruth thinks, if she had treated Sadie and Sylvia more like children and less like the responsible human beings and individuals she assumed they were, perhaps they wouldn't have turned out the way they did? Ruth doesn't know. You can't go back now, she thinks. Onward. *Trust yourself*, Ruth Swamp, *you know more than you think you do*.

Who organized Marvin's funeral? Ruth is sitting in her chair, wiping her eyes, and thinking. A relative? Who paid for all of this? The urn must have been expensive. The woman in the window? Did Ruth really see her? She is beginning to wonder. Maybe it was Reggie Reynolds. Who else could it have been? Marvin had no one else—the policeman said there was no one with him—and Reggie was almost like a son to him at the end. They did a lot together. Reggie was always around.

Ruth looks over at Reggie, sitting with Sadie. Sylvia is staring at both of them, her black hat askew on her fat head. Reggie is a bit like Marvin, Ruth thinks, if you ignore the sight of him and that constant rabbit smell. And, well, he certainly doesn't have the charisma. OK, he's nothing like Marvin. But he is the only real friend Marvin had. Marvin was a father figure to Reggie.

If anything, Ruth thinks this funeral should bring those two love-birds together. She thinks Sadie should be weeping into his shoulder. Ruth is not sure she understands kids today.

The firemen found nothing of Marvin's body and his urn is small and sad and Ruth has so much on her mind. The brief thought of who paid leaves her mind as quickly as it came.

A week after the funeral there is the horrible, bizarre lunch. The Swamps are all home at the same time, which is strange enough, but the lunch is loud and argumentative (Sadie's finally talking and boy is she talking. She won't shut up. She won't say anything nice). And then Sylvia has stomach flu. Or maybe she has just eaten too much? Ruth leaves the condo. She has decided to take a thoughtful, depressed walk alone, to clear her mind. She is always alone these days. She used to spend her evenings with Marvellous Marvin and now she is trapped in her condominium with her sullen daughter, her drab husband. Where is she in her life? Ruth needs to take stock. Toronto bustles around her. There is a strong wind. Ruth feels as if someone is standing on her chest, she is aching and sad and she finds it hard to breathe.

Suddenly she is standing in front of Marvellous Marvin's burnt out apartment—for what feels like the hundredth time (she keeps coming back here)—caution tape flapping in the wind, a construction worker continuing to board up the site—Ruth is standing there and worrying again about all the things she didn't know, about all the things she did, and she is thinking about what she is going to do next. Ruth thinks: fire and smoke, magic and reality. Life. If she doesn't have magic, if she doesn't have Marvin, then she is nothing. Then there is no point in going on. Who is she without that man? What has she done? Mr. Swamp isn't good enough, he doesn't count. Ruth wants to start again. She wants to find someone new to make her feel wonderful. She wants to lie down here, right now, and die.

Ruth feels she is always the stoic mother. She is the beam, the support. She thinks she holds up her family. Head high. Chest out. Swallow her sadness. Ruth walks home to her miserable condominium, to her emptiness and loneliness.

There are three police officers talking to Sylvia in the living room. Doesn't she know not to let anyone in when no one is home? Ruth doesn't care that they are police officers.

"Sylvia, what are you doing?"

"Ma'am," the police officer says. "You should sit down."

"Sylvia?"

Sylvia is trying to fold her arms in front of her chest. She is holding what looks like a chicken leg in one hand, hiding it but at the same time eating it quietly. Little snuffling licks and bites. Didn't she just vomit? Didn't we just eat lunch? Ruth thinks.

"Is that the chicken for dinner, Sylvia? Where is Sadie?"

Ruth studies her watch. It has been hours since she left. Where did the time go? Vomit. Eat. Vomit. Eat. The police officers start scribbling in notepads as Ruth enters the living room. Trying for a grand entrance. Is her lipstick fresh?

"Can I ask you where you were, Ma'am?"

"Walking. I went for a walk. Is that a crime?" she smiles. What does he want? "What's going on? What happened?"

Ruth recognizes one of the officers as the one she threw the plates at after he lied about Sadie in the baseball dugout. She can feel herself blushing. She touches her hair. Licks her lips. Composes herself. You are Ruth Swamp. You are beautiful and strong.

"Are you in trouble, Sylvia? Is anyone in this condominium ever NOT in trouble?" Ruth laughs lightly. Yes, make a joke out of it. Something has happened. The tension is palpable. Why won't they just say something? What are they preparing her for? Ruth places her purse on the floor, she changes her outdoor high heels for her indoor high heels, and she walks farther into the room and stands near Sylvia. She smells like animal fat, like grease, like body odour. Ruth's hips swing. Her head is held high. Nothing more can surprise her. She will not let herself fall apart in the face of grief or anger or despair. "Is it Mr. Swamp? Has something happened to Mr. Swamp?"

Sylvia shrugs. Takes a bite of her chicken leg. Swallows. The girl's lips quiver, her cheeks and jaw work to masticate the food. Ruth and the officers can hear her chew.

"Mrs. Swamp?" the police officer who knows Ruth says. "You might want to sit down." He points to the couch. He is dead serious. He is kindly even with their history of plate-throwing. Ruth's shoulders sag. The weight of the world. She thinks she might faint. She knows what is coming. She can sense death and disease and decay in the air. Leaning slightly, perching on the side of the couch, Ruth raises her hand to her hot forehead, and says "Yes?" in a meek voice. Is she to play the fallen heroine? Gloria Swanson in *Sunset Boulevard*: "I'm ready for my close-up, Mr. DeMille."

All Ruth wanted when she was a young girl was to be in the movies. To be up there, on the screen, in the spotlight. Her mother said, "No," her mother said, "You're already too proud, Ruth. Imagine what you'd be like if you were a movie star."

And now look at her. Ruth Mileford. Look at her life. For a minute there she had the spotlight, the sequined costumes, the applause. Now she has nothing and there are policemen in her living room and something has happened. Ruth sags down slightly, her shoulders fall.

The officer leans towards her.

"There's been an accident," he says. "Your daughter has been seriously hurt."

First Ruth looks at Sylvia.

"I don't understand. The girl is right here, in front of me." All over the place, spreading even as the man speaks. Huge. But of course it's not Sylvia, it's Sadie. Here's Sylvia pausing with the chicken half way to her open, gaping mouth. Here's Sylvia stifling a burp, her big belly rolls sticking out from her shirt. There is a pudding package on the coffee table. A potato chip bag near the TV. Sylvia is here and she's not going anywhere. Nothing will happen to her. But Sadie? Ruth's golden child? What did Ruth do to deserve this?

"What's happened?"

"Sadie is in the hospital. We need to get in touch with your husband as well. We need you to come to the hospital right away."

"But what?" It began with Marvin, now Sadie. "Is it fire? Did she burn up in fire?"

The police officers look at each other. "We have Reggie Reynolds in custody." Ruth doesn't understand. Has he been hurt too? Such a strange boy. And a little smelly. A little homely. He owns his own business, Ruth wants to shout. (Or is she shouting? Everyone is always telling her to hush but Ruth can never tell how loud her voice is.) He wouldn't do anything to harm anyone—only the occasional rabbit, but he's just feeding his snakes, or putting the bunnies out of their misery. It's natural, he has told Ruth this over and over. It's the way of the wild kingdom, he has said to her. Isn't it? "Your daughter here," the officer points towards Sylvia, "mentioned that he might be guilty and we found some evidence on him."

Sadie and Reggie are a couple, Ruth thinks. He wouldn't hurt her.

"Reggie Reynolds tried to kill Sadie," Sylvia says. Her big cheeks mashing down on the words. "But I don't know why."

Ruth watches her daughter's mouth open and close but she can't hear the words. She only sees Sylvia chewing, swallowing. Always eating. It's like a TV show. Where is the laugh track? Ruth wonders. This has to be funny to someone. Melodrama.

"Will you call your father at work?" the officer says.

"Yes," Sylvia says to the police officers. "I'll call my father. I'll take my mother to the hospital. We'll take a taxi."

She's the mother. Ruth, the child.

How will Sylvia do all of this? How does she put one huge foot in front of the other? How will she dial the telephone and speak to her father and help Ruth to the elevator? All with chicken in her hands? Ruth feels as if she is seeing Sylvia for the first time. Like when someone new comes into your home, she thinks, and you see the furniture through their eyes. Ruth is seeing Sylvia. Really seeing her. She's there, in front of her. Not part of Ruth. Just a child, really. A large child. Ruth feels, suddenly, so sorry. For Sylvia. For herself. For everyone. What could she have done differently? What did she do wrong?

"No proof," a police officer says. He is talking to Sylvia. "We only have the undergarment, the bra you told us about that belongs to your sister, as evidence. Reggie had it on him. In his pocket. But he has no alibi and his left hand is pretty bruised. A few cuts, although they are healing .... No one saw him but his snakes and rabbits. He says he was at his pet store. We also think he may have started that fire on Parliament Street. That magician. It could have been a crime of passion. Didn't Sadie have something to do with the magician? There are police records, a dugout—"

"Two crimes of passion," the other officer interrupts.

"Yes," Sylvia says. "That makes perfect sense. Passion." She looks suddenly fresh-faced and happy. "Fire."

"But that's not possible," Ruth shouts. This time she knows her voice is loud. "Reggie wouldn't hurt Marvin. Reggie loved Marvin. He was a father figure to him."

"Passion," Sylvia repeats. "That's it."

Everyone falls silent. Ruth is lost in her mind. Sadie is in the hospital. Ruth has to go to her. But she perches like a bird on the arm of the couch, holding onto the back. If she lets go she will fall off the edge of the world.

Reggie didn't start the fire.

"Sadie's hurt?" Ruth questions. "Are you telling me she is hurt?"

"More than hurt, ma'am," the officer says. "You'd better go to her now. She may not have long to live."

Ruth bites the back of her hand to stop the scream. She has seen this in the movies but now it seems natural.

"Would you like some chicken first?" Sylvia asks, and her voice carries strong over Ruth's groan. "We've got more in the kitchen. There's always more chicken in the kitchen."

Managing Young Children

"Play is serious business."

SADIE HAS BEEN attacked on the street somewhere between Parliament and Yonge, somewhere between Marvin's burnt out building and the Swamp's condominium.

"Wasn't she at school?"

Sylvia says, "She never went to school. You know that."

The doctor thinks the culprit is a lead pipe. (Sylvia says, between bites, "Like the one Colonel Mustard did it with in the Conservatory?" as if it's all some big joke.) Something heavy and powerful. Crashed into her skull over and over until there is barely anything left of Sadie, barely anything left of her beauty, her mind, her soul. This angry child of Ruth's, this teenager, is mush. First she is pulled into an alleyway and then she is assaulted near a dumpster loaded with food waste. The smell, they say, is horrific. Ruth knows that blood smells like iron. Like fish. Sadie is so thin, the doctor says, that a passer-by thinks she is merely a pile of old clothing.

"Thin is in," Ruth hears herself say. Did she really say that?

"No one heard her scream," the officer says. "That's why we think it was someone she knew."

"There was no rape. Nothing stolen. Just pure violence." The doctor shakes his head.

Violence for what? Ruth wonders. There has to be a reason for violence. Doesn't there?

Ruth is not sure what the doctor means by nothing stolen. No money stolen, no purse? Is that what he means? What about her life—nothing stolen? Ruth will spend the rest of her life listing all the things that were stolen from her Sadie.

Everyone will look at Reggie Reynold's picture in the paper the next day. "That's him," they will say. "Her boyfriend. He did it."

But Ruth is not sure.

"Nothing much left," the doctor says to Ruth and Mr. Swamp. "She won't be the same old Sadie you used to know. If she lives, that is. You might want to consider that. Think about what to do."

Sadie is hooked up to so many machines. Her head is wrapped in bandages. Her hands sport IV needles and tubes and bruising. Her eyes are closed. Her fingernails are shredded and dirty, caked in blood. From fighting back? Two teeth are missing. "Was she on birth control?" the doctor asks. "Any other medication? Drugs?"

They shrug. They don't know. And it hurts them not to know this kind of thing about their daughter.

"There was a lot of blood," the officer says. "We needed to get the fire department to open a hydrant to wash it away."

Ruth vomits into Sadie's hospital toilet. Over and over. There is nothing solid in her stomach but still she vomits bile and water. Perhaps, she thinks, I have Sylvia's flu or am I in shock?

Sylvia perches on a chair in the hallway outside of the room and eats a large pepperoni pizza she ordered and had delivered for all of them from the restaurant down the street. No one else eats.

Ruth paces the hall and looks at Sylvia's fingers holding slice after slice of pizza. They are dirty too. The nails are muddy and cracked. Like Sadie's. Can't she wash her hands? Can't she take care of herself?

"Can't you at least wash your hands before you eat?" Ruth says. "Your hands. They are disgusting. You need to learn to take care of yourself."

Sylvia tries to sit on her hands but can't get her arms around her hips. Ruth stifles the urge to shake her. She wants to take the pizza and smear it all over Sylvia's fat head and then shake her daughter by her fat arms until she wakes up and looks around and sees what she has done to herself and to her family. What she has done to Ruth.

Mr. Swamp has switched his grey cardigan for a beige one. It is nearing summer. There is a change in the air. The winds are less fierce.

Sometimes the sun shines brightly all day, warming up the hospital room. Mr. Swamp looks different in beige, he looks older, more complicated. He looks like someone Ruth doesn't know. How can that be?

"At least she won't miss much school now," he says one day.

"It's as if," Ruth can't help but say, "you haven't lived anywhere near us for years, Mr. Swamp. Do you think Sadie even goes to school? Do you think she's been at school at all this year? Where do you live, Mr. Swamp? Where is your mind?"

"You thought she was in school that day too," Sylvia says.

"Shut up, Sylvia. You're always talking."

The doctor says Sadie won't be able to talk, probably, let alone ever read or write again. He smiles condescendingly when the Swamps mention school. "Like a vegetable," he says. "Imagine that. No, she'll never go back to school. Or at least not a normal school. There are other ways to learn, though."

Sylvia says she can imagine the vegetable analogy. An eggplant or a turnip or a potato (is that a vegetable?) or a squash or a....

"Shut up," Ruth yells. "Can't you see my baby is hurting?"

"She might not live," the doctor says, casually. "You should prepare yourselves for that. Take it one step at a time."

"I'm technically your baby. Sadie is the oldest."

"What's with him?" Ruth says. "What's with the doctor saying things like that? Aren't they supposed to reassure us? Aren't they supposed to say, 'everything will be OK'?"

Sylvia says, "At least with all of this commotion we're finally doing something as a family again. Right?"

Mr. Swamp gives Sylvia money and tells her to go buy dessert for herself. "Head out and pick something up," Mr. Swamp says, "before your mother kills you."

"Whatever would make her say that?" Ruth asks Mr. Swamp as they stand at the hospital window and watch Sylvia waddle down the street outside, four stories down. They watch her stop traffic with her bulk, head out into University Avenue, and disappear around a corner towards the fast food of Yonge Street. "Doing something as a family? What does she mean? And, besides, we've always done things as a family. She's ridiculous."

"She's just a kid, Ruth," Mr. Swamp says. "We sometimes forget that, don't we? Because of her size. But she's just thirteen years old. She should be running around outside, not trapped in that body."

Sadie is behind them in bed, not moving, machines keeping her alive. Beeping. A wrapped mummy. Marvin is dead. Burnt up and buried in a tiny urn in a cemetery near the ravine. Reggie Reynolds is in jail. His bunnies and snakes and rats have probably all died slowly, Ruth thinks, because there was no one to take care of them.

"What would Dr. Spock do?" Ruth sighs.

"Who?" Mr. Swamp says.

Ruth turns and stares at this person, this man in the beige cardigan, her husband of seventeen years. "Do you even live with us? Do you even know who we are? Maybe Sylvia is right. Maybe we aren't much of a family."

•••

Naughty words

"They gaily insult each other, with expressions like 'You great big duty' and 'I'll flush you down the toilet,' and they think they are very witty and bold."

It is fall now and Sylvia is back at school. Mr. Swamp is at work. Ruth has a new job: she mothers Sadie from home. Sadie is set up on a hospital bed in the living room of the condo, her eyes glazed, her mind empty. There are tubes that feed her. Tubes that take the waste away from her. Tubes that keep her alive. She is a machine.

"If the power goes out," Ruth tells Sylvia, "I don't know what we'll do."

Occasionally Sadie wakes and takes a bite out of Ruth. If she is leaning close Sadie will chomp on her cheek. Hard. If Ruth is holding her hand she will draw Ruth's hand towards her mouth and crush the skin with her teeth. It seems, sometimes, that both of Ruth's children always have to have something in their mouths.

"Why would she bite me?" Ruth asks the doctor.

"Just be glad she wakes up at all," the doctor says. "Just be glad she's alive."

Biting Humans. "It's natural for a baby around 1 year to take a bite out of his parent's cheek."

"But what should I do?"

The doctor shrugs. He is no help. Sadie's biting is the least of his worries. He's got a patient this afternoon, he tells Ruth, who fell off her bike into the road and a car, would you believe, ran over her head. Crushed it flat, he tells Ruth, and his job, he jokes, is to unflatten it, to inflate it like a balloon.

Ruth looks at the ceiling, the cracks in the plaster, and she counts to ten so she won't kill him and she lets the doctor out the door. She watches him walk out of the condominium building on the street below and she sees him pass Sylvia on her way in. He nods. Sylvia nods back.

"Some mothers who have been bitten ask if they should bite back."

Sylvia comes in and heads straight for the fridge. Pops it open, pulls anything out. Whatever it is, it doesn't matter. Eats it. Sometimes she doesn't put things back and they have rotten milk on the counter, mouldy cheese. Ruth wonders if she cares what she puts in her mouth. Dirt? Dog shit? A pound of human flesh? Ruth picks up Sadie's hand and nibbles. It is salty, sweet.

"Is she talking yet?" Sylvia asks, mouth full. She asks this every day. Sometimes twice a day. As if whatever comes out of Sadie's mouth will be brilliant and she doesn't want to miss it.

"No." Ruth supposes that the silence coming from someone who was just recently so loud and obnoxious is wearing thin on Sylvia. Scaring her, perhaps.

Ruth and Sylvia turn on the TV. They sit on the couch. Sylvia eats. Sadie uses tubes to breathe. Her eyes are closed.

Float back in time, Ruth thinks. Remember the magic show? Remember the bright lights, the cheering audience, the sparkly costumes? Remember Marvin and his hands on her stomach, her neck, her back, her legs.

Ruth wonders if anything in her life will be like she wants it to be. It seems as if she's been fighting for so long. But, everything happens for a reason, she tries to tell herself. Inside, though, Ruth doesn't feel that way. Inside she feels as if there are no reasons for anything. Having children is supposed to make a woman feel accomplished, like she has done something good. Why doesn't it feel that way to Ruth? She had a job. She had true love. All of it gone now. She is an attractive, smart, wonderful woman. If her life is bad, she reasons, then others must be suffering even more.

How could anything get any worse?

There is a knock on the door. Usually people are buzzed up from the lobby first. It must be a neighbour, Ruth thinks. She pushes Sylvia off the couch, "You get it," and Sylvia reluctantly pulls herself up and, grunting, opens the door.

A woman is standing there. Ruth's age. Properly dressed—high heels, hat, gloves—clutching a black purse. As if she is going to church. The woman is taken aback when she sees Sylvia. She peers closely at her.

"Does Ruth Swamp live here?" the woman says.

"It's her," Sylvia shouts. "It's the woman."

Ruth stands. Yes, she thinks, it's the woman. Ruth recognizes her.

Sylvia is breathing heavily. Panting.

And there, behind the woman, is Mr. Swamp. He pushes his way in, around her, through the door. Back from work. The woman moves slightly to let him through. Sylvia turns towards Ruth and, by the look in her eyes, Ruth knows what she is thinking. She is thinking that she was right for once, she didn't imagine the woman. Sylvia looks scared, shocked. Her mouth is open (When is it not open? Ruth thinks. But that's beside the point). Ruth feels movement and turns to look behind her. In the corner of the living room, on her hospital bed, Sadie opens her biting mouth, opens one eye, looks at the woman in the doorway, looks at Ruth, looks back and forth with one peering eye, and says loudly and clearly, "Mama."

The woman steps into the condominium as if she belongs there and she shuts the door behind her.

•••

The Father As Companion

"Unfortunately, the father is apt to come home wanting most of all to slump down and read the paper." A girl needs a friendly father, too. "I'm thinking of little things he can do, like complimenting her on her dress, her hair-do, or the cookies she's made." A father should go light on kidding. "On the average, men seem to have more fierceness in them than women do.... Kidding is too strong for young children."

MR. SWAMP REACHES out and touches Sadie's cheek. She bites him. He recoils. The woman in the hall comes into the living room and stands back as everyone gathers around Sadie's hospital bed.

"She said something. Did she say something?" Ruth bustles around Sadie. "Did you hear that? Did everyone hear her?"

"Mrs. Swamp?" the woman says. "You are Ruth Swamp?"

Sylvia whispers, "Should I offer her something to eat?"

"My God," Mr. Swamp whispers. "Sadie said Mama."

Ruth called her mother Mama when she was little. Until one day she told Ruth not to, she told Ruth that only babies call their mothers Mama. Father. Mother. Ruth wasn't a baby anymore, she was a grown girl and, as she reminded Ruth, she was proud of her for that. Ruth was three years old. Yes, Mother.

"Mama," Sadie says again.

"Mrs. Swamp, I've come to talk to you."

Sylvia eats and eats and eats. Stuffing her mouth with peanuts from a jar. Pushing so many peanuts in that she can't speak herself. But the Swamps are so used to ignoring her that they pay no attention.

"Sadie is talking now," Sylvia says with her full mouth. "Can you believe it? I wonder what she'll say."

"I've come about Marvellous Marvin," the woman says.

"What?" Mr. Swamp says.

"You're the woman in the apartment, aren't you?" Sylvia asks the woman. "I did see you that day. I knew I saw her that day." Sylvia laughs nervously.

"Sylvia, honey, don't talk with your mouth full," Ruth says. "Marvin was very important to all of us. Was he a friend of yours?" Ruth wants time to process this.

Sylvia spits the chewed peanuts into her hand. "It's her, I saw her in the apartment. Kissing him."

"I know how important he was to your family." The woman looks down at the floor and then straight up into Ruth's eyes. Her neck seems to swell. Like a cobra. "And especially to you." She pauses. Dramatic flair: "I am his wife," she says.

"Whose wife?" Mr. Swamp says, rubbing his arm. "Ouch. Why did you slap me, Ruth? Who is she? What is she talking about?"

"What?" Ruth is frozen to the spot. She was his wife? A wife? Oh God, Ruth knew it. Just knew it.

Sylvia coughs up some peanuts. "Phew, I thought I made that up," she shouts, and they all listen to her now, even Sadie, one eye peering. "I thought I didn't see you really. I thought I didn't." She begins to laugh.

"I'm not sure I understand," the wife says. "See me? Where?"

"Mama," Sadie moans.

"I'm confused," Ruth says.

"The day of the fire. I saw you."

"When did Sadie start talking?" Mr. Swamp says. "Just now, or did she say something earlier? I really should call the doctor, let him know. This could be a breakthrough."

"Just now," Sylvia says. "She said Mama when you came in. She might not say anything else, right?" Sylvia turns to the woman. "Were you in the apartment fire?" She looks wide-eyed, scared. Is this woman a ghost coming back from death? She imagined this woman and now here she is, in the flesh.

"We were on stage together," the woman says. "Years ago. I taught him everything he knew. You could say he was my protégé."

A female magician.

"A female magician?" Mr. Swamp echoes Ruth's thoughts. Mr. Swamp looks pleased. Ruth assumes he's thinking he isn't the only one who got cheated on. He isn't the only cuckold in the condo. His mouth is wide. Grinning. For years Ruth has been sure that Mr. Swamp has known what was going on. Ruth assumed he was just too worried about what would happen if he admitted it to himself, or to Ruth. They avoided talking about it. Always skirted the issue. He was too overworked and too tired to deal with the consequences. He has no self-esteem. He has nothing else. That's what Ruth has always thought. He was too weak to stand up for anything.

"He didn't tell me he was married." Ruth clears her throat. He was holding this woman, spinning her, looking out at Ruth from his apartment window. His secret wife. His secret apartment.

"Mama."

"You were there," Sylvia says, "and then you were gone. And then the fire."

"Shush up, Sadie."

"She's finally talking and you want her to be quiet?" Mr. Swamp scratches his head.

"Yes, well, he didn't tell me about you either," the woman says. "For a while."

"About us you mean?" Ruth moves her hand around, encompassing her two daughters and her husband. "Sadie worked for him too."

"Would anyone like something to eat?" Sylvia suddenly says. "There are cookies in the cupboard. Doughnuts in the dining room. Bananas in the bowl."

"No, no thank you." The woman approaches the couch in the living room carefully, as if walking into a pen of lions at the zoo. "Although that is impressive alliteration." She laughs. Sylvia looks confused. "I thought we should have a little chat, Ruth," she says. "Iron some things out."

"Yes," Mr. Swamp says. "Yes, a chat would be good. Don't you think, Ruth? A good, long chat. Sit down please."

"No, I don't think so. Not right now." Ruth can't possibly stomach this. She pivots quickly on her heels and walks down the hall towards her bedroom. "I'm slightly tired. Just a bit. My brain-damaged child just spoke for the first time in quite a few months. It has shocked me. I'm not right. I need a nap. Another time." Ruth spits the words. He was married. He deserved everything he got then, Marvellous Marvin deserved the fire.

"I'll wait then." The woman sits in the living room with Mr. Swamp, Sylvia and poor Sadie in her hospital bed. "You take a little rest and then we can talk."

"I'll be awhile," Ruth says. "Maybe all night."

The three of them eat popcorn and watch television. Ruth peeks out occasionally from the bedroom and still they are there. They are not speaking. The light dims outside and it begins to rain. Sadie says, "Mama" over and over until even Mr. Swamp is annoyed and he turns the volume up on the TV. Sylvia has made everyone food, they are eating silently. TV dinners. Ruth lies in bed thinking. A wife. How? Why? What does she want from Ruth? She keep her shoes on, just in case she needs to run.

Oh, Marvin, Ruth thinks, why did you do this to me?

"Did you know Reggie Reynolds?" Ruth can hear Mr. Swamp ask the woman sitting close and warm beside him.

"No," the woman says. "Not personally. I heard, though. What he did to her, that girl. And the fire, of course. I know what he did to Marvin." The woman sniffs melodramatically from the living room. Ruth can imagine Mr. Swamp handing her a Kleenex.

"We did," Mr. Swamp says. "We certainly knew him. Sorry case. Sorry situation." Mr. Swamp is probably nodding his head towards Sadie.

"Umhm," says the woman.

Sylvia has made more popcorn, Ruth can hear it in the microwave, and she swears she can hear her munching on handfuls of it, getting most of it stuck in her lap, her shirt, her hair, Ruth is sure. Ruth is positive that Sylvia is sweating profusely and making growly noises as she eats. Breathing heavily. She can't seem to take one piece of popcorn at a time. A handful doesn't fit either. It's a messy event. She always needs to fill up her mouth. Desperately. Like she's trying to stop something from coming out.

"Mama."

Ruth falls into fitful sleep. Worrying, wondering. Her family.

And Marvellous Marvin's wife.

The Two-Year-Old

What He's Like

"The two-year-old learns by imitation."

IT IS ONLY after Marvellous Marvin's wife leaves, after the restless, tossing, excruciatingly quiet and long night, after Mr. Swamp and Sylvia go to sleep and then wake up, check on Sadie's tubes, get their breakfasts and leave for work or school, it is only after all of this that Ruth feels the strength to stand and emerge from the bedroom. She looks at Sadie. Sadie's eyes are closed but she senses her mother and one eye pops open and she says, "Mama."

Ruth sighs. "A fucking one-word wonder."

"Fucking," she says.

Ruth laughs. She rarely swears. Sadie used to swear a lot. This is good, Ruth thinks. Sadie is coming back.

Sadie laughs.

Marvellous Marvin used to hold Ruth in his arms, late at night, after lovemaking. He used to hold her tight and whisper all kinds of things; clues to how he performed magic, tales of his childhood in a broken family with a broken heart and a half-assed brother who died snowshoeing somewhere—got lost, Ruth thinks—his wishes for the future. But he never said anything to Ruth about a wife. He never talked about being married. Never. Ever. Not once.

Wouldn't it have been easy to say, "Oh, by the way, Ruth, you're married—well, so am I." How hard could that have been? Ruth thinks. Why would he ever need to deceive Ruth?

He talked about wanting a baby. Marvellous Marvin would hold Sadie when she was just a baby. He would hold her in his hands, study her and say, "I want this. I could eat her all up."

Oh God, it just occurred to Ruth. Does he have children with this woman? Ruth knows that you hear about this sometimes—men who have two or three families in different cities, families who know nothing about each other. But how could that happen to her? She is Ruth Mileford.

Magic. Marvin used to take two-year-old Sadie, hold her under her armpits, and spin her until she was so dizzy that when he put her back on her feet she fell down. "Helicopter," she would shout. "More." And then he would pull pennies from her nose, her ears, from between her fingers and toes. He would complicate scarves until there was certainly no way to untangle them. Then pull slightly. Wiggle them a bit. And they would come undone or, even better, be tied neatly together in one long rope. Magic.

Children. He said he wanted children.

And so one night Ruth decided not to use any protection, no control, and Marvellous Marvin—unbeknownst to everyone but Ruth—created Sylvia Swamp, aka Plath.

He deceived her. She deceived him.

Of course, Ruth had to have sex with Mr. Swamp a couple of times that month so he wouldn't get suspicious, but she knew in her heart that it was Marvellous Marvin's baby she was carrying. Poor Mr. Swamp. There were times Ruth felt sick about what she was doing, but, like a drug, Marvellous Marvin was hard to resist. He made life worth living.

With Sylvia, Ruth only wanted him to have something of his own. Something that carried him on when worms were feasting on his eyes. It was to be a surprise.

Eventually.

"Surprise," Ruth thought she would shout in the hospital when he came to visit. "This baby's all yours." They would keep their secret from the world. They would bask in their deception together. Marvin loved a good secret. Mr. Swamp would never know. After all, what good would it do to tell him? Who wouldn't want a baby to pass on their genes? And, Ruth reasoned, Marvin wouldn't have to spend a dime to take care of it. He was, after all, always worried about money. Surely this was a perfect plan.

But Ruth never shouted surprise. Mr. Swamp was in the room, having spent the night holding Ruth's hands and massaging her back as she screamed, as she pushed Sylvia from her, and Ruth just couldn't do it to him. Mr. Swamp was so taken with Sylvia. He cried happy tears. "Another girl," he whimpered. "Oh how lovely. We are so lucky, Ruth." Ruth guesses that she wanted to give Mr. Swamp a present, an apology for all of her unfaithfulness. And, besides, she had been arguing recently with Marvellous Marvin. About her weight, about her moods, about how she wouldn't let him do the things he wanted to do to her. "I'm pregnant," Ruth would say. "My breasts hurt. Can't you see that?" Ruth was always tired, Marvin said. He said she was not fun anymore.

Eventually, Ruth told herself, she would tell Marvellous Marvin. How could she not? The baby would look like him, act like him, walk like him, talk like him, perform magic like him. Wouldn't she? A little brown-eyed miracle. He would surely know.

Instead, Sylvia. From birth, chubby and slow. You could almost see her growing hungrier and larger every minute. And she looked nothing like Ruth's sexy magician. She looked nothing like anyone in any of the families involved. Did they give Ruth the wrong baby at the hospital? Dark, curly hair. Blue eyes, when Marvin's were so yellow-brown they shone like honey in the sun. It was as if Sylvia was a foundling, as if, like magic, she appeared out of nowhere. Out of no one. Snuggled (smuggled) into the wrong womb. Snuck inside and rested until she was ready to come out.

Ruth wouldn't put it beyond the hospital staff to have mixed up babies on the way back from a test. They seemed incapable of so much. But what could Ruth do?

Might as well keep up the facade, she thought then. What was the point in telling anyone? Marvellous Marvin was always slightly disgusted around Sylvia. As she grew, he said she reminded him of a cow, always chewing and staring, gentle but capable of a kick if you got too close. Mr. Swamp was the only one for Sylvia anyway. Imagine, Ruth thinks, how she would have felt if she found out that Marvellous Marvin was her daddy? She still thinks her daddy is alive. The one who sits in front of the TV and eats with her. That's good. That's the way it should be. Besides, there wasn't enough time to tell Marvin. Thirteen years isn't enough time? Ruth is not sure. But she didn't know he'd be dead so early in life.

Sadie there, mocking Ruth like a parrot. Imitating everything her mother says. Ruth wanders around the condominium picking things up and looking at them. Speaking their names. "Sparkle glue," she says and Sadie repeats it. "*TV Guide.*" As if there are answers in Christmas ornaments, half glued, half sparkled. As if there are answers in medicine and extra needles and tubes. In beeping machines. Everyone has gone and Ruth is here, alone, with Sadie, her echo.

Last night that woman, that Widow Of Marvellous Marvin, the Window Woman, that Magician Lady, came into Ruth's life and up surged all the jealousies, the odd feelings, the horrible sensations that were around when Sadie was flirting with Marvin, when he hired her and she was taking him away from Ruth. Up everything came again, like vomit, and Ruth wanted to tell all of them—Sadie, Mr. Swamp, the wife, even her Daddy at the rest home—that Sylvia was the spawn of Marvellous Marvin. That would fix them, Ruth thought. Put them in their places.

"Ha ha," she desperately wanted to shout. "I've got a piece of him that you can't have."

"Mama," Sadie says.

"What?" Ruth screams "What, what, what?"

"What?" she says.

All day Ruth walks the condo and thinks and all night she tosses and thinks. She pictures huge Sylvia in her mind's eye and wonders, would Marvin really have been that upset to know that Sylvia was his? Sylvia can be nice, and sweet, a little dumb, perhaps, but kind. Look at the way she watches her sister lying still on her hospital bed. Look at the way she can't take her eyes off her, like she herself was to blame for this crime. And Marvin is dead now. He'll never know. The only people her confession would harm would be Sylvia and Mr. Swamp. It would break their hearts, Ruth thinks.

Sixteen years old and Sadie won't ever be pretty again. She won't ever go to her prom (not that she would have anyway, because, after all, her lack of attendance, her horrific grades, guaranteed no graduation certificate—but still, someone might have asked her as their date). She won't ever have her own children (lucky? Ruth is not sure), or be blessed with reading Dr. Spock (that's something). She won't read anything, as a matter of fact, not just The Book. She won't read a *TV Guide* or a Shakespeare play. Mind you, she could watch a play and see a movie, Ruth supposes. If someone would take her. If someone had the energy to wheel her around and mop up the drool. If she could keep her one eye open and keep quiet long enough to listen.

Perhaps Sylvia will take her out one day. Maybe Sylvia will take care of her. Maybe Sylvia will lose weight pushing Sadie around in a wheel chair. It could be good for both of them.

Ruth clomps around the living room in her heels. She has smeared her lipstick on without staying in the lines. She can't control her hands anymore. She is sure she must look as crazy as she feels.

That woman. That Wife Of Marvin. How dare she come into their lives right now? What good will this do? What was she thinking?

How did Ruth not know? Ruth knew everything. She knows everything. She is Ruth Mileford Swamp. She is invincible and strong and beautiful and aware of everything around her.

It does explain who covered the funeral costs, Ruth thinks. That tiny urn with nothing much in it.

"Mama," Sadie says.

"What?"

"What?" Sadie says.

"You're copying me."

"You're copying me."

Ruth pauses and looks at Sadie. Her one eye is closed. She is still. Looks half dead. Her head bandage is dirty and needs changing. "You're copying?" Sadie says it again.

"Stop copying me."

"Stop copying me."

Great. A macaw and The Fat Lady circus freak. Ruth's two lovely daughters. A mysterious wife. A dead lover. A jailed rabbit boy and a husband who can't stop clearing his throat. What ever did Ruth do to deserve this?

Three to Six

Different Causes for Handling the Genitals

"Most of us heard in childhood the threat that masturbation would lead to insanity."

THEY MEET IN the diner down the street for coffee. Neither of them orders pie. They are watching their weight, they are watching everything the other one is doing, they are watching the way the other holds her coffee cup, her napkin, the way her lipstick is applied, the way she crosses her legs. Who flicks their hair first? Who smells better?

Ruth does. Ruth does. Ruth does.

"What do you want with me?" Ruth starts.

"You called me."

"But you came to me originally. You showed up in my condominium."

"Condominium is it? I thought it was an apartment building." She laughs.

"You know nothing."

"But there is a difference. A condominium is—"

"I know it. I know there is a difference."

Silence.

Her name is Rose. A tacky name. The name of a waitress at a drive-in A&W. When they used to wear roller skates. Rosie, they'd call, I want a Papa Burger. Or it's the name of a nanny from England in stiff walking shoes and tweed. A pitiful Mary Poppins. "Tea, Miss Rose?"

Rose—the name on the watch Marvin gave Ruth. You see, she hasn't forgotten.

Ruth left Sylvia in the condominium watching Sadie. She has instructed her not to touch any of the tubes or bags and to run (if possible) as fast as her chubby legs can carry her to the diner if anything starts beeping or leaking. Sylvia is supposed to be in school but instead sits there, in the kitchen, watching her sister from afar. She's happy. Doing just what she loves to be doing. Sitting. Staring. Eating. Why disturb that with school? It's not as if she is learning anything there.

Ruth is definitely not doing what she loves to do best right now. What does she love to do, though? She can't seem to remember. She loves reading The Book and trying to figure out what went wrong in her life. Nothing more, really. Ruth used to love being with Marvellous Marvin, being part of his magic, but then, if she is truly honest with herself, things were starting to taste sour because of Sadie's interest in him, because he hired her to work for him and was starting to ignore Ruth. She used to love thinking about all the many babies she would have, but after two hair-raising, hellish labours, after two little girls screaming, "Mine!" and occasionally slapping and often demanding, Ruth knew the loving was in the wanting, not the having. A novelist she saw on TV one night said the same thing. He said the fun was in writing the book, not publishing it. Ruth figures now, at the diner, looking at Marvin's wife, that at least she loves coffee. That's one thing she absolutely knows she loves. Ruth loves to sip coffee. That's a plus. She loves both wanting the coffee and having it. She loves how it makes her feel as if her whole body is one big electrical impulse. She loves the aftertaste on her tongue. She loves the smell.

Is that all Ruth loves? Coffee? How can that be?

"I don't want anything from you," Rose says, clearing her throat in an annoying manner. Ahem. Ahem. Just like Mr. Swamp. Why can't some people just deal with their phlegm quietly? "I just thought I'd introduce myself the other night. I'm in town for a performance and I thought I'd just say hello. After all these years of knowing about you why shouldn't you know about me? But if you don't want to talk, it's no skin off my back." Rose lights a cigarette. "It's not as if he's going to come back from the dead and have to pick between us." She snorts.

Was that a laugh? She snorts again. Louder.

Skin off my back? Skin off my back? Did she say that? Whatever does that mean? Is that a phrase a tough-magician-woman uses? And he would pick Ruth. She knows it. Look at this woman. Snorting. Using stupid sayings. Smoking.

"How did you find out about me?" Ruth says before she can stop herself. She was going to pretend that nothing, absolutely nothing—besides work experience on stage, of course—went on between herself and the magician. But now the cat's out of the bag. Skin off her back, cat out of bag. This whole situation, Ruth muses, is one big helpful saying.

Ruth blows Rose's smoke away from her face. She hates the smell of smoke. Especially after the fire, the inferno, now that Ruth knows Marvin was inside. Roof collapsing. Ash covering the area (Ruth's hair, Ruth's dress). The smell took days to leave her nostrils. She can still smell it sometimes. She searched The Book to find out if Dr. Spock had any advice on getting rid of the stench of fire, but he had nothing. Just a little bit on Burns, but Ruth didn't need burn advice right then and so she didn't read it. She wishes she had read it now, though, as everything Dr. Spock writes makes sense in ways that are beyond what Ruth can imagine. His burn advice might have applied to meeting the wife of a dead lover in a diner for coffee. Who knows?

"I just wondered," Rose says. "About you. I thought it would be fun to say hello." Rose snorts again. She's not so tough or attractive.

"Did you," Ruth says, "live together? Were you still together?"

"What do you mean?"

Ruth can't help but sigh. "I have never seen or heard about you. For sixteen years I've been ... with ... working with Marvellous Marvin. I never even knew he had an apartment."

"I travel with my job," Rose says. She laughs again. "I guess that's why he needed you. I was always travelling." Magically she pulls a lighter out of the space between her fingers (out of her cuff? But she's wearing short sleeves) and lights up another cigarette she finds behind her ear (or in her hair). "Where do you think he went after he was with you? When you were home with your husband. Besides," Rose pouts suggestively, "you didn't know about the apartment so you obviously didn't know everything. I figured you out a long time ago. And the others. There were others, you know."

"Sadie?" Not possible. Ruth refuses to believe it.

"Who's Sadie?"

Ruth shakes her head. How many women can one magician shuffle? Like cards. He was good at the tricks. The Double Cut. The In-Jog Dribble Control. It's all about looking casual. Magic. It takes one sly magician, skilled in deception, to fool this many women into believing that they are the only ones in his life. It is a joke: how many magicians does it take to screw in a light bulb? Punch line: One. He holds the light bulb up and the world revolves around him.

Ruth knew he cheated, she assumed he did, but only with magic. Sadie was an innocent thing. Just a small bit of flirting. Mostly on Sadie's part. What middle-aged magician wouldn't like the attention of a sixteen-year-old? But a wife? He had a wife?

"You were still married then? Why did you put up with this?"

"Yes. Eighteen years." She doesn't answer Ruth's other question.

"Do you have children?" Are they fat? Are they dumpy and dumb as chickens, Ruth wants to ask. Do they look like Sylvia Swamp? Or Plath even? Do they look like they should stick their head in a gas oven? Do they look like Marvellous Marvin? Do they wear toupées and have brownest brown eyes?

"No." Rose blows the smoke out of her nostrils. A mad bull. A steam engine. "Marvin couldn't have children. Besides, we didn't want any. They would complicate things too much."

No children. Ruth feels smug, sort of. She has a piece (a BIG piece) of Marvin this woman will never have. And she knows something that Rose doesn't. He couldn't have children? Oh yes he could.

"Why weren't you at the funeral?"

"I was in Montreal performing. I couldn't get back in time."

"You missed your own husband's funeral?" Not likely. Her eyes move up and to the left, over Ruth's shoulder. She blushes again.

"I told you." Rose blows smoke out of every open orifice on her face. Ruth swears it comes out her eyeballs. "I was in Montreal at the time."

"It's a six-hour drive. It's not the other side of the world."

"More coffee?" the waitress shouts from across the diner. She holds up the pot and signals to Rose and Ruth.

"We were a professional couple," Rose says. "Our careers, our art, were more important than being together. Perhaps that's why he thought he needed someone like you, why he turned to you. You had nothing in your life except him. Nothing that compelled you. You lived to please him. You live to please men. I, on the other hand, live to please myself."

"I have plenty of things. I have a family. I have my Avon. And my Christmas decorations. I sell them occasionally. And I have my children."

Rose smiles. "That's something, I suppose." She lights another cigarette. Ruth assumes that this is how she keeps her figure. "Christmas decorations." She snorts.

Rose says, "I just wanted to see you for myself. After all he says about you." She corrects herself quickly, "Said about you." She pauses. "When I was going through his dressing room at the hotel I found things of yours. I wanted to put the woman in the shoes, the underwear, the love letters, the lipstick, the toothbrush, so to speak. You know, Ruth, I never doubted that he loved me. I always knew. We would laugh about you and your children. Your messed up life. Your silly husband." She snorts. Ruth really wants to hit her. "The disaster you left in the hotel, your messiness just confirmed it. Marvin could never have loved you. Never."

"Oh." Ruth didn't clear her things out of Marvin's dressing room. She didn't think it was important. She didn't think anyone was left who would care. She sucks in her breath.

"Now that I've met you in person," Rose says. She pauses. She shrugs.

"What?"

"Nothing. It's just I've met you now. There's nothing else for me to do." Rose doesn't look impressed. She stands and begins to walk out of the diner. "Nothing else to do about it. He is, after all, dead." She snorts again. "He's moved on to bigger and better things, I suppose." She looks up.

"He did love me," Ruth shouts. "He honestly loved me. I know."

Rose turns at the door. "I'm sure you thought he did, honey." She waves. "Who wouldn't? You're a delight. A real keeper." And she's gone. A snap of the fingers and poof! The magician disappears behind a smoke screen, through the wind, up into the air. Ruth peers out the window and shakes her head. She has never been so insulted, so out of control, in her life. Her hands are shaking.

Ruth growls, "You didn't pay for your coffee," and the waitress immediately brings the bill over and places it next to Ruth's plate. She taps it with long, painted fingernails. Waits for Ruth to get her wallet out. "Where is Maeve today?" Ruth manages, but this waitress scowls.

Marvellous Marvin's second life. No, his first life—Ruth supposes she is the second life. Why can't men leave it in their pants? Why is it all about conquest and how many and how much sex? For Ruth it was about the magic. It was about the way The Book fell to the floor in the Book Barn when she needed it most, and about how she could barely bend she was so pregnant, scared and confused. She had to lean backwards, reach out, bend her cracking knees. Having a baby is no easy matter. And then, there he was. A magician with a spark. And Ruth was terrified of her life. And sad. And he was kind. He was a man who picked things up for her—books—and laughed with her and later took her in his arms. In his black tuxedo (Ruth couldn't see the tear in the shoulder then, she didn't smell the underarm odour, the sourness of it. At that time she didn't catch the flakes of dandruff on his shoulders, or the thread coming out from his cuff or the untrimmed hairs in his nostrils. And, later, when Ruth got her watch back, it was too late, she was smitten, and she forgave him for it all). He was a knight in armour. He was a movie star. He was the romance Ruth always wanted. He was new and original. Interesting. Who cares if he borrowed money from her all the time and never paid her for her work? Who cares if he destroyed Ruth's family?

Gone. Dead. All the magic has disappeared. Ruth is deflated. She walks back home to take care of Sadie. She walks towards the condominium with nothing more to do with her life but be a mother to Sylvia and Sadie, be a wife to Mr. Swamp.

Mr. _____ Swamp. Right now Ruth has to think really hard to remember Mr. Swamp's first name. She has to stop for a moment and gather her thoughts. Breathe deeply. Benjamin, that's right. Like Dr. Spock. But not at all like him. Not anything like him.

From Six to Eleven

"Do comics, TV, *and movies contribute to delinquency?" Stealing. "Aggressive stealing—His only hope is in good psychiatric treatment and being able to live with kind, affectionate people."*

REGGIE INSISTS HE isn't guilty. He tells the court he was at the pet shop feeding his animals when the fire in Marvellous Marvin's apartment broke out. He lies and says that Sylvia came to see him. Sylvia looks shocked, horrified. He tells the court that he was again at the pet shop the time that Sadie was almost killed by the lead pipe (or, rather, the hand attached to it, he corrects himself), when she was left by the dumpster. The court finds no evidence to disprove any of this. Only Sylvia, who says he is lying. They convict him anyway. After all the press, the judge, the jury, they look hard at Reggie Reynolds. Wouldn't you convict him? He's a grown man who lives alone with snakes and rats and bunny rabbits. A grown man with a face full of pimples and a dirty bra in his pocket belonging to the victim. He is a grown man who follows teenagers around in a menacing and stalking manner. What more evidence does the jury need than that? Look how his father died, for God's sake—he hung himself. Insanity must run in the family. Criminal minds. And where oh where is his mother—a man who grew up without a mother is not really whole, is he? No one knows where she is. Not even Reggie.

Three people on the jury are terrified of snakes (who isn't). Most of the jury don't like mice or rats. Everyone likes bunnies until they bite or poop. The thought of this boy-man feeding his snakes a bunny makes the jury all sick. "Lock him up," they say. Arms crossed in front of their chests.

Reggie has no record of any previous crime. Not even a parking ticket. Not even jaywalking.

"But the bra?" the prosecutor shouts. "In his pocket. Dirty. Grimy. Soiled."

"He wiped his nose with it," Sylvia says, shyly, up on the stand. "He made me get it for him." Barely able to fit in the witness box. They shove her in. Do they need a crowbar to get her out? Ruth worries for a minute, but then Sylvia pushes and pops out cleanly. "I saw him wipe his nose with it once."

There are two trials—Marvellous Marvin's first and then Sadie's—Reggie stands accused in both. And eventually Reggie is convicted in both. Sent away to a prison—far far away. Kingston, Ontario—which isn't that far away, really (Ruth has never been there, but, then again, Mr. Swamp takes her nowhere). But still. Far enough for now. Serving two consecutive sentences. The prosecutor says, "He'll be in there for life." And he means real, human life. Not the legal definition of life.

The snakes, Ruth assumes, die.

The rabbits die.

Ruth does feel bad about this.

The mice and rats probably manage to mostly escape into the back streets of Toronto.

Reggie's pet store closes down, goes under, dissolves. An empty building. And then, in time, an import store—Chinese handbags and parasols and dried fruit and carvings. Ruth visits sometimes (and, occasionally she gets a whiff of cedar chips and rabbit poop. It's subtle, but it's still there).

Reggie becomes morbidly depressed and Sylvia becomes morbidly obese. He is on suicide watch (as is Sylvia, sort of). Ruth is watching Sylvia but she really can't keep track of her every minute (or every pound). Miracle of miracles, Sadie is up and walking now. Limping. She has a limp and carries her right arm out in front of her as if it's still in a cast. The tubes and bags are gone. The hospital bed is gone. At times Ruth hears Sadie whisper "Mama" and occasionally she echoes what they say but nothing original comes out of her damaged lips. But saliva. Drool. Lots of it. Sadie's face is twisted, half-paralysed, scarred. She's a walking, echoing, mimicking, drooling monster.

It doesn't happen often, but sometimes there is nothing in Dr. Spock's book to help Ruth. There is nothing anybody can do. Mr. Swamp comes and goes, fades in and out of the scenery. Sylvia watches TV.

Everyone thinks that Reggie killed Marvellous Marvin because he was jealous. They think he noticed Sadie's affection for the magician. Then still Sadie rejected Reggie and so he tried to kill her. Left her for dead. It makes complete sense to everyone. Easy to figure out. However, something about what he did to Sadie nags Ruth at the back of her mind. Something small and worrisome. She didn't much know Reggie, but he didn't seem the type to do this much damage to her daughter. Did he? He wasn't smart enough, for one. He wasn't very organized. And he was lazy. Too lazy to complete the arduous task of attempted murder? Ruth thinks this kind of thing takes time and energy. It takes patience and determination. Getting him up before noon for an early afternoon show was a chore for Marvellous Marvin and Ruth. They cajoled and begged and pleaded. Called him, knocked on his door. "Come on, Reggie, get up. We need rabbits."

And, besides, Ruth knows for a fact that Reggie didn't start the fire.

Ruth talks to Mr. Swamp about this at the diner. They have been talking a lot more since Ruth met Rose (or Ruth is talking more, Mr. Swamp mostly listens and nods and clears his throat. Ruth is making an effort. She is trying to work on this marriage). Now that they are alone together, now that the elephant in the room has been swallowed up by fire, there seems to be more to discuss. Besides, no one else listens to Ruth and to be honest she is a little lonely these days.

"He wasn't a delinquent," Ruth says. She swirls her coffee with a spoon. "He had no police record. No previous convictions."

Mr. Swamp bites into his apple-blueberry pie. His lips turn purple immediately, a gothic effect that suggests suffocation. "I don't know," he says. "What did we really know about him?"

"He wasn't aggressive." Ruth has lately been wishing she smoked. Despite how it smells she realizes that she kind of liked the look of that Rose woman blowing smoke out her nose like an angry bull. It was effective punctuation.

"I once saw him wrestle a rabbit on stage," Mr. Swamp says, contemplatively.

Ruth tries a snort on for size. Mr. Swamp looks up from his pie.

"I did. The rabbit was making a bee-line for the edge of the stage. Marvin let him out of the hat too early. Reggie dove towards the thing and I witnessed the rabbit and Reggie roll head over heel towards the curtains."

"You call that violent?" Ruth imagines a cigarette in her hand. She imagines twirling it between her polished fingers. She tries it out on a straw. Did Marvellous Marvin like smokers? He must have. All the things Ruth didn't know about him. She gets teary-eyed just thinking.

"That was when Reggie hurt his leg, wasn't it?" Ruth says. "Sadie worked that night." Then she pauses and looks at her husband as he shoves pie into his mouth. "What were you doing there? I never saw you at a show."

Mr. Swamp blushes. "I went occasionally." He clears his throat. "I went whenever I wanted to see my two girls."

What else did he see? "They say he's seeing a psychiatrist in prison. They say he's talking all about his father, about his snakes, his rabbits. They say he's still in love with Sadie and says he wouldn't do anything to hurt her."

"If he could see Sadie now."

"I know. No one will ever love her now."

In the back of her mind Ruth is slightly pleased—well, not pleased. That's harsh. But sort of relieved. Sadie's beauty has gone out the window. This is hard for Ruth to even think. But it's difficult watching your baby overtake you in prettiness. It's painful watching all the men look at her instead of you.

Not anymore. That will never happen. Unfortunately. Fortunately. Ruth is being honest with herself here. She is opening up her soul. Don't judge me, she thinks.

And no one ever will look at Sylvia. Ruth in a sense has won the game. She gets to keep the trophy. What a messy game it is.

"Sylvia still thinks Sadie's the cat's meow," Mr. Swamp says as he puts money for the bill down on the table. "She told me yesterday that Sadie is just as pretty as she was before but in a different way."

"Was Frankenstein pretty? Kids. They say the stupidest things."

Mr. Swamp smiles sadly. His I'm-thinking-and-I'm-not-listening-to-your-chatter smile. "Kids," he echoes. "Diamonds in the rough."

"Huh?" Ruth turns out the diner door into the wind. She waves Mr. Swamp off to work (she even plants a little red-lipped peck on his scratchy grey cheek—see, she thinks, I'm trying. I'm repenting for my sins. Sort of) and she walks quickly down the street. Towards Sylvia and Sadie. Towards coal. Not diamonds.

"You always feel sorry for yourself," her mother would say.

But Ruth always seems to have reason.

•••

Schools

What a School Is For. "The main lesson in school is how to get along in the world."

THE MORE DAYS pass and months and years, the more Ruth realizes that it all began and ended with Marvellous Marvin. It being Life. Ruth's life. Everything that was fun or carefree in those short years—sixteen years—has ended. Nothing ever seems to happen to or for Ruth again.

She sits in the condominium with her hot glue gun and her Christmas decorations (which have grown so large in quantity that she can't sell them anymore and she's now taken to donating them monthly to a couple of local churches. Sometimes Ruth leaves boxes of them out on the street for the garbage collectors or the bums or the homeless. Something with sparkle and ribbons for their dingy lives) and she putters away the time. Sadie hovers by, watching. She occasionally helps (although she becomes mesmerized by the glitter and mostly stares. And the glue is a nightmare. Like a child, she smears it everywhere). Sylvia sits in the kitchen or in front of the TV and hums and eats and watches and says nothing much. She has turned into her father. A virtual mute. No one ever seems to talk. Just Ruth. Mr. Swamp comes and goes to work, seemingly happy that he finally has a family, even if they are all becoming like him.

Ruth's father eventually dies. The funeral is small and quiet. Surprisingly, it does not rain. Sylvia cries but tells her mother later that it's because she was hungry and her stomach hurt. Ruth pretends to have something in her eye that day. The wind. Perhaps dust. They are all sad in their own ways. And time passes.

And then the unspeakable happens. The unexpected. One day, in front of the TV, Mr. Swamp has a heart attack. Like everything in his life, it is a quiet heart attack. And slightly boring. No hysterics. No noise. He merely clutches his chest non-dramatically. He smiles kind of shyly. Ruth is sitting near him, Sylvia to one side, Sadie across the room. He makes a small burp noise and they all look over at him. Ruth is sure he has gas. He says nothing, no end-of-life confession, no apologies for his nothingness, no confessions of passionate love or even fear. He dies.

"I didn't see that coming," Ruth says to Sylvia and Sadie as they all stand over him, watching. "Did you?"

"Mama," Sadie says.

And although Sylvia's eyes are wide, she can't answer, because, as usual, her mouth is full. She collapses deeper into the couch and the springs complain wildly.

It is after Mr. Swamp dies that Ruth discovers the real reason Marvellous Marvin loved her. Or didn't love her. And she finds that Mr. Swamp loved her and protected her. Of course. Life is like that. In one fell swoop the outcome changes. It was about money, of course—typical.

Isn't everything always about money? Ruth thinks.

She is going through Mr. Swamp's desk at work (they've asked her to come clean it out so someone living can use it), and she finds bankbooks. They are old, from just before Sadie was born up until the week Marvellous Marvin died. Ruth doesn't know why she studies them. It seems peculiar to have them all there, in order, bound with a rubber band.

Ruth takes them home.

It takes her awhile but she finally figures out what must have happened. The fact that Mr. Swamp has these particular books saved and none from before or after is the first clue. This tells Ruth that he was keeping track of something, that he noticed something to do with their accounts, something wrong. And there is something wrong. There are consistent and regular withdrawals over the years from their joint account, withdrawals that have no explanation. Their grocery money, the mortgage payment, any other expense, this was always done with another account. In fact, there shouldn't have been much taken from the savings account. They used to say that they were saving for things.

Ruth doesn't know what, but they saved. But here there are withdrawals. Totalling almost two hundred and fifty thousand dollars over sixteen years. Not much to some people, Ruth thinks. When you do the math: just over fifteen and a half thousand dollars a year. That's about forty-two dollars a day. Almost three hundred a week. But to them, to Mr. Swamp and Ruth, that was a lot of money. Especially considering Ruth wasn't really making any money. Marvellous Marvin rarely paid her.

Ruth goes to the bank. She talks to the people there. They tell her to stop shouting. They show her the withdrawal forms. Signed by her, but, "That's not my signature." A woman, they say, came in every week. She was quite a regular. In fact, one of the tellers became quite chatty with her. They traded recipes. "A great butternut squash soup one in particular." No, she didn't look much like Ruth. She was taller. And she smoked. She had Ruth's identification, they said, but after a while they stopped asking for it. She claimed she was Ruth Swamp, married to the accountant, Mr. Swamp.

"Funny," the teller says, "she stopped coming in a couple of years ago. I haven't thought of her in a good long time."

"She had the funniest laugh," the teller says. "Like a snort. Like a pig."

"Really quite a character."

Ruth spends months trying to find Rose. Searching everywhere for a female magician who smokes and snorts. She would like to hire a detective but she visits a few and they tell her she can't afford them and that the money is probably long gone. Rose has disappeared off the face of the earth it seems. With Ruth's money. Gone. She is, after all, magic.

What they were up to was no good. Rose and Marvellous Marvin.

Dr. Spock is wrong when it comes to Ruth. Ruth doesn't know more than she thinks she does. She figures she knows virtually nothing.

Mr. Swamp knew this was going on and did nothing. Or, most likely, he thought Ruth was taking the money. Maybe he thought Ruth was giving it to Marvellous Marvin? What did he think? Poor Mr. Swamp, he spent his life disillusioned and sad. And quiet. And assuming all the wrong things. Why didn't he say anything?

Ruth was, in the long run, giving Marvellous Marvin everything. This magician took her money, her heart, her life, her love. He took

Mr. Swamp's life too. And Sadie's and Sylvia's. And now he's dead and Rose has probably remarried and has taken a new name (a new magician?), and there is nothing left to do but wallow in self-pity and guilt.

Which Ruth does.

She pities Mr. Swamp.

Poor Mr. Swamp. Ruth never did appreciate him and, now that he's gone, she is so very sorry for it. Too late, though. Too late for guilt and sorrow. Too late for apologies.

The funny thing is, the horrible thing is, the sad thing is (Sylvia would say, the ironic thing is), that Ruth never thought it was odd that Marvellous Marvin didn't pay her for her work. At the beginning, sure, he threw a couple of dollars to Ruth every week, here and there. But she worked for him for years and years because she loved him, not for the money. He was always short, he said, he would pay her next time. But after a while he stopped even saying that. He didn't need to anymore. He held Ruth captive. Like a woman in his box. It was always about the magic, about the show. And, the show must go on. The assistant was crucial to that. Without Ruth, he couldn't do anything. Ruth distracted the audience, she squeezed her legs up so he could saw her in half, she disappeared through the panel in the box.

The show must go on.

And it did. It does, It always will.

Ruth wonders if he paid Sadie. She can't ask her daughter now as Sadie doesn't even remember Marvin. She doesn't even remember herself.

Now Ruth studies her hands. They are old and veined. They are speckled with age spots. They are bony and the skin is thin. Her wedding ring circles round and round her finger. It won't stay still, it's always moving.

Rose is gone.

Reggie Reynolds rots away in prison. They tell Ruth that a psychiatrist visits him sometimes. Even though he isn't getting out anytime soon, they tell her that Reggie takes some classes through a release-reintegration program. Law, some Psychology (B.F. Skinner and Freud), an English Literature class (Great Canadian Writers—Atwood, Laurence, Munro, Engel and Gallant—why, Reggie asks, when interviewed for the prison newsletter, are they all women?). He writes Ruth a short story but she neglects to read it. His cover letter says it's about snakes in the grass and rats on the prowl. His cover letter says it symbolizes man's power over beasts, but Ruth has no interest and no idea what he means by that and whether the snakes or the rats represent Man. She has no idea why he would even write to her. "For God's sake, who mailed this letter to me? A prison guard? Is a prisoner really allowed to write to his victim's family?" Ruth shouts throughout the condominium. She scatters the Christmas ornaments she has been working on. They fall to the floor, Reggie's story on top of them.

Sylvia and Ruth send the letter and the story back to the prison. Ruth writes an angry letter and they both sign it. They sign Sadie's name for her. Full apologies come swiftly from the warden. A little financial compensation that they squirrel away. Everything is rapidly forgotten. Including Reggie. Ruth never hears from him again.

Ruth thinks of Rose often and she wonders what the woman is doing and if she's found another magician to marry. Ruth feels angry when she thinks these things. Why can't I find another magician she thinks. One day Ruth stands by the pile of a new edition of Dr. Spock, just released (updated and improved, if that is at all possible), and tips slightly on her heels and knocks into the stack. But no one, not one man, comes to help her pick them up (to steal her heart and her money). There is only, suddenly, a young female store clerk who noisily pushes Ruth out of the way and says, "Watch what you are doing, ma'am," with a bitter, underpaid, get-out-of-my-way-old-lady voice.

Old lady. Ma'am. Ruth feels old. She is older, sadder, wasted. No wiser.

What has she done to deserve all of this?

She knows what she has done to deserve this.

Sadie turns twenty just like that. Ruth snaps her fingers. One day she is sixteen and almost dead, the next she is twenty and dusting the walls. Sadie takes the feather duster and scurries around the condominium. She spends hours keeping the framed posters of Marvellous Marvin clean. Although Ruth has stopped looking at the posters, although she has been duped, she can't seem to remove them, to remove Marvellous Marvin from her life. Sadie doesn't remember who he is anymore, this man in the posters, but she is happy to dust him.

Sylvia now is seventeen and weighs more than Ruth can guess. More than her bathroom scale can handle, the little needle scurrying all over the place in confusion. The girl can barely walk anymore. She shuffles, limps, uses a walker in the condominium, is talking about a wheelchair. Sylvia doesn't go out much at all. She can barely dress herself and has taken up sewing in order to make the dresses she needs to wear. No stockings fit her and so in winter she is bare-legged. She wears a bathrobe as a coat. Ruth is astonished, horrified, chagrined. She feels as if she has no way of stopping this mountain. It is out of control. Sylvia is like a snowball rolling down a hill, picking up speed, growing bigger and bigger. Ruth feels... not responsible... but something else. Guilt? No. This cannot be her fault. Sylvia has always been large. Ruth blames it mostly on TV and snacks. On Sadie's situation. On their lack of money. On Sylvia's lack of education. On laziness. On Marvellous Marvin's genes? Or hers? On Mr. Swamp and Rose. She even blames it on Dr. Spock, although she takes that back as soon as it comes out of her mouth.

"Mama," Sadie says.

It is not Ruth's fault.

Or is it?

•••

Puberty Development in Girls

"Suddenly, at about 11, the brakes let go."

AFTER SADIE'S ACCIDENT and then after Mr. Swamp dies, Ruth attempts to focus more on Sylvia. The daughter she has been ashamed to acknowledge for all these years she now places in the limelight. Ruth puts her there on her stage and she studies her. There is Sylvia, peering out through the glare, listening to the boos and hisses from the peanut gallery: Ruth. Constant criticism. What else can a mother do? Praise is impossible. Support is crazy. She needs to be shamed. Ruth is hoping that she'll feel the need to lose weight to please her mother. There has to be something Ruth can get out of this Marvellous Marvin fiasco. Anything. Even if it is only one healthy daughter. He owes Ruth that.

Helping Sylvia makes Ruth feel as if she is making up to Mr. Swamp, as if she is proving that she is sorry for the pain she caused in his life. He loved Sylvia and maybe there was a reason for that. Maybe there is something inside of the girl other than fast food. Something wonderful that only Mr. Swamp saw.

Besides, it's not as if Ruth can help Sadie anymore. There is no way to improve her. Sylvia's weight loss seems easy in comparison.

Here's where Dr. Spock will help. Ruth scans the last several sections of The Book, looking, as always, for advice. In *Problems of Feeding and Development* she finds, *"The child who is worrying about bogeymen, or death, or his mother's going away and leaving him, may lose a lot of his appetite."*

"What good does that do me?" Ruth is at the kitchen table, reading. It is late. She has a part time job cleaning a few houses and she is tired and her bones are sore. Ruth's hands, once manicured and lovely, are chapped and her skin is raw. Sylvia and Sadie are asleep in their rooMs Marvellous Marvin, Grandma and Grandpa Mileford and now Mr. Swamp are buried deep underground. Rose is living off Ruth's money. Money she could badly use right now. Reggie is caged. His rabbits and snakes are free. Ruth rubs at her eyes, smearing her falsely advertised smudge-proof and waterproof mascara, unintentionally giving herself just the right amount of black liner to make her look desperately tired and sick. (Ruth discovers this later, her image reflecting back at her from the bathroom mirror.) Avon would never have sold such a bad product. Even wearing her nightgown, Ruth has heels on (one must always be prepared for a knock at the door, she thinks). Ruth taps them on the linoleum floor. She likes the way they sound. Hearing them she still feels young and beautiful. Hearing them she doesn't feel like a cleaning lady.

Ruth can hear Sylvia down the hall in her bedroom snoring. She has been having trouble breathing lately and so snores loudly in the night. The box springs creak whenever she turns. They have thrown away the bedframe, worried Sylvia would collapse it. The box spring might be the next to go. Sometimes Ruth frets about living in a condominium. With regards to Sylvia, she wonders about the floor, how sturdy it is.

"What if we went right through to the downstairs condo?" she asks. "What if Sylvia crushed someone?"

But the building owners have reassured her. This building, they say, is meant to withstand great stress.

But Sylvia is more than great stress. Sylvia is a war ship, Sylvia is an airplane, an elephant, a bomb.

She is the bogeyman. If the death of her own father didn't worry Sylvia into losing weight, if all Ruth's cajoling and bribing and yelling doesn't do it, then nothing will.

Sylvia is a drain on their finances. She contributes nothing but is eating them out of their home.

Snore, creak, groan.

Sadie is asleep in her room too, although Ruth can never be sure if Sadie really sleeps. That half a year of drug-induced coma gave Sadie enough sleep for a lifetime. Often Ruth will find her up and dusting, up and wandering, her thin frame clutching her nightgown, creepy in the glow of the moon, moving through the condo like a brainless ghost. Haunting: a word that explains the look in Sadie's eyes, that explains the way she floats through the place, never settling down for long.

If Sadie can't help support them either, Ruth can train her to do things around the condo. She has already taught her how to fold laundry, how to turn on the microwave and how to use potholders when she takes anything out of the oven. Ruth has shown Sadie how to plug things in and screw in light bulbs and help Sylvia into the bath. She is feeling old and ill and she can see the future and it looks grim. When Ruth is gone, if she goes before Sylvia, Sadie will have to look after everything. How does one leave a brain-damaged woman in charge of a handicapped fat girl? Ruth shakes her head, rubs her eyes some more, studies The Book.

Ruth is saving all the money she can. She hasn't even dipped into Mr. Swamp's pension. The girls will need it when she is gone.

Are all mothers disappointed with their lives? Do all women wish that more could be done to make them happy? Is Ruth being too picky? At least her children are alive. At least neither one of them is pregnant and unmarried. Really, in the big scheme of things, Ruth is doing well. There is a woman in her building whose only son, sixteen years old, got a fifteen-year-old girl pregnant. Now, with their baby, they wander up and down the streets of Toronto. They are both children themselves, playing house. They are covered in piercings and tattoos, they smoke constantly.

There is nowhere for them to go but down. Compared to this, Ruth's girls are just grand.

It hasn't been easy since Mr. Swamp died. Now that he's gone Ruth sees him in everything, she sees him everywhere. His greyness has turned colourful in her mind and his smile beautiful. There is no one for Ruth now. No one to eat at the diner with, no one to argue with, no one to pay the bills or make the money. Ruth tries selling Avon again on top of the cleaning, but it's not as lucrative as it used to be. No one wears Avon makeup anymore. People buy their makeup at the malls these days. There is too much choice, in Ruth's opinion. But even Ruth would be the first to admit that Avon perfume can't hold a candle to what's now available in Shoppers Drug Mart. All the movie stars and singers with their own fragrances.

Ruth remembers when Shoppers Drug Mart was called Koffler's. She is now officially one of those women who remember when things were different. Her mother would say, "I remember when," and it signified her age, it meant she was out of touch with the present day. Now Ruth is her mother. Will her children remember her as meek and quiet? As controlling or passive? As dominant or as a failure? How will Ruth make history? Or will she? Will Sadie ever remember anything? Will Sylvia eat herself to death before Ruth dies?

Ruth reaches up and snaps off the light. She takes a final look around at the dim kitchen, messy, disorganized. She has never been one for housework. Maybe if Ruth told Sylvia that Marvellous Marvin was her real father, maybe that would scare some skinniness into the girl? But she shies away from this admission. She cringes when she thinks of the reaction—good or bad—that would follow. Alone at night, Ruth refuses to admit to herself that this is the case. Mr. Swamp was a good daddy to Sylvia. Leave it at that. Ruth has done the best she could with the worst of situations. She has done the best she knew how. Ruth hears her mother in those words. But that's fine. There's nothing else to do anymore.

What else? What else?

Ruth itches her scalp. The once a week visits to the hairdressers have become too expensive and so they have ended and her hair now needs a good wash and style. It's just that she hasn't had time. The oven clock reads 2:34 am. It glows. Ruth needs to sleep.

But what more can she do?

She switches the light back on and continues to read. Dr. Spock, the only man faithful to her, stuck with her no matter what. Never talked back or disagreed. Didn't steal her money. Helped her raise her children. Dr. Spock gave Ruth the skills she needed to raise her children when her mother gave only ridiculous advice. She wanted Ruth to raise her children the way she was raised. Seen, not heard. As small accessories. Not human. Ruth thought Dr. Spock's book, his words, his common sense, would reverse this horrible trend, this like-mother-like-daughter cycle. Wouldn't it? Ruth needed that book and it fell into her hands. Dr. Spock was good to her. The best.

Mr. Swamp, too, was good to Ruth.

She reads, "*Many people think the cause is gland trouble, but actually this is rarely the case. There are several factors that make for overweight, including heredity, temperament, appetite, happiness.*"

"Happiness," Ruth sighs. "In which case I should be as large as Sylvia."

"*It's good for parents to know that this mild school-age obesity is common and that it often goes away later, so that they won't make too much of an issue about it.*"

Sylvia is now morbidly obese.

Once Marvellous Marvin stopped halfway through a performance and refused to go back on stage. He said to Ruth behind the curtain that he had suddenly seen the future. There he was, out there performing, making people ooh and ahh and clap, and twirling his tuxedo tails, topping his hat, rabbits running, cards flying fast and furious in his fingers, and there before him, in his mind, he saw death. He knew, he told Ruth, that whatever happened, whatever he did, whoever he was, it would all be over someday and so, instantly, like a flash of lightning, he saw that nothing he did made sense anymore.

Ruth whimpered. This scared her. Thinking of no more Marvellous Marvin. No more Ruth. She clutched at her sequins, picked her constantly creeping costume out of her bum. "Oh, Marvin, you're a young man," she said then. "You have lots of time left."

"That's not what I mean, Ruth. That's not what I mean at all." The dark clouds lined his face for a minute. Raced over his features. And then were gone. He was bright again, shiny. "I'm being morbid," he said. "Forgive me." And then went back on stage.

Now, when Ruth hears the word morbid, as in morbidly obese, the picture of those dark clouds moving across Marvin's face, the feeling of cold clamminess, of death approaching, all of this travels through her mind. She supposes that's what the doctors meant when they gave it that name. Sylvia is morbid. She has added the end of her life to her belly.

How is it possible to feel so distant from her youngest daughter? Ruth contemplates what it is that is missing in Sylvia, what it is that makes Ruth not able to connect with her the same way she used to connect with Sadie. It's as if Sylvia is lacking a spark, a twinkle. She's devoid of any personality. She's missing charisma. Ruth needs fireworks in her life and Sylvia has always merely fizzled out. And now, well, she's beyond help.

Ruth puts The Book down and stands and moves towards the oven. She opens the oven door. What did that author do? Sylvia's author? Put her head in the oven? Made bread or cookies or something first? Killed herself over a man. A poet. What good was that? The children lay sleeping, all tucked in their beds. SugarpluMs Visions. What more? What a thing to wake up to. "Mommy, why are you sleeping with your head in the oven?"

Ruth is tired. So tired. "I'm sick and tired of all of this," she says all the time, to anyone who will listen. In the grocery store lineup, at the dry cleaners, and especially at the diner, where half the staff won't serve her anymore. Even Maeve, who has aged with Ruth, who is sick and tired too, even she won't serve her. "She's way too depressing," Ruth heard one waitress say to the other as she passed on the way to her booth. She heard her clearly. "She takes me down, makes me sad."

But Ruth's old oven is not gas. It's electric. And even if it was gas she is far too tired to get towels to put under the door to keep her children safe and alive.

Still. Wouldn't it be nice not to have to feed Sylvia and Sadie in the morning? Wouldn't it be nice if she didn't have to think about Marvellous Marvin and his magic and her money, or about Rose living somewhere happily, or Reggie Reynolds in jail, or Ruth's poor husband or her mother and father? Wouldn't it be nice to be floating on a fluffy white marshmallow cloud somewhere looking down on all of this waste of potential, all the crap in the Swamp household, instead of being mired in it herself? If she were there, on that cloud, she would be with her husband and she would take his hand and turn to him and look him in the eyes (what colour were his eyes?) and tell him that she is sorry for everything. Ruth doesn't feel guilty, but she is sorry. She would tell him that she knows who started the fire. She would finally confess, get it off her chest. She would tell him and he would forgive her. Ruth thinks she would even enjoy hearing him clear his throat loudly.

But she can't blame herself. It's not her fault. Marvin did wrong by Ruth and he deserved what he got. He cheated Ruth. He tricked her.

Ruth never intended the fire to get that hot, to do that much damage.

Ruth carries The Book delicately down the hall towards her bedroom (her own, quiet, lonely bedroom), reading as she walks. Pages are falling out and brittle and ripped. Ruth remembers her mother saying, "You are to be seen, not heard, Ruth." She remembers Daddy spanking her whenever her mother said to. Shhhhh, they both said. Now there is only the tip tapping of Ruth's heels on the bathroom floor, soft pitter-patters as she crosses the carpet to her bed:

"Some people who have read popular articles on glands assume that every short person, every slow pupil, every nervous girl, every fat boy with small genitals, is merely a glandular problem who can be cured by the proper tablet or injection."

Dr. Spock knew that you can't blame everything on just one thing, on one glandular disorder. Problems aren't so easily solved. Ruth has finally learned her lesson. After those sixteen years surrounded by magic and excitement and love and applause, she has eventually come to the truth—nothing in life can be fixed. You just have to go on, move forward, get it done and over with. Life is short.

Of course, it's as easy as pie to pick one cause for your problems and stick with the cure. Glands (tablets, injections). Cheating (fire). Ruth puts The Book on her bedside table and climbs under the covers. She has lined her high-heeled shoes up beside the bed, and is ready for the morning. She is ready to face the new day. Whatever comes. Ruth flicks off the light, all alone in her cold empty room, and for what seems like the millionth time, she tries not to remember how she, Ruth Swamp, started the fire that killed Marvellous Marvin. How she sparked the match against the box and held it to the Sterno she had bought in the convenience store. It was certainly convenient. How Ruth poured the fire onto the curtains and then shut the window and stepped back onto the fire escape. She disappeared. Like magic. Ruth lies here now and tries not to let the flames into her head. It's hard, but she can do it if she concentrates. Ruth closes her eyes and drifts slowly to sleep.

Part Three

Sadie

Illness, First Aid and Special Problems

"You may have more confidence in an older man or feel that you are imposing less on a younger man, or you may prefer a woman."

I HAVE NEVER understood why people like me so much, why they think I am special. I have always felt just average, or even below average, a body trying to survive in this harsh, evil world. Jesus, look at all the stuff going on out there. Assassinations. Wars. A plague here and there. But all my life people say to me, or to my family, that I am different. I mean, shit. I'm not just Sadie Swamp, they say, I am a beautiful girl full of some sort of fire, some spark that moves things, some burning sensation that passes into souls. Ha. "She'll go places," the women on the bus tell my mother when I am small. "That girl is special." They pinch my cheeks and ruffle my hair. Golden Girl they call me.

My mother grunts. Humph.

And then Sylvia is born. And Sylvia is special too. But in a different way. And I'm the only one who sees it, even when she becomes bigger than a house. Even when her eyes seem to disappear into her eyelids. Even when the kids at school pull her into their circle and taunt and tease her.

So I guess I'm special in a normal way. A physical way. Far out, I think. I roll my eyes. Fun to do. Great effect. Sylvia loves it, the eye rolling.

It is the blonde hair. That's the first thing they all notice. My hair shines in the light as if it's the sun. Then there are my legs. They are thin and thin is really in (hey, that rhymes). Just because I'm taller, thinner, prettier than everyone else (in the whole world?), it doesn't mean I'm anything special. Just because I can make men swoon—and oh how I've made them swoon—that doesn't mean I, Sadie Swamp, have powers. I can't, for one, see into the future. I can't, for two, fly, and I certainly am not, for three, invisible. Wish I was. Wish I had one of those invisible planes that Wonder Woman flies too. And bracelets that reflect bullets. Rock-hard cone breasts. What do they want, these people who tell me these things? Do they want me to perform magic?

I am not a magician.

And I certainly don't believe in magic. I've seen enough of it in my life to know what's real and what's not real. And magic does not exist.

I pretend it does when Sylvia is little and her face lights up with the suspense of a card trick, when she squeals with delight as our mother is cut apart in the trick box.

I get to a point, though, when I am sick to death of living up to everyone's expectations. Be pretty. Be quiet. Be smart. Smile, smile, smile. So I think to myself, what's the best thing to do when you are sick of being perfect?

Disappoint?

Certainly.

Show them the opposite of what they expect. If they can't get what they want, then give them what they don't want.

I'm so smart.

"I'm disappointed in you," my mother hollers. "What has gotten into you?"

"Your grades are slipping," Dad says.

"I didn't see you at school today," Sylvia says. Her mouth always opening, closing, chewing.

"It must be her hormones," my mother says. "Let me just look it up in The Book."

And the boys. Ah, the boys. Trailing after me like I'm a cat in heat. Sniff, sniff. I love to watch my mother's face when I unbutton my blouse just enough to show the hickey, or when I hike up my skirt to give a peek of underwear. As if she doesn't do this stuff herself. You should see her with the cops, with the men in the diner, with the magician, of course.

"You're doing this to kill me," my mother shouts. "What did I do to deserve this?"

Marvin has been in the family, part of the family, if you can call this a family, since I was born. He flutters in and out of my life—sometimes he's there for days, hanging out, showing me tricks (card, string, thimble, coin)—sometimes he's gone for weeks. Months. Depends upon how his lovely Ruth treats him.

When I am a child I am only impressed by the magic. But when I become a teenager I am impressed by what I can do to the magician. I'm impressed by my effect on him. I can turn his magic, I can turn him, into jelly, into goo. So easily. He's sticky and sweet. Sometimes I think I might actually love him. Or do I just love what I can do to him? When I'm fourteen I am fully matured—everything in the right places, yep—and giving off a smell or a look, or something that Marvin can't resist. It's not love I'm feeling, really, it's familiarity. And the ability to make a difference. Like a pebble in a pool of water, I make ripples.

And it's not just what I can do to Marvin, it's what I can do to my mother.

"She's fourteen years old," my mother screams. "Stop looking at her like that or I'll have you arrested. And, Sadie, that blouse is see-through. You know better than that. Take it off ... Not here ... Jesus, Sadie. Take it off in your bedroom."

Sometimes, when you throw a huge pebble, a stone, I guess, the ripple goes on for days and days, months, years.

I don't know why I'm angry all the time.

Nothing can happen to a smart girl like me. After all, I'm so smart that I know I'm smart. It's the dumb people who don't know anything. Nothing can happen to me because I am a girl who is so smart that she pretends she is not smart. Dumb people pretend nothing, ever. Seriously. How can I get into REAL trouble when I'm so damn smart (I know about birth control. I know about STDs. I know how to make a man groan)? I'm so smart I don't need to go to school anymore.

I guess I am special. Not just because of my looks, but because of the way I think.

"When you've got talent and looks," I tell Sylvia, "why waste your time at school?"

Sylvia narrows her eyes. She says nothing. Just swallows more food. She hasn't got talent or looks so she has no idea what I'm talking about.

"How could any two sisters be more opposite?" I say. Sylvia has never been as smart as I am. She's fat and she can't seem to stop eating. She's stupidly happy, though, I think. Jolly?

When Sylvia's not at school she seems happy.

But everyone focuses on her fatness. Worry worry worry. "Don't eat that." "Watch your weight." "How about you wait for dinner?" No one says, "What pretty hair you have."

Poor, dumb Sylvia. I can't take care of her forever. She has to learn to fight.

Boys line up in the park to kiss me when I'm in elementary school. They falter and stutter and trip on their shoelaces. Their faces are beet red. Eyes wide open for a peck on the cheek. My nickname is Foxy.

When they are older those same boys fight for me, fight over me. Tear each other's hair out, punch bloody noses, black eyes, make tooth and nail marks on skin. All for me, Sadie Swamp.

The girls at school call me a tramp. They say I'm loose, a slut. I'm so smart I don't really care.

"She's a cyclone," Grandma Mileford says to my mom one day. I'm right there, sitting in the kitchen beside Grandma, watching Sylvia stuff her face. "She's a tornado. She wrecks everything in her path."

"Are you talking about Sadie?" my mom asks. "She's right beside you." She rolls her eyes at me.

"Are tornados and cyclones the same thing?" I ask. "I'm not sure they are."

"Mother." My mom tidies up the dishes, snaps off her yellow dish-gloves, stares over at me as I sit there at the table. I smile beatifically at her. "She's just a fireball. That's all, right, Sadie? You're not a wrecker."

"Wrecking ball," I say.

"You watch out. She's trouble."

"Grandma, Jesus. I'm right here."

"See. What did I just say? Listen to the swear words."

"I was a fireball too. Wasn't I?" my mother says.

I stick my tongue out, catch Grandma Mileford's eye, smile sweetly.

"Yes, Ruth," Grandma sighs. "She's just like you were. Exactly so. That's the problem. Up to no good all the time. Both of you. Sylvia, on the other hand, isn't like anyone. She's her own girl."

Sylvia looks startled. She puts the cookie down that she is snitching. She smiles. "Me?"

"She's not her own girl," I say. "She's her own girl and another one put together." We laugh. All of us. Except Sylvia.

If I am just like Ruth Mileford, then, I think, why not go all the way? I study her. The high heels come on, the red lipstick. I just can't talk as loudly as my mother. I'm not as commanding a presence. Not yet.

I don't know why I want to be like my mother. Except that she seems to have everything in control. She seems to have power over everyone. My father, my sister, Marvellous Marvin. Ruth Mileford Swamp is the boss of them all.

"Everyone thinks Sylvia is the shy one, the quiet one, the easy one, but you mark my words. One day she'll come out of her cocoon and I'll be afraid to see what—" Grandma Mileford says. And then stops saying. She never finishes the sentence. Imbecile.

I used to like my Grandma. I used to feel warm around her. Lately everyone annoys me.

"What is that supposed to mean?" I tap my fingers along the kitchen table.

"I have no idea, Sadie. Your grandmother is losing her mind."

"I am losing no such thing. Watch your mouth, Ruth."

My mother shuts up.

Maybe my grandma is the boss?

Sylvia swallows hard.

Enough said.

•••

Rectal Thermometers

"Instead, lay the palm of your hand across his buttocks, lightly holding the thermometer between two of the fingers, the way you'd hold a cigarette."

ANOTHER DAY OF taking Sylvia's hand and dragging her away from the beasts.

"Fuck off," I tell her, when we are out of sight of the school. "Find your own way home."

I am almost sixteen now and I have managed to alienate all of my friends. That's OK. They weren't really my friends if you think about it. A real friend sticks with you through thick and thin. A real friend doesn't say mean things about your mother and father.

I drop out of school. Without telling anyone. The school calls my mother. She doesn't seem to care.

"It's your life, Sadie, you do with it what you will."

Is that Dr. Spock? I'm never sure. My mother is possessed by a baby doctor.

Why wouldn't she care?

Everyone who thought I was special in school now thinks the opposite. Even the boys. I'm nothing to them anymore. I've become the girl who dropped out of school to hang around with an over-age magician who is "a weird-looking dude," (direct quote) and to work as his assistant. What's up with that? That's the opposite of cool.

"I mean," they say, "how are you supposed to go anywhere in life if you don't go to school?"

"If I jumped off a cliff, would you?"

"We're in downtown Toronto, Sadie. Where are the cliffs?"

"What I mean is, I don't have to do the same thing everyone else does."

"She's so uptight."

"What does she mean by that?"

"But you have to go to school."

I'm too smart for them. I move on.

Even when I go to the parties on Friday nights—the ones that start in Yorkville, then eventually move north to the suburbs and someone's back yard or basement—even when I let the boys line up to kiss me in the closest closet (tongue-twister)—even then I'm not part of anything anymore. I've fallen out of my place in the teenage scheme of things.

I guess when you don't want something anymore, then that something doesn't really want you either. It's such hard work being popular and I really don't have time for it. I'm a working girl. I have an older man who is interested in me. Busy, busy, busy.

This is why I quit school.

Ryan's parents are away and he's got me where he wants me, in his bedroom, and all the other kids are outside of the room drinking shit-mix and smoking tea-leaves, which is all they could find to smoke and which is making them cough and feel sick. He's got me on his bed. Me: Sadie Swamp. Jesus, she's hot, he's probably thinking, and he's got his hands all over me and I'm making little kitten noises to turn him on because I know those kitten noises work, I've seen them work in the movies. Ryan finally manages to find under my skirt, he manages to play with his fingers around the elastic between my legs, he manages to use his fingers to their best advantage until suddenly—I know he can't help it, it's like it exploded—he's wet and I sigh and pull away. Just like that. I tidy myself up, thinking it's no big thing, shit happens, and I leave to smoke a tea-leaf cigarette and later puke.

I forget all about it.

But Ryan doesn't.

Weeks go by and Ryan tells everyone I'm loose, he tells everyone he could have lost his hand inside, I'm that loose. He tells Sylvia even and Sylvia looks at me in a new way. So I stop going to school because, for some reason, this one really bugs me. Bugs me and makes me not care all at the same time. It's just, I'm sick of it, you know. First everyone looks at me because I'm beautiful and special, then they look at me because I have a huge sister, now they look at me because they think I'm a slut. I end up riding the bus up and down and walking all around Toronto for days and then weeks and then months (it gets easier and more natural every day), looking out the bus windows at the billboards and restaurants and people strolling up and down the streets. I give old ladies my seat, and old men, and they smile at me nicely. They look at me nicely. I pound the pavement in Yorkville. Or stand in front of Honest Ed's and stare in the window. Sometimes I hang out in the Eaton Centre and one day I take a bus to Mississauga and stare at all the strip malls. I get to know my city. And the people in it.

There are homeless people here, more than you'd even think. Lying on the subway grates, hoping to stay warm. There are people who speak no English who need help with directions. There are people in wheelchairs who can't get up the curb.

I feel useful. I feel good.

Who needs school anyway when you are as smart as I am? There are better things to do with your time, things that make money, or make you feel good. There are things I want to do that need money. Like travel. God, I would love to see the world: New York, Tokyo, London, Paris. I will take off and fly out of here. Leave everyone behind. Daddy and Sylvia can spend all their time together quietly and my mother will have no one to scream at.

"You are not wearing that," my mother screams. "You are not working for Marvin. What about school? You have to go to school in the day, Sadie. You are not working. You're only sixteen."

"I thought you said I had a choice, that it was up to me."

"But I didn't know you'd be working for him. Did I? You didn't tell me that."

I work at Marvin's shows in those sparkly outfits, green and blue and red, snug and tight between my legs, around my growing breasts, over my slim ass. They are my Wonder Woman suits. Marvin says he'll pay me later, when he has the cash. He says I look fine and sweet. Like a breath of fresh air. To the stage and then into the spotlight. There are people clapping, cheering for me. Amazed by Marvin. First I work for him. And then I go into his dressing room, where I "relax" after the show.

"There is nothing your mother loves more than to relax after a hard show," he tells me the first night it happens.

I collapse on the bed. Euphoric. The applause still rings in my ears. I throw off these too-high heels (how does my mom wear these things). I want to peel off the tight body suit, let my ribs expand. I want a bath.

"She likes a glass of wine. Are you old enough for a glass of wine?"

There were over one hundred people in the audience tonight. All the tables full. Two men pinched my ass when I walked out into the crowd to hold up items for Marvin to guess at. One man tried to slip a finger under the leg of my suit. I batted him away nervously. I can feel bruises where the too-hard fingers grabbed flesh.

Sylvia was there. Spilling into two seats, her arms on both armrests, she looked crammed in and tight. I couldn't catch her eye. She wouldn't look at me. Maybe our mother told her to come to the show to glare at me, make me want to quit.

"Feel free to put on a dressing gown," Marvin says. "If you're uncomfortable." He looks distracted, unhappy. For a minute I wonder what I've done. Was I that bad on stage? I did trip once. But that was because of Sylvia, because of the way she ignored me.

Is this my seduction scene? My big moment? Like in the movies, I think. Cameras flashing. Always smile nicely. Always fun.

Marvin throws me a dressing gown and turns away to make himself another drink. "I'm not sure that card trick works properly yet," he says. "But maybe it's the actual cards. Maybe I need a smaller deck." He's talking to himself now. Ignoring me. "I almost dropped them."

I take his cue—he's distracted? Bored? And start to unzip my body suit. Ah, I can breathe now. It's not like I don't know men, boys, whatever. It's not like I'm not feeling his vibes. I know he wants me. It's just that I don't know if I want him (yet, not yet). It hasn't occurred to me to want him yet (I laugh about this later). I am my mother, but I'm also not my mother. Finally released and able to breathe—the tights off, the heels gone, the gown on—I feel more than naked. I feel vulnerable. But that's the same thing.

If you learn how to perform the magic, if you know the tricks, will the magic go away? Is ignorance really bliss?

Suddenly his hands are all over me. His fingers everywhere. Like magic, just like it. One minute I am standing there, thinking, the next minute I'm on the bed in the arms of Marvellous Marvin.

And it's not bad. I mean, I think I love it. Don't I? Sparks fly. Fairy dust in the air. Abracadabra.

I love him (I think). Do I?

Does my mother love him?

What else can I feel? What more can I do?

I don't make enough money working for him to go anywhere, to do anything. He's always short on cash, he's always going to pay me next week.

But the sex is pretty good, I like the clapping of the audience, and it's not like I have anything else to do.

•••

Objects in the Nose and Ears

"Small children often stuff things like beads and wads of paper into their nose or ears. The important thing is not to push the object any further in, in your efforts to take it out."

"Foreign objects that stay in the nose for several days usually cause a bad-smelling discharge tinged with blood."

THERE ARE THE times I am with Marvin when I am aware he is much older, when I know he is boring and stuffy. The way he blows his nose, for example, upsets me. Boys don't blow their noses, they snort it in and spit it out into the street. Marvin takes a handkerchief (yes, he calls it that) and honks into it, checks it, honks again, rubs away, puts the handkerchief BACK into his pocket (that's so disgusting) and continues on. As if nothing has happened. As if he doesn't now have SNOT in his pocket. Ugh.

And the way he opens doors for me. That bugs me. I don't know why. It is polite. I am aware of that. And old-fashioned. It bothers me to no end.

"Stop it," I say. "I can open my own damn door."

He laughs and ushers me through as if he's the King of England or something. He bows and I can see the thinning hair on the top of his head. I shiver at the thought of him sometimes. Marvellous Marvin. What's so Marvellous?

When he's with my mother, the two of them together, I swear I can feel their electricity. I feel their connection. They spark. It infuriates and disgusts me. I want to barf. I want to hurl. I want to go back to school and stop needing him, stop wanting his touch, the way he makes me feel when the lights are out, when the wine is soft and warm inside my stomach, and his hands—magic hands—are roaming. He does have a certain way about him. It's just sometimes ... I feel too much like ... something.

Like what?

Like my mother.

If only he wouldn't speak. Stay perfectly silent.

"Tea? Would you like tea?"

Who asks that? Who wants tea? What is he—British? I have never met a boy in my life who would ask me if I wanted tea after seeing me strip out of my red and gold sequined body suit with the way-too-high sides and way-too-low cleavage. Tea?

"You're serious?"

He looks at me, confused. "Yes. Tea? Or I have coffee. It's chilly tonight."

"Fuck off," I say. And then I leave the dressing room gradually and head home to the overstuffed, overcrowded, over-tight apartment my mother insists on calling a condominium. As if the Swamp family are high class, hoity-toity, TEA-drinking people living in a glass building. Jesus.

And then the next night he has rolled me onto my stomach and is kissing, yes, kissing, all the way down my back. Slowly. Patiently. I'm ready to giggle. I'm ready to explode with lust. He continues on.

What young boy has such power? What young boy bothers to kiss like that? Soft, small puckers. Taking his time. I can forgive the tea-asking, the door-opening.

Besides, I guess I like what all of this is doing to my mother. There's always that. My mother has my dad. What does she need with Marvellous Marvin too? That's just plain greedy. And selfish.

Sylvia has shut up completely. Thankfully. She won't talk to me anymore. What more is there to do in life now but work and have sex and come home and scream at my mother and have my mother scream at me? I have stopped caring about Sylvia and her ballooning weight. She is not my baby. She has to take care of herself, fight her own battles, grow up (not out).

"I don't have time for you anymore," I say to Sylvia when she isn't paying attention. She is watching TV. "I'm a teenager now. Don't you know that? Get some friends."

Sylvia goes pale. Then red. Then purple like an eggplant. "Shhhh," she says. "I'm watching TV. I have friends."

"Where? I don't see any," I say. I wave my arms around the apartment.

Sylvia, distracted, has her finger up her nose.

I swat it away. "You are so disgusting." I clomp out of the room in my high heels.

It's a shame, watching my huge sister, it's a shame that Sylvia will never ever ever know what it's like to have someone lust after you so badly that your all-powerful, larger than life, loud mother becomes nothing more than a particle of dust in the wind, nothing more than a sound that is here and then gone. Not even lingering. Sylvia will never know the feeling you can get from watching our mother squirm with jealousy. A lovely, hot feeling. A sexual feeling.

I don't know what makes me so angry. Some days I feel fine. Other days I feel like I could easily start a war. My mother says it's my hormones, that I'm just a teenager, but it seems like so much more. That can't be the only reason I want to run as far away from this family as my legs will allow, I want to slam doors and push everyone hard into walls, I want to knock people over on the sidewalk. I want to say whatever it is that I want to say. I can't hold anything in. It's bursting out of me—anger. Fierceness.

"It's not that I want to be mean to you, Sylvia," I say one night when I'm having a normal day. One of those days when I remember what it's like to care about your little sister, or your mother, or your stupid father. "It's just that you have to hear it like it is. You have to know how your body is making all of us, everyone out there in the world, actually, sick, sick, sick. You are huge. You are full. You are so bloated you look like a marshmallow. You smell bad. Stinky. Foot-odoury and body rotting smells. You push food into your open mouth like you are starving and the hole needs filling. Are you starving? Don't tell me there is nothing you can do about it. Get a hold of yourself. Take charge. Do something. Shut. Your. Mouth. For. Once." I pat her on her head. I leave the room. Advice given. Advice taken.

In and out of the apartment. I own the world (I do own the world, you know). I don't stop for anyone. Dad gets a pat on the head. Just because I can. Sylvia gets words. And Mom. My mother gets blasted until it looks as if she's walking in a high wind. Tilted forward. Stooped. But she can return it. Oh she's capable of straightening sometimes and blasting back.

"Come back here. Where do you think you are going? Who do you think you are?"

My crowning achievement is when I throw The Book across the living room and it takes a powdered dent out of the drywall. Who knew The Book could damage anything?

My mom chases me then—cat and mouse—out the door, down the hall, down the stairs—why wait for the elevator at a time like this—into the main lobby, past a neighbour checking his mail, out into the street, past the diner. All on high heels. All screamy. Loud. Violent. I'm laughing. I look behind and see her stumbling. I'm scared, sort of, but this is kind of fun.

"You ungrateful little bitch," my mother shouts and then stops. Heads turn. I laugh. She looks shocked at herself.

I disappear into the crowds on the street. Toronto rush hour pedestrians. Everyone trying to get home before the rain. Black suits. High heel boots. They tilt their heads up to the sky, watch the beginning of the rain as the clouds darken. Hunker down and walk quickly away.

I am long gone before the first drops fall. I'm fast in more than one way. My mother doesn't know the half of it.

•••

Special Problems

Twins. "Help!"

THE IMPRESSION I have of the world is that it is to be absorbed and then conquered. It is to be fought and won. My competitive nature baffles my father but my mother finds it both appealing and infuriating (more infuriating than appealing, if she's honest with herself, I'm sure).

"I'm always right," I say one day. "I know everything. Really." And I mean it.

"Imagine," Sylvia says to our father one night while they are watching TV and eating chips. I can hear them from the kitchen, "Imagine if you had two Sadies, not just one. Imagine what that would be like."

Dad clears his throat, almost chokes on a chip. Ahem. Ahem. "Imagine," he says, quietly, in that tiny voice he uses when he's been stumped. Shell-shocked. Dad is Dad. There is no one like him. Luckily.

But then there are really two of me. Sort of. One older than the other. Other than that, pretty much the same. This gets me thinking, digesting, worrying. I do wear heels everywhere, like my mom. I am sleeping with her boyfriend. Do I really want to be exactly like her? I take up smoking just to be different, holding the cigarette out in long, polished fingers. It doesn't work (it makes me cough). Well, if I can't beat her, I might as well join her—I attempt to talk loudly but can't quite reach the volume without hurting my throat. It's a real skill, my mother's constant noise. I never fully appreciated it before I tried it.

Do I want to be like her? Do I want to be her, but better? I'm not sure. I'm just angry, that's all. There is so much I want out of my life and I'm stuck in this stupid apartment in this stupid city in this stupid country, too young for some things, too old for other things. Or so I'm told. Nothing works out the way I want it to work out. If I could just wake up tomorrow and be happy.

It's not that I'm sad. I'm angry. I'm happy. I'm sad. I don't know what I am. But there is no way I'm telling anyone that.

One day Marvin is performing his magic and I am lying awkwardly in the box waiting to be sawn in half. My legs are bent at the knees, up under me. The optical illusion. I am getting a cramp. The rabbit boy, that stupid stinking Reggie, is staring at me like he always does. Making me feel creepy. I am trying to smile at the audience, but the cramp is getting worse and worse. My fake legs and shoes are down there, out the bottom of the box. Marvin won't stop talking, flirting with the audience. Blue-haired old ladies. Putting on the charm. Oh, look at me—I'm so talented. Stupid old man knows some tricks, that's all.

"Jesus, Marvin," I finally say—too loudly, "hurry the fuck up."

After that I take my voice down to its regular level. Because Marvin obviously doesn't appreciate loud voices so it must be just something he puts up with in my mother. It certainly doesn't appeal to him. He sends me home alone that night. Doesn't invite me into his changing room. Turns his back on me.

"Never undermine a magician on stage. Or ever," he says. "If you know what's good for you."

My mother looks obviously elated that evening. I crawl into my bed, say I'm sick. Throw my black satin high heels on the floor. Rip my body suit taking it off.

That's why I take Marvin to the baseball field.

"It's raining," he says. "I'm getting wet."

"Over here." The dugout is dry, the bench, the roof overhead. Marvin sits down. It is dark, late. Rain is pouring down. A sheet.

"I'm sorry I yelled at you," I say. "The other night on stage."

He looks at me. Uses those brown eyes. Smiles slightly. I stand and pull up my skirt and then I climb onto his lap and that's when the police come, the lights flashing, and Marvin is hauled off, I'm taken home wet and ashamed.

"I don't believe you," my mother shouts. "You are lying." The plates fly, the policeman ducks. I head to my room.

She doesn't believe it. Why? Why couldn't I be sleeping with the magician?

There are four of us in Marvellous Marvin's bed—me, my mother, Marvin, and my mother's ego. I wonder, all the time, what I am doing. I take the bus up and down Yonge Street, day after day, watching the seasons pass, and I think about why, what, where, when, how. I think about my small life and what it amounts to, if anything. For someone who is always right, always perfect, I don't feel so great. I wonder for a minute if I could be pregnant. I mean, I feel so crappy inside and out. The thought of this makes me even sicker.

The anger inside me can't be normal. It's as if something is growing.

I worry for two weeks and then see the blood on my underwear and immediately trust the pill again. I forget that I was worried. It's easy to do.

Reggie, rabbit boy, begins to hang around the apartment. He is always there. A comic book character. Outside the building, leaning against a pole, waiting for me, smoking. Trying to look like James Dean but, instead, looking like a gross version of Richie Cunningham. Talking. Always saying things that make me want to slap him or puke. Why won't he leave me alone?

"Are you for real?" I ask.

Reggie stumbles. Trips on the curb. Twists his ankle. He's always falling. Off the stage, onto the road.

At the magic show Reggie wipes his face with a dirty piece of cloth. Constantly. I want someone to wash it for him. It's disgusting. I even mention it one day and it's like I've shot him. His jaw clenches. His hands fist up in his pockets.

"Just mellow out," I say. "You're so uptight. What is it? Like, your baby blankie?" I laugh. Head thrown back. Revlon Red lips flashing. Stolen lipstick from my mother's purse. I click my heels together and meander out on stage. Sashay, that's what my daddy calls it. Sashay. He says my mother and I have sashaying down to an art. Marvin dazzles the audience. I strut my stuff. My perfume, Charlie, probably wows everyone. Reggie's eyes burn holes through my suit.

There is a letter in our box one day from someone claiming to be "watching" me. I read it and then stuff it in my purse. I climb on the Yonge Street bus. Think, it's probably Sylvia, threatening to tell my mother about me and Marvin. But the letter says,

"I am watching you.

Day and night.

We will be together.

You and me."

Like it's poetry or something. Which makes me laugh because it doesn't rhyme. And Sylvia would never write poetry. She's really too stupid. She's nothing like that writer she was named after. So who could it be? Marvin? A weird love letter? Reggie? Or even my mother? But she doesn't want to be together with me. If anything she is pushing me out the door all the time, still furious about that incident with the cop in the park (I still blush when I think of it—Marvin's flabby ass stuck to the bench, my skirt riding around my waist, feet not touching the ground. In fact, that boy in the basement at that party calling me loose and that cop in my living room are the two most embarrassing moments in my life), still acting like she doesn't believe Marvin was with her daughter. Like she didn't see it coming. At least that's what she says now, but that night, throwing the plate at the policeman, screaming, that night I think she almost believed it. I think that my mother should stick to what she has—my father, Dr. Spock and all those fucking smelly women who are hanging out in our kitchen these days—and leave the magician to me.

"Why were you sitting on his lap?" she screamed that night. "You're not a child anymore." And then she looked all hurt and shouted, "You know, Sadie, you've had so many advantages. Advantages I never had. And you've thrown them all away. Think what you could do if you just had a proper education. You have your whole life to work. Think what you could accomplish if you went to school...." Blah blah blah. She rambles on and on.

Think what I could accomplish.

My father doesn't speak to me now. It's as if he decided that I wasn't worth anything if I didn't go to school.

"To be what?" I shout. "A fucking accountant?"

Stabbed him, straight through the heart. I don't mean to. He just makes me so angry. I want him to yell at me, drag me by my hair to school. I don't know. I just want a reaction.

After the blah blah blah, my mother usually heads back to Dr. Spock's index, looking up education (not there), academics (nope), then school problems (oh the list is long—my mother focuses loudly—like nails on a chalkboard—on *School Phobia 352-53*, reciting facts aloud. Drowning out any thoughts I might have). I leave the apartment and head out into the world.

What makes me happy? Let's see: makeup, a new hairstyle, my leather gloves, the audience applause, Marvin's mouth and lips and hands, the little rabbit I've named Jojo, mint chocolate chip ice cream, giving a quarter to the guy in front of the subway entrance, helping the woman in her wheelchair down the street in the snow, a good show on TV. But nothing much else. Nothing makes me really, truly happy.

I spend some of my days in the movies. Whenever Marvin gives me money. But every movie seems good compared to my boring life. Even the slasher flicks. Even the crazy, long, boring dramas. Everyone's house is nicer than my apartment, all the teenagers have better hair and jewellery and clothes, and no one is sleeping with an aging magician or has a mother who is so loudly shouting that it always feels as if your head will split in two.

I'm on the street.

There he is again. Reggie.

"Are you following me?"

"No, I just thought I'd walk with you a bit." To school? To the movies? To the hotel?

"You are following me." I say "jerk," but under my breath.

Reggie is fiddling with that cloth in his pocket. If I ever see him holding it I'm going to run away as fast as I can. He probably uses it to clean the rabbit cages. I've seen him wipe his nose with it. My stomach turns.

"I don't need you to walk me."

"I want to walk you," he mumbles. I can barely hear him. He talks to his feet.

I have left the apartment in a hurry today. Fighting again. With guess who. I can't wait to get to Marvin's. It is night. Marvin is waiting for me and I have my red-sequined costume, his favourite, on underneath my coat.

"Who are you?" my mother had shouted at me.

And I said, "Sadie Swamp, duh."

And then she stuck in the kicker. "He doesn't love you," she cried. "He loves me." A whisper (From her? Is this possible? But Dad and Sylvia were sitting in the other room).

I said I was sweet, that's who I was, and then took off. Sweet.

What does she mean, he doesn't love me? Of course he loves me. He doesn't love her. And, besides, I thought she didn't believe what the cop told her that night.

It's hard to believe she gave birth to me sometimes. She hasn't an inkling... a clue... about anything. She's creeping towards understanding my relationship with Marvin, but every time she gets close, she backs away again. Like what will happen if she really figures it out? Will her head explode?

He doesn't love me? Yes he does. Why wouldn't he love me? How could he not love me? I'd love me if I could love me. Ha.

Reggie scuffles along beside me like a crab. Sideways walking, always coming back, veering off. I say nothing to him until I get to the hotel.

"OK, see you on stage." I try to be nice. Why not? What harm will it do? Maybe if I'm polite he'll leave me alone.

Reggie turns fuschia and trips again. I take the elevator up to Marvin's room alone. There he is, the magician, with his hands in metal cuffs, his fly undone. Oh, it's funny. He looks so old and confused and timid and even a tiny bit scared. He's got himself in this position and needs my help getting out of it. I take the K-Y Jelly and smear it on his hands while he laughs and says he forgot to do that before he put them on. "What kind of a Houdini am I?" His new trick—getting out of things. When he laughs I can see his yellow teeth, his receding gums. I close my eyes, remember other things and massage.

Suddenly my mother charges in and startles us. I drop Marvin's hands.

"Ruth?"

"She's just a child," my mother screams. And I can't help it but I look around, I look for the child. Where? Who?

Looking back into Marvin's eyes makes me sigh. Suddenly I feel tired. Old before my time. I am no child. I have no energy for this kind of behaviour anymore. Is he worth fighting for? I turn, zip him up, and leave the room. Leave them together. But then something makes me turn back. Wait. Watch. Soon I catch myself watching too closely as they begin their heated fuck, like animals. Is that what we look like? The sounds they make. Slap-slapping. I know deep inside that watching this will probably damage me for life—how could it not? It's purely disgusting, but my interest in this right now overpowers any urge to shut my eyes and move away. It's almost medical. Like when you take a hand-held mirror and crouch over it to see what's going on down there. Besides, it has suddenly come to my attention that Sylvia has somehow squished herself under the food trolley in the hall and is breathing very heavily and admiring the view. She is crying. In a minute or two I'll have to unstick her, pull out her bulk, release her into the wild.

I pop her out from her tight space. I yank her hard. I am beginning to feel like an animal.

On the stage one night Reggie is particularly watchful. Part of me actually relishes this. I notice that Marvin notices this and my mother, behind the curtain, notices this and this makes me sort of happy. My mother seems to have won Marvin's heart (or another part of him) again—or he's seen the light (She's too young, perhaps he's thinking, but then I've got admirers who are half his age)—and Mother is now working behind the scenes, passing him things, smiling sickly.

After this, days go by and my mother shrinks herself back into her beaded costumes, cinches up her waist, fluffs up her large breasts. She's taken over again. I'm pushed aside. Part of her new routine is that she smiles at me a lot. Like a doll. Plastic.

"Really," she shouts one day in the kitchen at home. "You should get a job at that chicken place."

I close my eyes and turn away.

"You could bring dinner home for your sister. And your father. They both like a good chicken." She laughs. "Or two." Wink. Wink. Jokes about the fat sister. We're in this together, she is saying, but we're not. Not even close.

I open my eyes and look at Sylvia there on the couch with Dad. They are always there. She has her hand in a bag of Fritos Corn Chips and is balancing a Tab on her stomach. She is huge.

"When did she get so big?" I want to ask but I'm not talking to my mother. Look at her. Has she always been that fat?

And it's not just fat. It's absurd. She is becoming massive. She is out of control. The kids in school are right. She's a whale.

"What happened?" I want to shout. "Where did Sylvia go?"

I watch my mother clip-clop on heels out the door of the apartment. Then I turn back to Sylvia. Thirteen years old. How much does she weigh? She is humongous. Bigger than last week it seems. She breathes heavily, her mouth open all the time, even when she's not stuffing food into it. Sylvia feels me staring at her and her eyes narrow. She turns her large head and looks right at me. Hard. I have to swallow. It's like a horror movie. In all that chub there is something strange in her eyes, in the set of her jaw. Who said fat people are jolly? And nice? Like Santa? I turn nervously away from Sylvia's stare and head down the hall to my room. I put on a record, but I don't quite feel like dancing. Or doing much of anything. My mother has stolen my job. My mother has stolen Marvellous Marvin back again. And here I am, alone in my room. In the living room there is an angry fat person I don't know anymore, and a blank, quiet shadow of a man who calls himself my father, watching TV.

•••

The Working Mother

"To work or not to work?"

My headphones are on loud and I'm lying on my back, eyes closed, listening to music, and so I don't hear him come in. I can smell him, though. Suddenly I smell rabbits and cedar and piss. My eyes flash open quickly. Not quickly enough. It is dark out now, how long have I been lying here? I must have been asleep. Is this a dream? A nightmare? My room is dim. But then Reggie is on top of me in one giant leap, his hand covers my mouth. His stinky, foul-smelling, dirty hand, the nails jagged and bitten, the cuticles cut into bleeding strips from picking. His calluses scratch my lips, my cheeks. I try to take a deep breath in. I gag. Struggle. He must be joking. His other hand comes up. Comes down on my jaw, on the side of my head at my temple. He says, "Shit," and shakes his hand out. I see black. Pinpricks of light. I feel woozy. I taste blood. Half of his hand is covering my nose. I can't breathe. My headphones fall off my head and I can now hear the opening song from an old rerun of *Laverne and Shirley* coming from the living room. Sylvia is there, watching, sitting, not moving. Breathing heavily. Sylvia will come to help me. Won't she? I helped her out from the trolley.

"One, two, three, four, five, six, seven, eight.

Schlemiel, Schlimazel! Hasenpfeffer Incorporated!"

Why doesn't Sylvia come save me? Where is my father?

Reggie says nothing. His eyes are black. Fierce. Stop struggling. I've heard that it's better if you don't struggle, that they won't get as violent, they won't hurt you as much. (Who is they? Rapists? Men in general? Assholes?) But I only want to kill him. I wriggle and move my arms trying to attack, to scratch his eyes out. I want him dead right now. I want to hurt him.

Reggie pins my arms to my side with the insides of his thighs. He smells. The smell is putrid. I can smell alcohol on his breath. A beery smell. He is perched on top of me, looking confused, looking like, how do I do this? How do I hold her down and get on with it? I want to shout, to say, "I've got my period," or something. Anything to stop him. But then I wonder if maybe he didn't intend this, maybe he just came in and didn't want to startle me, sleeping there, and so jumped on me so I wouldn't scream. Maybe? In that case, he should take his stupid smelly hand off my face. My face is numb. I can forget about the punch—of course all he wanted was not to scare me. It was an accident, right? He didn't want to startle me. I, maybe, would have, after all, screamed bloody murder. Woken the entire apartment building. My father.

I will myself to relax slightly.

Maybe Sylvia let him in? Maybe my father went to bed and Sylvia snuck him in? Who let him into the apartment?

"Shhhh," Reggie says. "I didn't mean."

There, he said it. He didn't mean it.

And then, magic, he takes a pair of handcuffs out of his back pocket using the hand that is loose, the one not holding my face down. My eyes widen. I can feel my eyes bolting around in my skull. Trick cuffs? Marvellous Marvin's? Is this a joke?

"I don't want to hurt you." He says this. Like he's on TV. Isn't that what they all say on TV and the movies? The rapists? I don't want to hurt you. And then they hurt you. He's drunk. Wobbly. I buck and try to bite his hand. Reggie looks around for somewhere to clip my arms but my bed has no headboard (thankfully—if I believed in God...). What are you going to do now?

The thing is: usually I'm in control, usually I can take care of myself.

Reggie looks pained. His eyes water. His pimples are standing out on his cheeks like glow in the dark stars. Quickly he switches hands, not giving me time to make a sound. One hand up, the other on my face, covering my mouth. Now he has his left hand free, the handcuffs have been flung to the floor. He takes a deep breath, raises that left hand high above his head and smashes it down on the side of my face, on my temple. Again. Smashes hard. I can hear him swear again. He's hurt his hand. Then he hits my mouth and I taste blood again. A tooth wobbles in my skull. Instant pain. Blinding.

I feel my eyes blink once, then eyes wide open, then my eyes close and there is a whiteness suddenly, a glow, and my body goes stiff (there's nothing I can do about it) and then (quickly) relaxes.

•••

"Some mothers HAVE *to work to make a living. Usually their children turn out all right, because some reasonably good arrangement is made for their care. But others grow up neglected and maladjusted. It would save money in the end if the government paid a comfortable allowance to all mothers of young children who would otherwise be compelled to work."*

IT IS SYLVIA who finds me in the morning. It is Sylvia, shuffling in, loud like Darth Vader breathing through a mask, who puts a cold washcloth on my forehead and says, "What happened? What happened? What happened to your face? There's blood on it. What happened to your tooth?"

My mother is sleeping in.

"Shhhh, my head."

Reggie is gone.

My tooth aches. It is dangling. Sylvia says nothing but helps pull it out. Painfully. I cry a lot. I swat her arms away. "Don't touch me."

Sylvia's face is white and pasty. Her eyes are wide. "What happened to you?"

In the kitchen, my father looks at me quickly, coffee cup in hand. There is hurt in his eyes, like I've disappointed him somehow, but I don't know how. Hasn't he disappointed me? Why didn't he come to help last night? Surely he heard something? I'm having trouble remembering last night. My mouth aches. There is a bruise on my temple, swollen and green. Can't he see that? I am having trouble standing without leaning on something—Sylvia's arm, the kitchen counter, the kitchen table, Dad's grey-cardiganed shoulders. Can't he see this?

"Keep your voices down this morning," he says on his way to work (as if NOTHING happened). "Your mother worked late last night. And, Sadie, wash off that makeup, it's smeared all over your face."

Makeup?

We both watch our receding father recede. He is there one moment and gone the next and nothing in the apartment seems to change. It's as if he isn't really alive. As if he doesn't make even a tiny bit of a shuffle in the universe. And, therefore, he doesn't matter. So I guess it really doesn't matter that he doesn't notice me. What did I expect from him? He never does anything. I walk over to the living room window and watch as he walks, hunched over, on his way to work, his briefcase knocking lightly against his side. The pain in my head is severe.

How could he ignore the condition of my face? (I don't care, I don't care, I don't care!) How could he think it was makeup? My throbbing temple. I'm dizzy and exhausted.

"What is it with men?" I'm swallowing bile. But Sylvia is back in front of the TV, the volume low, watching cartoons. She placed my tooth on the bathroom counter and then said nothing more. It is as if she is disappointed in me. For what? Getting raped?

My head aches. My legs ache, my inner thighs are bruised. My mouth aches. My body cries. In the shower I do what girls in this situation normally (naturally?) do, what the sex-ed teacher at school (before I quit) told us would probably happen if you ever got raped. Scrub your body hard with a brush, a washcloth, soap. Get any trace of him out of you, off of you. You see it all the time in the movies but it's true. There is this dirtiness, smelliness, that you have to get off. If you can just scrub hard enough, deep enough.

Good thing I'm on the pill.

Part of me wonders if I deserved this.

I feel the scorching water streaming over my face. What is water and what are tears?

There is nothing but a blank hole in my mind. I am supposed to work Marvin's show tonight and I don't know if I can remember the tricks, or how to be a stooge if needed. Marvin plants me in the audience in a black wig and a boy's coat. When I quickly hide to change from that costume into my red-sequined bodysuit, throwing off the wig and parading out onto the stage, there isn't anyone in the audience who recognizes me as the tomboy whose mind was just read, whose pocket was picked and revealed by Marvellous Marvin. It's magic. Lately, my mother has been taking more and more shifts, lately I've been pushed out and away. Ever since the K-Y incident. The Houdini Hustle.

Reggie will be there. At work.

I pace in the kitchen, dripping wet, wrapped in a towel. My wet hair dangling over my face.

"Dry yourself," Sylvia says from behind, startling me. How can someone so big sneak up so quietly? She's always there. Tiptoeing in and surprising me. "I've made an appointment for you to see the dentist this afternoon."

"Thanks." Unexpected. But her eyes are cold.

Puddle of water on the floor. Sylvia stares at it. I stare at it.

"Did you let Reggie into the apartment last night?"

"Reggie?"

"Reggie, the rabbit guy, did you let him in?"

"No, why?"

"What do you mean, why?"

"Why would I let—"

She looks guilty. "I didn't hear anything."

"Just did you or not?"

Sylvia shakes her cow-head. Opens her mouth to speak. "Mom brought him home. Is that what happened to your tooth? Did he hit you? Did he hurt you?"

"How can you be so stupid?"

"What did you do to him?"

"Me? Shut up. Don't say anything. If you say anything to anyone I'll kill you."

My mother is in the kitchen then, suddenly, wearing a Cheshire cat grin and an orange bathrobe.

"You're wet, Sadie. You're making a mess on the floor." She pours coffee.

"When did you get home last night?" I ask.

"Why is that your concern?" She pours herself some orange juice from the fridge. "You're in a nasty mood." She hovers over the newspaper on the kitchen table. Sylvia wanders out into the living room again, to sit in front of the TV. It is a Saturday morning and the cartoons are good. I feel the pull of the Roadrunner but I'm too old for it now. I turn back to my mother. Look at my face, I want to shout.

She is now making toast. "Marvin says he doesn't need you tonight. He says I should come instead." She hasn't looked at me yet. She hasn't once taken a peek at my face. Toast is buttered, bit into, chewed and swallowed.

Am I suddenly invisible?

I stand still. Stare. Drip. I almost slip in my puddle. The world moves quickly around me but I am still. That's it. Stillness. Quietness. Silence. My head aches.

Then my mother's head comes up from her toast, from her paper, and she looks at me. Straight at me. "Did you lose a tooth, Sadie? I didn't think you had baby teeth anymore." She is looking closely at me (but maybe not close enough? Why can't she see me?). "I thought that stopped when you were younger? I'll have to check The Book. I'm sure all your baby teeth have already come out, haven't they?" My mother puts her hand (it's shaking slightly. She sees me. I know she does) up to touch my cheek, the bruise on my temple, but I duck out of the kitchen and slam my bedroom door. "And wash off that makeup. It doesn't look good," she shouts.

From that moment on, for the next week, until the fire, I stop talking. To my mother. To my father. To Sylvia or Reggie or Marvin. To anyone. I just shut up. Not a word.

Of course my mother is far too self-absorbed to notice. Marvin is back with her now, and that is all that matters. I am ignored by both of them. My father doesn't notice, really, because he hasn't said much to me in years. I've disappointed him somehow, I don't know when or why. Sylvia notices. She watches me. I can always feel her staring. The strain of not talking makes me feel strong and accomplished. And frustrated and angry. I am outside of myself now. I have something to work on. Self-control.

I do a lot of remembering. I remember when I was really little and my mother and father would take me to the zoo. The huge zoo, so big we rarely saw all of it. Me in my stroller, Mother and Father walking behind me, talking, laughing. Was it my mother and father or was it Mother and Marvellous Marvin? My father's face morphs into the magician's face and then back again. I'm not really sure. But I do remember being happy—arms would reach down and pick me up. I would cry and be comforted. And then Sylvia came along.

When I do finally go to work I shoot daggers out of my eyes at my mother and at Marvin. Marvellous Marvin messes up on some pretty easy tricks, he drops his cards during a shuffle, he gets the scarves tangled in a knot, another rabbit dies in his hat. He knows he is hated now and he's not sure what to do about it. My mother pretends to know nothing. She is back in the loop with her lover. She still doesn't believe Marvin and I were ever together. She believes, I think, that the cop was lying. Nothing else. In love with me? A mere child? When Marvin could have this Ruth Swamp, this woman of maturity and passion? My mother says as much to me in small bits. She notices nothing strange when I say nothing back.

After years of screaming, she doesn't even notice the silences.

And Reggie. God, I avoid him like the plague. My skin crawls when he walks by, his face blushing purple. His left hand is all bandaged and gory from my scratching and biting, I guess. I think about turning him in, going to the police. But what would they say? I know what they would say. They would mention the baseball dugout. They would look at my school records. They would tsk-tsk and shake their heads. Serves you right, they would say. Slut. Loose.

Foxy.

"I'm sorry," Reggie says and I feel as if my insides are falling out. It's better if he doesn't talk to me. My heart drops and hits my stomach. My stomach hits the floor. I vomit in the washroom behind the stage, over and over.

"I didn't mean—"

"I didn't want—"

"I'm so sorry."

"I was drunk."

I catch him crying once.

"Please forgive me?"

One lonely night before the fire, I find my mother's precious book, The Book, and I begin to read it for the first time. Really read it. Now that I'm not talking and my mother has taken over my work and my life I have plenty of time to read. I've never read The Book before, I've just held its pink hard cover (dust jacket off and preserved in a freezer bag) in my hands and oohed and ahhed at it as a child with Sylvia beside me, her fat fingers too dirty to touch it. I've just tossed it at the wall with a plaster-dust bang. Used it as a weapon. But my mother has become very relaxed about The Book since we have grown up and don't touch her things that much anymore (that she knows of) and so she leaves it out places she normally wouldn't. Like behind the cookbooks on the kitchen counter, or sometimes beside the toilet. Once she left it on the hall table in plain view where even Sylvia could have wiped her fingers across it while walking past.

And now The Book is lying on the bedside table, on my mother's side of the bed (it amazes me that they still sleep in the same bed), and she is at work and my father is working late and Sylvia is just there—where she always is—in the living room in front of the TV. I lift it, look at it.

"It's just a fucking book," I say out loud (like I expected fireworks).

"What?"

Sylvia's hearing is amazing. It's as if her senses, now that she's almost handicapped with her weight, have become stronger. Which means she must have heard Reggie. Which means she ignored the pain I was in. Why would she do that to me?

"I'm talking to myself," I say from the hallway where I ran when Sylvia said "what". The Book still in my hand. It still makes me nervous to touch it. It's just a book, I have to tell myself. A stupid book.

"Oh."

A little piece of paper falls out from The Book. Oh shit. I have no idea where that paper goes, a little spot-holding paper, a bookmark ripped from the pad of paper on the kitchen counter. Where would it go? I rifle through The Book looking for a good spot. Then stick the paper in anywhere. Then I realize there is paper everywhere. Stuck here and there. And writing all over The Book. Scribbly mom writing, barely legible. The pages are thin and the spine is broken. Glued parts of The Book are coming off. I juggle it back and forth between my hands, as if it's fire. On fire. Afraid to touch it for too long with one hand.

Standing there in the hall, I begin to thumb through to the index and look up some things. Some things that I think I need to know if I'm going to keep going on. If I'm going to keep living with this family, in this world. *Obesity (372-76), Sex Education (322-28), Sibling rivalry, (291-300); see also Jealousy, Sickness, see Illness, Mother, see also Parents.*

When I wanted to be my mother the one thing I forgot to do was to read Dr. Spock's book.

How could I be her without reading it?

I sink to the floor and begin to read.

•••

"It doesn't make sense to let mothers go to work making dresses in a factory or tapping typewriters in an office, and have them pay other people to do a poorer job of bringing up their children."

Music. Blast it through the apartment. When you refuse to talk, when there is nothing more to say, you can still make others hear your screaMs I lie on my bed, afraid to put my headphones on again, just in case anyone else hurts me or sneaks up on me. I crank my songs. I haven't seen Reggie all week, my mother says he's been sick, not coming in as much. She says the last rabbit died, several have died recently, and she's wondering if he's just not feeding them. Or maybe they have the flu? Maybe Reggie caught the flu from the rabbits. Is that possible? Can that happen? I wouldn't know. I wouldn't care. I haven't been in to see Marvin. My mother goes to work instead. Was it unspoken firing? Or unspoken quitting? Or maybe I'm still employed and the tables will turn once more.

I miss him. I do. Marvin. I miss his touch, I miss his toupée even, his eyes. I miss his eyes. And mostly I miss his magic, even though I don't believe in it at all. I miss the way that a little part of me still delights in his ta-da moves, when the rabbit comes out of the hat, or when the scarves are knotted. He makes me feel like a kid. And a woman. He never makes me feel like a sixteen-year-old.

I feel a storm coming, something in the apartment. Suddenly everything seems quiet, even though the music is loud. Something is happening. I get up and look out my window. That's when I hear it. Sylvia's voice from the kitchen saying, "Marvellous Marvin is married." How can I hear this over the music? It's as if she shouted it, but she didn't. A whisper. How is that possible. I turn off my music. Listen carefully. Nothing.

And then I am running towards the kitchen.

"And she's very, very skinny," Sylvia adds.

"You're kidding," our mother shouts. First she laughs and then her body slumps and sinks in upon itself. She knows that what Sylvia said could possibly be true. How could none of us have ever considered this? Of course he's married. Of course. This makes life suddenly very interesting.

"That's not possible." The first words I've spoken in a week. They come out hoarse and scratchy. I clear my throat. I want to be heard.

"Wouldn't we have known?" My father is there, wiping crumbs off his pants. The TV is loud but suddenly everything feels quiet and contained. As if the sounds are merely an echo, the real sound is silence.

Sylvia's lips are yellow. Jaundice? More likely candy.

"Parliament Street. Apartment. Shoe store."

Our apartment empties quickly. Typical. Instead of talking we all disperse. On my way out I see Sylvia standing in the kitchen looking around as if this wasn't what she expected, as if she is lost. There is a jug of orange juice on the counter. The fridge door is open. I see Sylvia take the ice cream out of the freezer and eat it with a spoon from the drawer. Ladling her germs in there because she knows she's the only one who will finish it. I leave the apartment like the snap of a finger. One minute I'm there, the next I'm gone. I know where I have to go to see this through. Poof. Magic.

This is what happens. I run, walk, limp when I stub my toe (which makes me cry a bit), push people aside, skirt the road, the sidewalk, rush all the way to where Sylvia said he lived. His apartment. Apartment? Him? It makes no sense. He had a hotel room, didn't he? Why wouldn't he have taken me there? Or, if not me, why not my mother? Did my mother know about the apartment? Parliament Street. Above a shoe store. That's what Ruth got out of Sylvia before her mouth filled up with ice cream.

I've already lost him to my mother, but now she's losing him. Who is this other woman? What does she look like? What does she have that my mother doesn't have?

When I get to Parliament Street, when I find the shoe store, I see my father standing there, then there is my mother. Then we all walk around as if we don't know each other. Ignore each other. Then I'm suddenly in front of the shoe store again, looking up, and there is an apartment there, like Sylvia said. A chair in the window. Curtains billowing and then smoke.

Smoke?

I'm watching a scene unfold. Fire trucks. Smoke billowing from the top apartment over the shoe store. My mother appears behind me. She puts her hand on my shoulder and, for once, I don't shrug it off. Her touch is warm. There is a crowd on the sidewalk. A fire truck comes whizzing around the corner and crashes into a fire hydrant. Did it hit someone? I hear screaming. Two people down. Is that possible? I'm stunned. I watch the firemen, I watch the apartment. Marvellous Marvin's secret apartment is on fire? My mother is crying. I narrow my eyes at her and watch the fire.

"Did you know this was where he lived?"

"I know nothing," she says. As if she's Colonel Klink on *Hogan's Heroes*. I almost laugh. Is she trying to be funny?

"I thought he lived in that hotel," my father says.

We all nod together. The Swamp family. Minus Sylvia. We watch. There are two people under the fire truck. They are taken away in an ambulance. It seems to take forever.

"So much for knowing anything," I say. It feels weird to talk again. My mother faints, I have to (want to) kick her to wake her, and then I turn and sees Marvellous Marvin's stuff coming out of the apartment door in the hands of firemen. His top hat ends up in my mother's hands. But where is this wife? I wait and watch, wanting, willing a body to appear. But the firemen work on and the ambulances leave and no one—dead or alive—ever comes out.

On the way home, my father buys us all green popsicles. Why? My popsicle tastes like ash and smoke. My mother's popsicle paints her lips sickly green. My father eats his with great big bites. Relishing the flavour.

•••

"What about the mothers who don't absolutely have to work but would prefer to, either to supplement the family income or because they think they will be more satisfied and therefore get along better at home? That's harder to answer."

FUNERAL. STUFF. I feel tired all the time. My body seems to be shutting down, turning off. Grief? Marvellous Marvin was part of my life for so long. Reggie is there beside me at the funeral. I'm almost afraid to move my chair. What if he gets mad and comes at me again? I've gone from tough girl to wimp so quickly. My mother cries all the time. Her hands shake. She looks nervous. My eyes are dry. Sylvia looks strangely content. Like a wise old whale from a kid's book we used to have. Big ol' smile, grin from eye to eye. Loopy. She's eating celery at the funeral and munching so loudly I can't hear myself think. I can't even hear the service (which is OK because I don't actually want to hear the service, but I would like to hear my own thoughts).

There are many women here. Old women, like my mother. Crying, laughing, talking about Marvin as if they knew him. I mean, really knew him. Like we did.

Or thought we did.

"Remember when he used to wear that blue tuxedo? Before the black one. Oh, it made his brown eyes so lovely. Baby blue."

Yuck.

Women from as far away as Texas—the wife of a CEO from the annual convention held at the hotel. She says she never went anywhere else for her magic fix.

"Just Toronto. Just to see Marvellous Marvin."

"Oh," another woman says. "What about Las Vegas? I mean, Marvin was great, honey, a real treat, but what about Las Vegas? Haven't you ever seen a show in Vegas?"

I try to drown out their voices. I try to drown out Sylvia's celery. I hum a little. I focus on what the minister is saying—about life being just a precursor to death. Precursor—what the hell does that mean? He's making no sense. And he's giving me eyes. I know he is. Looking at me over his Bible, even though he's pretending not to. Reggie stiffens beside me. He plays with the dirty bandage on his hand and that friggin' cloth in his pocket. After the funeral the minister takes my hand, assumes I am Marvellous Marvin's daughter ("What the fuck?" I can't help saying, and then I blush). He turns red from the tips of his ears to the point of his nose, across his pale freckled face. He says, "Well, what relation were you then?"

"Lover," I whisper, I can't help myself, someone needs to know. I need it to be said, acknowledged, admitted. I follow the small groups of people off toward the cemetery. The minister stands shaking at the door of the church, too confused to put one foot in front of the other. It would be funny if it weren't so tragic.

What are they burying if there was nothing left of him but ash? A small, piddly urn. This is plain ridiculous. Everyone cried when they carried the urn out of the service. I sigh a lot (what else can one do at a funeral) and try to walk as far from everyone as I can—far and fast away. Sylvia can't catch up to me. She tries. Puffing and panting and sucking/crunching on celery. Reggie closing in behind ("I'm sorry, I'm sorry." Will he ever shut up? I almost want to forgive him to make him stop bothering me. But I won't. I won't ever forgive him). My father and mother (Dad is wearing all black. He should have been the minister. Much more appropriate than that pedophile—but then if he's a pedophile what was Marvin?) move slowly back behind the crowd of old biddies. Are my parents comforting each other? That seems unlikely, but things have been changing since the fire. Suddenly I have been feeling like the sixteen-year-old I am. Not the twenty-one-year-old I assumed I was. I want to go to bed at nine o'clock these days. And I want to go back to school (I know, it shocks me too). Really. I want to start being a kid again because, like the minister just said, life really is just a precursor to death. And death happens fast. Snap the fingers fast. One minute you are smooching your invisible wife, the next minute you are nothing but ash being scooped up by a fireman. One day you are lying in bed listening to your headphones, the next day you've become a victim of rape. Not everything is easy. Not everyone stays smart. Things happen quickly and completely. Life just ends. No matter what.

"Trust yourself," I say to myself. It has become my mantra. Ever since I started reading The Book.

Kicking dirt around the tiny open hole I contemplate that today is a day where I might just make some resolutions. I'll change my life. For the better. A different school? A different perspective? Maybe Marvin's death was a gift? I feel melodramatic. I wonder if I'm getting my period. No more working right now, strutting myself in the stage lights, showing off my body. I have my whole life to work. I want to be me for once, Sadie Swamp, sixteen years old.

Sylvia creeps around behind me and fakes pushing me into the hole that has been made for the urn. I grab my sister's hands and trip, almost falling.

"Jesus, Sylvia. Don't do that. I could have sprained my ankle. What's gotten into you?" So much for being a new person. I'm already screaming at my kid sister again.

Sylvia giggles nervously.

Everyone else finally forms a circle around the little hole. The urn comes with the minister. My mother and father. The ceremony takes on the appearance it is supposed to. Darkness and solemnity. The sky opens up and the rain pours down.

"Why," my mother says, loudly, popping up her umbrella, "does it always rain at funerals?"

"It breaks my heart," I say.

"But," Sylvia whispers. Almost no one hears her. But I hear her. "It's for the better now."

I don't know if she means the rain, or life, or Marvin's death. What is better? Nothing. Absolutely nothing. Things are only different now.

In the future I may wish that I had said, "Yes, everything is better now. Even the rain."

My mother wails, "What am I going to do now?"

And Dad says (again, for the hundredth time), "Don't worry, you'll get another job."

The old women cluck and coo, comfort my mother as if she's the widow. The urn is placed into the ground. So slowly. So final.

Where is the widow? Where is she? I scan the crowd, peer behind tombstones, under trees in the distance, through the rain. No one. Nowhere.

Sylvia eats and eats and eats her celery until it seems like the whole world gets swallowed up by her. One piece after another. Stuffing herself.

I think it may never end.

•••

"If a mother realizes clearly how vital this kind of care is to a small child, it may make it easier for her to decide that the extra money she might earn, or the satisfaction she might receive from an outside job, is not so important, after all."

IT DOES END, I suppose. One late afternoon, a week and a bit after the funeral. Behind a dumpster. In an alley between Parliament and Yonge.

The last things that happen: I am out walking towards Marvellous Marvin's burnt-out shell of a building. Just out for a walk. Feeling blue. Saying goodbye? Starting again? It's a mystery. At lunch I fought with Sylvia. And said some really mean things. We've spent our lives living in the same vicinity but we don't really know each other. Like two planets rushing around a hot, angry (mother) sun, never crossing paths. Ever since the funeral, though, Sylvia has changed. She's been acting really strange. She has been saying things like, "I told you so" whenever she can. She is suddenly bossy and loud (crunching, chewing, swallowing, laughing, everything is loud), thumping her huge, unwieldy body around the apartment and waking me up in the middle of the night with her noises. Sylvia is often standing in my doorway late at night, watching me while I sleep. Beady eyes. Sallow grin. I lock my door. My little (big) sister, staring.

And then the vomiting at lunch today, the French fries. It was horrible. I know she needs help, but I couldn't stop myself. She makes me feel gross and sick and sad. And so I blurted out some things that I wish I could take back.

And so I am walking down the street, minding my own damn business. Thinking of Sylvia and of Marvellous Marvin. And of my mother and sometimes of my father (although he is harder to focus on. His lines are blurry). Thinking of magic and how it draws people in—me, mother, even Sylvia and Dad—how the concept of trickery is so lovely, but also so open and apparent to me. Pick a card, any card. I am bothering no one on the street. I am innocent.

I have a brand spanking new tooth. It hurts a bit and I have trouble chewing on the left side. It's like it's too high or something and my mouth doesn't fit together right anymore. I snap my jaw open and closed as I walk and think of Reggie and then quickly stop thinking of Reggie because it makes me feel so gross and angry inside. I'm trying hard these days to push away the anger, I'm trying to control it. Marvin is dead. What's the point of being angry? But Sylvia made me so angry at lunch. Because I'm trying to change and she makes it hard. And my mother makes me angry, of course. And Reggie. I can't really help it. But I am trying.

Change is slow. I know that. I just need time.

I have my large canvas bag with me. In it is makeup (lots, mostly eyeliners, blue, black, brown), a hair brush, a hair pick, cigarettes (Virginia Slims), a green lighter, watermelon bubblegum, a large leather wallet with $40 in it and a book, *Helter Skelter*, by Vincent Bugliosi. I bought it in a second-hand bookstore about a month ago and I've been reading it off and on. I was wondering if Manson was as angry as I was. Was that his problem?

So I'm walking and thinking about life and about *Helter Skelter*, about Sharon Tate and all the rest of them. How can I not be thinking about this? The tragedy of it. The whole thing is so scary, worse than scary, how can anyone be that cruel? I admit, I've been up to no good most of my life, but not in that kind of way. The anger I feel wouldn't go that deep. It wouldn't shatter, alter, destroy life like that. Would it? Am I capable of such anger? I am not. I'm trying so hard to alter my life right now. I'm moving on, moving up, moving away from what I was and heading straight into the good, smart future. Before, I just thought I was smart. Now I'm going to make it a reality. I wonder if my mother will see it that way. And Sylvia? After lunch today, I told her I hated her. Right to her face. And she looked like she'd been slapped. Perhaps she's only just now acting out all the pent-up anger she's had over having a non-existent older sister these last few years. Perhaps she's now going through the things I've been going through. I mean, after all, we are sisters. Maybe she's angry too? Things have changed so quickly that maybe Sylvia is having trouble dealing with the change. I really should apologize. From now on my mother will be home every day, every minute, every second. That's enough to make anyone crazy angry. Sylvia's going to get an earful every day now about her weight, her eating habits, her TV watching time. She will be our mother's project. I really should try to be a little nicer to everyone at home.

"Now" my thoughts go. Walking along, almost happily. A little skip to my step. Thinking, "things are going to be different—"

I hear shuffling behind me. Heavy breathing. I turn.

And then everything stands still, time pauses, and, just as quickly, crashes down. A sharp pain, a burning sensation, body ripped away from me. Mind and body disconnect. I feel only blackness. Numbness. My purse is torn from my arm. A tugging, heaving, panting sound. Dragging me. I am being dragged (drugged?). Sliding roughly across concrete. I feel burning pain in my head. The smell of iron, shit, garbage in the air. My eyes are wide open but I can't see anything. What I can see I don't understand. I can't feel anything. I can't understand what I feel. White, hot pain. My hands clutch at whatever is around me, scratching and digging. Skin, I grab skin, and blood and pebbles, garbage.

Alone. Dark. Cold.

The last things that come out of my mouth are vomit and blood.

And then that's it.

The show is over.

The magician bows, flourishes his scarves in the air—a rainbow—tips his top hat, blows kisses to the thundering audience, and exits the stage.

Things will be different now.

The Handicapped Child

"He'll be happy without your pity."

"It breaks my heart."

"Her brain injury is diffuse."

"If you mean it is spread all over why can't you just say that?"

"A craniotomy is necessary to drain the blood that is creating pressure, Mrs. Swamp. The injury is substantial because Sadie's brain ricocheted in her skull causing more damage. Like a squash ball in a white court."

"There are many lacerations to the skin, causing hemorrhaging. She was covered in dried blood, which the nurses attempted to wash carefully off. There was cerebral contusion or bruising of the brain tissue. And concussion and coma."

"Punch-drunk syndrome, something boxers get when they've been injured too many times."

"She doesn't seem funny drunk to me. More like continuously distracted. More like she always has something better to do."

"Shut up, Sylvia."

Seizures. Vomiting.

"She can't focus or speak. Her right eye won't move anymore. There is memory loss."

"What is that?"

"Cerebrospinal fluid leaking from her ears and nose. Not a pretty sight."

"Put away that pizza. How can you eat when you look at her, Sylvia?"

Adopting a Child

"It's not the words but the music that counts."

I HEAR MY MIND. Music. I hear sounds, dings, bells, sweet symphonies. I hear birds twittering, crickets in summer, seagulls. I hear trilling, an opera star, the deep bass of a mating bullfrog. The looping sounds of wind in the trees. A melody of traffic. I shudder. Twitch. Lost in the sound. Music.

All the voices around me. I hear, but cannot understand who is speaking, what is going on.

In the hospital. In bed in the living room. In my own bedroom. Time passes. Then voices. Music. Sounds. Feelings.

First wheeling, then limping, then walking. A riddle. "What walks on four legs in the morning, two legs in the afternoon, and three legs in the evening?" Steady now.

Time passes.

But Sylvia moves slower. I learn to help out.

"Help out," Mama says. "See. This is how you do it."

A snow globe. Fix the crack. Glitter leaks on the dining room table. Dusting. The baby sailor outfit, the pink lacy one.

"Humph," Mama says.

Daddy disappears. I do not know where.

Then days, weeks, months, years.

Time passes.

And suddenly Mama is gone. One day Mama shows me how to butter toast, "For the hundredth time, Sadie. Pay Attention. Help out now." The next day, time passes, (although it could be weeks, months) Mama is gone. Sylvia says dead. She says cancer. The music in my head stops, time passes, and then starts up again. Louder. Sylvia's TV set. Her creaking bed. Her calls, "Come, Sadie. I'm hungry. Feed me."

Sylvia is a snake eating its tail.

Going through the motions. I've heard that before. Get up. Wash. Make breakfast. Serve breakfast. Wash Sylvia. Make lunch. Wash dishes, clean kitchen, dust living room. Fix ornaments. Make snacks and dinners and snacks and dinners. Late night dinners. Whole BBQ chickens, dipping sauces, coleslaw, potato salad and French fries. "I'm hungry, I'm hungry, I'm hungry. Feed me."

Time passes. Slowly, quickly. I'm never quite sure.

"And it breaks my heart," Mama once said. "It breaks my heart, my heart, my heart."

I don't know happy or unhappy. I watch my reflection in the hall mirror, delivering food to Sylvia—bedridden Sylvia. Poor Sylvia. Time passes. I watch my face, one side hangs down, they say: paralyzed. I watch my hair, stringy yellow, long. It wasn't always like this. Was it? Shaking my head the music of my greasy hair hits my ears. A wisp. Wisp. A helicopter passes outside the apartment. Startling. Sounds everywhere.

"And it breaks my heart."

"Come. There's something good on TV," says Sylvia. I find my eyes in the mirror. Searching. Dark blue, my eyes. Black middle pools of water drawing me in. Drown in your water-pool eyes. I've heard that somewhere. Dripping pool eyes.

"Pooools," I hum. Face paralyzed. The sound a melody, an underlying tune, the beat to a song. The tray tips. Sometimes food falls onto the floor. I know how to clean it. Sometimes food falls onto the floor. I do not remember. Does it matter?

The apartment smells. Sylvia smells. I smell. I wash, dust, wash again. Time passes. It's overwhelming. It's comforting. Thousands of Christmas decorations. Ceramic ones, glass orbs, snow globes, cotton angels, metal crosses, red and green balls, paper stars.

Time passes. Nothing happens. Sylvia gets bigger. Meals on Wheels. Grocery delivery. A social worker. Another one. Sylvia "handles the finances." Welfare cheques. By phone. By mail. Sometimes a man or a woman comes to the apartment. "Checking up on us," Sylvia says. Sometimes a doctor. He tsks and says Sylvia is slowly killing herself. He says I can't look after myself, let alone Sylvia.

"Up on us," I whisper. "Checking up on us." Music, a waltz. Most words are a dance, contain a dance, make me want to dance.

"You're happy," Sylvia says, laughing. Her great body quakes and I think: the room in the sky that we live in will fall.

But I don't dance when I am happy because I am not happy or unhappy. I am not sad or unsad. I dance only when I hear the music in things. In my head. And it breaks my heart. It will break my heart.

An old movie on TV one night. Late. *Whatever Happened to Baby Jane?* Sylvia settles us in to watch it. Me beside her. Her beside me. Food in bed. Snuggle down.

"This movie is about two sisters," Sylvia says. "They are horribly jealous of each other. Wait till you see what happens."

Sisters. Together. Bette Davis and Joan Crawford. Sylvia and Sadie.

Sylvia loves this movie, she says. "It's really creepy. How much hate they have for each other. One actually tries to kill the other. You won't believe." I watch the black TV long after the movie is over.

There were two sisters. And hate. And jealousy.

There was hate. Jealousy. Two sisters.

"Isn't that a great movie?" Sylvia sighs contentedly. "A real drama. Emotionally tense. Intriguing. Dark." She smiles. "Did you like it? Did you understand it?" Sylvia, munching on popcorn. Drinking Diet Coke.

"Sisters." I leave the room. I wander into the kitchen. Look at everything. The clock. The microwave. The fridge. Dust the picture frames. A Marvellous Magician stares at me. I watch him. I look at the cabinets, the counter top, the toaster. "Sisters." I feel sick suddenly. Confused. All this time I thought it was mothers and now I know. Sisters. I know like I know about the music in my head, like I know about the sounds that make my heart break. Suddenly I know. It's not only mothers, it's sisters. Or ... mothers AND sisters. And what they can do together. Apart. They can break your heart.

Or just you.

Ten? Fifteen years? Time has passed. Over ten years and things, small things, feelings mostly, are coming back. Not memories. Instead flashes of light and colour. Images. Movie scenes. Creeping into my mind. A large figure on the street behind me. Arm raised. Heavy pipe.

I am damaged. I know this now.

I existed once. Suddenly I am sure of this. I was alive. Water-pool eyes. Yellow lovely hair. Special. I am now the walking dead. I am the housekeeper in the movie we just watched, *Whatever Happened To Baby Jane?*—Elvira. Murdered with a hammer and disposed. I am murdered. I am disposed. Is Elvira's family worried? Is mine? Clean, cook, clean, cook, wash, clean, cook. El-vi-ra. Mama is gone now. Dead. Sylvia says cancer. The music is loud and ringing. There is a hole in my sweater pocket and I worry it until the hole is so big I can stick my hand in and see it down there on my hip waving at me. Sylvia wouldn't be alive if it weren't for me. For Sadie. Would she?

Mama said, "Take care of Sylvia. She can't get up anymore." I am a good girl. I take care of my sister.

Sisters.

My hand moves in and out of my sweater pocket-hole. It is a gopher. See the light. See the dark. See the light. I watch my hand.

I am scared. I am nervous.

I think, one day you are going to miss me. Aren't you?

Sylvia is twenty-eight years old. I am thirty-one. I am not a day over sixteen. There are noises that come from Sylvia's room at night. Horrible groans. Pain. Deep, gulping breaths.

"We'll all outlive Sylvia," Mama said. And then Mama went away.

Sylvia is calling for a washcloth. "My hands are sticky," she says. "Come help me, Sadie." Instead I take the envelope of money from the hall table—just small bills to tip the delivery boys—and I shuffle in slippers out the door. Stand in the hallway of the apartment building, suck in smells, sounds of the world. Out there. There are things, I think, that I will do. That I will see. Perhaps?

Sylvia says I have always wanted to travel.

"Sadie?" Sylvia calls. "Where are you?"

One foot in front of the other. Someday you will miss me, I know. Someday. Out into the world. I catch the next elevator down.

Part Four
Benjamin

Emergencies

Animal Bites

HE SEES HER. There, across the park. She has golden hair and wide, red lips. She is wearing a sundress the colour of the sky. She is spreading a blanket on the grass, annoyed with it, and the spark of anger, the loveliness of this girl with her parents at the park, stops him in his tracks.

"Can I help you with that?"

Benjamin sits down on the blanket and talks to the mother. The girl looks off into the distance, she looks at the band in the park, at the dog walkers and closes her eyes at the sun. Benjamin can't stop smiling. This girl is frustrated with something, a tomato drip on her dress, a bug in the grass, but she is enjoying the music.

His heart has been captured by her. He has been bitten by her beauty, her wrinkled brow, her short temper.

"Can I see you again?" He takes her hand over by the ice cream cart. He can't help himself. New to the city, fresh from his parents' house, feeling overwhelmed with her loveliness, the smell of her, with his newfound freedom and fresh linen suit and new job, he asks her again, "Can I see you sometime?"

She shrugs. He takes that to mean yes. They exchange phone numbers and within months, he is walking down the aisle with her and then standing in the diner with her and then toasting her with coffee and telling her to call him Mr. Swamp.

Benjamin's mother called Benjamin's father Mr. Swamp, but only in an endearing way. The name came out of her mouth with a drop of love. When she was mad she would call him Frank. But Mr. Swamp was her pet name. She would bite into her meatloaf, smile at her husband, and say, "Mr. Swamp, how was your day?"

Benjamin marries Ruth Mileford and thinks, there, at the diner, that his life is complete. His life can't possibly get any better. He is newly employed, newly married, and happy.

•••

Artificial Respiration

AND THEN HE can't breathe. She smothers him with her hard words, with her anger.

Why does she hate him so much?

Ruth looks in on him as he relaxes in front of the TV. "God, you're lazy," she says. "Get up and do something." But Benjamin has been working all day, dealing with numbers, looking at them until he can see them with his eyes closed. He turns off the TV.

"Do you want to go for a walk?" he asks.

Ruth sighs. She is wearing a new dress, new pink shoes.

"We could get an ice cream? Go to the park? Or have dessert at the diner?"

"You never want to do anything fun," Ruth says. She pouts. Stamps her little foot. Leaves the apartment and goes out into the early evening. Benjamin wants to follow her, take her in his arms, breathe happiness into her lungs with his kiss, but instead he decides it's best to let her calm down. He'll talk to her later. They'll laugh about their fight. They'll get into bed and spoon together and think how silly they were to get angry so quickly—or how silly she was. Benjamin doesn't think he did anything wrong.

Did he?

•••

Bleeding

BENJAMIN'S PARENTS ARE GONE. Suddenly. A car accident on a county road during a winter storm. Their bodies are unrecognizable. He buries them alone and returns to his pregnant wife who doesn't even notice that he has gone and come back.

What is happening? he thinks.

Sadie comes out of her like a shot. Benjamin hears the last scream coming from the delivery room and then he hears Sadie's cry. Her shout. "I'm here," she wails. When he takes her in his arms for the first time he can't get over how perfectly formed she is.

Ruth whines in her bed, "You have no idea, Mr. Swamp, how badly that hurt."

Benjamin sighs, takes his daughter in his arms, and kisses her forehead. She wrinkles up her eyebrows, barely there, and her milky eyes look into his.

"Sadie," he whispers.

"Your dog?"

"Her name."

"Why do you get to name her? I pushed her out." Ruth leans to one side to get a better look at her new daughter. "She looks a bit like me," she says. "That's good."

She has my blood, Benjamin thinks. That's all that matters.

•••

Broken Bones

BENJAMIN HAS NO idea how little blood matters until he sees Sylvia enter the world. He knows in his heart that Sylvia is not his child, he knows about Ruth and Marvellous Marvin, about their time together. Benjamin goes to work each day, creeping out of the apartment quietly to avoid any confrontation. He thinks about his parents and what their last thoughts were before they died. He thinks about what they felt, if there was any pain in their mangled bodies. When he comes home each night Ruth has a glowing look about her, her face bright and cheerful, she has showered but the smell of Old Spice still lingers.

His mother-in-law tells him that Ruth drops Sadie off at her house all day, goes off with the magician, does magic. Benjamin knows what she does.

His heart is broken.

So when she is pregnant again, Benjamin knows that the only way to hold onto her, to keep Ruth (why he wants her, he doesn't know) and Sadie, is to pretend that the baby is his. Fake stupidity. It's easier than he thinks. Especially since Ruth isn't paying attention. Benjamin doesn't know how to get out of his situation. He wants to take care of his family, he wants to be happy, he wants to feel that feeling he had in the park that summer day.

Benjamin wants his parents back, his old life, his yellow dog and farm.

Sylvia is born.

"She just about broke my hips," Ruth shouts. "I can't believe how hard it is to have a baby."

Blood is thicker than water but Sylvia is like glue. She sticks to Benjamin's heart, heals it almost. Gives it that extra strength to keep him together.

If it weren't for Sylvia, Benjamin often wonders what he would have done. But he knows that he has nothing else in his life but this.

This family.

•••

Burns

THE FIRE IS devastatingly hot. Benjamin can feel it from across the street, the heat and noise of it. Louder than he would have thought. Sylvia hovers around the periphery but Benjamin is too concerned with what his wife has done to pay any attention to her. Sadie is talking again, and this is good, although what she's saying dismays him. Like her mother, she complains loudly.

Benjamin knows that Ruth has set the fire. He watched her do it. Saw her take a box of matches out of her pocket and climb the fire escape at the side of the apartment and light the curtains through the open window. He saw the Sterno container. He saw the flames leap up and shoot out the window, almost knocking her over. He saw the look of horror and realization on her face when she finally figured out what damage she has caused.

And Benjamin saw Marvellous Marvin and a woman leave through the back of the apartment, out the patio door that emptied onto the deck. He saw Marvin and the woman carefully climb down, using window ledges and patio supports, and he saw them head off behind the apartment, down the alley, into the city. And that was the last of the man. Benjamin never saw him again.

After the night Benjamin confronted Marvin about the money, and then after Sylvia came into their apartment and told them about Marvin and the woman, Benjamin was sure this would happen. He knew the magician would disappear. After all, Benjamin asked him to leave.

He didn't know his wife would have the gall to set fire to a building. He didn't know his wife would live her life thinking she killed a man. He didn't know she wouldn't change a bit because of it.

If he had known, maybe he would have told her about Marvin's disappearing act.

In the long run Benjamin waited for her to feel something. And while he waited she felt nothing.

•••

Choking

Marvin says he doesn't know why he took the money.

"All these years," Benjamin says. "Do you know how much you've hurt my family?"

"She doesn't know," Marvin says. "What good would it do to tell her?"

"Which her do you mean? Sadie or Ruth?" Benjamin sinks to the sofa in Marvin's hotel suite. "You've hurt me so much." He cries. It shocks him that he is crying in front of this man. It shocks him that he is crying at all. Benjamin thought in his heart that he was over all of this, that the jealousy was long gone, that he loved his wife, but understood what it was she had to do to make herself happy. He thought he was OK. But here he is, choking on his words, trying to control his sobbing.

Marvin backs up. Sits on the bed. Sighs. "I can't pay you back," he says. "I have no money."

"It isn't just the money, you know that." Benjamin looks up at the man who has taken everything from him.

"What do you want me to do?"

"I want you to leave. Get out of here. Never come back. Leave both of them alone."

Marvin nods. "I can do that," he says. "It's about time. I don't often stay in one place for so long." He rubs his eyes. "This has been a long stretch."

Benjamin imagines all the women in the world left by this magician. He imagines all the tricks this man has played on other duped husbands, wives, daughters. If Benjamin had seen a show about this man on TV he wouldn't have believed it. He wouldn't have believed what he was capable of. He would have thought the show was pure fiction, all made up. What would make a man take money, love and happiness, away from another man? Benjamin feels old-fashioned and sad. He feels stupid.

Even after all these years Benjamin wishes he could tell his father about this situation, ask his advice, listen to what he'd have to say.

"You have to know," Marvin says. "She wanted it too. It wasn't just me. I'm not solely to blame. There was something missing in her life—"

"Their lives?"

"Yes, their lives. I just gave them what they wanted and took a little for myself. How else do you expect me to live?"

"And what was that? What was it that you gave them, Marvin?"

"Magic."

•••

Concussion

BENJAMIN DOESN'T KNOW what Reggie did to his daughter until much later, until it is too late. He knows that Sadie never forgave him for not seeing the bruises, for thinking it was makeup. In the trial, when it comes out that Reggie raped his daughter, Benjamin falls to the floor, collapses, can't get up.

"Get up," Ruth hisses. "You are making a fool out of me."

Benjamin goes back to the hospital and touches Sadie's tubes and machines. He walks around the room looking at everything that is keeping her alive. He unwraps her head and looks at her face, her bashed-in head, the damage. He tells her that he didn't know, that he assumed she had invited Reggie into her bed, that he was ashamed of her and didn't know what to do. He didn't know what was going on.

What could he do?

Benjamin wonders if he had just said something, or if maybe he had talked a little, told them how he felt about everything, then maybe their lives would be different? He isn't sure. There are times when he knows that being quiet is the best way to be. Being quiet lets them think about what they are doing. He assumes this. But there are times when he thinks that if he had just complained a little, or stood up for himself, lived his own life for awhile, maybe those times things could have turned out better.

There were so many times he wanted to talk to Sadie, but he never knew what to say, how to act or react. She was wildfire, she was hot pepper, she was a spark of light, an electric shock. And now Sadie is nothing.

Benjamin feels sometimes as if he's already dead. Sometimes he feels that if he watches a lot of TV and thinks of nothing but work and sleep, if he thinks only about how to breathe, or how to put one foot in front of the other, then he'll be OK. He'll get there. Somewhere. Somehow.

•••

Convulsions

It was Sylvia.

Benjamin knows this. His beautiful, quiet, sad daughter. His thoughtful daughter.

Benjamin knows that Sylvia isn't his daughter, he knows that Ruth set fire to the apartment building, that Marvellous Marvin stole money and then disappeared, he knows that Reggie raped his daughter, and he knows that Sylvia tried to kill Sadie.

What more must he learn about his family?

Sylvia tried to kill Sadie. It's almost impossible to contemplate. But Benjamin knows this deep in his soul. He can tell by the way Sylvia watches her battered sister, he can tell by the way Sylvia eats, by what she puts in her mouth and how she puts food in her mouth. Full-fisted.

Ruth told him later about the lunch, Sylvia vomiting everywhere. Benjamin found speckles of vomit on the cabinets in the kitchen, he smelled it when he came into the apartment after two days straight at the hospital with Sadie. But even before he knew about the vomit, he knew. Benjamin knows his daughter, the daughter who isn't really his, more than he knows himself. When they sit together in front of the TV he can feel her body beside his and it feels as if he is wrapped in a warm blanket. She is the only one who seems to care for him. Always there with him, when everyone else has left the room.

What made her do it?

The fighting, the arguing, the shouting, the magic, magician, tricks? The costumes, the heaviness, the food, the weight of the world?

If Benjamin was a different kind of person, a person of action, not thought, then he thinks he might have done the same. Not to Sadie, but to someone else, some complete stranger on the street. One day, just having had enough, he might bash a pipe, he might batter in a skull. Why not? What more can happen?

The weird thing about all of this, all this knowing, Benjamin thinks, is that if anyone else out there looked into his life, saw it from the outside, they would think that this family is normal—they would think, "accidents happen," they would think, "one screwed up rabbit-man and the whole world turns to pot," they would think, "arson, magician dead—poor Ruth and Sadie, out of a job."

Only he knows how everything is connected. Only Benjamin knows how Sylvia vomited up her food and then destroyed her sister. Benjamin knows how it was done, but not why.

Even though Benjamin always says *what is going on* he actually knows a lot. He knows what, but he doesn't often know why.

In the meantime, while he's thinking about it all, he'll watch TV with Sylvia beside him on the couch, he'll eat with her, he'll enjoy her company, and he won't blame the girl for anything. Because it's not her fault, really. If you think about it. None of it is her fault.

•••

Fractures

SHE COMES INTO the apartment the night Sadie says her first word and Benjamin thinks, "Ah, it's all finally going to be over." This is the woman Marvin escaped with—she is going to tell Ruth all about it. He is convinced that everyone will suddenly jump up and confess their sins. Instead, the Swamp family fractures even more.

Her name is Rose. She is busty and lovely and tall and commanding. She didn't look this way when he saw her scale the beams of the patio during the fire. Benjamin is smitten. She sails into their apartment and settles down for a while, for the evening. He smells the cigarette smoke on her and some flowery perfume. He catches a glimpse of her cleavage when she bends to grab a handful of popcorn from the bowl on the coffee table. And when Sylvia finally goes to bed, Benjamin finds his hand on her lap and her hand on his hand and then his hand up her skirt and finding warmth between her legs.

He is shocked by what he is doing. This woman helped steal money from him. This woman took off with Marvin and is in his apartment to rub his wife's nose in her good luck. But she's a magician and she plays him with her magic, she tricks him and seduces him and he falls for it.

Just like Ruth fell for Marvellous Marvin.

If everyone in his family is guilty, why shouldn't he be, too?

Benjamin lets her out of the apartment and climbs into bed next to Ruth. He is fully satiated, he is filled up with happiness and requited lust, he is emptied out, he can smell her on his hands, in his nose, around his lips. She smells like a rose. This is what Ruth must have felt, all these years, climbing into bed with him, Marvin's musk all around her.

He feels lovely—until suddenly he realizes that Sadie was there, in the living room on her hospital bed, her one eye open, watching him make love to Rose.

•••

Head Injuries

THERE ARE TIMES when Benjamin comes home from work at the end of a busy day, and settles down with his family on the couch in front of the TV and thinks, this is the life. Finally everyone is quiet and fairly content—as far as he knows. The trials are over, Sadie is now up and walking a bit. She will never be the same but this is the new Sadie and at least she's alive. Reggie is in jail. Ruth seems settled now. She isn't complaining too much. Every day she looks more like her mother. Her head in The Book, she is bent over at the kitchen counter running her hands through her greyish hair. If Benjamin comes into the kitchen quietly, so as not to disturb her, she jumps, rattled, when he drops a spoon.

"God, you scared me." She runs her fingers through her thinning hair. She touches her temples with her fingertips, massages her head. "I have such a headache."

Benjamin stands behind his wife and kneads his sharp fingers into her shoulders. "You've been reading for hours. You should get up and stretch."

It is at times like this that Benjamin Swamp thinks he has everything he has always wanted. He came about it in a crazed, wild way, but finally he is at rest and at peace. This kind of stillness reminds him of the farm and his quiet, lovely parents. It reminds him of a childhood of satisfying physical work and bone-tired evenings on the porch, his mother reading aloud, his father smoking and looking out on his property. This is all Benjamin ever wanted. This feeling.

And Sylvia. She is altered, different, more internal, thoughtful, but she is still beside him. He loves her. She has taken to holding on to him when she gets up from her seat, leaning all her weight onto him. He takes it, all this weight, he uses all his muscles, all his strength, to hold her up. His daughter.

•••

Hemorrhage

AT NIGHT SOMETIMES Ruth moves up close to his back as he lies on his side, and she pulls her warm, full body into his and they stay there, quiet, and feel the beating of their hearts as the blood rushes through.

•••

Objects in Nose and Ears

SYLVIA'S FACE HAS blown up bright red. She is breathing heavily, holding onto her side, cramping.

"Come on, you can do it." He is trying to get her to walk down the stairs.

"Dad, oh God, Dad."

"Sylvia, you can do anything you want to do."

"But I don't want to do this. I want to go home. I want to have dinner. I want to watch TV."

"One more step?"

"No, I can't. One more step down means one more step up."

"One more step down and we can take the elevator up. I'll make you dinner. Something you love."

"Meatloaf and gravy?"

"Sure, yeah."

"Mashed potatoes, beans?"

"Sylvia, yes." Benjamin laughs.

"And what about dessert?"

"Anything you want."

"I'll think about it. Let me rest here for a minute and think about what I want for dessert."

Sylvia sits on the step and begins to cry. Benjamin sits down beside her and puts his arm around her and hugs her tight.

"You are brave and strong and smart and beautiful," he says, but she can't hear him because she's crying too loud, because she's blowing her nose on her sleeve, because her ears are ringing from all the pressure as the blood pushes wildly around her body, trying to pump through her damaged heart.

•••

Poisoning

HE'S BEEN HAVING shooting pains in his side. But he's ignoring them. Benjamin has to take care of his family. He thinks it's indigestion and swallows bottles of Pepto-Bismol. The chalky pink stuff stains his mouth, makes it difficult to take in anything else. And so he loses weight while Sylvia gains.

Ruth is decorating Christmas ornaments with a passion. Sadie is dusting the walls. Sylvia is sitting, watching everyone, occasionally humming. The TV is on. Mr. Swamp comes in from work and heads straight to the bathroom. He vomits up Pepto-Bismol. He stretches, trying to relieve the cramp. He feels like he has been running great distances and is finally ready to lie down.

"Daddy," Sylvia calls from the quiet living room. "Our show is on."

•••

Smothering

BENJAMIN THINKS MORE and more of the farm. They had a lot of property in the country with a barn full of old hay, with fields to run in, with corn and barn cats and swallows and a dog named Sadie. Now he lives in the city with Ruth, Sylvia and Sadie.

Lately, when he puts his head down on the pillow at night he can sometimes smell hay. When he rubs his nose in Ruth's hair as she sleeps soundly beside him he can smell it. When he holds Sylvia's hand sitting together on the couch he catches a whiff. When Sadie dusts around him, sometimes pats his balding head, he feels as if he can taste it—the hay. The smell of hay in the barn heated up by the sun. Sadie, the dog, bounding around him, barking. His mother over there, by the clothes line, sheets flapping in the breeze, waving her hands happily at his father driving the truck back from town, "Hello, Mr. Swamp," he is coming down the long driveway towards the house, beeping the wonky horn.

This smell is all Benjamin could ever ask for. This smell of hay, this feeling of warmth, of being smothered, of being weighted down by his family.

•••

Swallowed Objects

BENJAMIN SWAMP SWALLOWS his after-dinner coffee and then closes his eyes at the TV set. It was all worth it, he thinks. The curtain closes quickly and Benjamin is gone.

•••

When To Call The Doctor

"I DIDN'T SEE that coming, did you?" Ruth says.

Index
SYLVIA

Animal Bites

WHAT GOES AROUND comes around.

I am around.

I am round.

"You OK, Ms Swamp?" the garlic paramedic is grunting as he and the others push my platform down the halls of the veterinary hospital. It took forty-five minutes to get me out of the ambulance. The whole time I feared for their lives. Squished paramedics. I pictured it. A flat doctor or two.

But now I'm being wheeled down white corridors, the smell of wet dog in the air.

"I'm doing fine," I say. "How are you all?"

They nod. All of them. My garlic man looks winded and sore, as if he's pulled muscles. There is a line of sweat, a sheen on his upper lip.

"You've been moving in and out of consciousness, Ms Swamp," the doctor says. I assume she is a doctor. She is wearing a white coat. A stethoscope is draped around her neck. "I'm afraid your blood pressure is dangerously high. Your heartbeat is elevated. We want to make sure you are back to normal before we do the CT scan."

"You know," says my paramedic. "It's not actually the scanner that is bigger here, it's the support table. It's specially made for horses and cows and such." He says this and then blushes. "I'm so sorry. I didn't mean—I just thought—"

"That's fine," I say. "It's interesting. I understand."

"The scanner is bigger too," the doctor says and the paramedic and the doctor continue walking with me down the white hallway.

"I was hoping to see some animals," I say. And then I laugh and then my breath catches and suddenly I can't breathe. A white-hot pain shoots across my eyes and the ceiling, lit up with fluorescent lights, is quickly dissolving into a fine mist.

It seems as if Sadie is there. Above me.

I loved her so much. I also hated her. How else could I have hit her so hard?

Sadie Swamp took my life and turned it into a freak show. As she grew into her beauty I grew out. As Sadie's legs stretched, mine bowed and bent and widened. As her personality shone, her mouth flashed red, her eyes twinkled blue, my personality, mouth and eyes dulled. It may have been different if she had, just once, helped me. Protected me. But she turned from me on the playground at school—even when we were very young—she turned away and laughed with everyone else. Pointed at me. Taunted me. The interesting thing is: she always thought she was good to me. How many times did I hear her say, "I tried to help you today, Sylvia, but it's impossible to help someone who won't help herself."

But then I changed her. I took her and moulded her, bashed her, into a lovely person. My Sadie Swamp with wrecked face and limp and brain damage. She was wonderful at the end. Just perfect. She was what a big sister should be. Kind and helpful. Dignified even.

"Flat-lining," the doctor shouts. "Code Blue."

I want to see that CT scan and the table. I want to see the animals all around me, watching me get my test. The cows and sheep and goats and horses, all waiting their turns. Two by two, like Noah's ark.

Now that it is time to die—and it is time, I can feel it, see it, white lights and everything—I don't want to die.

I am drowning in my flesh. I am drowning in my guilt.

In the long run, though, I did make everything better. Didn't I?

Tubes. Intubation. I'm choking, coughing. "Tie her hands tighter." That garlic smell is strong and the sweat from my body mixed with this reeks.

What a big mess I am.

What a big mess we are. The Swamps.

I am falling. Sadie, wherever you are out there, catch me. All I wanted was for everything to work out. But she vanished.

Was I wrong?

•••

"We're losing her," the paramedic says.

The doctor sighs. The other paramedics look at each other, at the floor, at the walls, at anything but the enormous woman on the platform in the hall. Her bulk is still, her mouth and eyes are open.

"We've lost her." The doctor wipes her forehead with the back of her hand. "Well," she says.

"Yes, well." The paramedics look down upon this woman, this mound of flesh. They cover her up gently. They roll her down the hall, towards a room where they can do all necessary paperwork.

"Is there anyone to notify?" the garlic paramedic stops, turns and asks.

The doctor is heading out the door, back towards her car, towards more patients at the hospital in the city. She turns. Checks her chart. Reads. "A sister," she says. "Ms Swamp has an older sister. We'll have to find her. Let her know what happened."

"What did happen?"

"What do you think? She couldn't take it anymore."

"Take what?"

"This." The doctor waves her hands over the mountain buried under the sheet. "This."

"The weight of the world?" the paramedic says.

"I guess you could say that." The doctor smiles a little. "I'll make sure we find her sister. Surely she'll want to know. How can this much of something be gone without someone caring?"

"Yes." The platform turns a corner and is gone. Squeaky wheels. A door opens and closes.

A puff of spring air. The smell of wet earth and drying rain.

Three Blank Pages At The Back Of The Book

SADIE

HAPPILY EVER AFTER?

After living in alleys and on the streets, people offering her food and warmth, Sadie finally finds her way home again. But Sylvia is gone and the door is broken in. A neighbour, passing in the hall on his way to the garbage chute, sees Sadie standing in the living room staring at an empty TV set, and he calls the police.

Police come. Social workers come. They talk. They tell her that people have been trying to find her. Sadie nods and accepts their help. Days pass.

Eventually Sadie visits Sylvia's grave. Eventually Sadie proves to the welfare people that she can live alone. Eventually Sadie is hired in the diner, replacing Maeve, who has retired. She serves silent, grumpy couples their breakfasts. She walks to and from the apartment every day and manages to take care of herself. She doesn't remember her mother, her father, her sister, Marvellous Marvin or Reggie Reynolds.

One day, on the way to work, she sees a poster on a hydro pole:

Sadie can't read, but she is intrigued and charmed by the pictures of top hats and rabbits and magic wands that adorn the poster. She touches them lovingly and feels some sort of connection, a spark. And then she continues down the street to the diner.

At first Sadie is sad and melancholic. At first she is contemplative and worried.

But soon she forgets to be anything and just is.

She just is.

Acknowledgements

Dr. Benjamin Spock's widow, Mary Morgan, has been nothing but kind. She personally answered e-mails and we struck up a small correspondence. At one point she sent me a photo of herself surfing in San Francisco and another of Dr. Spock on his sailboat. Both inspired me. Dr. Benjamin Spock was an incredibly thoughtful and intelligent doctor, his advice still holds true today, and Mary Morgan's tenacity and strength has ensured that he will not be forgotten.

The thrill of winning the inaugural Enfield & Wizenty Colophon prize for fiction was only the beginning. Working with, and finally meeting, Maurice Mierau made the win that much better. Who would have thought I would place my bizarrely structured novel with an editor whose recently published poetry (*Fear Not*) followed a similar concept? Maurice understood my constraints because he also worked with them. Gregg Shilliday, publisher of Enfield & Wizenty, and Catharina de Bakker, assistant to the publisher, have worked tirelessly with me. I thank them for their patience and kindness.

I would like to thank the Ontario Arts Council for the much-needed and much-appreciated Works in Progress Grant. It came at just the right time. All grants come at just the right time, but this one boosted my self-esteem as well as my bank account.

Hilary McMahon at Westwood Creative Artists. How many years have we been together? Hilary is my friend, mentor, editor, psychologist, and most of all, my cheerleader. Every time I think she's going to give up on me, something good happens. Thank you for your persistence and determination. And thank you to Chris Casuccio at Westwood, without whom Mr. Swamp would not have a voice.

Charlie Foran, thank you for reading this novel and saying all you said. Your support is immeasurable. Thank you to Margaret, Edward, David and Nicola Berry—my wonderful family. To Stuart Baird, my husband, who always seems to get my jokes even when they aren't funny. To Abby and Zoe, my tireless, witty, incredibly intelligent daughters. You make my life.

Thank you to Julie Johnston who, being a writer herself, was not even shocked when, out for a walk with her dog past my house, heard me shout out from my office window, "Hey, Julie, what can you buy at a corner store that will ensure a quick and devastating apartment fire?" Julie immediately answered, "Sterno," and, I'm pretty sure, kept walking.

My body thanks Karen Kretchman who kept me jogging, dog-walking, biking, skiing and weight lifting through it all. Thank you to Dawn Carr whose character advice was a turning point in this novel. And my extreme gratitude to Dr. David Carr for his medical advice. All mistakes are my own.

Lastly, thank you to the 2009-2010 National and Executive Council of The Writers' Union of Canada.

The idea for this novel started with a seed, and that seed was the *New Yorker* article "Mother's Helpers: A Century of Child-Rearing Manuals," by Joan Acocella, published May 5, 2003. The magic references come from *The Art of Magic and Sleight of Hand* by Nicholas Einhorn (Hermes House, Anness Publishing, 2002). I tried some of the tricks, but the only thing I could make disappear was any notion of time as I wrote this book.

—Michelle Berry, June 2010